Peabody Public Library
Columbia City, IN

FICTION SOBANET
Sobanet, Juliett⌐
Dancing with
Sobanet.

W9-ARQ-236

MAY 0 6 2016

REMEMBER WHAT YOU READ

USE THIS SPACE FOR YOUR

MARK OR INITIALS

BRODART, CO.   Cat. No. 23-221

ALSO BY JULIETTE SOBANET

Sleeping with Paris

Kissed in Paris

Midnight Train to Paris

JULIETTE SOBANET

Peabody Public Library
Columbia City, IN

Montlake
Romance

The characters and events portrayed in this book are fictitious. Any similarity to real persons, living or dead, is coincidental and not intended by the author.

Text copyright © 2013 Juliette Sobanet

All rights reserved.
Printed in the United States of America.
No part of this book may be reproduced, or stored in a retrieval system, or transmitted in any form or by any means, electronic, mechanical, photocopying, recording, or otherwise, without express written permission of the publisher.

Published by Montlake Romance
PO Box 400818
Las Vegas, NV 89140

ISBN-13: 9781477805916
ISBN-10: 1477805915

For Karen,

I am forever blessed to have you as

my writing teacher and friend.

And for my Grandma Martha,

who would've loved to dance in Paris.

ONE

"Claudia, what do I always tell you? Salsa comes from the hips! Now, *move!*"

My face flamed as Kosta, my Serbian-born salsa instructor, squared himself in front of me, then grabbed my hips and tried to emulate the smooth gyrations that were coming from his own. When I snuck a glimpse of myself in the mirror, I decided I looked more like a swollen purple balloon jiggling atop a pair of stilts than the Latin dance goddess Kosta expected.

And of all nights, tonight was *not* the night to look like a swollen *anything*.

But I wouldn't let the growing baby bump hiding underneath my loose violet tank stop me from telling Édouard the truth. Tonight was my last chance.

If only he would get here.

I glanced at the clock as my feet stumbled to keep up with the rapid Latin beat booming through my grandmother's San Diego dance studio.

It was already seven thirty. He'd never been this late before.

Kosta grabbed my chin and swiveled my face back to his. "He'll be here, Miss Claudia. And in the meantime, you need to focus. Focus on the movements. On the hips. On the *sex*. Like I always teach you." Kosta twirled me around, then pulled me back into his chest as he flipped his full head of wavy brown hair over to one side. "After all, what do you think Édouard is going to want to do with you tonight once you make your confession?"

Peabody Public Library
Columbia City, IN

1

I pulled away from Kosta's grasp and shot him a scowl. "The point of telling Édouard the truth about me being pregnant is not to get him into bed."

Kosta raised one perfectly plucked eyebrow, his hands on his bony hips. "What? A thirty-five-year-old woman cannot make the sex just because she is pregnant? If sex is not the point, Miss Claudia, then what is?"

Over the past five years that I'd been taking lessons at my grandma Martine's dance studio, Kosta *and* his inappropriately tight black pants had become like family to me. And just like family, sometimes I wanted to smack him.

"The *point* is that for the past three months, I've told Édouard everything about myself, *except* for the most important thing of all: that I'm pregnant. And that I'm going to be a single mother. Because I was too…I was too—"

"Cowardly? Scared?"

I sighed. "Yes. Thank you for that. But really, when Édouard and I first became dance partners, what was I going to do? Tell him that I just found out I'm pregnant and that the father of the baby turned out to be a married asshole who wants nothing to do with his child?"

Kosta shrugged, his twenty-five-year-old eyes revealing their naivety. "Why not?"

"Édouard didn't even know me. You can't blurt out that kind of humiliating information to a perfect stranger. *Especially* not to a handsome, famous actor like Édouard Marceau. But then once we got to know each other more and started going out together after class, and I…I started falling for him, I just never found the right time to tell him. I mean, seriously, what man would want to date a woman who's about to have some other man's baby?"

Kosta pulled at my loose purple tank. "Well, you can't hide behind these poofy tops forever."

"Besides the fact that I'm just starting to show, you know it's Édouard's last night here before he leaves for Brazil for three months to shoot his next film, and if I don't tell him now—"

"You will always wonder, could I have gotten that sexy French actor into my bed? Even with a pregnant belly that will soon look like a small basketball?"

This time I did smack Kosta. Once on the right arm. And again on the left.

"I am sorry, Miss Claudia. You know, I kid. You are beautiful. And while Édouard is a little too *French* for my taste, he is clearly a much better man than Ian, that bag of scum. Plus, I have never seen you dance better than you do with Édouard. There is a…how do you say in English? An energy? Yes, an energy between the two of you. It is intense. It is sexy. I have never seen anything like it."

The flush on my cheeks crept down to my neck. "Let's not get carried away," I said to Kosta, although as I searched the studio to make sure Édouard hadn't walked in unnoticed, I knew Kosta was right. I felt that energy, that inexplicable connection. I'd felt it the moment Édouard had first walked into the dance studio three months ago.

But now, as I waited for him to make that same entrance, the only person I spotted was my elegant grandmother, practicing a waltz with one of the many older men who frequented the popular studio just to have the opportunity to dance with the infamous Martine Porter. Her soft, springy red curls coupled with her dazzling smile and her ability to tear up a dance floor still drew them in from miles away.

I clearly hadn't inherited my grandmother's man-magnet skills.

I pulled away from Kosta, the clock above the open window now reading a quarter till eight, my heart sinking into my chest.

Édouard wasn't coming.

"Kosta, I think I'd better call it a night. It's been a long day." I turned from him as I blinked away the warm tears that had sprung to my eyes.

Damn hormones.

I walked over to the bench on the far side of the studio, and my gaze immediately caught the scarlet-red journal sticking out of my purse. I couldn't help but open it up and pull out the small black-and-white sonogram picture I'd tucked inside after my doctor's appointment earlier that day.

As I gazed down at the cute little blob that was my baby's head, a gush of warmth laced with a twinge of sadness rushed through me.

"Looks like it's just going to be me and you, baby girl," I whispered as I patted my belly then tucked the photo back into my journal. But just as I was closing the book, the *other* picture I kept inside those worn pages slipped into my hands.

It was a photo of me as an innocent-faced little girl, sitting on my father's lap, smiling at him as if he were the only man on earth worthy of my love.

And completely oblivious to the fact that he would be taken from me only a year later.

I shook off the familiar feeling of guilt that threatened to engulf me as I gazed into my dad's eyes, an endless sea of blue that mirrored my own. I wondered, if he were here now, would he be disappointed in me?

What would he think of the fact that I made my living as a marriage and family therapist, counseling *others* on how to keep their families together, yet somehow here I was—thirty-five, pregnant, and single? *And* on the night I was finally going to open up to the man I truly cared about, he wasn't even going to show.

If I couldn't keep a man around, would I really be enough for my little girl?

Tucking the old photograph of me and my father back into my journal, I blew a strand of my long, chestnut-brown hair out of my eyes and plopped down on the bench, exasperated. But just as I was bending over to take off my glittery red heels, a sweet, rose-scented perfume wafted my way.

I closed my eyes and inhaled the scent, feeling a strange calm momentarily wash over me. My shoulders relaxed, the knot in my chest loosened, and when I opened my eyes, I found a striking older woman sitting next to me. She looked older than my grandmother and not nearly as glamorous. But as her silvery hair glistened underneath the bright lights of the dance studio and her oval-shaped violet eyes sparkled back at me, I felt as if I knew her somehow.

"Did you lose this?" she asked, stretching her weathered hand in my direction.

I gazed down to find my grandmother's heart-shaped ruby-red pendant dangling from the woman's fingers.

"That's my grandmother's favorite necklace. It must've slipped off her somehow. She'll be so happy you found it."

A mischievous gleam flashed in the woman's eyes as she unhooked the clasp on the silver chain. "It looks like your grandmother is busy over there, so why don't you wear the necklace tonight? The ruby will bring out that gorgeous sparkle in your blue eyes."

My cheeks flushed as I gazed down at the vintage necklace, which I'd never once seen my grandmother take off. The gorgeous stone twinkled in the old woman's hands, and before I could say no, she had already reached behind me and fastened the silver chain around my neck. She arranged the sparkling ruby heart in the center of my chest then beamed back at me with a warm, knowing smile.

"Just like I remembered. Stunning."

"I'm sorry. Have we met?" I ran my hand instinctively over the finely cut stone. But when a sharp spark flashed under my fingertips, I jumped in my seat.

"What the heck?" I said, shaking my hand out as the jolt of electricity sizzled underneath my skin.

The old woman chuckled, then raised a silvery brow. "Sometimes all it takes is a little jewelry to bring the spark back to your life, no?"

A bubble of nervous laughter escaped from my lips as I bent over again to slip off my heels. "No, I think this is a case of pregnancy exhaustion paired with mild delirium. Thank you for finding the necklace, though. I know my grandma will really appreciate it."

The old woman laid her warm hand on my arm. "I wouldn't take your dancing shoes off quite yet, if I were you," she said with a wink before lifting her striking eyes toward the front of the studio.

I opened my mouth to ask her what she was talking about, but when I followed her gaze, my breath caught in my lungs and refused to exhale.

With his head of jet-black unruly hair, his smoky-gray eyes, and his rugged five o'clock shadow, Édouard bounded across the shiny hardwood floors straight toward me.

"Breathe," came the old woman's soothing voice. "Just breathe."

I finally puffed out my bated breath and glanced quickly to my left, but the silver-haired woman was gone. All that remained was the lingering scent of roses and the distinct feeling of Édouard Marceau's gaze piercing through the cool, salty air in the beachside studio and straight into my soul.

Where had the woman gone? And why did I feel as if I'd met her before?

And why on earth was my hand still tingling?

When I lifted my eyes back up, I found Édouard standing over me, his breath heavy and his gaze serious.

"Dance with me, Claudia." He stretched out his hand, the determined look in his eyes telling me he wasn't going to take no for an answer.

I rested my hand inside Édouard's; more tiny sparks ignited under my skin at the mere feel of his touch. Hope rose in my chest as he swept me onto the dance floor.

"I hope you didn't think I wasn't coming," Édouard whispered in my ear as we fell into the natural rhythm we'd had since that first night he'd asked me to dance.

As our feet and hips swayed in perfect unison to the sultry beat of the salsa music lacing through the air, and my baby filled the tiny gap between us, I couldn't get a single word past my lips.

He'd shown up.

And before he walked back out those doors tonight, I had to tell him the truth.

Édouard wrapped his arm around my waist and pulled me closer to him, his grip tighter, more urgent than the other nights. As if there wasn't a moment to lose.

His deep voice cut through the music before I had a chance to speak. "I've been wanting to tell you since the first night we met... you're a stunning dancer, Claudia."

A blazing heat fanned over my cheeks as I focused on keeping my balance. "You're not so bad yourself."

He gave me his first sultry grin of the evening. "*Merci*. I must make a confession to you, though. These are not the only dance lessons I have ever taken."

"Oh?"

"When I was growing up in Paris, it was my mother who taught me how to dance. You see, in the fifties, she was a dancer near the famous Latin Quarter of Paris."

"Really? I can't believe you've never mentioned that." *God, I was one to talk.* "My grandmother spent some time dancing in Paris when she was younger too. She never talks about it much, but I can only imagine how glamorous it must've been. I've never even been to Paris."

"Ah, *Paris*. There is nowhere in the world like it," he said. "When you leave your apartment in the morning, you smell fresh *croissants*, *le café, et le chocolat*. You see couples kissing on the streets, not caring who might be watching. You sit for hours at cafés with your friends and drink wine and talk about nothing and everything." Édouard blinked away the wistfulness in his gaze, then twirled me around and pulled me tightly into his chest. "You must go someday. I am sure you would adore Paris."

Suddenly, a scene of a busy Parisian boulevard packed with old cars and lively French cafés flittered through my mind. I could almost feel the soles of my shoes on the rough cobblestones; hear the

French chatter swirling around my head; and smell the coffee, the buttery croissants, and the chocolate, just as Édouard had said. It felt so strangely familiar, as if I'd actually been there.

But then Édouard's hips shifted against mine, jarring me back to the present, erasing the vivid scene from my confused head.

I told myself that the vibrant picture of Paris I'd just envisioned must've been from all of the old films I'd watched with my grandmother.

But it felt so real.

Shaking off the bizarre notion that something strange was happening, I told myself I was simply nervous. I focused on Édouard's handsome face, his hands around my waist. It was time to come clean.

But as the salsa tune came to an abrupt halt and a dark, seductive tango took its place, for some reason, in my jumbled mind, the sexy beat rang a bell of recognition.

Focus, Claudia. Focus.

I cleared my throat over the loud music and focused on Édouard's slate-gray eyes. "Édouard, there's something I need to—"

"Shhh," he whispered as he leaned closer to me, his lips brushing softly over my ear, his hot breath warming my already flaming skin. "Just for tonight—for our last night—let's forget about everything else that is going on in our lives. Just dance with me."

Édouard's firm shoulders locked into place, his strong arms enveloping me as he led me around the dance floor. All words escaped my lips once more, and as his silent gaze cut through me, I wondered what was going on in *his* life that he wanted to forget. Perhaps whatever it was had made him late tonight.

Before I could ask, a gust of bitter cold air swept through the dance studio as two teenage girls bounced through the front door. A chill rolled down my spine as I wondered how the temperature had dropped so fast. December in San Diego had *never* felt this icy.

My eyes stayed on those girls and their long blonde ponytails, which bobbed as they tossed their purses onto the bench and sat down to change into their heels. But when one of their designer bags toppled over, a magazine slid out and skidded to a stop right next to our feet.

I peered down at the glossy cover of the latest *People* magazine, and my heart stopped.

Édouard's charming smile beamed up at me, and next to him stood a young, rail-thin French actress named Solange Raspail, one hand on her emaciated hip, the other draped loosely through Édouard's arm.

And above her chilly smile, I read the word *engaged*.

Édouard snatched the magazine up off the floor before I could reach it then marched it over to the girls. "I believe you dropped this," he snapped at them before tossing the magazine onto the bench and striding back over to me, a flare of anger present in his gaze.

He was engaged. Édouard was *engaged*.

All this time, I'd never asked if he was seeing anyone. And he'd never shared.

And here I stood, a complete and utter fool about to tell him the truth about me being pregnant, as if it even mattered to him. Édouard was leaving the next day for Brazil to shoot a film where he would play a sexy dance instructor, and it was clear now that he wouldn't be making the trip alone.

A spurt of rage flowed through me as I thought about all the chances he'd had to tell me about Solange. Then again, I'd had just as many chances to tell him I was pregnant. Even if I *had* told Édouard the truth from the start, I was now certain it wouldn't have mattered.

"Claudia," he said, placing a firm hand on my arm.

I tore away from his grip, unwilling to meet his gaze—the same gaze that had melted me from the inside out these past months. The gaze that, for once, had made me drop my defenses and be vulnerable.

That was over now. *This* was over. It was time to go.

But just as I turned to leave the studio, a jarring pain ripped through my chest, directly underneath the ruby pendant. The pain intensified then soared down through my stomach. I doubled over, hands clasping my tight, round belly, my eyes squeezing shut from the intensity of the pain rushing through me.

"Claudia, what is it? Are you all right?"

I vaguely felt Édouard's hands wrapping around me as my knees buckled and I crumpled to the floor.

Another jolt of pain rattled my insides, and I let out a low whimper. What was happening? I'd lost everything else. Was I going to lose my baby now too?

Édouard's strong voice boomed through the studio, ringing through my ears. "Stay with me, Claudia. Stay with me." He knelt on the hardwood floor, cradling me in his arms.

I will not lose my baby. I will not lose her.

Another frosty draft whipped through the studio, chilling me to the bone, numbing me only slightly to the pain that now rolled through me in waves.

I closed my eyes and felt Édouard's warm breath blowing over my frosty skin, his face only inches from mine.

"Why is it so cold in here?" I whispered, my whole body trembling.

But before I could hear his answer, I saw something in the darkness—it was Édouard's smoky-gray eyes dancing before me. I remembered the way his strong hands had felt on my skin, his warm breath grazing over my neck, his sexy hips and broad chest shifting in tune with mine to the same tango beat we'd danced to just moments before.

Only there was something different about Édouard. His hair was shorter, the lines around his eyes were more deeply pronounced, and his lips were a bit fuller, happier even.

The vision slipped away when another burst of pain ruptured inside of me. I opened my eyes and gasped for breath. Édouard's face—the one I knew—hovered over me, his mouth moving in slow motion, but no sound coming out. The chill that shot through me intensified, spread from my toes up to my chest, my neck, and finally, to my head.

I shivered as Édouard's concerned face distanced from me. Farther and farther away he drifted, his message to me unclear. But by the urgency in his eyes, I knew it was important. No matter how hard I tried to focus though, I couldn't hear him.

I tried to yell, to reach out to him, to tell him that no matter what, he needed to save my baby. But I couldn't because the blackness was quicker. It closed in around me, eerily dark but strangely comforting in its obscurity. And just as the last flicker of light left my sight, I inhaled the strong scent of roses and heard my grandmother's voice whisper in my ear.

"Ruby. *My Ruby.*"

TWO

"Ruby, wake up," a soft, familiar female voice whispered off in the distance.

"Qu'est-ce qui s'est passé?" *What happened?*

It was a different voice—a man's. And something was odd about the way he spoke. Was he speaking French?

Ruby, Ruby, Ruby.

I went in and out of consciousness as that name flooded my ears, ricocheting through my pounding head.

Then a hand, cool and steady, cupping my chin.

"Ruby! *Lève-toi!"* *Wake up!*

He was definitely speaking French. Was it Édouard? No, Édouard's voice wasn't that demanding or harsh. But I'd understood him. And I didn't speak French.

My brain spun in circles as the skin on my face blazed with heat. I'd never felt so hot in all my life.

Warm breath engulfed me. Where was I? Who was standing over me?

I blinked a couple of times, noticing the weight in my eyelids. It was different. My eyelashes were so long they clouded my view.

The hand on my chin slid up my boiling cheek.

"I'm so hot," I murmured.

But whose voice was that? It wasn't min,e.

I opened my eyes fully and focused on the man's face which hovered only inches from mine. He knelt over me, his brown eyes widening and his thin lips forming words as if in slow motion.

"Ça va, Ruby? Ça va?" *Are you okay, Ruby? Are you okay?*

Jean-Pierre. The name soared into my brain as the gruff sound of his voice trickled through my ears. He leaned closer, his breath a mixture of cigarettes and peppermint. I didn't know anyone named Jean-Pierre. Who was this man? I blinked a few more times and refocused on his face—his dark five o'clock shadow and his lips, drawn into a tight line.

Those lips. I knew those lips. As I lay flat on my back, my limbs as heavy as cement, their weight keeping me strapped to the floor, I could almost taste those lips.

"Ruby, you're awake," he said, the corners of his mouth relaxing slightly.

"Jean-Pierre?" I whispered before I could stop myself.

"That's right, baby. Have some water and you can go back onstage."

Onstage?

"Jean-Pierre, she needs a break! We've been rehearsing since six in the morning and she hasn't eaten a thing. You can't keep pushing her like this, not after what happened this week. *Putain.*"

It was the female voice from before, its inflection and feistiness more familiar to me now. But this time, she'd spoken French, hadn't she? And again, I'd understood what she'd said. But how?

I swiveled my head to the left, away from Jean-Pierre, and found a pair of silver strappy heels right in front of my face. The toenails protruding over the edge of the shoes were painted a blood red, and the feet attached to them were small and heavily arched. I worked my eyes up the length of her body to see a pair of legs, short and slim, covered in tan panty hose, then a red sequined leotard with feathers sprouting from the shoulders, and finally a gaudy red-and-silver feathery headpiece.

She knelt down beside me, taking my hand, and immediately the scent of lavender swirled underneath my nose. "We're going to get you something to eat, sweetie. Don't you worry."

I stared into her eyes. They were a crystal green, gleaming in the dim light that surrounded us.

What in the hell is going on?

Suddenly, a vision of me dancing with Édouard flashed through my jumbled head. I'd been planning on telling him the truth about being pregnant. But why hadn't I told him?

And where was he now?

I gazed up at the two concerned faces hovering over me and wondered why Édouard had been replaced with this man and woman who both looked so familiar to me. Why were they calling me Ruby? And why were they speaking French?

Where am I?

"I'm not Ruby," I said, my voice still foreign yet strangely familiar. "My name is Claudia. Do you know where Édouard is? Or my grandmother?" My hand shot up to my neck, but I only felt warm, bare skin where my grandmother's necklace should've been. "And the necklace. Where is it?"

"You see, Jean-Pierre! She doesn't even know her own name. She needs a break. We all do," the woman spouted, hurling daggers at him with her eyes.

Panic seized my chest as I flicked my head toward Jean-Pierre, who towered over me, shaking his head. "After what happened to Gisèle last weekend, no one is in their right mind. Get her some food and water and be back onstage in an hour. We have already replaced the star of the show once this week, and I refuse to do it again. *Merde.*"

Gisèle.

As soon as that name left his lips, the blood drained from my head and the insides of my palms coated with sweat. I closed my eyes, hoping the nausea would leave. Instead, a rush of terror boiled over inside of me.

Why did the simple mention of this woman's name make me want to crawl out of my skin?

My eyes shot open as I reached for the woman with the red feathers in her hair. "Where am I? What's going on?"

A hint of fear passed through her eyes before she glared up at Jean-Pierre. "Bastard," she murmured under her breath. "Come on, Ruby. Let's get you up. You'll feel better once you get some rest."

As she peeled me off the ground, I noticed a crowd of women surrounding me—all of them dressed alike in their low-cut red leotards, feathers, silver high heels, and cherry lipstick. They whispered and stared at me, a few of them with concern etched in their brows, but one of them—a tall brunette with hazel eyes and cheekbones that almost reached her forehead—glared at me so hard I thought my face would break.

I didn't have time to process the ominous feeling that crept into my stomach, because the woman with the familiar green eyes ushered me through the throngs of red and silver and into a messy room lined with mirrors and bright lights and makeup scattered all over the countertops. As my eyes darted frantically around the clutter, a hauntingly vivid sense of déjà-vu suddenly came over me.

I've been here before.

The smell of lipstick, the missing lightbulb over the mirror in the right corner, the racks of skimpy, sequined costumes shimmering before me.

My mind took a mental snapshot of each item, each color, each scent in this room, and for every single one, my brain told me that I'd already touched it, seen it, smelled it.

But how could that be possible?

"Here, doll. Just lie down on the couch and I'll get you some water and something for your head. You'll feel better in no time. Tomorrow's a big night, and we're *not* letting Véronique weasel her way into your role. *La salope.*"

Okay. That was it. I had to let this woman know that although I was having a *major*, inexplicable case of déjà-vu, I did not belong here. I had to get back to my home in San Diego. To my grandma Martine, to my clients, to Édouard...and to my *baby*.

"I have no idea what you're talking about. Who are you? Where am—" I started, but my strange voice caught in my throat as the reflection of a young woman I didn't recognize stared back at me in the mirror.

She wore an outfit almost identical to the other girls, skintight and low-cut, except her leotard was all silver sequins, and a lone red feather stuck out from the soft blonde curls piled atop her head. Her breasts were voluptuous and bursting; her skin as pale as a first snow; her cheeks rosy; her lips full, round, and bathed in crimson lipstick; and her legs long, thin, and toned.

She was undeniably gorgeous.

It was when I gazed into her eyes that my entire body went ice-cold.

She had *my* eyes—the exact same iridescent blue eyes I'd seen each time I'd gazed into a mirror, for all of my thirty-five years as Claudia.

How were *my* eyes in *this* body?

I peered down at my stomach—at *her* stomach—and the air constricted in my lungs as the flat, sequin-covered abdomen confirmed my worst fear.

My baby girl was gone.

I remembered then. I remembered why I hadn't gotten the chance to tell Édouard that I was single. The magazine cover announcing his engagement. The pain that had ripped from my chest down through my stomach.

Lights and sequins blurred around me as I stumbled backward and landed with a thud on the couch.

"Oh, dear. You really bopped your head hard, didn't you?"

I barely heard the woman as she fumbled around the dressing room. How could I have woken up in someone else's body?

Where is my baby? Am I losing my mind?

The woman appeared at my side with a cup of water and some pills. "Here, take these. They'll help with your head."

I pushed her hand away. "No, I can't take pills. I'm pregnant. I'm eighteen weeks along. But something really strange is happening to me. Did I lose her? Did I lose my baby?"

Small lines crinkled around the woman's sea-green eyes, replacing the feistiness I'd seen earlier. "Calm down, sweetie. You haven't lost anyone. And you're not pregnant. I think you just bumped your head a little too hard."

I pushed myself up to a seated position as hot tears filled my eyelids. "I told you, I'm not Ruby. My name is Claudia. And I *am* pregnant. I'm not that girl in the mirror! Tell me where I am. What is going on?" I struggled to breathe the stale, smoky air in the dressing room as I gripped the side of the couch.

The woman reached for my hand. And through my panic, I felt another jolt of déjà-vu…but this time it was one of comfort. I gazed into her green eyes. *Those eyes.* How did I know them?

As if she was talking to a child she said, "My name is Titine. You and I, we grew up in New York City together and we're best friends. We moved from New York to Paris a little less than a year ago, and we dance at the club together."

When I didn't respond to that absurd statement, an exasperated sigh escaped her lips. "Don't you remember any of this?"

"No, I don't. What club? What are you talking about?"

Her brow creased in concern as she pushed a lock of strawberry-red hair off her shoulder. "Ruby, you're a singer and dancer at a famous jazz club near the Latin Quarter called Chez Gisèle."

I'm in Paris?

What is this? Some sort of messed-up version of *The Wizard of Oz?*

Before I could form a coherent response, Titine continued speaking, her eyes revealing a sadness I hadn't noticed before. "And as of this week, after what happened to Gisèle…never mind, we don't need to talk about that tonight. It's been a tough week on everyone. You're the star now, sweetie. And you took a really bad fall onstage.

Let's get you upstairs to your apartment and fix you something to eat. I think you're just exhausted."

The dread that had consumed me earlier at the mention of Gisèle's name reared its ugly head once again. "What happened to this Gisèle woman?" I asked. "And why am I the star of the show now?"

Titine squeezed my hand and lowered her glittery eyelids before speaking. "Gisèle *used* to be the star of the show, and she was our closest friend here. But on Saturday night she…she was found dead in her dressing room."

"How did she die?" I asked.

Titine shook her head at me. "You honestly don't remember?"

"Just tell me. Please. What's going on? What happened to Gisèle?"

She let out a weary sigh before looking me in the eye. "Ruby, *you* were one of the first people who found her. And I think you're still in shock."

I swallowed hard and stared back at Titine, my entire body paralyzed with fear.

"When you found Gisèle, her neck was broken…and she'd been shot," Titine continued.

"Did they catch the murderer?"

She bit her lower lip. "Talking about this right now isn't going to help you feel any better."

From the way Titine suddenly avoided my gaze, I knew there was more to this story. And even though I didn't want to acknowledge the possibility that any of this terrifying experience could be *real* by asking another question, I couldn't stop the words as they burst from my lips. "What aren't you telling me?"

Titine stayed silent, her eyes combing the floor for what seemed like hours before she finally lifted her deadpan gaze to meet mine. "The police are investigating you for Gisèle's murder, Ruby…*you* are their main suspect."

THREE

I had to be dreaming. There was no other logical explanation for this insane situation.

If I'd suddenly morphed from a pregnant, straitlaced therapist into this blonde-bombshell performer who was wanted for murder, hell must've frozen over.

I closed my eyes in an attempt to snap myself out of this insane dream, but then I remembered something else about my dance with Édouard.

Before I'd seen the magazine announcing Édouard's engagement and passed out in his arms, Édouard had spoken to me about Paris. This was making more sense now. Of course I would dream about being a dancer in Paris after that conversation. After all, my mind always liked to grab on to the last conversation I'd had, the last song I'd heard, or the last movie I'd watched, then concoct some bizarre dream about it.

But why was everything and everyone so familiar here?

I shook my head and told myself not to overanalyze. If this was a dream—and I was *sure* it was—all I needed to do was go back to sleep within the dream, and I would wake up in my grandma's dance studio in San Diego. I just hoped that when I woke up, my baby would be okay. I had to get back there *now*.

"You said my apartment is upstairs?" I asked Titine, still startled at the sound of this voice, much deeper and more seductive than my own. This was one absurd dream.

She nodded. "Yes, let's get you up there."

Even with her tiny frame, she was able to hoist me up off the couch and support me as she led me to a dark, winding staircase. A familiar musty smell assaulted my nose, and the sound of our heels tapping on the hardwood stairs made me remember walking this exact same path before. With each step, the feeling of déjà-vu grew stronger and the panic returned.

This is only a dream. I'll follow this woman, go back to bed, and when I wake up, everything will be back to normal.

It had to.

Five flights later, we arrived at the top floor, and I found myself gravitating to the tall blue door on the left. Titine reached for the doorknob.

"Does this ring a bell?" she asked as she ushered me into what I was assuming—and *praying*—was my dream-state apartment.

I glanced around the cluttered abode, taking mental snapshots of the rickety black desk in the corner and the piles of newspapers that littered the dusty surface, the pairs of sleek high heels carelessly strewn over the hardwood floors, and the cherry-red scarf draped over the stark white couch. A strong perfume masked the distinct smell of cigarette smoke, and a frosty draft sent shivers up my arms.

I know this apartment. I've been here before.

I leaned against the wall and closed my eyes, telling myself this would all be okay.

This has to be a dream.

But just as I was about to open my eyes, a vision of a man with hair the color of dark chocolate and broad, muscular shoulders appeared in my mind. He stormed toward the window on the far side of the small apartment, and standing there, topless, was the woman I'd seen in the mirror earlier—the woman whose body I was currently *inside*. The man reached for her and kissed her forcefully on the lips as he cupped her breast in his palm, then whispered something in her ear.

My cheeks flushed as I remembered the way his hands had felt on my skin, the way I'd yearned for him to take me. I tried to make out his face, but I could only feel his strong hands, caressing my entire body, their force, their strength unmatched by any other man's.

"Ruby? Are you okay?" Titine asked, snapping me back the present moment.

My eyes jolted open and I forced in a breath, the panic and confusion now settling deep into my core. "I need to lie down. Please, just get me to bed."

She didn't mask the alarm on her sweet, pale face as she ushered me through the living room, her hands wrapped tightly around my shoulders, keeping me from collapsing out of sheer bewilderment.

When I turned the corner into the bedroom, I didn't even have to look to know that the walls would be painted a deep violet and the sheets on the bed would be red.

And they were. *Scarlet* red.

I ignored the flashes of déjà-vu that assaulted me from every direction and instead climbed into bed, desperately hoping for a reprieve from this madness. But just as my head plummeted and I curled up under the red satin sheets, something crinkled underneath the pillow. I slipped my hand beneath the silky scarlet pillowcase to find a small piece of paper folded in half.

I stared at it, knowing somewhere deep in my gut that whatever was written in this note wasn't going to help me get back to sleep.

Just go to bed, I told myself. *None of this is real.*

But my desire to uncover the information hidden inside the paper overpowered my reason.

As Titine left me alone in the bedroom, I unfolded the torn, faded paper. Inside, I found a note scrawled in French in eerie, thick red handwriting. And as I frantically skimmed the words in this foreign language I'd never learned, my brain translated the message directly into English.

My dear Ruby,
I know what you did, and if you even think about talking to
A., there will be consequences.
Yours truly,
T. R.

Goose bumps prickled my arms as I squinted to get a better look at the signature. Was it signed *T. R.?* Or *S. R.?* And who was *A.?*

As I gazed down at the hands that held this freaky note, I realized again that they weren't mine. They had long, manicured fingernails painted a deep red, and they were smaller and daintier than my own.

Okay, that was it. I *had* to be dreaming. I wasn't crazy. I wasn't an insane person. These were definitely *not* my hands, and this was definitely not my body.

I needed to wake up *now*. But I couldn't just lie here in this foreign bed and expect it to happen. I had to take action.

I jumped out of bed and ran into the kitchen, where Titine was reaching for a glass in the cabinet. Yanking the glass from her hands, I filled it with cold tap water, closed my eyes, and dumped the chilly liquid over my head.

"What in the hell are you doing, Ruby?" Titine shrieked.

I took a deep breath, peeled one eye open, then the other, but my chest deflated when I realized I was still in this stranger's apartment. Nothing had happened. I was now not only confused and in a complete state of panic, I was also soaking wet, and Titine was staring at me with her mouth wide open.

"Have you lost your mind?" she asked, snatching the glass from my death grip.

"This isn't my life," I announced once more as I paced through the apartment, trying to come up with another method to wake myself up from this insane nightmare. "I'm not Ruby. My name is Claudia. I'm a marriage and family therapist who lives alone in San Diego. And I already told you: I'm pregnant. This life, this body, this apartment—none of it is mine! I just need to wake up," I shouted, hoping the shrieks would snap me awake, but I was still here, in this foreign life, this foreign body, this foreign apartment, with no idea how in the hell I'd gotten here.

"You need to get your act together, Ruby," Titine scolded. "I know you're scared after what happened this week. We all are. We'd all like to conveniently *forget* what's been going on around here, but you can't go around pretending you've lost your memory and saying you're someone else just because you're under investigation for Gisèle's murder! It's only going to make you look guiltier, not to mention insane. Plus, tomorrow night is the biggest performance of our lives, and you cannot mess this up."

Titine charged toward me and grabbed me by the shoulders. "I need this chance just as much as you do, Ruby. This could be it for us. Our way out of these sleazy clubs forever. We could become real stars! But you have to stop this nonsense." She squeezed my shoulders, her lavender perfume engulfing me, her emerald eyes feisty and severe. "Do you understand me?"

I pulled away from her grasp and pointed toward the door. "Get out."

"Excuse me?" she said.

"Please, just leave me alone."

Titine shook her head at me and sighed. "Fine. But your dramatics aren't going to work, Ruby. I'm your best friend, and if I'm not buying it, no one else will either. Please calm down, eat something, and meet me downstairs for rehearsal in an hour." Titine walked toward the door, but before she left, she swiveled back around on her pointy heel.

"Don't even think about spouting off any of this nonsense about being a therapist living in San Diego." The corners of her mouth turned up into a teasing grin. "I mean, if you were going to fake a fall and pretend to lose your mind, couldn't you have come up with a better story than that?"

+≈≈+

Ignoring the little voice inside my head telling me that this was all too real and entirely too vivid to be a dream, I raced over to the window, ripped the cherry-red curtains apart, and opened up the French windows to find a small black iron balcony jutting out into the wintry air.

Clutching the ice-cold railing, I climbed onto the tiny platform, fully prepared to jump—not to my death, but to my real life back in San Diego.

But instead, I could only gasp.

A scene from the old black-and-white films I used to watch with my grandma Martine played out right before my eyes. Except it was in color. And it was as real as the freezing water still dripping down my face.

Classic cars in cherry red, sky blue, forest green, and jet black chugged along the busy boulevard below, while men clad in black and gray trousers, long overcoats, and dapper black bowler hats escorted women down the crowded, narrow sidewalk. Some of the women wore dark fur coats with matching hats and hand muffs while others kept warm in less-showy peacoats and sleek white gloves. Elegant, colorful scarves adorned their necks, completing that look of pure sophistication that only a French woman could possess.

Cafés and brasseries lined the boulevard, their heated terraces filled to the brim with smoking Parisians leisurely sipping wine, reading the *journal*, or enjoying tiny cups of coffee. Chic clothing stores revealed gorgeous window displays of the most beautiful vintage dresses, hats, and heels I'd ever laid eyes upon. Rows upon rows of black iron balconies just like the one I was currently glued to lined the elegant apartment buildings that surrounded the boulevard.

Sounds of the French language drifted up to my perch on the balcony, my stupefied brain immediately recognizing the words… even though I'd never before spoken French in my life.

I'm really in Paris.

Titine hadn't been lying. But unless a movie crew was shooting a period film right outside my window, this was *not* Paris of the twenty-first century.

I lifted my gaze over the tops of the old stone buildings, past the rows of skinny red chimneys, and caught a glimpse of something I'd longed to see in person all my life—La Tour Eiffel. But as I stared at the top of the majestic tower until swirls of thick gray clouds swallowed it up, a terrifying realization overcame me.

I'd never dreamed in color before. Ever.

And even more shocking was the distinct feeling that I'd stood on this exact balcony, gazing out at this exact view of the Eiffel Tower many times before.

But *not* in my life as Claudia.

It hit me then. Like another shot of ice water to the face. But this time the harsh freeze traveled all the way down to my bones.

I'm really here. I'm in Paris, in some other woman's body, living some other woman's life. A life I remembered. A life in the past.

I'm not dreaming.

Overwhelmed at the magnitude of the situation and utterly confused as to what it all could mean, I hobbled back from the balcony and turned to search the apartment for something that had the date on it. Because at least I knew for sure where I was, but now I had to figure out *when*.

As I riffled through Ruby's clutter, I didn't find a computer or a cell phone or even a television, which confirmed what the old cars and outdated fashions on the street below had already shown me. Then, on the messy black desk in the corner of the living room, I found a copy of *Le Monde*, a French newspaper. And sure enough, just underneath the heading was a date stamped in bold black ink— *lundi 1 décembre 1959.*

Holy shit.

1959?

But I was born in 1977.

How in the hell did this happen?

I stumbled into the wobbly desk chair, then scanned the paper once more just to make sure this was real. That I'd really gone from being pregnant and dancing with Édouard Marceau one minute—in the year *2012*—only to pass out in his arms and wake up in a completely different and absolutely *stunning* body in Paris in 1959 the next.

A bold headline in the center of the front page caught my eye, and my brain—or *Ruby's* brain?—effortlessly turned the elegant French words into English as I skimmed the page.

> *Sister of Esteemed Surgeon Found Dead in the Latin Quarter*
>
> *Twenty-six-year-old Gisèle Richard, longtime star of the booming Latin Quarter cabaret club Chez Gisèle, was found murdered in her dressing room after a performance on Saturday night. Survived only by her older brother, renowned obstetric surgeon Antoine Richard, Mademoiselle Richard lived a lively and scandalous existence until her untimely death earlier this week.*
>
> *Replacing Mademoiselle Richard as the lead singer and dancer at the popular nightclub will be Ruby Kerrigan, a transplant from New York City who arrived in Paris less than a year ago. It was this beauty of Irish descent who reportedly discovered the body of her fellow dancer on the floor of the deceased's dressing room, with a broken neck and a bullet wound to her chest.*
>
> *The club's owner, Jean-Pierre Fontaine, refused to comment on the circumstances surrounding the young performer's death. Police confirmed a murder investigation is under way.*

A chill slithered down my spine as an unwelcome image invaded my mind. I saw a woman lying on the ground, her neck twisted at an odd angle, her long black hair tangled up in her feathery red costume, her eyes open but motionless, and a crimson stream of blood pooling off her chest.

It was Gisèle's lifeless body, just as I'd found her.

Shaking off the sickening memory, I tried not to overthink the fact that I hadn't even been here for an hour and I'd already found this new name of mine on the front page of a major French newspaper, connected to a gruesome murder…a gruesome murder that I vaguely remembered. But even more shocking than seeing Ruby's name in print were the tingles that shot through my body at the mention of Gisèle's brother's name.

Antoine Richard.

I tossed the paper back onto the desk and ran into the bedroom. I threw the pillows from the bed, and there, crumpled underneath the red satin sheets, was the threatening note I'd found just a few minutes earlier.

> *My dear Ruby,*
> *I know what you did, and if you even think about talking to A., there will be consequences.*
> *Yours truly,*
> *T. R.*

Was the *A.* mentioned in this note referring to *Antoine*? And what *had* Ruby done?

I rushed back out to the living room and riffled through Ruby's mess of a desk searching for more information. Anything that could help me put together the puzzle pieces of Ruby's life, find out who was threatening her, if she had, in fact, been involved in Gisèle's murder, and why I felt so light-headed simply upon reading the name *Antoine Richard*.

But as I flung useless, empty notebooks, papers with meaningless scribbles, and old newspapers from the pile, I began to wonder if this was all in vain…and I even began to wonder if I really had lost my mind.

Maybe my life as Claudia had merely been a figment of my—or Ruby's—imagination. Maybe I had multiple personality disorder or schizophrenia.

Maybe none of my memories—my baby, Édouard Marceau, my life in San Diego—were real. Maybe I really was Ruby and *only* Ruby, and I'd snapped under the trauma of finding Gisèle's body and being accused of her murder. And as a result, I'd created another life to focus on, to hide behind.

But as I threw the last newspaper from the desk in exasperation, my eyes landed on two objects that proved otherwise.

There, lying on Ruby's desk, was *my* red journal, and next to it, the *People* magazine dated December 1, 2012, with Édouard Marceau's and Solange Raspail's faces smiling back at me.

FOUR

The sight of Édouard with that wispy French woman draped all over him and the word *engaged* printed over their happy faces made me want to rip the glossy magazine to shreds. At the same time, I felt immense hope over the fact that I hadn't lost my mind. If both of these objects had traveled here with me, it meant my future life as Claudia really *had* existed and that all I needed to do was tap back into whatever force had landed me here and hope that it would return me to 2012.

Maybe it's the journal.

My fingers brushed over its worn spine and thick, yellowed pages, but I didn't feel myself falling or transporting anywhere. I stayed right where I was, grounded in this surreal moment where I was living in someone else's life, touching a journal I'd brought back with me from the future.

I opened the cover and flipped frantically through the pages, just to make sure my life was still all there. The good *and* the bad of it. I didn't want to lose a single moment, a single memory.

But with each turn of the page, the dark-blue ink I'd always written in began to fade. Lighter and lighter it became until whole dates, lines, and stories disappeared right before my eyes. I swallowed the knot forming in my throat, hoping I was imagining it. Hoping my life, my memories, wouldn't be gone forever.

I wasn't imagining it, though. Not any more than I was imagining this entire bewildering experience.

When I reached the middle of the journal and watched yet another line of my neat handwriting vanish into thin air, suddenly the sonogram photo of my baby girl slid out from between the pages. I picked it up, praying the picture would transport me back to my life. But when I focused on the ultrasound picture, I noticed the tiny black-and-white specks that made up my baby's head beginning to fade too.

The room spun around me as I clutched my flat stomach, wondering what in the hell was happening to me, to my life, to my baby. Where could my unborn child possibly be if I was here? Would I ever get her back?

I didn't care anymore that her father had turned out to be married, that he wanted nothing to do with our child, or that I was going to be a single mom. I'd give anything to go back and have that amazing opportunity again.

In a desperate rage, I shot up from the desk, ran to the open window, and shouted into the freezing winter air, "I want to go back! Send me back!"

Meeting my frantic plea, a violent torrent of wind whipped through the small apartment, snatching the photograph from my hand and swirling it up above my head. I lunged for the picture of my baby, not willing to let this crazy experience leach anything else from my grasp. But the wind grew stronger, scooping up every loose piece of paper in Ruby's apartment and spinning them around like a tornado until I couldn't see straight.

I grabbed onto the chair and closed my eyes. The unmistakable scent of roses drifted past my nose, surrounding me like a pillow until I couldn't feel the ground beneath my feet.

Within seconds, a harsh beeping noise replaced the howling wind, and my feet landed on solid ground.

And when I opened my eyes, I spotted a green 1950s Renault Dauphine rambling down a busy Parisian boulevard, its beady round headlights heading straight for me.

I lunged out of the way, stumbling onto the uneven cobblestone sidewalk and gasping for air. It took me a few moments to gain my bearings, but as I stood in Ruby's skin and gazed at the chilly Parisian streets and the life that buzzed all around me, I realized this was the exact view I'd seen from Ruby's window just moments ago.

But standing here now, with my feet firmly planted on the sidewalk, the wind whipping my new curly blonde locks against my face, and the landscape of *Paris* laid out before me, I had to steady my entire body against the building to keep from passing out.

Newsstands and crêpe stands dotted the sidewalks, *boulangeries* speckled the narrow little *rue* to my right, and the picturesque cafés I'd seen just moments before now looked all too familiar. I could see myself—as Ruby—packed inside their smoke-filled interiors with groups of fellow dancers, drinking wine with handsome men dressed in suits, their ties loosening with each glass, each flirtatious glance, each brush of their hands on my thin, toned legs.

Shaking myself from the vivid memories, I noticed a woman smoking a long, skinny cigarette, walking her tiny dog with an air of elegance and sophistication of which I knew nothing from my beach life back in California.

I tried to wrap my mind around my mysterious voyage—not only to 1950s Paris, but from Ruby's fifth-floor apartment down to the street below—but instead, all I could think about was the distinct notion that I'd stood on this tree-lined boulevard before.

I'd seen the way the thin branches twisted and reached toward the sunlight, hoping, waiting for spring to arrive in Paris. I'd breathed in these same mouthwatering aromas of strong French coffee and freshly baked baguettes. I'd heard the bizarre sounds of sirens and squeaky car horns. I'd smiled to myself as the elegant music of the French language swirled endlessly through these bustling Parisian streets.

Many times before.

And I didn't even need to peek up at the street sign to know that I was standing at the corner of Boulevard Saint-Germain and rue de l'Ancienne Comédie.

I simply *knew.*

With my back pressed up against the cold stones of Ruby's apartment building, and chic Parisians raising their brows at me as they strolled past, I recalled again that bizarre vision of Paris that I'd experienced while dancing with Édouard. Except this time I knew for certain that it hadn't been my imagination. The soles of my shoes really *had* stood on these rough cobblestone streets before.

But how?

"*Suivez-moi.*" *Follow me*, said a female voice, shaking me from my confused trance.

Another strong whiff of roses encapsulated me as I flipped around and caught a flash of silvery-gray hair and luminous violet eyes.

It was her.

The elegant older woman who'd been in my grandmother's dance studio in San Diego, in the year 2012, less than an hour ago.

And she was jetting through the crosswalk, not even giving me a second to catch my breath.

Three teenage boys clad in old-fashioned trousers and black caps hooted and hollered at me as I pushed past them to catch up with the woman, my mind struggling to make any sense of this insane situation.

"*Attendez!*" I yelled to her as she zipped with ease across the lively boulevard.

It was only after I'd rounded a slow-walking older gentleman that I realized I'd just spoken French. In a perfect accent, no less.

I'd never spoken French before in my life. In my life as *Claudia*, that is.

What a freaking trip.

Spotting the woman's silvery hair and long indigo peacoat ducking into a café a block down the boulevard, I only hoped she wouldn't magically disappear before I could reach her.

A few moments later, I burst into the crowded café and exhaled a sigh of relief as the woman raised a brow at me from a tiny table nestled in the corner. I rushed over to her, my legs shaky from the cold, the adrenaline, and from the confusion of it all.

"*Asseyez-vous.*" *Sit down*, she said with a deliberate nod as she took a sip of what smelled to be a steaming hot chocolate.

I stared at her incredulously as I took a seat, a plethora of questions hanging at the tip of my tongue, burning to be answered.

"Mmm, a tasty *chocolat chaud* in the middle of winter in Paris," she said, with that same mischievous gleam in her eye I'd noticed in the dance studio. "There is nothing better, *n'est-ce pas?*"

"Hot chocolate? You're seriously talking about hot chocolate when I just saw you less than an hour ago in San Diego in the year 2012? How—" But I stopped speaking when the woman calmly pushed another steamy cup in my direction. There hadn't been a second mug on the table just a second earlier, had there?

"Try some, dear. It'll warm you up. You really must start dressing for the weather. It's not always springtime in Paris, you know." She unwrapped the silky red scarf from her neck and placed it in my hand.

I gazed down and realized that I was still wearing the tight, silver-sequined leotard I'd woken up in, with Ruby's outrageous cleavage bursting over the top.

Oh, dear God. No wonder those boys were drooling and shouting as I ran past them.

I wrapped the rose-scented scarf around my neck and chest, telling myself it didn't matter that I'd just dashed, half-naked, across a busy Parisian boulevard. Because I wasn't planning on staying here for much longer.

"You did this, didn't you?" I said to the woman. "I don't understand how or why, and I can't believe I'm acknowledging that this is really happening, but I know it was *you* who sent me here. And I need you to send me back right now. Back to my *real* life."

Peabody Public Library
Columbia City, IN

A soft chuckle danced from her full red lips. "It's not that easy, my dear. I do suggest you eat something, though." She nudged a plate in my direction—which, much like the cup of hot chocolate, seemed to have materialized out of thin air. Thick slices of ham and melted cheese spilled out over a warm baguette, the aroma making my stomach ache with hunger.

"Go on. Take a bite," she urged. "And in case you were wondering, I am aware that Claudia is a vegetarian, but Ruby, my dear, is not. Now, *mangez*."

"Who are—?" I began, but as my eyes landed once again on those juicy slices of ham, I realized that I didn't feel a single ounce of the usual distaste I'd garnered toward meat in my life as Claudia. Instead, my mouth watered.

Oh, screw it.

After taking a huge bite of the hot, buttery sandwich, I washed it down with a steamy sip of *chocolat chaud* and gazed up at the stubborn old woman. "Happy?"

"There, that's better." She leaned forward in her seat, her penetrating violet eyes piercing right through me. "These past-life trips can really take a toll on you, so it is imperative that you take care of yourself while you're here. You don't have much time, after all."

I almost choked on the second piece of buttery baguette I'd just bitten into. "Past-life trips?"

"Like I said, you don't have much time to accomplish what you were brought back here to do. Five short days, to be exact. So the sooner you recognize what you already know to be true, the smoother things will go. That's not saying this is going to be easy, though. A past-life revisit is rarely a walk in the park. Especially in your case."

"Are you saying that the reason I remember Jean-Pierre, Titine, Gisèle, Ruby's apartment, and her view of the Eiffel Tower, is because I *used* to be Ruby? That…oh, God, I can't even believe I'm going to say this. I've never believed in this nonsense before. But you're saying that I was Ruby in my past life?"

She nodded, her sparkly eyes suddenly taking on a grave regard. "That is exactly what I'm saying. And if you listen to your intuition, you will know, my dear, that this *isn't* nonsense. *Au contraire.* Your situation is quite serious; your position here in this lifetime is vital. And there isn't a single moment to waste."

"What do you mean?" I asked, letting the baguette slip from my fingers, my heart pounding inside my chest.

"There is a specific reason you were sent back to this lifetime—a specific task that you must accomplish. And like I said, you have five days to do it."

"So what is it? I mean, whatever it is, I'll do it right now. Then can I go back to being Claudia? To being pregnant and living in San Diego, in the twenty-first century?"

She raised an eyebrow. "We often don't realize how wonderful things are until they are taken away from us, no?"

"Listen, I've lost enough in my lifetime to understand how precious life is…and how easily we can lose it. Just tell me how to get back. Tell me what to do."

Her long eyelashes batted quickly before a shadow crossed her face. "That information, I do not have. Such is the nature of a past-life revisit. Only the soul in question will know the time and the hour of this one monumental event. Only *you* will know yours. And only you will know what action to take when that moment comes. That is, if you are listening."

"Listening to what? To who?" I asked, feeling panic overtaking my system.

The old woman tapped her weathered hands over her heart. "Listen to Ruby. After all, you used to *be* her. You know her better than you think you do."

I closed my eyes and rubbed my throbbing temples in my hands, wishing I could just go back. Wishing this wasn't really happening.

The old woman continued, "If you engage in this life—*fully engage*—the answers will come to you when you need them. But you must listen carefully, Claudia. Pay attention to everything you see and everyone you meet. And above all, no matter how frightful this experience becomes, you mustn't run. For the fates of countless people—including yourself, your future husband, and your future child—rest on your shoulders."

She took another leisurely sip of hot chocolate, making me want to smack the cup out of her hands and force her to tell me what in the hell she was talking about.

"But I'm not married. In case you didn't know, I'm a pregnant, single, thirty-five-year-old." I glanced down at my flat, silver-sequined tummy. "Well, I used to be pregnant."

"Tell me, Claudia, have you ever felt as if the events that have happened in your life weren't supposed to happen? Your father's murder just before he was about to run for Senate, your mother blaming you for his death, you getting pregnant right before you finally meet the one man who feels right to you? The first man you've ever truly loved? Haven't you ever wondered why life has played out in sometimes tragic ways for you? Haven't you found yourself bewildered over the irony of it all?"

Goose bumps prickled my arms as I searched her violet gaze. "Who are you? And how do you know all of that stuff about my father, my family, and my life?"

"You can call me Madame Bouchard. And as for how I know what I know…there is a long explanation, which we, or *you*, rather, do not have time to hear. Nor is it relevant. The important question at hand, my dear, is haven't you ever wondered about fate? And why yours seems destined to be on the wrong track?"

"I don't believe in fate. I believe that these are the cards I've been dealt, and it's up to me to figure out how to live with them. Fate, destiny, all of that is just nonsense people rely on so they don't have to take responsibility for their lives."

The old woman gazed around at the Parisians smoking cigarettes and sipping their strong French cafés before a knowing smirk glided over her lips. "You didn't believe in past lives before, and yet, here you are."

I opened my mouth, ready to retort with more of my therapist drivel, but Madame Bouchard was right. Here I was. In Paris. In 1959.

"Suppose I did believe in fate, that I thought there was some grand reason why my life has gone so off course, what does that have to do with this?" I asked.

She set her *chocolat chaud* down in the saucer, then leaned over the table and whispered, "Because, my dear, now you have been given the chance to correct your ill-fated course. *All* of it."

"But how will I know—"

She reached across the table and squeezed my hand, sending those familiar sparks soaring underneath my skin. "If you listen, if you pay attention, you'll *know*. And no matter what happens, do not lose your dancing shoes. After all, you have rehearsal in ten minutes."

I peered underneath the table, and for the first time since I'd woken up in Ruby's body, I noticed that the shoes on Ruby's dainty feet were the *exact same* pair of sparkly red heels I'd been wearing in my grandmother's dance studio.

"How did—" I began, but when I lifted my gaze, the old woman was gone, her rose-scented perfume lingering in the smoky air of the café, drowning out my questions, mocking my search for answers.

And when I peered down at my tingling fingers, there, resting in Ruby's soft palms, was the photo of my baby, its faded colors like a ticking time bomb in my hands.

FIVE

Struggling to grasp the utter insanity of this situation, I discreetly tucked the photograph into my sequined leotard, then pushed past a bewildered Parisian waiter and rushed out of the café.

I wrapped the cherry-red scarf tighter around my neck as a gust of wind barreled down the boulevard. Combing the street, I searched for Madame Bouchard's silvery hair and her indigo peacoat, but she was nowhere to be found.

How could she just leave me here like this? After telling me I had some monumental task to accomplish in my *past life*? After telling me that I could potentially change my future? My fate?

How is this happening to me?

Another bitter draft whipped past, reminding me that I was standing on a busy Parisian boulevard in the middle of winter in a tight, wet, silver-sequined leotard with bare legs and sparkly red heels—heels that had traveled back in time with me, no less. And besides, the bitter air was beginning to turn my fingertips and nose into ice, and the sophisticated Parisians all bundled in their chic winter clothing were beginning to stare. I needed to get inside.

Turning back toward the club, I smacked straight into someone.

"Mais qu'est-ce que tu fous là?" *What in the hell are you doing out here?*

It was Jean-Pierre, the bossy club owner from earlier. I opened my mouth to respond, but what was I supposed to tell him? That I'd been magically transported from Ruby's apartment to the street, had just eaten a sandwich and a hot chocolate that appeared out of nowhere with an old woman who vanished into thin air? And, oh yeah, I'm not actually Ruby. Well, I used to be her in my so-called past life, but my real name is Claudia and I'm from the year 2012. Somehow I didn't think any of that would go over well.

Luckily, Jean-Pierre didn't wait for my answer. He stripped off his long black coat and wrapped it around my shoulders as he ushered me back across the boulevard. *"Allez, viens."* *Come on, let's go*, he said firmly, his eyes nervously combing the street around us.

Neither of us spoke another word as we entered through the side door of the club and wound through the dark hallway to the dressing room where I'd been with Titine earlier. Jean-Pierre closed the door behind him, then charged toward me, the anger in his gaze making me flinch.

"What in the hell were you doing out there? *Merde!* Roaming the streets of Paris in the middle of winter in barely any clothing! *Les policiers* are watching us, Ruby. The last thing we need after Gisèle's murder is to bring more negative attention to the club." He grabbed my arm and lowered his voice. "And in case your little fall made you forget, the police think *you* could be the one responsible for Gisèle's death. Pretending to lose your memory right now will not help. It will only make you appear more suspicious."

"I'm not pretending. I don't even know what I would tell the police if they came to question me."

He shook his head and huffed out an angry breath. "You would tell them exactly what you told them the night you found Gisèle. That after the show, you drank a little too much at the bar and suddenly didn't feel well. You went up to your apartment to take a rest, but half an hour later, you felt a little better and decided to come back downstairs to mingle. On your way through the wings, you heard a commotion, and that is when you found Gisèle lying on the floor in her dressing room."

When I didn't respond, Jean-Pierre raised a brow. "This *is* what you told the police, correct?"

"Is the story true? Did I really go up to my apartment because I was feeling sick?"

Jean-Pierre took a step closer to me, his brown eyes severe and unforgiving, his grip on my arm tightening. "I do not like these games you are playing with me, Ruby. You know exactly what you were doing before you found Gisèle, and if you even think about mentioning François Lefevre's name to the police, you will lose everything: your career, your apartment, your reputation, everything."

I yanked my arm free of his grasp and pointed to the door. "You need to leave."

Jean-Pierre muttered something under his breath, then turned and reached for the door handle while I braced myself against the makeup counter to keep my knees from buckling underneath me.

But before he left me alone, he turned back around one last time, the edge in his gaze and the sharpness of his tone not softening one bit. "You have five minutes to get yourself together, change out of that wet costume, and be back onstage to rehearse. Tomorrow is the single most important performance of your life, not to mention the most important performance this club has ever had. And in case you have forgotten, the arrangement we have for after the show is still on. Do not even think about backing out now."

"What arrangement?" I hurled through the lonely space only seconds after he had left. God, that man was a pushy, chauvinistic lunatic.

I steadied myself against the counter, my knees still shaking from the cold, but more so from fear. What in God's name was I expected to do after the show? And *who* was François Lefevre? I closed my eyes and remembered the way his name had rolled of Jean-Pierre's tongue in his thick French accent, and somewhere in my confused, terrified head, "Lefevre" rang a bell.

But when I couldn't remember a face to match the name, I shook my head and gazed over at the rack of sparkly leotards and shimmering, provocative costumes lining the wall. How was I supposed to rehearse, let alone *perform*, when the most dancing I'd ever done was taking lessons at Grandma Martine's studio?

I squeezed my eyes closed, hearing the old woman's voice from moments before come soaring back to me.

No matter how frightful this experience becomes, you mustn't run. For the fates of countless people—including yourself, your future husband, and your future child—rest on your shoulders.

But to be the star of the show? And to pull off the most important performance of Ruby's life?

Listen to Ruby. After all, you used to be her. You know her better than you think you do.

All I knew for sure about Ruby in that moment was that she needed to get out of this wet costume because she was freezing. *I* was freezing.

I crossed over to the rack of slinky leotards, picked out the most conservative one I could find—which, with its dangerously low neckline and equally low scoop-back, was not something I would've ever worn before this insane time warp. But at least it was dry.

I slipped Jean-Pierre's coat from my shoulders, pulled the fading photo of my baby from my chest, then peeled off the tight mass of silver sequins. But just as I was about to slip on the dry leotard, I couldn't help but gaze at this new, naked body of mine in the floor-to-ceiling mirror before me.

And there she was.

There *I* was.

My long, chestnut-brown hair had been replaced by a head of thick, shoulder-length, wavy blonde locks. My cheekbones were higher, my eyebrows more heavily arched and perfectly plucked. My lips were full and luscious, and when I smiled, a set of straight, pearly white teeth glistened back at me. Even my skin was much paler in contrast to the olive complexion I'd had my whole life as Claudia.

My gaze lowered to my new neck and shoulders. They were thinner and bonier than my old ones, and they gave way to a set of round, perky, and, I couldn't deny it, *gorgeous* breasts.

Thirty-five-year-old breasts did *not* sit up this tall. How much younger was I?

But just before I tore my gaze from the shocking reflection in the mirror, I spotted a small, thin scar on my lower abdomen and another thicker, more jagged scar stretching around my side and across my lower back. Running my finger over the deep, nasty gash, my stomach curled and my head became woozy. I reached for the edge of the mirror to steady myself, but as I closed my eyes, instead of finding blackness, I saw a shiny knife pointed straight at me.

A gruff, scarred hand held onto the knife, but no matter how hard I focused, I couldn't see past that hand. And before I could stop it, the knife came swirling around my side and sliced into my back.

The sound of my own bloodcurdling scream woke me from the vision. I ran to the trash can in the corner of the dressing room and hurled the contents of Ruby's last meal into the plastic bag.

I slid onto the ground, but refused to close my eyes out of fear that I would see that hand, that knife, coming at me again. Feel it slicing me across the back, feel the blood running down my legs.

Each shallow breath burned my lungs as my stomach contracted for one final purge.

Someone had tried to kill Ruby. The memory was so absolutely terrifying and clear, and the scars on my back and stomach were fresh enough, I knew it couldn't have been long ago.

And on top of all of that, Ruby was now a murder suspect.

I was a murder suspect.

And I had no clue what I'd really been doing the night of Gisèle's murder. Or who François Lefevre was, or what the *arrangement* was for after the show.

I had no idea what any of this madness meant, or what monumental task I was supposed to accomplish in only five days.

And I didn't want to know.

All I wanted was to go home.

But as I turned my weary face back toward the mirror and spotted the gray circles forming around my own blue eyes—the eyes that had traveled back in time with me into this other woman's body and her mess of a life—I wondered if I'd brought enough strength with me to fight back and find my way home.

SIX

"Ruby, what happened?" Titine appeared in the doorway of the dressing room moments later, her sparkly green eyes gaping down at me in horror. "We're all waiting for you on stage, and Jean-Pierre is livid! What did you say to him? And why on earth are you naked on the floor?"

When I responded with a violent shiver, Titine crossed the dressing room, grabbed a throw off the tiny couch, then crouched down and wrapped it around me. She sighed, tucking a strand of hair behind my ears. "Oh, Ruby. My Ruby. What am I going to do with you?"

My trembling body snapped to attention at her words.

Ruby. My Ruby.

I'd heard someone else say those exact words in the dance studio, just before I'd woken up in Ruby's body in Paris.

Is it possible? Could Titine really be...?

I focused in on the strawberry color of Titine's hair, the way the curls bounced off her neck, the shiny strands swept up into a messy bun. Her skin was pale and dotted with tiny freckles—freckles I knew. Although in her old age, she would have even more freckles, and her smooth skin would become paler and lined with thin wrinkles. But her gorgeous eyes—her sea-green, sparkly eyes—those wouldn't change a bit.

There was no mistaking it. I just couldn't believe I hadn't seen it earlier.

Titine was my grandmother.

"Ruby, what is going on? Why are you looking at me like that? You look like you've seen a ghost."

Hadn't I?

"I'm sorry," I mumbled as I tried to put the pieces together in my head. I knew my grandmother had spent time dancing in Paris when she was younger, but she'd never elaborated much. And why was she called Titine? And how would I ask Titine these questions without making her think I was completely nuts?

"Don't be sorry, sweetie," she said as she reached past me for the costume I'd dropped on the floor. "Just get dressed. With everything that's going on this week, you have to pull yourself together. You have to finish rehearsal."

I stared back at Titine, at my young grandmother, completely mesmerized by her, and wondering how in the hell this could be happening. Her movements, her hands, her words, even the rhythm and inflection of her speech—it was all the same. A bit bouncier and livelier than the seventy-six-year-old version, but really, not much had changed.

But why had my grandma Martine called out Ruby's name just before I'd passed out in the dance studio? Had she seen Ruby in me that night? Had she somehow known this would happen?

Titine pushed the costume into my hands, snapping me back to reality, or whatever the hell this was. "Come on, Miss Drama. Not a moment to waste. It's time to get dressed and show Jean-Pierre what a great choice he made in making you the star of the show. Otherwise, that little tramp Véronique is going to try to mosey her way in. And I'll be damned if I let that happen."

Yes, Titine was most definitely my grandma Martine. Sassiness and all.

Just as she was about to stand up, I grabbed her wrist. "Titine, I need to talk to you."

"We can talk while you change into your costume. I'm serious, Ruby, we need to go. *Now.*" She clasped my hand and pulled me up to my feet.

"I'm sorry, but this can't wait. Are you…" I trailed off, not sure how to approach this without coming off as if I'd completely lost it. The fact that I was naked, shivering, and wrapped in a blanket would not add points to my credibility either.

"Yes?" she said, her foot tapping the ground impatiently. Grandma Martine always did that when she was in a hurry.

"Was your name ever Martine?"

A hint of fear punctured Titine's determined gaze, but she quickly blinked it away. "Ruby, I'm serious. We don't have time for games. I know you want to pretend you don't remember anything. I know you want to run from all of this. But you can't run. Not from me, anyway."

"So your name *wasn't* ever Martine?"

Titine stomped her high-heeled foot on the floor and threw her hands into the air. "Ruby, my name *is* Martine."

"So why are you called *Titine*?"

"Because in France, Titine is the nickname for Martine, plus we thought it would be a better stage name. And your new nickname is going to be *Amnesia Ruby*. Do you really not remember any of this? Do you not remember *me*?"

"Of course, I remember you." *She had no idea how much of her I remembered.* "It's just that the details of my life here, of *our* lives, are a little fuzzy to me."

"Do you think you can get through rehearsal at least, and then we can call the doctor to come tonight, before the big show tomorrow? Does your head still hurt from the fall?"

"No, my head feels fine. I mean, physically it feels fine. But I still don't think I should dance today. If that girl Véronique wants my part, she can have it." Right as those words exited my lips, though, I felt a strange pang of…*something* in my gut. Was it jealousy? Before I could figure out why I felt that way, though, the feistiness I'd seen in Titine's eyes earlier returned in full force.

"Ruby, for the last time, we have to go *now*. I know what happened to Gisèle was horrific, and that finding her like that must've really taken a toll on you…we're all scared here. But to be honest, you're the strongest one of us all, and you've been through *much* worse." Titine's hands shot to her hips as she leveled her determined gaze at me. "If you're honest with the police, they'll have no choice but to find you innocent. As far as we know, they have no real evidence to convict you. They haven't even found the murder weapon. Plus, you and Gisèle were friends. You had no reason to want to harm her. I know the other girls might not think so now that Jean-Pierre has given you her role, but *I* know you're innocent, Ruby, and I'll do everything I can do help you. Acting as if you don't remember anything is not going to help, though. It's only going to make you appear guilty."

"Titine, what was I doing the night Gisèle was killed? Where was I when it happened?"

"You went up to your apartment because you didn't feel well, but then you decided to come back down a little while later. That's when you heard one of the younger dancers, Delphine, screaming in Gisèle's dressing room and ran in there. I still don't understand why the police aren't placing much weight on the fact that you weren't even the first one to find Gisèle, but we can talk more about that later."

Titine gazed back at me with a genuine look in her pretty green eyes. Old or young, I knew my grandmother. And I knew when she was telling the truth. From her point of view at least, the story Jean-Pierre had told me was true. But she hadn't mentioned that man's name—François Lefevre. And for some reason, my gut told me not to say anything about him yet—not until I knew who he was, anyway.

"If I didn't have anything to do with Gisèle's death, then do we have any idea who did?" I asked.

Titine shook her head. "No, we don't. Gisèle had a lot of admirers—including a few scary ones—and just as many enemies. The club was so crowded that night…it could've been anyone. That's what's so frightening about the whole thing." She reached down and squeezed my hand. "But we have to keep going, Ruby. We can't let this stop us. This was our *dream*. To be dancers in Paris. And you're the star of the show now. You can't throw it all away before the biggest night of your career just because you're scared. You're the strongest woman I know, Ruby. You can do this."

My brain grasped on to what Madame Bouchard had said to me earlier at the café. That I'd been brought here for a reason...that I'd been given the chance to correct my *ill-fated course*. Although I hadn't a clue what that reason was, or how in fact I would go about correcting my fate, I knew without a doubt that it must have something to do with my young grandmother. After all, it was *not* a coincidence that she just happened to be my best friend in my past life.

And in that moment, even though I didn't feel an ounce of the strength Titine insisted I possessed, and I would have much rather booked a one-way flight to the States, I knew I had to do this. I had to engage in Ruby's life if I wanted to have any shot at making it home. At seeing Édouard again.

At having my baby.

Swallowing my fear, I took Titine's hand and nodded toward the door. "Let's do this."

SEVEN

Dressed in a skintight red leotard, black tights, and my sparkly red heels, I stood at the edge of an empty stage, my newfound cleavage overflowing and my confidence waning.

What in the hell was I doing here? I was a fraud. And the minute I stepped out onto that stage, everyone would know it. I stared down at the three-inch glittering red heels on my feet and wished I could click them together three times and be magically transported back to San Diego—to the life I was comfortable in, to the life where my grandma was actually my *grandma* and not my best friend.

But again, that only worked in fairy tales, didn't it? And sending me onstage to do a solo song-and-dance routine, that was a nightmare.

I peeked out from behind the curtain and spotted Jean-Pierre leaning over the piano, talking with the accompanist. I probably only had a few more seconds until he'd summon me.

What am I going to do?

Closing my eyes, I forced myself to inhale, but my breath caught in my throat when a warm hand landed on my arm.

"Ruby?"

I opened my eyes to see whose hand was resting on my skin, whose deep voice had whispered in my ear. But by the lack of arrogance in his tone, I knew even before I saw his face that it wasn't Jean-Pierre.

Before me stood a tall, distinguished man, his black top hat, crisp black suit jacket, and red tie giving off an air of professionalism

I hadn't yet encountered in this dank, smoky nightclub. His dark-brown hair shone in the low light of the wings, and the tiny lines surrounding his smoky-gray eyes crinkled as he gazed at me in anticipation.

Before a simple *Yes, I'm Ruby* could escape my lips, I realized that I knew those tiny lines, those smoky eyes, those classic, yet unbelievably handsome features.

Antoine.

My heart raced as his name shot into my brain.

Was this *the* Antoine Richard? The renowned surgeon I'd read about in the newspaper article? Gisèle's brother?

And possibly the *A.* from the note who I was *not* supposed to speak to?

"*Suivez-moi,*" he whispered, as he gestured toward the darkest area of the wings, where we wouldn't be seen by any of the dancers milling around *or* by Jean-Pierre.

My hand effortlessly slipped into his as I followed him into the shadows. We squeezed behind the last curtain, and as I breathed in the scent of cold air and cologne on his clothes and felt his hot breath grazing my cheeks, I felt as if my legs might give way underneath me.

What was it about this man that was making me feel so... *off-balance?*

"Where were you this morning?" he whispered in my ear. "I waited for you at the café, and you never arrived. I need to know what you were about to tell me yesterday...what you saw before you found Gisèle." He glanced over his shoulder, and as the sounds of the dancers' heels and Jean-Pierre's voice shot past us, he squeezed even closer to me, his lips barely brushing my ear. "There is something else...something important that has come up today, after my meeting with the police. But now is not the time to discuss this. I know what Jean-Pierre will do if he finds me here with you, so we will talk later. Meet me at Café de Flore at five o'clock. And remember, don't tell anyone you're talking to me, especially the police."

Our eyes locked in one final, intense gaze, and it was then that I noticed the pain in his regard, the pain that permeated his entire being. He'd lost his only sister, Gisèle, and I'd found her dead in these very wings. Of course he wanted answers. I would too.

And even though I knew I wasn't supposed to talk to him— that doing so could endanger me further—I felt an instinctual pull toward this man. I wanted to hear his deep voice echo through my ears again, feel his hand brush against my skin once more, breathe in his cool, masculine scent. But most of all, I didn't want to lose the strange sense of comfort and familiarity I felt from these few brief seconds in his presence.

Of course, I had no idea what information I could give him, seeing as how I wasn't *actually* Ruby anymore and her memories were only coming to me in short, jagged pieces, but even so, I knew I couldn't refuse his request. I had to help him.

"I'll be there," I said, recognizing that the sensation coursing through my veins at that instant was a feeling I'd only experienced one other time in my life—when Édouard had taken me in his arms and danced with me.

And since nothing had ever made me feel so complete, so whole, I knew I wouldn't be able to stay away from this man if I tried.

With only a nod and a whisper of a good-bye, Antoine disappeared as quickly as he'd come, leaving me alone in the wings trying to catch my breath.

I stepped out of the shadows and set my gaze on the stage as the spotlight flickered on. In the front row, Jean-Pierre glanced down at his watch and took a puff of the cigarette dangling from his thin lips. As I watched his building impatience cause his nose to twitch, I dreaded ever having to speak to him again. Instead, I found myself wishing it was five o'clock so that I could find out more about Antoine—the mystery man who'd appeared like a lightning bolt straight out of the sky.

"There you are. I've been looking all over for you." Titine slid up beside me and placed a microphone in my hands. "It's time."

I wrapped my sweaty palms around the microphone, holding on to it for dear life, and wondered how I would fill up the stage with a song I didn't have the words for and a dance I'd never done.

But as my long legs carried me toward center stage, I figured I was about to find out.

⊹══ ══⊹

It felt like my first day of kindergarten—except it was like kindergarten on acid. My ankles trembled, my mouth went dry, and my stomach balled up in so many knots, I felt like I might throw up.

The haze that had engulfed me since my encounter with Antoine dissipated completely as I focused on Jean-Pierre leaning back in his chair, legs crossed, a smug look of entitlement on his face. The other dancers, along with Titine, filled up the wings, their anxious gazes set firmly on me. And as a group of musicians began playing at the foot of the stage, I had the sickening feeling that I never should've agreed to rehearse because there was no possible way I could follow Ruby's legacy.

But then, something happened—I recognized the song they were playing. It was "Fever" by Peggy Lee. It was an old song, but it was one that I knew from my life as Claudia too. Though even stronger than the memories I had of this song from my twenty-first-century life, I remembered it *here*. From *this* life. On this exact stage.

Suddenly, the lyrics and the dance I was set to perform flooded into my consciousness like a tidal wave—forceful and unapologetic. The bass player plucked away, and just when I reached the chair in the middle of the stage, my body—*Ruby's* body—took over. Without thinking, I flipped my back to the audience, grabbed on to the chair with my left hand, and lifted the microphone to my mouth with my right. I cringed on the inside as I sang the first few notes, expecting to hear my usual off-pitch singing voice. But when the most sultry, seductive sound I'd ever heard escaped from my very own lips, I could hardly keep from grinning.

I snapped my fingers in time to the song, which magically flowed from my own mouth as my long, toned legs strutted around the stage, my graceful arms knowing exactly where to go for each dance move, my body moving in perfect sync with the beat of this sexy tune.

And as the musicians picked up the pace and I belted a high note into the microphone, I suddenly felt a oneness with Ruby I hadn't yet experienced since I'd arrived here. For that brief moment, I didn't feel separated from her, but instead felt for certain that I *had* been Ruby in the past, and that somewhere, deep down, she still lived inside of me.

With my connection to this life and this stage taking root, I felt that same rush I'd known each time I'd stepped foot into my grandma Martine's dance studio. But this time it was stronger—it was laced in my bones, in my entire being, like a drug.

I *loved* performing.

This was something I'd felt a hint of as Claudia, but now it was clear to me *why* I'd always felt that odd pull toward the dance floor. It was because in this life as Ruby, I *was* a dancer. I *was* a performer. And judging by the sly grin that had transformed Jean-Pierre's otherwise harsh features, I was a damned good one.

Halfway through the song, ten other dancers joined me on stage, and as I took my place in the front and kicked and shimmied and sang my heart out, I'd never felt so utterly alive. Titine's words from earlier rang in my ears, a truth that I knew now, I couldn't deny.

This was our dream. To be dancers in Paris.

I remembered then. The feeling of wanting to sing and dance and perform more than anything. The rush, the incredible high I'd felt each time I'd stepped on stage. The excitement at taking over the starring role. The burning desire to go even further—to make it to the top.

And the willingness to do *anything* to get there.

Ruby's hopes and dreams burned themselves on my heart, and I knew that I would never again be the same. But as I fueled my performance with this renewed desire, a terrifying thought shot into my mind.

Ruby had wanted to be the star of this show—it was her absolute, number one dream. And if she'd been willing to do anything to make it to the top, was it possible that she—that *I*—had been responsible for Gisèle's death? Was that why Jean-Pierre had insisted on me telling that story to the police about where I'd been while Gisèle was murdered?

Was *I* the murderer? And did this François Lefevre man have something to do with it as well?

"*Arrêtez!*" Jean-Pierre's agitated yell cut through my frantic thoughts. "Ruby, what are you doing? I've never seen you dance so well, and then you just stop and stand there like a lost puppy. *Qu'est-ce qu'il y a?*" *What's the matter?*

I grabbed on to the chair as my gaze slid over the other dancers, the spotlight's red glow highlighting the chilly disdain on their faces.

With the exception of Titine, my only friend in this world, each of those dancers believed I'd done it. There was no mistaking the scorn in their eyes.

They thought I'd killed Gisèle to steal her starring role.

Were they right?

Before I could search Ruby's memories for the answer to that burning question, the blinding overhead lights flickered on. In the audience stood a French detective, the glare from his shiny badge only slightly less daunting than his stern gaze.

EIGHT

Clad in a crisp black suit with a gun sitting comfortably in a holster at his hip and a large manila envelope in hand, the tall, lanky detective marched up to the stage and nodded at me.

"Mademoiselle Kerrigan. *Suivez-moi, s'il vous plaît.*" *Follow me, please.*

Jean-Pierre's face had visibly paled at the detective's arrival. He raised his eyebrows at me and motioned for me to go ahead.

But I didn't budge. What was I supposed to say to this man?

"*Mademoiselle.*" The detective's impatient voice boomed once more through the silent club.

The heat of the other dancers' glares burned into my back as I walked across the stage and met the detective face on. The minute I got a closer look at his olive complexion, the frown lines around his mouth, and his dark-brown eyes, I knew I'd met him before. Feeling one of those eerie déjà-vu flashes coming on, I reached for the wall as I trailed him to the rear of the club and out into a damp hallway. Every time I blinked, I saw a vision of the detective's face, his brow furrowed, the corners of his lips turned down as he leaned over and examined something.

And just before the he opened up an office door, I remembered *what* he'd been examining.

Gisèle's dead body.

This must've been the same detective who'd arrived on the scene the night I had found Gisèle, the same detective who'd questioned me, and the one who'd heard the story that Jean-Pierre and I had apparently told him of where I'd been before the murder.

Inside the cramped office, framed photographs of topless dancers wearing enormous, gaudy headpieces stared down at us as the detective rounded the desk and took a seat at what I assumed was Jean-Pierre's desk.

His deadpan gaze sent a chill down my spine. "Detective Duval," he said with a cold nod. "But I trust you remember my name by now since we have already met twice this week."

Trusting me to remember anything accurately right now was a terrible idea, but I wasn't going to tell him that.

He gestured to the chair facing him. *"Asseyez-vous." Sit down.*

I lowered myself into the stiff wooden chair, my mind running a mile a minute, wondering if I really *was* the guilty party he was searching for and praying with all my might that I wasn't. But when a whiff of pine and musk passed under my nose, a new memory flooded my mind and made me forget that I was about to be questioned for Gisèle's murder.

When I closed my eyes, I saw myself as Ruby, strutting around the desk of this exact office, wearing a scanty red-sequined costume that barely covered my firm behind and flat stomach. And like the dancers peering down at us from inside their picture frames, my voluptuous breasts were completely nude. I didn't seem to be the least bit concerned about my lack of apparel as I gazed at the man waiting for me on the other side of the desk. His faint wrinkles and thinning dark hair told me that he was at least forty-five, but his sapphire eyes, which traveled deliberately down the length of my body, and his cheeks, burning red with desire, told me that he *very much* liked younger women.

"Mademoiselle Kerrigan, you are enjoying your new position as zee star of zee show?" The detective's heavy French accent distracted me momentarily, but when the memory continued playing uninterrupted in my head, I forgot all about his horrible pronunciation.

In the vision, the man with the thinning hair and blue eyes shot me a devious grin before I straddled his lap, then leaned over and kissed him on the lips.

It was that sly, conniving grin that made me remember his name. *François Lefevre.*

And I knew immediately. For lack of a better term, *he's* what I'd been *doing* the night Gisèle was murdered. In this office. On this desk.

Oh, God. Was Ruby a prostitute?

"Since it appears that you do not want to make zee small talk, let us go down to zee business." It was the detective again, in his intense accent, pulling me back to the present moment.

I opened my mouth to tell him that the night Gisèle was murdered, I'd been here, in this office, sleeping with some man named François Lefevre, and all we had to do was find Mr. Lefevre and he'd surely verify that he'd been with me that night.

But one question remained: Had I actually been with Mr. Lefevre *while* the murder had taken place?

Before I spoke, I remembered Jean-Pierre's words.

If you even think about mentioning François Lefevre's name to the police, you will lose everything—your career, your apartment, your reputation, everything.

"Mademoiselle Kerrigan, is something the matter? I need you to focus. I do not have all zee day to speak with you, you know."

But who *was* François Lefevre? And why couldn't I at least mention his name as an alibi? Was it because after we'd been together in this office, I had killed Gisèle to win the starring role? I closed my eyes again, trying with all my might to remember what had happened after Ruby and François's romp in the office, but this confused mind of mine refused to oblige.

"I do not have time for your games. You will either focus and answer my questions right here, or I will take you to zee station. It is your choice."

"I'm sorry, Detective. I'm ready."

"*Bon.* I am here to give you one more chance to tell me *la verité* about what happened the night of Mademoiselle Richard's death."

I cringed internally as I realized I was going to have to stick to the story I'd apparently already told the police. I hated lying, but I couldn't mention my tryst with François Lefevre until I found out who he was and *why* I shouldn't mention his name to Detective Duval.

Gripping my knees underneath the desk, I cleared my throat, determined not to show him an ounce of the fear that was making my palms sweat and my chest ache. "After the show, I didn't feel very well, so I went up to my apartment to rest. After about half an hour, I started to feel better, and I came back down to the club to mingle. But on my way back through the wings, I heard a scream coming from Gisèle's dressing room, and that's when I ran in and found Delphine lying over Gisèle's body."

Detective Duval leaned back in his chair and drummed his long fingers on the desk. "I see. You have nothing new to add to your story? No details you may have...*forgotten?*"

Damn.

"No, Detective. That's all."

"I see." He grabbed the manila envelope he'd been carrying, opened it up, and slid an eight-by-ten black-and-white photo across the desk. "Maybe this will refresh your *mémoire.*"

I glanced down at the 1950s photograph and saw myself— Ruby—standing outside on a shadowy street corner, my back up against the building, a seductive grin on my lips. Leaning over me, with one hand on the wall, was the same man from my vision— François Lefevre.

In his other hand was a wad of cash, which he appeared to be handing over to me.

Oh, dear God.

It was official.

In my past life, I wasn't *only* a bombshell blonde performer, I was also a prostitute.

"This photo was taken the night of Gisèle's death. Just before you supposedly *found* her lying on her dressing room floor, already dead. Can you explain to me what is going on in this picture?"

I barely heard the detective's pointed questions, though, because my gaze caught something else in the photograph.

A female silhouette lingered down the alley, just beyond Ruby and François. The dim glow of one lonely streetlamp reflected off what appeared to be a dangly diamond earring.

I closed my eyes, willing the memories from that night to come into focus. But beyond my steamy romp with François in this office, I couldn't recall anything else…anything *except* seeing that slithering silhouette and that impressive diamond earring.

"Mademoiselle Kerrigan!" Detective Duval pounded his fist on the desk. "*Répondez à la question*, or I will not hesitate to take you to zee station."

A bead of sweat dripped down the back of my neck as I slid the portrait across the desk and pointed to the creepy woman hovering in the shadows. For all I knew, she was another dancer stepping outside for a smoke, but I had to at least try to take the focus off of myself until I could figure out what had really happened that night. "Do you know who this woman is?" I asked the detective.

Detective Duval leaned forward, the unforgiving expression on his face making me wish with all my heart that I was anywhere but here. "Your plan to distract me will not work, Mademoiselle Kerrigan. Let us go back to the matter on hand. Monsieur Lefevre is a powerful man who comes from an even more powerful family. I imagine you are aware that he holds a prominent role in the French government as a *député* of France's *Assemblée Nationale*. And I am sure you did not miss the part about his father being an advisor to the newly elected *Président* de Gaulle. So, tell me if I am wrong, but if you happened to have some sort of *arrangement* with Monsieur Lefevre, he would surely be able to use his political connections to clear your name from a murder investigation. In exchange, you would, of course, keep his indiscretions a secret from his family and from the press."

"No, Detective. That's not what is going on here. I…I didn't realize he was—"

Detective Duval ripped the photo from the desk, his olive-colored cheeks suddenly a blazing red. "You are wasting my time,

Mademoiselle Kerrigan. I will give you one day to get your story straight, and when I come back, you and your *petit-ami* François Lefevre better be ready to tell me the truth about what happened that night."

"Have you spoken to him about this already?"

"I do not make it a habit of sharing investigation details with the *suspects*." He raised a black eyebrow at me. "But I am sure you can imagine what would happen to Monsieur Lefevre's career, to his family, and consequently, to you, if this photo were to find itself in the wrong hands. However, if the two of you decide you want to talk, I can assure you that will not happen."

"I hardly doubt it's legal for you to use blackmail as an investigation tool," I spat.

Detective Duval raised a brow. "And I hardly think a *prostituée* who is having relations with a top official is in any position to lecture me on my morals." He walked purposefully toward the door, clearly finished with me.

"I didn't kill her," I called out just as his hand reached the doorknob. "We were good friends, and I never would've harmed her. You have to believe me." I sincerely hoped the words that had just flown out of my mouth were true…but I also knew that whether Ruby had been involved in Gisèle's murder or not, my time here was limited. And I surely wouldn't find a way home to my real life, or to my future child, if I was locked up in a cold French jail cell.

"If you are truly innocent," Detective Duval said on his way out the door, "I will need *la preuve*."

NINE

La preuve. The French word for *proof.*

Proving my innocence in this case would undoubtedly *im*prove my grim circumstances as Ruby, but would it bring me any closer to finding a way back home to my life as Claudia, to Édouard, and to my baby?

When I thought of my ultrasound photo and the way it had faded right in front of my eyes, I knew that whether Ruby was innocent or not, I had no other choice but to try.

A jazzy piano rhythm and the clatter of high heels echoed down the long, shadowy hallway as I let myself out of Jean-Pierre's office. I suspected that if he or any of the girls noticed that I'd finished speaking to Detective Duval, I would be expected to rehearse for the rest of the day. I didn't have time for that, though. I needed to speak with François Lefevre and find out if our little office *rendez-vous* had taken place during the time of Gisèle's murder. If it had, and if François was willing to *discreetly* admit our affair to the police, I could potentially clear my name from this investigation.

On the other hand, if Ruby *had* killed Gisèle just after the steamy office romp, François's statement could be a one-way ticket to prison.

Plus, there was still the pressing issue of the threatening note I'd found under my pillow, and despite its clear order not to speak with *A.*, I'd still agreed to meet Antoine tonight. And none of that was taking into consideration the haunting memory of that scarred hand coming at me with a knife. Who had wanted to hurt Ruby so badly?

Was he here in Paris right now? Could he have something to do with Gisèle's murder? Could he have written the note?

My head spun from all of the unanswered questions, and before I realized where I was going, I emerged to an area of the wings that had been blocked off with yellow police tape.

Gisèle's dressing room.

I knew I should stay out. But my desire to know the truth about that night won over. Maybe I would remember something that could help me find a way out of here.

I scanned the wings to make sure no one was watching, then stepped over the glossy yellow tape and let myself into the forbidden dressing room.

With its big, round lightbulbs hovering over tall, mirrored walls, makeup strewn all over the countertops, and racks of scanty, gaudy costumes dangling from metal racks in the corner, the dressing room didn't look much different from the one I'd been in this morning.

But when my eyes met the reddish-brown stains splattering the concrete beneath my feet, I remembered.

The blood.

I flinched and jumped to the side to get away from where she'd been lying, from where she'd been killed. I didn't want to remember anymore. I didn't want to be involved in the murder of this innocent girl. I didn't want to be *here*.

But it was too late. The scents of lipstick and blood carried me right back to that moment, to the gruesome image that had plagued me when I'd first woken up as Ruby...except this time it was much, much clearer.

My sparkly red stilettos pound through the wings toward the desperate screams emanating from inside Gisèle's dressing room.

Only they aren't Gisèle's screams. The cries are higher, younger, more frantic.

I burst into the room, nearly slipping on the silky red blood pooling at my feet.

A young dancer still in her silver sequins and red feathers is kneeling over Gisèle, shaking her shoulders and screaming, crying, begging the lifeless body laid out before her to wake up.

The dancer turns to me, tears pouring out of her big, brown doe eyes, thick streaks of mascara and eyeliner smearing her rosy cheeks. It's Delphine, the youngest girl in the troupe, only seventeen. Too young to see this. Too young to find the star of the show murdered in cold blood in her very own dressing room.

"Delphine, qu'est-ce qui s'est passé?" *What happened?* I ask her, my voice surprisingly calm. I've seen this before. The blood. The body. I just need Delphine to get out. She'll only make things harder.

Delphine doesn't respond, but instead keeps crying, her little hands trembling as she kneels in the blood, unable to get up.

"Lève-toi." *Get up,* I tell her. *"Va trouver Jean-Pierre, et appelle la police."* *Go find Jean-Pierre and call the police.*

I hoist the girl up from the floor and pull her away from the body, from the blood.

"Vas-y!" *Go!* I yell when her feet refuse to move.

Finally, Delphine flees the dressing room, leaving me alone with Gisèle.

Beautiful, beautiful Gisèle.

Like a porcelain doll's, her luminous skin, dainty pink lips, and sweet, delicate features are eerily frozen into place. I kneel by her side, ripping the red-sequined bodice off her tiny figure to find the wound. A bullet hole to her chest, right over her heart, spills warm blood onto my hands, soaking right through every piece of cloth I can find to stop it.

I've seen a wound just like this one before. I know it's too late. She's gone.

"Did you have a nice *rendez-vous* with the detective?"

The smooth, cool voice snuck up on me like a rattlesnake in a desert, startling me from that vivid, chilling memory, bringing me back to the present. The fresh blood was gone, and in its place stood a rail-thin brunette with hazel eyes and outrageously high cheekbones. She circled me like a lion would its prey, her pointy silver heels stomping over the bloodstains, the sound ringing in my ears. She stopped a few inches from me, one perfectly manicured hand hoisted on her bony hip.

Véronique.

She was the dancer who'd shot me the evil eye earlier this morning. The one who, according to Titine, wanted my new starring role in the show.

"This little memory loss act you are playing, Ruby…it will not work, you know," she said, her voice cool and unforgiving.

I didn't respond, though, because as I studied her face, another memory burst through my consciousness. I'd seen Véronique that night—the night I'd found Gisèle. I'd bumped into her in the wings, not far from this dressing room. The flash or the vision or whatever it was played out clearly in my head—Véronique's dash toward the front of the club, then her startled expression when she'd nearly knocked me over. We'd met eyes for only a second, and in that time, I'd registered that her cheeks were red and splotchy, not from a bad makeup job as much as from adrenaline. And her hazel eyes had darted frantically over my face, like she was scared. Like she was running from something.

As quickly as it had entered my mind, the memory faded to nothing, leaving me standing in front of the ice-cold, collected woman who appeared so opposite of the racing, frenzied dancer I'd bumped into that night. Had I run into her *before* I'd found Gisèle? Or after?

"You don't have to pretend with me, Ruby. I know it was you. We all do. And it's only a matter of time before the detective finds *la preuve* he needs."

"I saw you that night," I said coolly, my voice refusing to reveal even a trace of the nerves that swam just below the surface.

Véronique's eyes flickered, and for a moment, I detected a hint of the fear I'd seen in her that night. But then it was gone, the iciness returning in full force. "*Mais bien sûr.* We both dance here. Everyone was here that night. Do not be *stupide.*"

"No, I mean, I *saw* you. Running from something. Scared. What were you doing back here?"

She crossed her arms over her chest and drummed her long fingernails over her tiny bicep. "I thought you lost your *mémoire, non?*"

An intense stubbornness coupled with a deep-seated rivalry overpowered my best reasoning as I took a purposeful step toward Véronique, squaring my face directly in front of hers. "Some of my memory appears to be intact. What did you see that night, Véronique? Or more important, what did you *do?*"

She puffed an annoyed breath into my face and narrowed her eyes. "First, you are sleeping with Jean-Pierre, then you are the second one to supposedly *find* Gisèle's dead body, and finally, Jean-Pierre gives you the starring role when you have only been performing here less than one year. And you actually think anyone is going to be looking to me? You are a *salope,* Ruby. And it is only a matter of time before the police and everyone else see right through you, the way I already have."

True to form, I understood her. She'd called me a slut.

I told myself to walk away. I didn't know the whole story with Véronique. Why she hated me so much. What she'd been doing that night in the wings. And as for the slut accusation…well, Ruby *did* do her fair share of sleeping around.

But Ruby's instincts won out yet again over my practicality. And before I could tell my hand to stop its swinging motion, I'd slapped Véronique across the face.

"*C'est toi, la salope,*" I said, the French insult rolling off my tongue as if I'd been practicing for years.

Véronique barely registered a flinch on her stone-cold face whereas I stood, frozen in place, stunned at what I'd just said, what I'd just done. Again, I was speaking perfect French. And more important, I'd never slapped someone in my life. Not even Ian.

Not after I'd told him I was pregnant and he'd returned the favor by telling me he was married and that he wanted nothing to do with the child.

I hadn't even slapped him then.

Yet I'd smacked this woman across the face without a second thought.

Who had I become?

Véronique shook her head at me and curled her lips into a wicked grin. "Such petty arguments won't matter when you are in prison for the rest of your life." She turned on her heel and sauntered out of the bloodstained dressing room and back toward the stage, where the scarlet-red lights swallowed her secrets.

<hr />

Since I did not plan on spending the rest of my days in a French prison, I needed to find François Lefevre and try to put together the rest of the pieces from that night.

Now.

I turned around to head to the staircase that led up to my apartment, but just as I was taking off in the opposite direction from the stage, a tiny hand seized my arm.

"Ruby!" It was Titine, her green eyes flashing. "Where are you going? Rehearsal isn't over yet."

"I can't rehearse right now, Titine. I have to go."

"Listen, Ruby. I don't know what has gotten into you, but you're really making things difficult. What did the detective say to you? Doesn't he believe you?"

"That's why I have to go. I have to take care of something important. I can't rehearse right now."

A few of the other dancers filtered through the wings and walked past us, their eyes not hiding their curiosity…or their blame.

Titine took a step closer to me and lowered her voice. "I don't know what happened in there or what on earth you could possibly need to take care of since you were not the one responsible for Gisèle's death. But we don't have the time or the privacy to talk about any of that right now. The detective is with Jean-Pierre, but as soon as he gets back, you *have* to be out on that stage. You'll lose your role if you don't do this, Ruby. And you might even lose your job."

I could see the determination in my young grandmother's eyes, and I knew that she wouldn't let me go anywhere, no matter how hard I tried. I'd seen the stubborn, diva-like fits she'd thrown as a seventy-six-year-old woman. I could only imagine what she'd been like in her twenties when she didn't get what she wanted.

"How much longer is rehearsal?" I asked.

"A couple more hours. Then we can talk about whatever is scaring you, okay? Well, besides the obvious problems of you being investigated for Gisèle's murder and losing your memory." She ran the back of her hand over her forehead and let out a sigh. "If we can just make it through the next few weeks in one piece without anyone going to jail or to a hospital, it will be a miracle. Come on, Ruby, let's go."

As I followed Titine toward the stage, the red lights faded and the glaring overhead lights flickered on once more. I noticed that Titine's rosy cheeks had paled, and gray circles surrounded her gorgeous eyes.

"Are you feeling okay, Titine?" I asked.

"What? Me? Oh…I might've just caught a little bug or something, but I'll be fine."

Grandma Martine had always been a horrible liar. But as the young Titine, she was even worse.

"Titine, are you sure—"

But I didn't have the chance to finish my sentence, because as we made it into the brightly lit space where the troupe of long-legged, busty performers awaited, I spotted Jean-Pierre and Detective Duval looming at the edge of the stage.

My stomach curled at the sight of the detective, who knew I'd been lying. Couldn't he just leave? What more could there be?

Jean-Pierre's nose twitched again, the crease lines in his brow revealing his agitation. "Ladies, the police need to investigate the club once more," he said in French, my mind needing no instruction to translate immediately into English. "Rehearsal is off for today. I expect to see you all tomorrow morning at ten sharp."

Then, as Jean-Pierre's eyes squinted down at us, his hard gaze landed on me. "That means no messing around tonight. Tomorrow is a big performance."

No rehearsal meant I could go upstairs and ransack Ruby's apartment to find François Lefevre's contact information. Surely Ruby had kept his phone number somewhere.

I tore my eyes from Jean-Pierre's menacing stare and pushed my way through all of the scantily dressed dancers. I needed to get out of here before he stopped me. I was sure he'd want to know what I'd said to Detective Duval.

Just as I made it to the foot of the stairs, Titine's urgent voice came from behind. "Ruby, wait!"

"I really have to go, Titine. I'm sorry."

She laid a shaky palm on my arm. "I'm sorry if I've been a little hard on you. I know this week has been awful, and to tell the truth, you haven't been yourself at all since you fell this morning. You're scaring me, Ruby. Do you want me to come upstairs with you? We can call the doctor to come, now that rehearsal is off. What do you think?"

I couldn't get my young grandmother involved in this mess with François Lefevre. Based on what she'd said earlier, Titine didn't even know that I'd been involved with him. Plus, I needed to think through the details of the vivid memory I'd just had of finding Gisèle. I needed to find out what Véronique had been doing that night, *why* I'd stayed so calm in the face of a gruesome murder—a murder of one of my supposed friends, no less—and why I'd felt that unmistakable notion of having seen a gunshot wound just like Gisèle's before.

Was it because I'd killed her just moments before Delphine had found her?

That would explain the absence of panic.

But something in my gut told me it wasn't that simple. There was more to this complicated story. And I needed to speak with François Lefevre. Alone.

"Thanks, Titine. But I just need to get some rest. I'm sure I'll feel better soon."

"Ruby, what happened with the detective? He believes you, right?" Desperation seeped through her usually strong voice, and her cheeks grew paler than before. "Why do they have to search the club again? This is insane! They already spent three days right after she died. We just opened back up yesterday, for God's sake, and they're already taking our rehearsal space away the day before a huge performance."

"I'm sure they're just covering their tracks again, making sure they didn't miss anything."

"So why were you and Jean-Pierre the only ones they wanted to talk to today? Do they really think you did it, Ruby?"

I opened my mouth to tell her that she didn't need to worry, but stopped when I noticed Jean-Pierre speaking with two new police officers in the wings. The sight of more badges and guns kicked my adrenaline into gear.

I didn't have much time. I had to go.

"I'm sorry, Titine. I really need to get some rest." I tore my arm from her grasp and ran toward the staircase. I took the steps two at a time, not even noticing that I was in three-inch heels.

Once in my apartment, I flew over to the desk and riffled through the papers that the crazy windstorm had whipped to the floor earlier. Ruby's scribbles had seemed meaningless to me this morning, but now I scanned every inch of her messy, handwritten notes, desperately hoping I would find a phone number, an address, anything that could lead me to François Lefevre.

When I came up empty-handed, I headed to the bedroom dresser—the place where I had always hidden my journal in my regular life back in San Diego. I was hoping Ruby had had the same idea.

But stuffed inside her tall black dresser, I did not find the usual stacks of conservative cotton bikini underwear I normally wore. Instead I found piles upon piles of skimpy *négligée*: bras in hot pink, purple, red, and black, and pairs of silver and black thigh highs trimmed in lace. After digging through the fourth and last drawer and realizing the entire dresser was filled with nothing but racy undergarments, I swallowed the realization once more that I, Claudia Davis, a single, thirty-five-year-old therapist who wanted nothing more than to marry Édouard Marceau and have my baby girl, had been a prostitute in my past life.

Unbelievable.

The only comfort was in the fact that even though Ruby had been a full-blown prostitute in the past, she sure as hell wouldn't be one now that I was running this show.

I gave up on the lingerie-filled dresser and turned to the closet, where Ruby housed her *regular* clothes.

There were no sweats or chunky sweaters here. No T-shirts. No pencil skirts and crisp collared shirts to match. No sundresses. No flip-flops. No sneakers.

Instead I found short, tight black dresses; flowing evening gowns in red, silver, and gold; sequined headpieces; and rows upon rows of the most elaborate, gorgeous high heels I'd ever seen. It was a full-on costume closet.

If she wasn't wanted for murder and involved in life-threatening circumstances, I would've thought that playing around in Ruby's glamorous life for a little while could actually be fun.

But as I recalled the vision of that jagged knife coming at me and slicing through my back, I knew that no amount of dazzling clothes could ever compensate for the dark sides of this woman's life.

In the midst of tearing apart Ruby's beautiful closet, a jarring slam rattled the apartment, making me drop the shoe box in my hands.

It was the front door.

The hairs on the back of my neck stood up. I'd locked that door. I was certain of it.

I crept to the bedroom doorway and peeked out, only to find Jean-Pierre charging through the apartment, his cheeks and ears blazing red, his brown squinty eyes focused on the kitchen cabinet.

I stared at him incredulously. This man was out of control. And he needed to leave. "How did you get in here? This is my apartment. You can't just barge in like you live here!"

He didn't acknowledge me as he removed a bottle of liquor, poured himself a half glass, and downed it on one violent gulp. He filled the glass back up again, this time to the brim, then marched over to me.

"You seem to be forgetting who pays for this apartment," he spat, the strong odors of alcohol and cigarettes wafting from his mouth and making me feel nauseous.

I took a step back, my eyes combing the space around me for a letter opener or a pen, anything with a sharp end. But I didn't have time to find something to defend myself with because Jean-Pierre moved in on me, pinning me against the wall.

He lowered his mouth to my ear, his hot breath scalding my skin. "You may be the new star of the show, but I can take everything away from you in the blink of an eye, Ruby. This apartment. Your reputation. Your money. Your dreams."

"Get off of me," I hissed in his ear.

But Jean-Pierre didn't budge. Instead, he hurled his glass against the wall, the shattering sound piercing my ears, the stench of liquor pooling at my feet. Then he seized my shoulders so forcefully that I couldn't help but let out a low cry.

"What did you say to Detective Duval?" he growled as he pressed his sweaty, hot body into mine.

"I told him exactly what you told me to say."

Jean-Pierre's jaw hardened as he tightened his hold on my shoulders. "Then can you tell me why they are searching *my* club again? And why did the detective not seem to believe a word I told him? And *why* did he mention François Lefevre's name to me?"

When I didn't respond, he ground his teeth together, the sound like nails down a chalkboard. "*Putain!* Tell me, Ruby! Why?"

I swallowed hard, but didn't break his gaze. "Detective Duval has a photograph of François Lefevre paying me outside the club. He thinks I killed Gisèle to take her starring role and that I'm hoping to use my relationship with François Lefevre to keep me out of prison."

"*Merde.* And what did you tell him?"

"I told him that it isn't true and that I never would've harmed Gisèle. He didn't believe me, though, and said he's coming back tomorrow. And that if Mr. Lefevre and I don't start talking, he will release the photo to the press."

"What is wrong with you, Ruby?" Jean-Pierre kept me pressed against the wall as he ran a warm finger down my cheek. "You had the detective alone in my office. Why did you not make him an offer he couldn't refuse?"

I strained to get out of Jean-Pierre's grasp, but he was too strong for me, his hold too overpowering. "You know, *ma chérie*, there isn't a man in this world who can say no to you. In fact, I know I have promised you to that American film director who is coming to the performance tomorrow, but I will have to have you at least once before he does." He lowered his face to mine, his thin lips barely brushing over my mouth. "And since you didn't give me what I needed last night, I think now will be a good time." He plunged his face into my neck, his hands groping my breasts, his erection filling up the space between my legs.

I swallowed the bile that rose in my throat and pushed against him with every ounce of strength in my body. He was ready for my opposition, though. He grabbed my wrists and pinned them up over my head, then blew his offensive alcohol-and-cigarette breath straight into my face.

"Fine, Ruby. I will not *force* you to make love to me. That is not how a *relationship* works, *n'est-ce pas*? In case that little bump on your head is making you forget, you do not have a *relationship* with François Lefevre. He pays you to fuck him." Jean-Pierre thrust his groin hard into my hips then cupped my chin in his hand. "You have a relationship with *me*. You fuck me whenever I want you to, and I do not have to pay you for it. And if you do not keep your end of our *relationship*, I am sure Véronique will be happy to take your apartment, share a bed with me, and of course, steal your starring role."

"*Va te faire foutre*," I growled under my breath, my instantaneous inner translation revealing the words that had flown out of my mouth—I'd just told him to go fuck himself.

And although I'd never talked to *anyone* this way before, the anger rising in my chest wouldn't let me stop there. I took a deep breath then spat right in Jean-Pierre's horny, greedy little face.

He released his grip on me, stumbling backward and wiping his right eye with the back of his palm.

"An innocent girl lost her life here, under *your* watch, and the only things you care about are your damn reputation and having sex," I said. "You're disgusting."

Jean-Pierre slammed his fist on the desk then turned to face me. "You think I do not care that Gisèle is gone? That I opened this club up four years ago with *Gisèle* as my vision, and now someone has killed her here, in the place that made her a star. Of course I care, Ruby! But she is gone now, and there is nothing we can do to bring her back." Jean-Pierre walked up to me and squared his cold eyes directly in front of mine.

I didn't flinch this time.

"*Mais la vie continue.* The show, it must go on. And I need *you* to do what you promised, Ruby. In fact, I do not think you have lost your memory. I think you are *choosing* to forget that I was the one who took you away from your horrible life in New York, from that despicable man. I saved you, Ruby. And now *you* will fix this problem with François Lefevre. I don't care what you have to do, but you will fix it before the detective comes back tomorrow. And you will keep the agreement with the film director for tomorrow night. And if you fail to do either of those two things, you are finished here."

Jean-Pierre shot me one last cutting glance then turned and stalked out of the apartment, the door slamming behind him.

His threats rang in my ears as I collapsed against the wall and sank to the ground, my entire body trembling.

I was the one who took you away from your horrible life in New York, from that despicable man. I saved you, Ruby.

I wrapped my arms around my legs and closed my eyes. And there, in Ruby's dark memories, I found the jagged knife again, and the scarred hand that held it. And while I still couldn't see the man's body or his face, I could see something else behind the knife—a floor-to-ceiling window with a clear view of the New York City skyline.

If it was true, if Jean-Pierre had really *saved* me from that *despicable* man, whoever he was, and brought me and Titine to dance at this club in Paris, it was clear that his service to me did not come without a price...or several of them.

This apartment.

My livelihood.

My *body*...which I was apparently selling to some American film director tomorrow night.

With my face buried in my knees and vicious thoughts about Jean-Pierre churning through my mind, I wished I could curl up in a ball forever and pretend that none of this was happening. How would I fix this unthinkable situation in only five days? Where was my magical fairy godmother when I needed her?

But then, in the silence of this old Parisian apartment, a ticking sound above my head made me remember.

Antoine.

The clock hanging above me read a quarter till five. I'd agreed to meet Antoine at five o'clock at Café de Flore. I squeezed my eyes shut and told myself that I should focus on finding François Lefevre and clearing my name from this murder investigation.

But before I could exhale, I was already on my feet, running to Ruby's bedroom, digging through her mess of a closet. I threw on a shimmering violet sweater and a pair of sleek black pants with matching black heels. Then I crossed back through the living room and pulled her red peacoat and silver scarf from the hall closet before slipping out the door.

TEN

The urge I felt to spend time with Antoine Richard—a man with whom I'd only shared a few brief words, a whisper of a touch—overpowered any rationale that may have tried to stop me. I didn't know Antoine, but after everything that had just happened, I knew I had to see him again.

I raced down the stairs of my building, surprisingly still not hindered by my tall heels. And from what could've only been explained as muscle memory, I easily found my way to the large black door that opened to the streets of Paris.

The glare of the setting sun blasted through the clouds and blinded my vision as I stepped straight into a bitter, cold draft. But as soon as the fiery orange ball disappeared over the tops of the buildings, I stopped walking, my jaw dropping once more at the 1950s Parisian scenery unfolding before my eyes.

A pale-green 2CV car, which resembled a larger, more classic version of a modern-day Volkswagen Beetle, rambled down the chilly boulevard, honking its squeaky horn at a curly-haired brunette in the crosswalk. The gorgeous French woman, who looked as if she could've been straight out of a vintage issue of *Vogue*, paid no attention to the approaching vehicle.

Cinched at the waist by a shiny black belt, the woman's long red dress billowed in the wind as she sauntered across the street in a pair of chic black pumps. She fastened the buttons of her gray wool coat all the way up to the high neckline of her dress as she reached the sidewalk. Sleek white gloves covered her tiny hands, and a dainty violet hat pinned atop her curls gave way to a thin layer of netting, which shielded her forehead.

She dashed past me, her pretty green eyes radiating the kind of bold, sophisticated confidence I only wished I possessed. Whatever handsome Frenchman was awaiting her arrival tonight was going to be happy to see her, and she knew it.

Strolling leisurely in the other direction, a man in a long black coat, gray trousers, and a black bowler hat grinned slyly at me, *le journal* tucked neatly underneath his arm.

"Vous êtes ravissante, Mademoiselle." You are ravishing, miss, he said to me.

But he didn't stop to wait for a response. Instead, he tipped his hat and continued down the boulevard, just another day in Paris.

I watched him walk away and was suddenly and completely hit over the head with the impossibility of this situation.

I was really here. Living in *Paris* in the year 1959 in the body of Ruby Kerrigan, with her memories, her acquaintances, her abilities and experiences all imprinted in this body and in this soul I now shared with her.

How could this have happened?

Another frosty draft snapped at my cheeks, and I remembered.

Antoine. Café de Flore. Five o'clock.

As I took off down the sidewalk, I didn't need a map to tell me that I was on Boulevard Saint-Germain, in the sixth arrondissement of Paris, on the left bank of the Seine. I just knew.

And as my heels combed the cobblestones, I realized that I also knew exactly how to find Café de Flore.

Along my brisk walk to meet Antoine, I pushed the disturbing argument I'd just had with Jean-Pierre out of my mind and instead marveled at the *pâtisseries* dispersed among the cafés, their windows lined with delicate French pastries—works of art begging to be eaten. The aromas of fresh buttery croissants and melted chocolate oozing out of their doors made me hungry and nostalgic all at the same time. I remembered those scents—and it wasn't from living in San Diego.

Endless rows of brasseries and cafés welcomed Parisians in from the cold, and quaint little boutiques boasted more styles from that classic 1950s wardrobe, making me wish I could forget about all of this disastrous nightclub and murder business and take myself shopping instead.

Bold French men didn't hesitate to hold my gaze, tipping their hats at me as they walked past, again reminding me that I was not walking the streets of Paris in my thirty-five-year-old pregnant body, but instead in the body of a striking blonde *Américaine*.

I crossed rue de Seine, then a few blocks later, passed by the Église de Saint-Germain-des-Prés. My head snapped back as I took a double take of a young couple all but undressing each other on a green bench facing the old church. They didn't care that it was freezing outside or that the church was only a few steps away.

They were young and in love. And in Paris.

It was just like Édouard had described to me. I only wished he were here now.

My ears tuned in to the church bells chiming five o'clock. I needed to get moving. I picked up my pace, crossed rue Bonaparte, then spotted the green awning of Les Deux Magots café. Café de Flore was *juste à côté*, Ruby's memory told me.

And there, at the corner of rue Saint-Benoît and the bustling Boulevard Saint-Germain was Café de Flore. A sign that read *Terrasse Chauffée* was posted on the outside of the restaurant's lovely windowed terrace, making me bolt to the door, my new body craving the heat even more than it craved food.

Bright interior lights, swirls of cigarette smoke, and sounds of clinking wineglasses mixed with bubbles of soft laughter spilled out into the early Parisian night as I opened the door. I stepped inside to find a bustling, lively café, its cherry-red booths filled to the brim with more of those sophisticated Parisians, stripping off their dark coats and scarves as a blast of heat swept through the dining room.

I scanned the tight tables, one squeezed right next to the other, the Parisians not seeming to mind the invasion of space. And there, in a back corner, sipping a steaming cup of French *café*, was Antoine.

It had been so dark earlier in the wings that I hadn't gotten a proper look at him...not like this, anyway.

He'd changed out of the suit and tie he'd been wearing earlier into a dark-gray sweater, which accentuated his broad shoulders. The lamplight overhead made his eyes gleam as he searched the crowded café. I stepped to the side of a tall, ivory pillar, just out of his view, so I could gaze at him another second longer.

A sexy five o'clock shadow graced his smooth face, his features exuding strength and warmth all at the same time. Like a strong cup of steaming hot coffee, I wanted to drink him in...and when I finished, I wanted to pour another cup.

I shook my head, told myself to get it together. I may have known Antoine in this lifetime the *first* time around, but right here and now, I did *not* know him.

Certainly not well enough to give merit to this overwhelming desire brewing inside of me.

But still, as I stepped aside from the pillar and weaved through the cramped café aisles to reach him, my heart squeezed a bit tighter with each step. And when his striking gaze landed on me, I couldn't ignore the heat that spread through me like a wildfire.

✦═══✦

"Please, sit down," he said, gesturing to the red booth across from him.

Right as I took a seat, a server clad in a crisp white shirt and a spiffy black vest appeared at my side with a steaming bowl of *soupe à l'oignon gratinée* and a beautiful salad covered with thick slices of ham, cheese, egg, and tomatoes.

"*Bon appétit, Mademoiselle*," he said, placing the dishes in front of me.

"*Merci, Monsieur*," I said, without a second thought. French onion soup and a salad—covered in meat, no less—had never looked so delicious to a former vegetarian.

I looked up to Antoine. "Aren't you having anything?"

His gaze flicked toward the window. "No, I have not had much of an appetite this week. But please, go ahead. The Salade Flore is superb, and besides, I thought you might be hungry after your rehearsal. I remember Gisèle telling me that Jean-Pierre did not allow the girls to eat much. *Le connard.*"

Hearing Antoine call Jean-Pierre an asshole in French made me smile for the first time all day. "I couldn't agree more." Totally and utterly ravenous, I picked up my large soup spoon and dug into the thick layer of golden-brown cheese melting over the sides of the bowl. I hadn't eaten anything except a few bites of that magical ham-and-cheese baguette this morning.

After a few spoonfuls of the most delicious soup I'd ever tasted, I lifted my gaze to Antoine and smiled again. "Thank you for ordering this for me…"

The tiny lines around his smoky-gray eyes had reappeared, his expression one of confusion as he searched my face. "Where were you this morning? You said you saw something that night… the night Gisèle was murdered. What was it, Ruby? What did you see?"

I set the spoon down on the table and cleared my throat. "I…I'm sorry I missed our meeting this morning. I fell during rehearsal and passed out, and ever since I woke up, my memory is…well, it's almost completely gone. I don't remember what I was going to tell you." I wished I could tell him the whole truth, that I wasn't *only* Ruby anymore, that I was confused and scared and wanted to go home. But if I confessed what was truly going on, he would have no choice but to cart me off to an insane asylum.

And I wouldn't have blamed him.

Antoine's jaw hardened, the lines on his forehead tightening. "Is this a game? You are under investigation for my sister's murder and you are telling me you have *conveniently* lost your *mémoire* of what happened that night?"

Pain and anger seared through Antoine's eyes, making me wish I could remember more. Making me wish I could help him.

"I remember bits and pieces…but not everything."

Antoine leaned forward in his chair, the clamoring of silverware against plates and the incessant French chatter swimming around us seeming not to distract him at all. He gripped my wrist from across the table. "I need to know everything you can remember. I don't trust the police, Jean-Pierre won't tell me a damn thing, and Delphine is too terrified to talk. You are the only one who will speak to me, Ruby. Now tell me what you know."

The intensity in Antoine's tone made me afraid that I'd made a mistake in coming here. But I had to answer him. I had to at least try to help. "I remember seeing Véronique in the wings, running from something, looking scared and out of breath. Do you know who Véronique is?"

Antoine nodded. "Yes. I remember my sister talking about her."

"I don't know where she was running from, but when I asked her about it today, she got really angry and skirted around the question."

"When did you see her running? Was it before you found Gisèle?"

"I'm not sure. I can't remember the timeline of that night very well. Like I said, since this morning—"

"Do you think Véronique has something to do with this?" he interjected. "Do you think she could've murdered Gisèle?"

"I…I'm not sure. It's possible. I know she's really angry that she didn't get the starring role. But I don't know if that means she's capable of murder."

"Tell me what else happened that night. I know there's more."

I opened my mouth but hesitated when I thought of the photo of me with François Lefevre. Of the money I'd taken from him. Of the sex we'd had in the office. I gazed deep into Antoine's eyes and knew I couldn't tell him any of that. I didn't want him to know who Ruby really was. What she'd been willing to do.

After all, I wasn't Ruby anymore. Deep down, I was still me, Claudia. Someone who would never dream of living the type of life Ruby had lived.

And even though the circumstances under which we were meeting were horrible, I wanted Antoine to get to know me, the *real* me.

But Antoine had other motivations at the moment. His fist clenched over the shiny wood table, his cheeks reddening. "Ruby, we spoke yesterday at the club and you told me you had information surrounding Gisèle's death. I'm not leaving this café until you tell me *exactly* what you know. When did you run into Véronique?"

Suddenly I realized that coming here may not have been a good idea after all. I couldn't give Antoine the information he needed or the justice and closure he craved after what had happened to his only sister. "I…I'm sorry. I don't know. I told you, I don't remember everything. Just bits and pieces."

"Are you scared, Ruby? Did Jean-Pierre threaten you not to talk? Did he have something to do with Gisèle's death and he's forcing you to be quiet? To make up this *histoire ridicule* of memory loss?"

I gazed down at the steaming bowl of soup and the perfectly arranged salad, realizing I didn't have an ounce of hunger left in me. "I don't know what Jean-Pierre did or didn't do. All I know is that he's a horrible man."

"A horrible man who you are sleeping with, and who gave you the starring role the minute my sister was dead, no?"

I lifted my eyes to Antoine's, searching for that same look of blame I'd seen in the dancers' eyes during rehearsal. But despite his accusatory tone, the disdain wasn't there. His expression was unreadable, his cheeks drawn, his face pale.

"There is something else," he murmured as he reached into his coat pocket and removed a crumpled paper bag. When he turned it over, a broken silver chain slipped out onto the table.

On the end of the silver chain was a beautiful heart-shaped ruby pendant.

It was shinier and newer than I remembered, but there was no mistaking it.

That was my grandma Martine's necklace. The same necklace the old woman had placed around my neck in the dance studio in San Diego, the one that had made my skin spark, just minutes before I'd been zapped back in time to Ruby's life.

"How did you get this?" I asked him, my voice trembling almost as much as my hands.

Antoine raised a brow. *"C'est à toi, non?"* *It is yours, no?*

My hand instinctively went to the bare skin on my chest. "Tell me how you got this," I demanded.

Antoine picked up the broken chain, rolling the smooth ruby pendant around in his hand. "When I met with the police today, they gave me a bag with Gisèle's personal effects. This necklace was lying underneath Gisèle when they found her. It was stuck to her costume, the chain already broken. The police said the fact that it was broken showed evidence of a struggle. This, I agree with. But the police have *assumed* that the necklace belonged to Gisèle, which is why they turned it over to me. I did not tell them that they were mistaken. That *this necklace*, Ruby…belongs to you."

My blood ran cold. None of this was making sense. The only thing that was becoming crystal clear was that Antoine believed I'd murdered his sister.

Antoine leaned forward in his seat, the intensity in his gray eyes burning right through me. "Tell me, Ruby, how was *your* necklace found *underneath* my sister's body?"

"Ruby would never kill someone," I declared, my gut instinct telling me to protect this woman I'd become overnight, this woman who, in another life, I had already been.

Antoine tossed me a strange glance, and after his expression morphed to one of complete confusion, I realized my mistake.

I had talked about Ruby in the third person. *Damn.*

Antoine leaned over the table, his heavy breath deepening as he inched toward me. "Come closer," he whispered.

I eased toward him, wondering if he was going to smack me across the face or kiss me.

But he did neither. Instead he dropped the necklace onto the table, then cupped my chin in the palm of his hand and gazed pointedly into my eyes. "They're blue," he said, the shock in his voice sending a chill down my spine. "*Bleu comme la mer.*"

Blue like the ocean.

"My eyes?"

He nodded slowly, the confidence he'd shown just moments ago draining from his face. "But your eyes aren't blue, Ruby. They're green. They've always been green."

Antoine dropped his hand from my chin and stared at me like he'd seen a ghost.

"You're wrong," I told him, my cheeks flaming up. "My eyes have always been blue."

"You're lying. Who are you?"

"What are you talking about? How would you know the color of my eyes, anyway?"

"You're not Ruby. You talk differently than she does. More refined, more sophisticated. Gentler, even. Are you her sister? Does Ruby have a twin? Did she run after the murder and send you in her place?"

Ruby could've had an identical twin or a whole brood of siblings back in the States for all I knew. But I couldn't come up with any more excuses, and I couldn't tell Antoine the truth. I had to get out of here.

"My name is Ruby and I have blue eyes. That's all I know right now. I don't know who that necklace belongs to, and I don't remember anything more about your sister's death. I'm sorry." I threw my napkin on the table, shot up from my seat, and ran out of the café, the frigid air smacking me like an unexpected slap to the face.

ELEVEN

I ran back past Les Deux Magots, then swung a left on rue Bonaparte. I knew this wasn't the way to my apartment, but I didn't want to go back there. I didn't want to risk seeing Jean-Pierre again or having to face this mess of a life I'd found myself in.

I needed air. I needed to breathe.

Squeezing down the narrow sidewalks of this chic neighborhood, I raced past fancy art galleries, ritzy hotels, *chocolateries*, and quaint bookstores, *librairies*. As I pushed past a classy Parisian couple all dressed up for a night on the town, I thought of Antoine, of his incredibly handsome face, those smoky eyes…and instantly wished I was in Paris on different terms.

Ruby's young body had much greater stamina than I'd ever had as Claudia. I reached the quai of the Seine River only slightly out of breath, my legs still keeping their fast pace, my lungs sucking down the cool air like water.

As soon as I spotted a break in traffic from the long line of Renault, Peugeot, and Citroën cars—their classic styles and bizarre-sounding horns an ever-present reminder that I was so far away from home—I jetted across the street and turned right toward the Pont des Arts.

My heels pounded onto the hard wooden planks of the bridge, the yellow glow of the tall lampposts lighting my way. I stopped when I reached the middle, realizing I was the only pedestrian crossing on such a bitterly cold evening. The river, which stretched out before me, was black and choppy, and just like my mind, the water spun in circles, an endless pool of unanswered questions drowning in the chaos.

The striking sights of Paris lit up the dark night—the Île de la Cité straight ahead and Notre Dame Cathedral off in the distance, its gothic towers reaching far up into the ominous night sky. The Palais du Louvre loomed to my left, and a riverboat passed underneath the bridge, its guide most certainly telling the tourists about all of the glamour the City of Lights has to offer.

The words I'd spoken to Édouard the last night we'd danced shot through my head, their irony so thick I could've choked on it.

I can only imagine how glamorous it must've been. I've never even been to Paris.

Leaning against the ledge, I curled my hands around the frosty railing and squeezed my eyes shut. I breathed in the smell of the icy water as the freeze traveled up to my brain, soothing my spinning head.

And just as the numbness set in and I could feel the air and the water sucking every last worry from my mind, I heard a voice. It was so soft, I thought I was imagining it. But as I remained on the bridge, my eyes still closed, my fingers wrapped around the ledge, I heard it again.

"Ruby."

My eyelids shot open as if a blast of ice water had woken me up from a bad dream. I turned and scanned the bridge, but no one was there.

He wasn't there.

That voice. It belonged to the man with the scarred hand. The man from New York who'd given me the scars on my back and stomach. I was sure of it.

The hairs on the back of my neck and arms stood on end, and despite the tension between me and Antoine and the fact that he believed I'd had something to do with his sister's murder, he was the *only* person I wanted to see.

I shot back across the bridge, my legs acting on muscle memory, adrenaline, and fear. I retraced my path to rue Bonaparte, praying that the man who'd whispered my name hadn't followed me to Paris. Praying I would make it back to Antoine, back to Ruby's apartment, unharmed. Alive.

Just as I rounded the corner, I plowed right into someone, our heads colliding in a cold, hard crash.

"Where did you go? I came looking for you, but I couldn't find you."

I let out the breath I'd been holding when I realized it was Antoine.

"*Ça va*, Ruby? Why are you running so fast? What is going on?"

"I…I don't know what's going on. I don't know why I'm running or who I am or what has happened to my life. I just want to go back," I said as a tear streamed down my cheek, its warmth painful on my cold, raw skin. "I just want to go home."

Antoine didn't respond. Instead, he wrapped his arms around my shivering body and pulled me into his chest. "I'll take you home, Ruby. I'll take you home."

+≈≈+

Antoine put on the teakettle and rummaged through Ruby's tiny kitchen as I sat on the couch, shivering inside the wool blanket he'd wrapped around my shoulders only moments before. I knew after what had happened at the café that it was stupid of me to bring Antoine back to my apartment, but I couldn't be alone right now. Not after hearing that blood-chilling whisper on the bridge.

What if that man was here in Paris, following me? Just waiting to strike again?

I shuddered once more, trying to erase the memory of his deep, haunting voice from my mind, but it wouldn't budge.

Antoine handed me a steaming mug of tea. "Here, this will help," he said before taking a seat opposite me in the armchair.

Closing my eyes, I poured the hot liquid down my throat, hoping it would calm me down. Make me feel safe again. But the truth was that the only thing making me feel safe right now was having Antoine next to me.

"What happened back there? What were you running from?" Antoine asked, his intense gaze fixated on me.

"I…I can't tell you. It's going to sound crazy," I said through chattering teeth.

"Crazier than your eyes changing color? Crazier than your speech, your personality, and your entire demeanor changing overnight?"

When I didn't respond, Antoine stood up from the chair and sat down next to me on the couch, forcing me to look into his eyes. "I don't want to hurt you, Ruby. I only want to know the truth. The truth about who you are, what or *who* you were running from back there, and why you are refusing to admit that the necklace found underneath my sister's body belongs to you."

"I still don't understand why you think that necklace is mine. It belongs to my…I mean, it belongs to Titine," I blurted, immediately regretting my words. Why would I want to implicate my young grandmother in Gisèle's murder?

Antoine reached past me, grabbed a framed black-and-white picture off the coffee table and thrust it into my hands. "If it belongs to Titine, why are you wearing it in this photograph?"

I glanced down at the photo of Ruby and Titine, all dolled up for a night out on the town in their chic black hats, white gloves, and dark lipstick. And sure enough, Ruby was wearing the heart-shaped pendant around her neck, just like Antoine had said. *Damn.*

So the necklace *had* belonged to Ruby, and at some point, Ruby must've given it to my grandmother. And the night I was zapped back in time to this insane life, the old woman in the dance studio put that very same necklace on me, and somehow, it had landed me here.

I shook my head, the confusion and the improbability of it all rattling me to the core.

"Tell me the truth," Antoine urged.

Puffing out a frustrated breath, I shoved the framed photograph back into his hands. "I told you, I don't remember everything! And just because my necklace was found underneath Gisèle, that doesn't make me a murderer. After I found her, it must've slipped off my neck and gotten caught in her costume."

"When you found Gisèle's body, did you move her around? Did you turn her over?"

"I…I don't know. I don't think so."

"Then why would the necklace have been *underneath* my sister if it just slipped off your neck as you are saying? What aren't you telling me? And why are you suddenly so different from the Ruby I spoke with just yesterday?"

Shoving past Antoine, I shot across the living room to get some cool air by the window.

I couldn't handle the heat of his gaze, the way he made me want to admit everything. The way he made me want to tell him who I really was: that beneath this façade of a gorgeous dancer who sold her body—and her *soul*—for money, I was really a woman who desperately wanted to find a way home, to my real life and my baby.

And that this necklace he was questioning me about had more of a story to it than he could possibly imagine.

I leaned my forehead against the chilly windowpanes, searching for that glimpse of La Tour Eiffel I'd seen earlier, but a cold, black darkness had swept over the Parisian skies. "Why are you giving me a chance to explain? Why didn't you just tell the police the necklace doesn't belong to Gisèle? Why didn't you have them arrest me?"

Antoine's footsteps bounded through the apartment, stopping only once they'd reached me. "Because, Ruby, I don't think you murdered my sister. But I think you know who did."

Antoine laid a palm on my shoulder, sending a jolt of electricity down my spine.

"Let me see your eyes again." His voice came as a deep, raspy whisper behind me. The urgency laced into his tone was palpable. He needed more than I could give him.

But still, I couldn't say no.

My arms fell to my sides, leaving me vulnerable as I turned to face him.

He took a step closer to me, our bodies now only inches apart. His other hand found my shoulder before I could break his gaze. "I know they were green. I'm positive."

I froze, unable to mutter a single word as I looked up at his sincere gray eyes and rugged face, feeling the weight of his palms on my shoulders. My cheeks flushed at his touch, my hands and my whole body tingling and warm.

And again, there was that familiar feeling. That comforting yet exhilarating sensation I'd felt when he'd taken my hand earlier in the wings. When I'd smelled his cool, masculine scent. The same feeling that had surged through me when I'd watched him from a distance in the café.

I remembered Antoine. This moment, his expression, his touch. I remembered all of it, but just in the same way I'd remembered everything so far in this life, it was like a lightning flash through my mind. And as soon as the blast hit the ground, the memory was gone, leaving me standing there, breathless and dizzy.

"It's not just the color," Antoine said, his deep voice resonating through my body, jarring me from my déjà-vu. "Your eyes are softer now, more naïve. And you are too."

"People change," I said softly, hoping against all reason that Antoine wouldn't take his hands off of me, that he would stand here and look at me this way forever.

He shook his head slowly, his eyes searching my face, his hands lingering on my shoulders. "Not in this way, though."

"You should go," I told him, the warmth and comfort I felt from his touch draining at the sound of my own words. I didn't want him to go. But this was an impossible situation. He wanted information

I couldn't give him. About Gisèle. About what Ruby had really been doing the night of her death. And about *me*—the me who stood before him tonight, a changed woman from the one he'd spoken to only a day earlier.

Antoine flinched just the slightest bit before his hands slipped from my shoulders, his pained gaze telling me he didn't want to leave. He wanted answers, he wanted justice for his sister…and maybe he wanted more.

But I couldn't give any of that to him.

I took a deep breath in an attempt to shake off the tingling, the burning, and the need that had manifested in my body over the past few minutes, and I stepped past him, showing him to the door.

On his way out, he turned and lingered in the doorway, the grief emanating off of him like a thick fog, engulfing us both in its haze of confusion, secrets, and lies. I wished I could take his pain away. I knew what it felt like to lose a family member, to lose someone you loved more than anything.

I only hoped *I* hadn't been the one who'd taken her away.

"Thank you for coming back here with me," I said softly, trying to mask the desire and the need in my voice. "And thank you for not saying anything to the police about the necklace. I know it's probably impossible to trust anyone right now, let alone me, but I'm telling you the truth about my memory loss. I'm so sorry about what happened to Gisèle. I wish I could help you more, I really do."

Antoine's smoky-gray eyes blinked down at me underneath long, thick lashes. "Will you be okay alone here tonight? Whatever you were running from on the bridge…are you safe?"

"I…I think so. I hope so."

Antoine nodded, but the concern in his eyes showed me that he was still worried. He reached inside his coat and pulled out a white business card. "If you need anything, or if you remember anything, anything at all, please call me. The hospital where I work is close by, so I can be here quickly."

"Thank you," I said, knowing that as soon as his hand let go of mine and he left my sight, I would already want to call him. Tell him to come back. Because no one I'd met so far in this crazy day as Ruby had made me feel as safe as I felt standing here with him.

He squeezed my hand. "Take care of yourself, Ruby. And please, be careful." With one last wistful gaze, he let go of my hand and disappeared down the stairwell, the scent of pine and cold air lingering under my nose, making me wish that I hadn't let him leave.

TWELVE

Alone in my apartment, I dead-bolted the door and forced myself to breathe.

What a day.

I turned around to face the cluttered apartment that was, for the moment, my own, and remembered the reason for the clutter.

François Lefevre. My frantic search for his contact information. I needed to ask him if we had been together during the murder, and if he would confirm my alibi with the police to clear my name from this investigation.

Antoine had merely been a distraction, I told myself. The feelings I'd felt for him were *not* real. I didn't even know the man. Closing my eyes, I wished away the tingling and the warmth that had flooded me the moment he'd first laid his hand on my arm, the moment he'd first said my name.

But no matter how hard I tried, I couldn't ignore the fact that I'd felt this feeling only once before—in Édouard's arms.

What did any of this mean?

I opened my eyes and scanned the apartment for answers, for something that could help me. Again, where was the silver-haired woman when I needed her?

All I had to go on were my gut instincts.

And right now, those instincts were telling me to forget about Antoine and Édouard and find François Lefevre.

I ran to the desk and searched once more through the mess of papers scattered around and underneath it. When I didn't find any mysterious phone numbers or notes leading me to François, I ripped open the desk drawer. There, on the top, were my journal and the *People* magazine with Édouard's and Solange's faces on the cover—still faded, just as they had been earlier. A shiver ran down my spine as I gazed a little too long at her icy smile and cold eyes, and found myself wondering how Édouard could be with her.

I pulled the faded sonogram photo from my coat pocket then tucked it inside my journal before my hands instinctively ran over my stomach. Disappointment flooded me yet again as I remembered that my baby wasn't there anymore. That I didn't even know if she would survive.

I couldn't stand here and be sad about it, though. I had to act. I had to get her back.

I tossed my journal and the magazine back onto the desk and resumed my search, refocusing my efforts in Ruby's cluttered bedroom. I picked once more through the plethora of gowns and high heels bursting from the closet, the piles of lacy lingerie shoved into the dresser drawers, and the empty shoe boxes and hatboxes that littered the floors.

But still, nothing.

I ransacked the hall closet, the bathroom, and the kitchen, my desperation rising with each opened box, each empty drawer, each dusty cupboard that yielded not a single piece of useful information.

Exhausted and defeated, I slid onto Ruby's dusty bedroom floor and curled my knees up against my chest, wracking my brain for ideas. The window above my head revealed a massive full moon lighting up the otherwise black Parisian sky. I followed the moon's glow along the windowsill, down the wall, and along the dark wooden panels of the floor when suddenly a gleam of light shimmered underneath Ruby's bed.

Unbelievable. In all of my searching, I hadn't thought to look under the bed. Clearly I wasn't cut out to be a sleuth.

Stacks of old books, dusty fashion magazines, and designer shoe boxes filled up the cramped space. I removed everything out from under the bed, but one lone magazine sat just beyond my grasp. I lay down on the floor and wiggled my fingers as far as I could reach, but before I got to the magazine, my hand hit something hard. When I peeked into the space, I realized something was weighing down the fabric underneath the box spring. I scooted farther underneath the bed and ran my hand along the lump, which I could now tell was in the shape of a box. With a little more probing, I was able to find a tear in the box spring material. With my heart pounding just a little bit faster, I slipped my hand up inside the box spring and pulled out a medium-size black box, its silver clasp reflecting in the soft moonlight.

With shaky fingers, I unhooked the clasp and opened the once-hidden box, desperately hoping to find something—*anything*—that would lead me to François Lefevre, and ultimately lead me back home.

I found a stack of old black-and-white photographs lying on top. I leaned closer to the window, allowing the moonlight to brighten the faces that smiled back at me. The first one was of a little girl wearing Mary Janes and a peacoat that stretched down to her knees. She was holding onto a small boy's hand and two adults stood behind them, their hands resting on the children's shoulders.

By the way warm tears sprang to my eyes, I knew that the little boy had been Ruby's brother, the adults had been her parents, and that cute little girl was Ruby.

Looking at this picture gave me such a profound sense of grief that I wondered if something bad had happened to them. I closed my eyes and tried to remember, but all I saw was Ruby as a little girl, leaning into her father's legs, smiling as if she hadn't a care in the world.

I pushed the memory from my mind and flipped through the rest of the pictures. Most of them were more recent photographs of Ruby and Titine in costume together, Ruby's piercing gaze and beautiful features so captivating, so alluring, I couldn't take my eyes off her.

I couldn't believe I *was* her.

But as I flipped to the last photograph, my chest tightened. It was the only one in the stack that was in color, and it was a picture of Ruby, Titine, Delphine, and Gisèle, all in their red sequined costumes, cleavage abounding, silver and black feathers in their hair, their arms draped around each other as if they were the best of friends. Ruby wore the red, heart-shaped pendant around her neck, proving once more that Antoine was right. But that wasn't what was upsetting me.

I'd seen this picture before.

This wasn't the typical déjà-vu feeling I'd experienced over the course of the past day, though. It was a memory I had from my life as Claudia.

Grandma Martine had a copy of this exact photograph hidden in an album in her home in San Diego. I'd come across it back when I was a nosy teenager, rummaging through a box of her old things. It had been stuffed behind another photo, as if she'd wanted to forget about it but hadn't had the heart to throw it away.

"When was this taken, Grandma?" I'd asked as I revealed the old, crinkled photo to her.

Her eyes had flicked toward the photograph, but when she focused in on the image, she immediately tore her gaze from it. "Oh, that was a long, long time ago. During my young dancer days in Paris."

"Were these good friends of yours?"

"Yes, dear. They were my best friends."

"Did you keep in touch?"

"No, dear, we didn't."

"Why not?"

My grandmother's distant, sad eyes fluttered toward the window. "Because, sweetie, the girls to either side of me, Gisèle and Ruby…they both died shortly after that photo was taken."

Back in Ruby's room, my grandma's words ringing through my ears like a busy signal on a dead phone, I let the picture float from my hands, its jagged edges *swoosh*ing through the air and landing softly on the hardwood floor.

If Gisèle and Ruby had *both* died shortly after that picture had been taken, that meant there wasn't much time left for *me*.

Since this was my past life, it made sense that Ruby must've died young. Because how else would I have been reborn as Claudia in 1977?

I recalled Madame Bouchard's words from this morning about my past-life revisit. About having only five days to accomplish some monumental task, which would forever correct the course of fate.

As a bitter draft squeezed its way through the cracks in the windowpane and sent goose bumps running down my arms, I wondered if I'd been brought back to stop Ruby's death altogether?

But if I did figure out how she was going to die and somehow found a way to stop her death before it happened, what would that mean for my future life? Would I ever be reborn as Claudia? What would happen to my baby? Would I go on living this life as Ruby instead? And on the flip side, if I let her death happen, would I wake up as Claudia? Pregnant, in the dance studio, with Édouard by my side?

Or maybe my purpose here had something to do with my grandmother. After all, it was beyond insane that we'd been best friends in this life.

I leaned my forehead up against the cool glass, trying to calm the burning in my chest and the racing of my heart. No matter what any of this meant, I was afraid. I was afraid of *how* Ruby had died so young, and scared that I was going to find out all too soon.

My eyes flickered down to the black box sitting at my feet.

There was more.

I picked up a folded, yellowed piece of paper and opened it up to find Ruby's birth certificate. I remembered this piece of paper. I remembered the way it smelled like an ancient library book, the way the lower left-hand corner had been torn just the slightest bit, and the way Ruby's name was spelled out in faded black print.

Ruby Fiona Kerrigan born on December 18, 1933, in New York City, New York.

To father, Rowan Patrick Kerrigan, and mother, Katherine Elise Walsh.

So the blonde hair and green eyes made sense; Ruby's parents—or my *former* parents—had been Irish. And by her date of birth, I knew that the body I was now inhabiting was only twenty-five years old going on twenty-six. The thought of being ten years younger should've excited me, but as I stared at the names Rowan and Katherine on the birth certificate and glanced over at the family photograph I'd laid out in front of me, I remembered them. And by the sorrow that engulfed me, I knew they were gone.

What Titine had said to me earlier made even more sense now.

To be honest, Ruby, you're the strongest one of us all, and you've been through much *worse.*

I took a deep breath in an attempt to shake off the grief. I didn't want to unearth the deep-seated memories of *how* Ruby's parents had died. First, I had to find out what else Ruby had stashed away in this box.

My hand hovered over a delicate violet handkerchief that stretched over the remaining contents. I ran my fingertips over Ruby's initials, embroidered in white at the corner of the soft fabric, before unfolding it.

A photograph torn into four jagged pieces spilled to the ground.

Arranging the pieces of the photo together, I discovered a picture of Ruby with another man—one I hadn't yet met. His arm was wrapped so tightly around Ruby's shoulders that his knuckles had turned white. Ruby smiled into the camera, but it wasn't the same seductive, carefree smile I'd seen in the other photos. The corners of her lips were tight, her jaw clenched, and fear traced her brow.

As a chill worked its way up my arms, I tilted the photo toward the moonlight to examine the man's hand, already knowing what I would find.

A long, jagged scar.

This was the man who'd pointed the knife at me in the apartment with the New York City skyline. The man who that sleazebag club owner Jean-Pierre had *saved* me from. The man who'd left that deep, awful scar on my back.

And it was *his* voice I'd heard on the bridge earlier tonight. I was sure of it.

He'd come to Paris for Ruby…for *me*.

One more glance at his slick, black hair, his hard jawline, and his eyes that were as dark and empty as a night with no stars brought a name to the tip of my tongue.

"Thomas," I whispered. "Thomas Riley."

A quick flip of the torn photo pieces confirmed my memory. Scrawled in faded black ink, a message from *him* made me shiver with fear.

> *My dearest Ruby,*
> *Until the day you die, you will forever be mine.*
> *Yours truly,*
> *Thomas*

Thomas's wording made me remember the threatening note I'd found underneath my pillow when I'd first arrived. I was fairly certain now that these notes had been written by the same hands. All I needed to do was compare the handwriting.

But just as I was standing up, the final contents inside Ruby's secret box grabbed my attention.

Lining the bottom of the box were three large envelopes filled to the brim with cash—clear evidence of Ruby's *side projects*.

And to the right of the cash, a shiny black pistol.

My blood ran cold at the sight of the gun. Could this have been the gun that had taken Gisèle's life? Was Ruby really a murderer? Someone who would kill a friend just to make it to the top?

Why else would she have a gun hidden *inside* her mattress? If it was for self-defense against this Thomas creep, wouldn't she have kept the gun somewhere accessible, like inside a dresser drawer?

Suddenly, I remembered Titine's words from earlier this morning…

As far as we know, they have no real evidence to convict you. They haven't even found the murder weapon.

They hadn't found the murder weapon because Ruby was no idiot.

She'd hidden it well.

I ran a finger over the shiny, cool metal and remembered the last time I'd held a gun like this. It was the night of my father's murder. I was only ten years old, and after that night, I'd sworn to myself that I would never again hold a gun in my hands.

But as I stared down at this one, I felt a strange, instinctual urge to pick it up.

My new hands acted on muscle memory, picking up the gun with ease, wrapping my long, delicate fingers around the trigger and aiming the barrel straight ahead. Closing my eyes, I saw these same hands, the fingernails painted a blood red, pointing this gun at something…or *someone*.

But just as I focused in on the incomplete memory to see who Ruby—or who *I*—had been pointing the gun at, a shrill *ring* pierced through the silence of the apartment.

The gun clattered to my feet, my heart pounding like a hammer to my chest.

It was the phone.

⊷≒≓⊶

I fumbled to answer the old telephone, my hands shaking so hard they almost dropped the shiny black receiver on the floor.

"Allô?"

"Ruby, *c'est François.*"

It took me a moment to regain my bearings. To forget about the creepy photo of Thomas, the night I'd lost my dad, and the memory I'd been having of Ruby pointing the gun.

But then it clicked. I recognized his voice. François Lefevre, the politician who could potentially clear my name from the murder investigation.

Thank God.

"François, I'm so glad it's you. I need to ask you—"

"No, Ruby. You do not need to ask me anything," he spat in a thick accent, clipping me off with his sharp tone. "It is you who will be answering the questions. Why have the police just been to my home? What have you told them about me? About us? And why do they think I am involved in the murder of that *pute?*"

François had just called Gisèle a whore. This wasn't going to go as smoothly as I'd hoped.

"I didn't tell them anything about you or about us. But they have a photo of us outside the club…of you paying me. It was taken the same night that Gisèle was murdered."

"*Merde.* How do they have a photo of us? Who gave it to them?"

"I'm not sure. Detective Duval didn't tell me *how* he got the photo. He did tell me, however, that if you and I don't tell him the truth about what we were doing together that night, the photo could be leaked to the press."

"*C'est pas vrai. Putain.* Do they know who I am? Do they know what I can do to their careers if they even think about releasing that photo?"

"Yes, François. Detective Duval knows exactly who you are. But an innocent woman was murdered that night, and they think *I* could've been the one responsible, and that I was hoping to use my connection with you to keep me from getting caught."

"*C'est ridicule.* After all, you are the only woman I have ever met who knows *exactly* how to get what she wants. Certainly, you would not be so stupid to murder someone to get it, *would you?*"

Stealing a guilty glimpse of the pistol at my feet, I swallowed hard. I didn't know *for sure* if Ruby had killed Gisèle, and although signs were pointing toward the possibility that she had, finding a way home to my baby had to take top priority…even if it meant lying.

"Of course not," I said, hoping my hesitation hadn't convinced him otherwise. "The problem is that I had a little fall this morning during rehearsal, and I'm having a hard time remembering what exactly happened that night. Were you and I together *during* the murder?"

"*Oh là là.* You are serious? You do not remember what happened that night?"

"Yes, I'm serious. Anything you can tell me about the way things played out, and specifically the timing of events, would be really helpful."

"Time is something I do not have a lot of. My wife will be home any minute. I do not know if we were together when the murder actually took place, but it is likely that even if it happened in the next room, we would not have heard anything."

"Why is that?"

"*La musique*, of course. It is so loud. And so were you, *ma chérie.* You are always loud when you come to me."

I swallowed my disgust and forged ahead. "Were you still in the club when I found Gisèle?"

"My driver had already picked me up when I saw the sirens racing down the street. I only read about the murder in the papers on Monday. I did not know that you were the one who found her. Nor do I care. What I do care about is that my name is not connected to this murder, and that the photo is *not* released to the press."

"I understand. Just answer one more question for me: You don't happen to remember me ever mentioning anything about wanting to harm Gisèle, do you?"

"Ruby, in case you have forgotten, we don't do a lot of *talking* when I visit you at the club."

"Please, just answer the question."

"No, you have never said anything of this nature to me. You are driven, yes, but mean-spirited, no."

A buildup of tension released from my chest. At least this was a step in the right direction.

"So in order to clear this up, would you be willing to *discreetly* admit to the police that you were with me that night, *during* the murder, and that I've never mentioned anything to you about wanting to harm Gisèle? If we both tell them the truth about our relationship, they will have no reason to release that photo to the press, and this will all be over."

"No, Ruby. This will not be over. There is still the question of *who* gave the police that photo in the first place. Someone was watching us. And whoever it was either wants to harm my career *or* they want to frame you for this murder. Or both."

I gripped the phone, thinking of the potential enemies I'd met—or remembered—in my first twenty-four hours as Ruby.

Véronique and Thomas Riley.

Could one of them have taken the photo of us?

"I understand your predicament, Ruby. But you are asking a lot of me. You are asking a married man with a high-profile political career to admit that he was having sex with a *prostituée*. And still, since we do not know who took the photograph, there will be no guarantee that it won't somehow find its way into the wrong hands."

I wanted to ask *why* a married man with a high-profile career would be paying women for sex in the first place, and doing so *outside* the club in plain view, but now wasn't the time to take the moral high ground. I was, after all, the *prostituée* in this scenario.

"I understand what I'm asking. But telling the police the truth could at least buy some time. For both of us. And with your connections, it won't be too difficult for you to make *sure* the police do not release that photo and maybe even find out who gave it to them in the first place, *n'est-ce pas?*"

"*Merde.* It was only supposed to be sex."

Peabody Public Library
Columbia City, IN

"Please, François. I know you don't owe me anything, but I need your help."

Silence traveled through the line while I waited for François to say he would help me. To say that he didn't want me to go to prison for a murder that *he* at least believed I didn't commit.

"*D'accord*. If this is the only way to keep that damn photo out of the papers, I'll do it. I refused to answer the detective's questions today without my lawyer present, so I will arrange a private meeting with the detective first thing in the morning to clear up this mess. I will admit to our *liaison* and tell him that you had nothing to do with the murder. That you were with me the entire time. And although I never intended to use my political stature in such a way, I will do what I must to keep the integrity of my family name. I trust, in return, that you will continue to keep our relations quiet, except for your conversation with the detective, of course."

I breathed a sigh of relief. "Yes, of course. Thank you so much, François."

"One more thing, Ruby." His voice took on the same hard tone he'd had at the beginning of the conversation, making me wish there wasn't anything else.

"I ask that in return for my confession to the police, you continue our *liaison* at my command...and for free."

He wanted me keep sleeping with him after this? And for free?

I shook my head. Of course that's what he wanted. What did I expect? That just because he'd agreed to tell the detective the truth about us, he'd suddenly become a decent man? These were exactly the kind of politicians my father had hated when he'd been in office.

"*Bien sûr*." *Of course*, I said, telling myself this promise was only a means to an end.

And that it was a promise I most certainly would break.

Just before we hung up, I remembered one last thing.

"François, did you see a woman with dangly diamond earrings exiting the club that night? When the photo was taken?"

"No." He sighed, the sound of fatigue lining his once-powerful voice. "I only saw you."

━━━

Later that night, I curled up in bed with my journal, flipping through the worn, faded pages once more in the hope that this object I'd carried back with me through time would somehow send me forward again. Take me the hell out of here.

The entries were fading even more now, some of them completely gone. It was as if someone had taken an eraser to my most important memories and carelessly wiped them away.

With another turn of the page, I discovered one entry that was still intact...and it was one that I hadn't read in ages.

There was a reason for that. But as I sat alone in this cold Parisian apartment with these foreign hands clutching my journal, I longed to be carried back to *my* life...even to the darkest moments of it.

July 22, 1996

I arrived in California today, and I've never been so happy to see the beach and the sunshine. But more than the gorgeous scenery, I needed to get away from her. I've felt her hatred coating me like a toxic virus ever since that day. The day we lost Dad.

And no matter how hard I've tried to make it up to her, no matter how many times I've apologized, I know now, my mother will never forgive me. I don't know if I'll ever be able to forgive myself for hesitating that night, my finger hovering over the trigger, too afraid to pull it.

How many times I've replayed that moment over and over in my head, wishing I could've shot that evil man who took my father away from us. I could've stopped it all from happening. But I hesitated. And that one second of hesitation will haunt me forever.

Dad, if you're listening, I'm so very sorry.

Unwilling to relive the grief I'd worked so hard to overcome, or to allow myself to think about the loss of my handsome, loving, larger-than-life father, I turned to the back of the journal, where a blank page awaited me. I decided to write down every last detail of what had happened to me at the dance studio the night I'd been transported back in time to Paris, and hopefully, I'd remember something that would help me to find a way back, to stop my life from disappearing altogether.

And so, with a shoddy red pen I found stuffed in Ruby's desk drawer, I began composing a new journal entry.

December 5, 1959
This morning I woke up in Paris in the body of a woman named Ruby Kerrigan. But my name isn't Ruby. My name is Claudia Marie Davis. I'm eighteen weeks pregnant with a little girl, and I have to find a way back to her…

THIRTEEN

I rolled over in bed and squinted at the harsh morning light piercing through the window. The clock on the nightstand read eight thirty. I hadn't slept this late since I was in my twenties.

But when I ran my hand over my flat stomach—the ever-constant reminder of the fact that I was *not* pregnant—I remembered. I *was* in my twenties.

My red journal and my future copy of *People* lay next to me on the red satin sheets of Ruby's bed, the magazine's edges crumpled and slightly torn. The night before, after I'd convinced François to speak to the police, and after I'd finished my journal entry, I'd held on to the faintest of hopes that maybe I'd already accomplished what I'd been sent to this life to do. And so I'd gone to sleep with my journal, my magazine, and my sonogram photo, hoping against all hope that I would wake up in Claudia's body, still pregnant, as if none of this had ever happened.

But it hadn't worked. I was still here. And although I was hopeful that with François's confession today, I could potentially clear my name from the murder investigation, there were still many *major* issues to be dealt with.

Before I'd gone to bed the night before, I'd cross-checked the eerie note from under my pillow with Thomas Riley's handwriting on the back of the torn photo. The handwriting didn't *quite* match up, but those initials did appear to be T. R., so I had to believe the threatening note had come from him.

Which meant that he was here, in Paris, stalking me in some jealous rage. He could've taken the photograph of Ruby and François outside the club that night and turned it over to the police. And there was always a chance that he had something to do with Gisèle's murder.

Whether my theories about Thomas Riley were accurate or not, I knew one thing for sure. Ruby's life—or *my* life—wasn't going to last much longer. And, if the silver-haired woman was telling the truth, I only had four more days to figure out this impossible mess and find a way back home.

My stomach growled, reminding me that there were other, more basic needs that also had to be met.

Wrapped in Ruby's silky lavender robe, I ransacked the kitchen but only found a half-empty bottle of liquor and a stale baguette. In my ravenous state, I actually considered eating the rock-hard bread, but then I remembered Ruby's stash of French francs under the bed.

I wasn't sure if she'd been saving the money for something else—like to move out of this apartment and out of Jean-Pierre's control—but first things first. Whether or not Ruby was a bona fide murderer, a girl's gotta eat.

After showering in the coldest water I'd ever put my head under, I threw on a soft, snow-white sweater, smooth gray pants, and a pair of closed-toe red heels. Ruby's *only* shoes were heels. Thank God her young feet were accustomed to wearing them.

I bundled up in Ruby's red peacoat and white scarf, tucked a wad of francs into her cute black purse, then headed out to find food.

The minute I exited the building, a blast of cold air slapped me in the face, but I quickly forgot about the bitter winter temperatures as the scent of warm, buttery croissants floated past. I turned to the right, toward that heavenly aroma, and headed up rue de l'Ancienne Comédie. With my eyes focused on the red awning of the *boulangerie* a few storefronts down, I barely heard the voice calling Ruby's name.

"Ruby! Hey, Ruby, wait!"

It was Titine, her red hair swooped into a bun, a few curly auburn tendrils cascading down her cheeks. I had to stop myself from gasping. This was exactly how my grandmother always wore her hair.

I still couldn't believe Titine was my young grandma. This was insane.

"Are you okay?" she asked. "You look surprised to see me or something."

I cleared my throat and smiled. "Yes, I'm fine. Just really hungry, that's all."

"Let's get some breakfast, then. I was on my way to your apartment anyway…just in case you *forgot* about rehearsal this morning." She winked at me as she led the way toward the *boulangerie*. "Are you feeling better after yesterday? Is the good ol' memory back in business?"

I eyed her up and down, still reeling at her sassy little attitude, the way her emerald eyes danced back and forth when she was hyper, the way her smile could warm me up no matter what the circumstances. "Not quite. I went through my apartment last night to see if I could find anything that would help me jog my memory, and I have a few questions to ask you."

Inside the quaint *boulangerie*, my eyes melted at the sight of baskets filled to the brim with freshly baked baguettes, fluffy croissants, buttery *pains au chocolat*, and swirly *pains aux raisins*.

"Sure," Titine said, completely unfazed by the gourmet spread of pastries before us. "What do you want to know?"

"Let's get food first. I'm so hungry, I can hardly see straight."

Titine shot me a strange glance then ordered for us both. "*Deux pains au chocolat, s'il vous plaît*," she told the petite French woman behind the counter.

A flash of déjà-vu hit me as Titine and I settled into a tiny table in the corner of the *boulangerie*, gooey chocolate croissants in hand. I closed my eyes and could see Titine and myself sitting at this exact table, only it must've been springtime, because we were wearing knee-length skirts, fitted white blouses, and tall, classic pumps.

"Ruby? *Hello?*"

I snapped my eyes open and tried to ignore the memories swimming around in my head. But as I took a bite of the most buttery, fattening, and *delicious* chocolate croissant I'd ever tasted, I remembered this taste. I'd been to this *boulangerie* and had eaten many a *pain au chocolat* here before. If anything, in my second day as Ruby, the memories felt stronger.

"Ruby, what are you thinking about? I know things have been crazy lately, but you're acting really strange." Titine searched my face, as if she could almost see the difference that had taken hold in me, but she just as quickly dismissed her questioning gaze with a dainty bite of flaky pastry.

I finished the bite I was devouring and forced a smile. "I'm sorry, Titine. I know I'm not really myself right now...but like I told you, after the fall, I don't have my full memory. Only bits and pieces. And with this whole murder investigation going on, it's not exactly great timing, you know?" I stared deep into my young grandmother's eyes, wishing I could tell her the truth about what I really remembered. About my life as Claudia and my relationship with her as she would grow older. But she would think I'd lost my mind.

"Tell me about it." She peeked down at her watch. "We have half an hour until we need to get to rehearsal, so ask me your questions and let's see if we can't get your head straightened out a bit. And then maybe we can talk about what the detective said to you yesterday and why you ran off in a tizzy."

I nodded, taking another bite of my scrumptious croissant, then wiped the corners of my mouth and launched in with my first question. "What's the story with Véronique? What's her problem and why does she hate me so much?"

The eagerness in Titine's eyes waned. "You sure you really want to go into all of this? I mean, *some* things are better left in the past."

"I need to know as much as I can about what was going on in Ru...I mean, in *my* life before I fell yesterday morning." *Note to self, stop referring to Ruby in the third person.*

Titine shot me a questioning glance but kept going. "Véronique didn't like us from the start...especially you. She saw how Gisèle took to us immediately and how much Jean-Pierre favored you over the other girls. Then she turned most of the other dancers against you by spreading rumors...and even though some of them may have been true, she still had no right to do that."

"What kind of rumors?"

Titine sighed. "Are you really sure you want to dig all of this up? I don't see how it's going to help anything."

"Titine, you said you would answer my questions."

"Okay, fine. She told the other dancers that you were sleeping with Jean-Pierre just so you could bump Gisèle out of her starring role. *And* she told them that you were sleeping with the club's investors to keep Jean-Pierre happy."

Ah. François Lefevre wasn't *only* paying Ruby for sex, he was also investing money into Jean-Pierre's club. That explained why Jean-Pierre had been so insistent about keeping François's name out of the murder investigation. Jean-Pierre didn't give a damn about ruining François's reputation; he was only scared he might lose one of his investors.

It was all about the money.

"Did you believe the rumors?" I asked.

Titine shifted uncomfortably, her gaze drifting out the window. "Well, you've always been *motivated*...to say the least. And of course I know you're sleeping with Jean-Pierre, but I never believed that you were doing it to push Gisèle out of her role. I mean, we all would've loved to be the star of the show. But we became really close friends with Gisèle. She was different from the other girls. She was actually nice to us when we first arrived, and she was the only one who wasn't afraid of Véronique. I know that you never would've intentionally hurt her career. Unfortunately, though, that's not how the other girls, especially Véronique, see things."

"What about the other rumor—the one about me sleeping with the club's investors to keep Jean-Pierre happy?" I already knew the answer to this one, but wanted to find out how much Titine knew.

"You always denied it, but…"

"You didn't believe me?"

"If you really want to know, the truth is that no, I didn't believe you. I saw one of the richest businessmen who frequent the club leaving your apartment one morning when I was on my way over, but I never said anything to you. I figured you would've told me if it was something you wanted me to know."

"So it makes sense that the other girls would believe I'd want to get rid of Gisèle. I mean, look at everything else I was willing to do to make it to the top."

Titine reached across the table and squeezed my hand. "It's not like that, Ruby. In this business, we've all had to do some questionable things to get where we want to be. It doesn't make you a murderer, for heaven's sake. All of those girls are just terrified of having Véronique turn against them. They saw how livid she was when Jean-Pierre announced that he'd given you Gisèle's role."

"Well, I'm not going to keep this charade up. I don't want the lead role anymore. I'll figure out another way to earn my living."

"Ruby, don't talk like that. You've dreamed of this your whole life. And if there's anyone who deserves this opportunity, it's you. Tonight is your big chance. *Robert Maxwell* is coming to see us perform. You can't quit now. I won't let you."

"Who is Robert Maxwell? Is he the film director Jean-Pierre keeps talking about? And why is it such a big deal that he's coming to see me perform?"

Titine shook her head. "Jeez, Ruby. I can't believe you don't remember any of this. I think you really do need to see a doctor, but if you can get through tonight's show you'll have to wait until tomorrow." She took another bite then began talking again, her eyes lighting up. "Robert Maxwell is a famous film director from *Hollywood*, Ruby. He was here about a month ago, on a night you filled in for Gisèle, and I took your usual spot. He saw the show and was so impressed with us, he asked Jean-Pierre to schedule this special performance just for him. And based on how we do tonight, he's considering casting us in one of his films."

"What? Are you serious?"

"Yes! That's why Jean-Pierre chose that new Peggy Lee song, 'Fever,' for you to sing. He figured it would be better to sing a popular American song as the main act. And if all goes well, Robert will make us stars, Ruby. *Real* movie stars."

A twinge of excitement rose up in my chest, but it was quickly squashed when I remembered what I was supposed to do with Robert after the performance. He would make Ruby a star *if* she complied with his demands, and even then, once he had Ruby, would he keep his end of the bargain? And would Ruby then be expected to continue sleeping with Robert *in addition* to Jean-Pierre? *And* François? If she—or *I*—lived long enough to do so?

I buried my forehead in my hands. "I can't do this, Titine."

"Did you not hear me correctly? He's going to make you a star! That means you can be finished with nightclubs and with sleazy Jean-Pierre. This could be it for both of us, Ruby. You can't let what happened to Gisèle stop you from—"

"Titine," I cut her off. "Do you know what I'm supposed to do with Robert, in order to become a *star*?"

"What are you talking about? He's coming to see you perform in the show tonight. That's it."

I shook my head. "No, that's not it."

"I don't understand."

"I think Robert might be one of Jean-Pierre's investors."

Titine's cheeks paled. "You're supposed to sleep with him? With Robert?"

I rubbed my forehead in my hands. "Jean-Pierre told me they've made an agreement. And he says if I break it, I'll lose my job. My apartment. Everything."

I thought of the picture I'd found, and of my grandmother's words. Gisèle and Ruby would die soon after the photo was taken.

"There's something else I need to tell you, Titine. I'm afraid something bad—"

But I didn't have time to get the words past my lips before Titine gripped her stomach, shot up from her chair, and dashed out of the *boulangerie*. She left no explanation, just an empty seat and a whiff of her lavender-scented perfume.

Outside, I spotted Titine doubled over next to a newsstand, getting sick on the cobblestone sidewalk.

I rushed to her side and laid my hand on her back. "Titine, are you okay?"

She clutched her stomach as she stood abruptly, shrugging my hand off. "I'm fine. I must have a stomach bug or something."

"Do you think you need to see a doctor?"

"No, there's no time for that. Rehearsal starts soon." Her tone was suddenly as chilly as the wind that whipped against our faces. She refused to meet my gaze as she wiped the tears pooling at the corners of her eyes.

I laid my hand on her arm. "Are you sure you're going to be okay to rehearse? I mean, you just got sick and you don't look too good."

She puffed out an annoyed breath and once again shrugged my hand off of her. "You're not the only one with things going on, you know. I have to go get ready." And with that, she turned and left me alone on the sidewalk, wondering what in the hell had just happened.

A strange car horn beeped behind me, and as I turned and took in the shiny teal Citroën DS weaving down the crowded side street, I remembered again. I was in Paris. In the fifties. But before I lost myself in the next déjà-vu flash, I bumped smack into the newsstand behind me. Flipping around to see if I'd caused any damage, a familiar image on the front page of today's *France-Soir* newspaper caught my eye.

It was the photo of me and François Lefevre outside the club, my back against the stone wall, François leaning over me, slipping a wad of cash into my hand. It was the same photograph the detective had shown me yesterday, and as my eyes darted over the rows of *Le Monde* and *Le Figaro* newspapers lining the stand, I found the incriminating image splattered across every single front page.

With a shaky hand, I reached for one of the papers, nervously skimming the headline that read: *Le Scandale Lefevre.*

"C'est vous sur cette photo, Mademoiselle?" It was the old man behind the kiosk counter. He'd recognized me from the photo.

I shook my head at him. *"Non, c'est pas moi, Monsieur,"* I snapped as I threw a few francs on the counter and took off toward my apartment, tucking the newspaper *and* its announcement that I'd sold my body to a married politician tightly under my arm.

+≍≍+

Back in my apartment, I read the newspaper article, only to find my worst fears confirmed.

Not only did the article expose François Lefevre's extracurricular activities *and* my full name, it also named François, *député* of France's *Assemblée Nationale*, as one of the club's primary investors. The article went on to state that an investigation was under way to find out if the well-known politician had been stealing government money to fund his exploits.

Despite France's stereotypical blasé attitude toward infidelity, I doubted even the most liberal of its people would be too excited to learn that one of their top officials—whose father was an advisor to the president, no less—was being accused of smuggling government funds to invest in a scandalous nightclub.

And as if that wasn't enough, the writer of the article went so far as to connect both me and François to Gisèle's death as potential murder suspects.

Examining the photo once more, I noticed that the picture had been cropped to *only* include me and François. That female silhouette with the dangly diamond earrings had been cut out of the image. When I closed my eyes, I could still only conjure up a flash of that long string of diamonds but no face to go with it. The club would've been packed that night. She could've been anyone. And since my broken memory still refused to serve up a perfect timeline of the way things had gone down that night, speculating about who this woman was or what she may have had to do with the murder wouldn't do me any good now.

I tossed the newspaper onto the desk and reached for Ruby's telephone. My new set of hands effortlessly turned the dial on the black rotary phone, to reach a number I hadn't been able to remember for the life of me yesterday—but that suddenly flowed from Ruby's memory and straight to the dial without a second thought.

"*Allô?*"

"*François, c'est moi, Ruby.*"

His sigh came hard and defeated over the line. He'd seen the headlines too.

"*Putain.* What a *désastre.* Whoever took that photograph and turned it in to *les journaux* wanted to ruin my life, and they have succeeded."

"Does your wife—"

"*Elle est déjà partie.*" She already left. "*Et elle a pris les enfants.*" *And she took the kids.*

"I'm so sorry."

"There is no time for sorry," he snapped. "The police will want to speak to us both again today, no? We must have our story straight."

"Yes, of course."

"My lawyer is on his way over as we speak. If you want any chance at not being arrested for this murder and spending the rest of your days in a French prison, you must come over right away. My lawyer will advise us both on how to proceed with the police…and with the press. And if you see Jean-Pierre, tell him he is on his own now. All of my money will be going to legal fees."

A harsh dial tone rang in my ears as I closed my eyes and called to memory a picture of François's apartment building. I didn't need him to tell me the address. Thanks to Ruby's strengthened memory, I knew exactly where he lived.

As I tucked the newspaper into my purse, I spotted Antoine's business card on the desk. A flush of heat crept up my cheeks as I thought of his gaze, of his electric touch the night before. Surely he would see the headlines today. And the photo. He would know now what I'd really been doing the night Gisèle was killed.

And he would realize that I'd lied to him…or at least that I'd omitted the truth.

And even though I knew that his offer to call him if I needed anything would probably be revoked after he caught wind of today's news, I tucked his card into my purse anyway. If I had the opportunity to see him again, I would tell him the truth this time. At least what I remembered of it.

On my way out the door, I remembered one last thing. I rushed back into Ruby's bedroom and pulled the black box out from under a pile of lingerie in the dresser. After lifting up the silver clasp, I ran my hand over the smooth black pistol.

I didn't want to bring the gun with me. I didn't want to hold one in my hands ever again.

Especially a gun that may have taken the life of Antoine's only sister, and of my friend.

But when I thought about the eerie whisper I'd heard so clearly on the bridge the night before, the torn photo I'd found of Thomas, the red scars lining my lower back and abdomen, and my memory of the night he'd given them to me, I lifted the gun from its resting place and tucked it into my purse.

I would do whatever I had to if it meant a chance at making it back to my life as Claudia, a chance at saving my baby.

FOURTEEN

Heavy gray clouds swirled over the city, hurling fat drops of freezing rain onto the sidewalks as I took off down rue de l'Ancienne Comédie toward François's apartment. Rehearsal back at the club was set to begin any minute, and I knew that Jean-Pierre would be livid when I didn't show up, but I couldn't worry about him right now. Making sure I didn't go to prison before my five days were up clearly took precedence over the demands of that sleazy, ruthless club owner.

Bundling my red peacoat and wispy white scarf tighter around my neck, I turned the corner onto the confined sidewalks of rue Saint-André des Arts, Ruby's memory telling me exactly where to go. The rain pelted down even harder as I took another left toward the river, the long, winding stretch ahead of me now completely deserted. I broke into a run, praying my tall heels wouldn't slip on the icy rain that now poured over me in sheets, soaking my hair and clumping up my long eyelashes, making it nearly impossible to see more than a few steps ahead.

I lowered my face and focused on the ground, knowing that in only a few more blocks, I would find François's apartment building overlooking the Seine. Suddenly the rain let up, leaving only a chilly mist filtering through the winter air. And in the quiet of this miniscule Parisian side street, an earsplitting footstep clumped behind me.

I told myself there was no need for my heart to begin racing as it had at the sound of a simple footstep. The rain had stopped, so people would be making their way back outside now. But when I heard another pounding step, followed by another and another, the clicking of heavy shoes against pavement, coming closer and still closer, I couldn't help but whip my face around to see who was behind me.

There, less than a block away, stood a tall man cloaked in a stiff black trench coat, his slick, black hair blowing in the wind, his haunting black eyes staring straight at me. The blood drained from my face as the corners of his mouth turned upward into a crooked smile and his pace quickened.

Thomas.

I took off down the sidewalk, running faster than I ever had in my entire life. I couldn't tell if I was still hearing his footsteps against the concrete or if it was the pounding of my own heart drumming inside my ears. I wasn't going to stop to find out, though.

I reached the Quai des Grands Augustins, the Seine River just across the street, and knew that François's apartment building was only a couple of buildings down on the right. I flew around the corner, my heart pumping so hard I thought my chest would burst. As I reached the massive navy-blue door I distinctly remembered walking through before, I lunged for the buzzer.

I shot a harried glance to my right to see if the man in the black trench coat was still following me. But when I scanned the crowded sidewalks lining the Seine, a sea of long black trench coats and large umbrellas mocked me. The air in my lungs constricted as I buzzed François's apartment once more, praying for him to open the damn door.

The door finally clicked open, so with one last look over my shoulder, I ran inside, slammed the door behind me, then took off down the hallway toward the staircase. Beads of water flung off the ends of my hair as I took the stairs two at a time all the way up to the top floor and François's penthouse apartment.

Lifting a hand to bang on the door, I realized it was already ajar. With one final breath, I slipped inside, then closed and bolted the door behind me.

Thank God.

The chill from the freezing rainstorm settled into my bones as I leaned against the wall to catch my breath. A dimly lit foyer with shiny hardwood floors opened up to a large salon with floor-to-ceiling windows overlooking the choppy waters of the Seine, but François was nowhere to be seen.

"François?" I called, walking slowly through the silent apartment, my voice echoing off the tall ceilings. "François, it's Ruby. Are you here?"

A door creaked shut at the end of the hallway, closely followed by the sound of running water. Ah, he must be in the bathroom, I told myself as I continued my private tour of his home.

I walked past the perfectly set dining room table and headed down a long hallway, the walls to either side of me lined with photographs of François with his wife and kids. A pang of guilt hit me as I gazed into his children's eyes. A cute little boy with a dark mop of hair and a playful grin. A dainty little girl with bouncy curls and a round face. Had I taken this away from them? Their family? Their father?

I startled to attention at the sound of the shower turning on at the end of the darkened hallway. Hopefully François wasn't expecting me to come in there after him—surely not under these grim circumstances, with his lawyer set to arrive here any minute no less.

I continued slowly down the corridor until I reached the last door on the left, which I knew was his bedroom. And as I glimpsed the grand antique bed filling up the center of the beautiful master bedroom, I remembered being in that bed with François. I could see our two sweaty bodies intertwined on top of the sheets, his quivering fingers undressing me, the forbidden act in his own marital bed making him moan with pure excitement.

But the bed was empty now. The soft white pillows fluffed, the forbidden lust washed from the sheets. His wife knew. She knew he'd been paying me for sex.

What kind of a person had I been?

Someone who would break up families to earn a living?

Someone who would murder a friend in cold blood to steal her starring role?

I sank onto the edge of the bed and buried my face in my hands, my stomach curling at the guilty memories that plagued me, my heart still pounding from the fear of the man who could be waiting for me down on those damp Parisian streets.

This was all too much. François needed to get out of the shower and tell his lawyer to hurry up. I didn't have any more time to waste.

I shifted off the bed to get up, but something sharp poked me in the thigh. When I raised my leg up, the sparkle almost blinded me.

It was an earring.

A dangly diamond earring.

I snatched the silky string of diamonds off the bed and examined them in the light streaming through the window. Without the photograph in front of me, I couldn't be 100 percent certain, but my gut told me that *this* was the same earring I'd seen on that female silhouette outside the club the night of Gisèle's murder. The same one in the picture the detective had shown me of François paying me in the alley.

This earring must belong to François's wife. Which means she was there the night Gisèle was killed, watching her husband pay me for sex.

Maybe she'd hired an investigator to photograph us…and maybe she'd been the one to release it to the press.

Or, was it possible that François's wife had had something to do with Gisèle's death? Could she have found out about my relationship with François and tried to frame me for the murder?

My stomach clenched as I wondered how much deeper Ruby's mess could possibly go, and how I would ever solve this mystery. Clasping the diamond earring in my hand, I made a split-second decision and tucked it into my purse. I stood on shaky legs, prepared to knock on the bathroom door and tell François to hurry up, but my heel slid on the hardwood floors, nearly causing me to fall.

A stream of silky red liquid trickled down the shiny wooden panels, straight into my red heels.

Oh, God.

The running water in the bathroom suddenly sounded like a roaring steam engine, barreling straight at me as I stepped around the blood and peered toward the other side of the bed.

There, between the flowing blue curtains and the antique bed, lay François Lefevre, his eyes frozen open, his own scarlet blood flowing from a deep slit in his neck.

"François!"

I lunged to his side, my adrenaline kicking in and overpowering my gag reflex. Tossing my purse to the ground, I yanked off my white scarf and pressed it against the open wound in his neck, the endless flow of blood immediately soaking through the thin, silky material and onto my hands.

"François, wake up. Please, François. Wake up. Wake up!" I pleaded as I pushed the blood-soaked scarf into his neck and folded over his body, knowing it was too late.

He was already dead.

I searched the floor around his body, looking for the knife he'd used to end his own life, but I found nothing. His hands lay completely still by his sides, and the entire space around him was clear except for the blood, which continued to flow like a river from his open neck.

The sound of running water coupled with the eerie stillness in the apartment made me realize what was going on.

Someone had buzzed me into this apartment, only moments ago…the same someone who'd turned on the shower. And by the gruesome scene before me, it clearly had *not* been François.

I dropped the bloody scarf from my hands and searched the room for something to defend myself with, my grandmother's words returning to my memory with a vengeance.

Gisèle and Ruby died shortly after that photo was taken.

Was this it? Had I been sent back to this life just to die here in this foreign apartment, at the hands of an unknown killer?

I thought of my baby and of Édouard. Engaged or not, I couldn't bear the thought of never seeing him again. I needed to find a way back to both of them. Was Ruby's death my way back?

But when my eyes landed on my purse, lying right next to François's gray, lifeless face, my gut told me this was *not* Ruby's time.

Lunging for the purse, I wrapped my trembling hands around the cool black pistol inside. I pressed the gun up against my chest, then backed against the wall and inched my way over to the door.

Hot steam squeezed through the crack in the bathroom door, billowing out into the damp hallway, when suddenly the floorboards creaked in the other direction, near the salon.

Whoever had killed François was still here. They'd buzzed me up. They'd left the door open for me.

They wanted me too.

As my hand closed in around the trigger, I told myself I could do this. I had to do this. I knew I couldn't let Ruby's life—*my* life—end like this, in the middle of this senseless scandal. Madame Bouchard had told me I had something important to accomplish here, in this life, and I couldn't let it all end like this.

And so as I readied myself to turn the corner into the hallway, I promised myself that this time, I wouldn't hesitate.

I would pull the trigger.

Taking a deep breath, I pointed the gun out in front of me and crept around the corner. But there was no one waiting for me in the hallway.

A loud *click* toward the front of the apartment made my insides jump, but I kept the gun steady, facing forward, as I crept back down the long hallway. My ankles shook and my stomach threatened to hurl my chocolate croissant from this morning all over the shiny hardwood floors.

But I didn't cave. I kept going. I had no other choice.

As soon as I reached the foyer, something jumped out at me. I screamed and watched helplessly as the gun flew from my hands and a wiry black cat skittered across the floor.

I lunged toward the gun, which had flown into the front door, but stopped when I realized the door was now unlocked and sitting ajar.

I'd closed and locked that door behind me when I'd first entered the apartment.

Whoever had been here had just walked right out the front door and had left me alone in this apartment with a startled cat and François's dead body.

FIFTEEN

Shivering in a stiff blue chair in the fancy living room, I pulled the wool blanket that smelled of François's cologne tighter around my shoulders. Police milled around the apartment, speaking in hushed tones whenever they walked past me, until finally, one I recognized took a seat in the chair opposite me.

It was Detective Duval.

"You are making a habit of showing up at crime scenes, no?"

I responded with a shiver, my pants and hair still soaking wet from the rain, the shock of finding François's dead body and my own close call with the murderer still chilling me to the bone.

Detective Duval pulled a pad of paper and a pen from his front coat pocket and scooted his chair a few inches closer to mine. "Tell me, Mademoiselle Kerrigan, what were you doing at Monsieur Lefevre's apartment, *alone*?"

"I am assuming you saw the photo on the front page of the newspaper this morning?" I asked him, trying to control the trembling in my voice, the incessant spinning in my head.

He nodded.

"Can you tell me who leaked it to the press?"

"If you are suggesting it was my department, you are wrong, Mademoiselle. I only said that to you yesterday as a scare tactic. To get the two of you to talk. But seeing as how there is only *one* of you now, you will have to talk. You have no other choice."

"Who gave you that photo?" I asked.

He shifted in his seat, his gaze not breaking mine. "That is confidential information."

"Was it François's wife? Because I am fairly certain she was at the club the night of Gisèle's murder, watching me and François in the alley."

"What makes you think this?"

I nodded toward the coffee table where I'd laid the diamond earring. "I found that earring lying on François's bed when I first arrived, and I'm almost positive it's the same earring the female silhouette in the photo is wearing. I think she was there, and if she was, it's possible that she had something to do with Gisèle's murder."

Detective Duval sat back in his seat, the corners of his mouth twitching. "One murder at a time, Mademoiselle Kerrigan. Do you have any other suggestions for me, or are you ready to let me do my job?"

I sat up straighter in my chair, determined to stay strong. I would not let this man wear me down. "Yes, I do, actually. Besides François's wife's possible involvement in all of this, I need you to look into a man named Thomas Riley from New York City. He's my ex-boyfriend, he's extremely dangerous, and I think he's here in Paris following me. There's a strong chance he may be involved in these murders as well."

Detective Duval jotted something down on his notepad then raised an eyebrow at me. "How interesting that every time I meet with you, you point the finger at someone else. And in this case, at two other people. I have noted the name of this so-called ex-boyfriend of yours, but first I need you to answer my questions. How did you enter Monsieur Lefevre's apartment?"

"Someone buzzed me in from upstairs, and when I got up here, the door was already open. I thought François had left it open for me, but when I came in, I didn't see him anywhere. I heard the water turn on in the bathroom, so I assumed he was taking a quick shower. I walked back to his bedroom, and that's when I found the earring on the bed...and then I saw the blood." I closed my eyes, another violent shiver shaking me to the core. This was a nightmare. An absolute nightmare.

"And back to my original question: *Why* did you come here alone in the first place?"

"After I saw the photo and the article in the paper, I called François. He told me that his lawyer was on his way over, and if I wanted a chance at proving my innocence, I needed to be here."

Detective Duval tapped his pen against the notepad, the sound like sharp gunshots to my ears. "I can understand why Monsieur Lefevre would need a lawyer—after having all of his corrupt activities exposed in the papers. But if you and Monsieur Lefevre truly had nothing to do with the murder of Gisèle Richard, why then would *you* be seeking legal counsel?"

"Because *my* name is splattered all over the papers too, and you've been after me as if I'm the prime suspect in Gisèle's murder! Of course I would take him up on his offer for legal counsel."

"*Calmez-vous,* Mademoiselle. You can understand why I need you to answer my questions. Two murders both connected to you, all in the matter of a week. *Ce n'est pas normal.*"

"I know it's not normal. But it doesn't mean I'm responsible for either of them."

A twitch of doubt passed through Detective Duval's eyes. "Back to Monsieur Lefevre's lawyer. Did he ever arrive?"

"No, he never arrived. But someone else was here. Like I told you, someone buzzed me upstairs and turned on the shower to make me think it was François…but it wasn't. He was already dead."

The detective scribbled on his notepad. "Did you see the murder weapon lying anywhere near the body, or anywhere in the apartment?"

"No, they must've taken it with them."

"If the murderer was in the apartment with you, I find it difficult to believe that you didn't see this person exiting."

"After I found François and realized it was too late to save him, I crept back out to the living room and saw that someone had unlocked the front door and left it open. Whoever killed François walked right out the front door while I was back in the bedroom.

I ran down the stairs to find them, but it was too late. They were already gone."

"How convenient," he said with a snarl.

I ignored the detective's snide remark and forged ahead. "You need to find whoever did this, Detective. And you need to find that man I was telling you about, Thomas Riley. Because I'm afraid…"

"Yes, Mademoiselle?"

"I'm afraid I'm going to be next."

<hr />

Two hours later, after I'd answered lists of questions from two other police officers, I was desperately hoping they would let me leave when Detective Duval entered the room once more. He nodded to the police officer who'd been questioning me, then walked up to me without taking a seat.

"You mentioned that you did not find a knife in the vicinity of Monsieur Lefevre's body. Is this correct?"

I nodded as I wrapped the wool blanket tighter around my body, wondering where he was going with this, and hoping I'd done a good enough job at convincing him I was *not* involved in this murder in any way.

"And did you happen to bring anything with you? *Un sac à main, peut-être?*" *A purse, maybe?*

My eyes flickered over to the hall closet, where I'd thrown my purse just before the police had arrived. Showing the police the loaded gun I'd stashed inside for self-defense obviously would not help my case…*especially* if that gun would link me to Gisèle's murder.

Though the fact that there was now a *different* murderer on the loose gave me the slightest inkling of hope that maybe Ruby hadn't killed Gisèle after all. Whoever was responsible for François's murder could've had something to do with Gisèle's as well…and with the discovery of the diamond earring, I was beginning to think that someone may be François's wife.

Either way, I needed to get out of here fast...and somehow snatch my purse on the way out.

This wasn't going to be easy.

I shook my head. "No, Detective. I must've forgotten my purse in the rush to get over here."

His eyes searched the immediate area around me in the elegant living room, but when he came up empty, he shook his head. "Even in a hurry, it is unusual for women to travel without a purse of some sort, no?"

"In case you haven't noticed, I'm not like other women."

"So I see."

Just then, the medical examiners wheeled a stretcher through the living room, a long black body bag on top.

"I believe we have asked you everything we need to know, so you are free to go now, Mademoiselle Kerrigan. But while *both* of these murder investigations are under way, you must not leave the city. I will pass by the club or by your apartment for further questioning in the coming days. *Vous comprenez?*"

I barely heard him as I watched them wheel François's stiff body out into the hallway. A wave of dizziness hit me, the enormity of this horrific situation finally settling in. My gut clenched, my breath constricting in my throat. I doubled over and gagged, emptying the contents of my stomach onto the floor.

One of the medical examiners rushed to my side. "*À l'hôpital, Mademoiselle?*" he asked.

I shook my head as I wiped my mouth, wondering if my days here as Ruby were ever going to get any easier. "*Non, merci,*" I said. "I know a doctor I can call."

SIXTEEN

He arrived only ten minutes after I'd called him, his soft gray eyes and handsome face a breath of fresh air to the stale apartment, which smelled of death and rubber police boots.

Antoine flashed me a startled look as he took in the officers circulating inside the apartment.

"Let's go," I told him as I discreetly slipped my purse back onto my shoulder when I was sure Detective Duval wasn't in the room. "I'll explain everything outside."

We filed down the six flights of stairs together as I silently prayed that none of the policemen had seen me take my purse from the closet. The arm of Antoine's wool coat brushed up against my back as he ushered me out onto the street, reminding me that at least I wasn't alone.

Outside, the sky was still somber and gray as I combed the busy boulevard for any signs of Thomas. When I didn't see a man wearing a long black trench coat in the immediate vicinity, and when I realized the police weren't coming after me to search my purse, I said a silent thank-you to whoever might be listening. I was safe...for now.

We weaved around the police cars parked in front of the apartment building and crossed the street to the banks of the Seine. As we headed left up the quai, toward the Pont Neuf, our breath formed little white puffs at our lips.

"Thank you for coming, Antoine. I'm sure you saw the article in the papers this morning, and I was probably the last person you wanted to see today."

Antoine's expression hardened. "Why didn't you tell me the truth about your involvement with François Lefevre? Did he have something to do with Gisèle's murder? Are you covering up for him? And what happened up there? Were you hurt?"

His words hung in the air between us. He knew what hordes of police meant. He'd already been through this once in the past week.

"François is dead, Antoine. That was his apartment we were just in. He was just murdered this morning." A memory of François's blood pooling at my shoes, the gaping slit in his neck, and his lifeless gray face flashed before my eyes. My knees weakened, my stomach clenching once more.

"Here, Ruby. *Asseyez-vous*." Antoine wrapped his arm around my shoulders and led me over to a bench on the Pont Neuf nestled between two lampposts. "Just breathe," he told me, his warm breath blowing softly against my ear. "Breathe."

I looked into Antoine's eyes and felt all of my defenses melting away. I wanted to tell him the truth about who I was. The whole truth. I wanted to ask him if he would help me find a way home to my real life as Claudia. I didn't want to be here anymore. In this nightmare of a life with my name now linked to *two* murder cases, an ex-boyfriend hunting me down, and a mess surely waiting for me back at the club.

I wanted to go home, and yet, as Antoine's strong embrace shielded me from the harsh Parisian winter, I realized I also didn't want to leave his side.

"Are you ready to tell me what is going on now, Ruby?"

I breathed in the cool, moist air and proceeded to tell Antoine everything. I told him every detail I'd originally omitted from the night of Gisèle's death—that I'd slept with François in the office, that he'd paid me outside the club, and that at some point after I'd accepted his money, I'd come back inside, only to find Delphine lying over Gisèle's body in the dressing room.

I told Antoine about Detective Duval's theory that I'd killed Gisèle to steal her starring role, and that I'd planned on using my liaison with François Lefevre to clear my name from the murder investigation. I told him about my conversations with both Titine and François, confirming that I'd never planned to harm Gisèle, and that Gisèle was one of my closest friends at the club. I even mentioned the diamond earring in the photo and its possible connection to François's wife.

After I finished the first part of my explanation, Antoine remained silent, taking it all in.

"I'm sorry, Antoine. I'm sorry for not originally telling you the truth about what I was doing the night I found her. I still don't remember every single detail, like how my necklace ended up stuck to Gisèle's costume, or *when* I saw Véronique running and out of breath backstage. But I promise you, I'm telling you everything I can remember."

A pang of guilt swept over me when I recalled the gun hidden in my purse. That was the one thing I knew I couldn't tell him. Not yet, anyway.

Antoine's jaw tightened, his eyes not willing to soften as they had the night before. He looked away, out at the river. "If I have learned anything in my life, it is that the truth will always find a way to present itself, even if we, ourselves, aren't willing to face it." He turned back to me, his gaze searching my face and finally landing on my own ocean-blue eyes.

I fiddled with the hem of my coat, not able to hold Antoine's intense stare for another second. "I didn't tell you because I didn't want you to think of me that way. I know this probably won't make any sense, but I'm not *her* anymore. I would never do those things now."

His deep voice rose in frustration, drowning out the cars that zipped past us on the bridge. "Explain what you mean by this, Ruby. That you are not *her* anymore. You are not Ruby? Like I asked you last night? Because your eyes, they are still blue. And I am certain they were green just two days ago. And the way you talk, it is still different. Like you are a completely different person altogether. How is this possible?" Antoine ran his hand through his short, dark hair then shook his head. "Please, tell me what is going on."

"I've changed. I can't fully explain it to you, but after I woke up from that fall, I was different. And the things I would've done a week ago, I wouldn't do now."

Antoine shook his head. "I still don't understand, Ruby."

I looked to the ground. "I don't either."

Another rush of loud cars buzzed along the Pont Neuf, Parisians on their way home for lunch, completely unaware of the murder of one of their top officials that had just taken place only a few blocks away.

Antoine broke our silence. "If what you are saying is true, that you still do not remember the entire night of my sister's death, but that you *believe* you were with François Lefevre when it happened, then why did you not simply ask him to confirm your alibi with the police? Now that the photo is in the papers, everyone knows what he was doing anyway. There would be no reason for him to hide this information from the police...unless, of course, it is not true."

"What I've told you so far is true, Antoine. Gisèle was my friend. I would never have harmed—"

"But you are a different person, now, no? You said so yourself. There are things you would have done just last week that you would not do today. Does this include murder?"

I couldn't say with absolute certainty that Ruby hadn't killed Gisèle, so all I could go on was the gut instinct that if Ruby had held even a tiny piece of me—of *Claudia*—inside of her, she wouldn't have gone so far as to murder a friend. No matter how badly she wanted that starring role.

I looked into Antoine's eyes and detected the pain hiding beneath his anger. "No. I didn't do it," I said with more conviction than I'd anticipated. "I didn't kill Gisèle. And François *was* going to confirm my alibi with the police today, but then the article was released, and now he's...he's dead."

The color drained from Antoine's rosy cheeks. "Did you find him?"

I nodded as I focused on the dark river that stretched out before us, the gray apartment buildings lining the Seine, the happy couples strolling along hand in hand, not a care in the world. I wished I could switch places with them for a day—anything to forget about the blood, to forget about François's haunting face.

"I'm afraid that whoever did this knew that François was about to tell the police I had nothing to do with Gisèle's death, and they killed him so he wouldn't have the chance. So that everyone, including the police, would think that I'd killed her. Whoever did this wants *me* to take the blame for Gisèle's murder." I rubbed my forehead with my hands, my temples throbbing from all of this madness. Then I lowered my icy hands into my lap and looked over at Antoine to find his eyes searching me once more, the truth in his regard suddenly too much for me to bear.

"It's clear that you're not going to believe me either," I said to him. "I'm sorry I called you today, Antoine."

Leaving his side, I took off down the bridge, back toward my apartment. I felt like an idiot for calling him in the first place. Just because he'd made me feel safe in this life, just because I felt something for him in the short time I'd known him, didn't mean he would ever believe me.

I was on my own here. And I didn't have much time left.

But just as I reached the quai, a warm hand grasped mine. "Wait, Ruby. Please, wait."

I refused to look him in the eye, his gaze too powerful for me, too overwhelming.

Antoine squeezed my hand tighter in his. "If it is possible that whoever was responsible for killing François Lefevre also had a hand in my sister's murder, we have to find out who it was. And I won't let what happened to my sister happen to you. We must keep you safe."

I lifted my gaze to his, not able to hide the hope I felt coursing through me. "So you believe me?"

"I do not understand what has happened to you, or why you are so different all of a sudden. But I cannot look into those eyes...

your eyes, and believe that you could be responsible for harming my sister. Now we just need to find out who did."

⊹⊱══⊰⊹

Antoine held my hand the entire walk home, his touch making me feel warmer than I'd felt in my entire day and a half as Ruby. Knowing that he believed me, that he wanted to keep me safe, gave me such a profound sense of relief, I almost forgot about what had happened when I'd walked these same streets alone, earlier today.

Thomas Riley was here in Paris, looking for me. And whether or not he was connected to these murders, I knew he was dangerous. And even with Antoine by my side, I wasn't safe.

"There's one more thing I have to tell you, Antoine. Remember how I was running from something on the bridge last night?"

"Yes. And you wouldn't tell me. What was it, Ruby?"

"I heard a man's voice whisper my name, and now I know who it was. His name is Thomas Riley. He's an ex-boyfriend of mine from New York, and I'm almost certain I saw him today, following me on my way to François's apartment. I think he's here, in Paris, looking for me."

Concern etched into the lines around Antoine's eyes as we rounded the corner onto rue de l'Ancienne Comédie, only a block away from the club. "Is he dangerous?"

I thought of the scars that stretched across my lower back and abdomen...and Thomas's hand around the knife. "Yes. He's extremely dangerous."

"Do you think he had something to do with what happened today? Maybe he saw the photograph on the front page of the paper and became jealous."

"It's possible, but he would have to be working with someone because if it really *was* Thomas that I saw on the street, there was a different person already inside the apartment, which means someone *else* killed François." I shivered again at the thought that it so easily could have been me leaving the apartment in a body bag.

"Do you remember what happened with Thomas in the past? Why he would be here, looking for you? Wanting to harm you?"

We arrived at the front door of the club on the bustling corner of Boulevard Saint-Germain. "I only remember one incident—one really *awful* incident—in bits and pieces. My memory…it's still not all there." I searched Antoine's eyes for the doubt I'd seen in them last night and earlier on the bridge, but it was gone.

Antoine really believed me.

"Is there anyone you can ask about this man, to get a better idea of what happened with him before?"

"I can ask Titine, my best friend. She would know."

"Talk to her as soon as you can. We need to gather as much information as possible because I have hired a private investigator to help me with Gisèle's case. I will ask him to find this man, Thomas Riley, and also to investigate François's wife and Véronique. I will call him as soon as I get back to the hospital. In the meantime, you should not be walking around the streets alone, in plain view. With everything going on, it is not safe."

I eyed the door of the club, knowing it was time to go inside and face the music. But as Antoine squeezed my hand, I realized that if I had to be in this crazy world, there was nowhere I'd rather be than standing next to him.

"You are not too excited to go back in the club, I see. You have a show tonight, *n'est-ce pas?*"

"Yes, a big show. And between the article that came out this morning and me missing rehearsal, Jean-Pierre is *not* going to be happy. Let alone once I tell him what has happened to François." My temples began to throb again.

"Let me come inside with you."

I remembered the way Antoine had snuck into the wings yesterday to find me. "That probably isn't the best idea. Jean-Pierre doesn't like you very much, does he?"

"He doesn't want me here, asking questions, trying to find out who killed my sister. He wants to pretend it never happened so business can run as usual. *Le connard.* But I am not so stupid. And from everything I heard about him from Gisèle, I know that things are not going to go well between you and him today. I am coming with you." Antoine started for the door, but I placed a firm hand on his chest, stopping him.

"Antoine, thank you, really. But I have to do this on my own. I don't want you to involve yourself in any more of this mess than you have to. You have enough to deal with right now. And you've already helped me so much. I'll be okay."

"Are you sure?"

"Yes, I'll deal with Jean-Pierre. I'm sure you have to get back to the hospital."

"Only if you are sure, Ruby."

"I'm sure."

"I will call you later today if I receive any information on Thomas Riley, or on the other suspects. And please call me if you need anything. Anything at all." He squeezed my hand one last time, his intense gaze piercing right through to my heart, making my legs weak. And just like I had so many times already, I remembered Antoine. I remembered this moment. His hand wrapped around mine.

A bitter wind swept down the busy Boulevard Saint-Germain, taking my flash of a memory with it.

"Thank you, Antoine. Thank you for believing me."

SEVENTEEN

The sound of jazzy piano keys and the plucking of bass boomed through the air as I walked through the dark lobby and into the club. I spotted Titine, Véronique, and Delphine all onstage, lined up with about seven other dancers, an empty spot in the middle where I should've been.

Jean-Pierre loomed at the foot of the stage, his arms crossed, a cigarette permanently glued to his lips. "*Encore!*" he growled at the dancers.

Just before the women took their places, he flicked his cigarette into an ashtray and met eyes with me. "*Arrêtez la musique,*" he called to the musicians.

The dancers followed Jean-Pierre's heavy gaze until every eye in the club was on me.

"Nice of you to grace us with your presence, Mademoiselle," he spat from across the club.

With my head held high, I stalked toward him, determined not to show how scared I really felt. *Ruby* surely knew how to handle this raging, immature man. So I could too. "Jean-Pierre, I need to speak with you in private about why I haven't been here all morning. Something has happened."

He met me in the center of the club, his dark eyes flashing. "Yes, Ruby. Something has happened, hasn't it?" He leaned into me and whispered in my ear. "You did not handle the situation with François, and now it is all over the papers. I assume he will not want to *contribute* to the club any longer, which means your career here is suddenly not looking so stable."

I cringed at the scent of his stale cigarette breath while a violent, hot rage threatened to boil over inside of me. I knew I should keep my mouth shut and stick to telling Jean-Pierre what had happened to François this morning, but I couldn't stifle my ill feelings for this man any longer.

"You sick, pitiful man. All you care about is money. You don't care that the woman who made your club a success was killed in cold blood right here, under your roof, less than a week ago. You expect everyone to keep on going, to pretend it never happened, all so you can keep the money flowing into your greedy little pockets! And you want me to hide the truth: that you were whoring me out to François Lefevre just so he would keep investing in the club."

Before I could get another word out, Jean-Pierre slapped me across the face, the sting of his hit making me stumble to the ground. When I lifted my throbbing head, I spotted a fist slamming into Jean-Pierre's jaw.

It was Antoine's.

"*Fils de pute*," Jean-Pierre mumbled as he cradled his jaw in his hand, then walked toward Antoine and spat in his face.

Gasps erupted from the dancers onstage as Antoine tackled Jean-Pierre to the ground and punched him once again, harder this time. "Gisèle would still be here if it weren't for you," Antoine seethed in French. Then he climbed off of Jean-Pierre and stood over him, shaking his head. "If you ever touch Ruby again, I will not be as kind as I was this time."

Jean-Pierre winced but chose to stay silent this time. And judging by the way Antoine was still eyeing him, Jean-Pierre had no other choice.

Antoine walked toward me and offered his hand. "Come, Ruby. Let's get you upstairs."

He wrapped his arm around me and led me back past Jean-Pierre, who was still scowling on the ground, Véronique now kneeling at his side. "Do not forget, *ma chérie*," he called after me. "You were the one who arranged the deal with François Lefevre in the first place. You *wanted* to be his whore. But after what you have done to his career, I doubt he will want you anymore."

Antoine clenched his fists at his side, but I held on to his arm and fought this one for him.

"You're right, Jean-Pierre. He won't want me anymore because he's dead."

⊹══⊰

Upstairs, Antoine rinsed his bleeding knuckles in my bathroom sink while I stood in the doorway, noticing the way his chest rose and fell in quick, heavy breaths, the red splotches of anger on his cheeks that wouldn't disappear.

I remembered feeling that same anger after my father had been taken from me. I'd wanted to blame everyone and anyone, but mostly, I blamed myself. I'd felt so helpless, so lost. I wanted to tell Antoine that I knew what he was going through, but how could I open up to him when the stories I would share were not even from Ruby's life?

Antoine lathered his hands so violently, the bleeding actually worsened. I reached past him, turned off the water, and laid a hand on his arm.

"I know how this feels," I said softly. "To lose someone you love."

Antoine gripped the edge of the sink, his voice tinged with desperation. "Gisèle, she…she was so much more than a sister to me. She was only a little girl when we lost our parents, and with no other family, I was the one who raised her. It was up to me to protect her. To make sure nothing bad ever happened to her. This wasn't supposed to happen, Ruby. I never wanted her to be the star. Not with that monster downstairs running the show. So I came to every performance…every *single* show, to make sure she was okay. That none of these men were harming her, taking advantage of her. But last Saturday, I was called to the hospital for an emergency surgery, and I…I didn't make it to the show. I wasn't here to protect her."

Antoine lifted his face to mine, the look in his eyes so full of regret, it was almost impossible to bear.

"And now she's gone," he whispered, shaking away the emotions, the pain that engulfed him.

Antoine turned to me, a broken man. A man who wouldn't rest until he found justice for his sister. I knew that look in his eyes. It was the same one I'd carried with me my entire life.

"When I said earlier that I knew how you felt, I meant it," I said. "When I was ten years old, my father was murdered in front of me."

Antoine blinked then refocused on my face, as if he hadn't heard me right. "I am so sorry, Ruby. I had no idea."

"I had a chance to stop it, but I hesitated. I couldn't do it."

Antoine's hand found mine, the warmth of his touch making me lose my defenses. I hadn't talked about my father's death in years. I'd locked the terrifying memories up in a bottle and thrown them out to sea long ago.

But here in the safety of Antoine's gaze, his touch, his embrace, I couldn't hold it in any longer.

"My father came from a big family of politicians...a family that had a lot of supporters and, unfortunately, its fair share of enemies too. My dad was just about to run for a seat in the United States Senate, and if all went well, he even had hopes of one day running for president. He was handsome, intelligent, caring, larger-than-life, and the people loved him. He would've won the election. I know he would've. But the night before a huge debate was supposed to take place, someone broke into our home...and they weren't there for money.

"I was upstairs, asleep. My mother's cry woke me up. I knew something was wrong right away, by the way she was whimpering, pleading. She was so young—only twenty-eight at the time. I heard my dad's voice too. It was firm but calm. He was like that under pressure, always in control. He was used to speaking in public, used to being put on the spot. But when I heard him telling the intruder he would give him as much money as he wanted, I knew the man must've had a gun pointed at them. Otherwise my dad would've already taken him down. He never would've let anyone harm me or my mom."

"But I do not understand. If you were only ten, how could you have stopped this from happening?" Antoine asked.

"Somehow, I just knew it was up to me to save them. So I tip-toed into my dad's bedroom, found the gun he'd always stashed in his nightstand—the gun he'd told me never to touch—and crept down the stairs. The man who'd broken in had a black mask drawn over his face and a gun pointed at my parents. My dad told him to take anything he wanted from the house, but it was clear that the man in the mask wasn't there to rob my parents. He was there to kill my father. I pointed the gun right at his back and held my finger over the trigger. My mom saw me, and in between her cries, she nodded at me to do it. She wanted me to shoot him...but I hesitated. And that one moment of hesitation cost my father his life."

Antoine stared deeply into my eyes, and for the first time since I arrived here in Ruby's body, in Ruby's life, he really saw me. The *real* me.

He reached up and gently tucked a strand of hair behind my ears. "You were only a child, Ruby. It wasn't your fault."

"It took me years to believe that...and sometimes I still don't think I do. There are days when the guilt consumes me, makes me wonder what the point is. But I guess the point is that I survived." I laid a hand on Antoine's chest. "And you will too, Antoine. You will. In the mean-time, I'll do anything to help you find out who did this to your sister."

Antoine lowered his face to mine, his eyes not masking the pain that had taken over his life, the loss that I knew all too well ruled every waking moment. He breathed heavily as he stepped closer to me, then wrapped his arms around my waist, fisting my sweater in his strong hands.

I tilted my head as his lips hovered over mine, his racing chest pressed up against me. He pushed my back into the wall, traced his hands up the sides of my body and over my shoulders, sending shivers down my spine. I wanted him to kiss me so badly, I could hardly bear it.

Finally he cupped my chin in his hands and brushed his lips over mine, the warmth of his kiss so inviting, I could've stayed locked in the heat of his body, of his kiss, forever.

Our mouths pressed together a little harder as Antoine wrapped his fingers around my hips and pulled me closer to him. An aching, an intense desire I'd never before experienced, crept from my chest down to my stomach and finally settled in between my thighs, where Antoine's hips ground into mine.

His lips roamed over my mouth, then down the nape of my neck, his pent-up need pouring into his touch, into this intense connection we shared.

But as quickly as he'd taken me into his arms, he pulled away, his lips distancing from mine. He traced the outline of my face with his finger and blinked as he took a step back.

"I'm sorry. I didn't mean to…it's not the right time." His hand dropped from my face, leaving a cool draft in its place…and a desire for more.

"I should go, Ruby. This will only complicate things."

I smoothed out my sweater and tucked my ruffled hair behind my ears. "Of course," I said, my gaze running past him, not wanting to admit what I really felt. That nothing in my life had ever felt so good, so right, as his lips on mine. That if I could take anything back to my life as Claudia, it would be him.

But that was foolish…and impossible. What was I thinking?

A knock on the door made me jump, made me thankful that Antoine hadn't left yet.

A familiar voice sounded from out in the hallway. "Ruby, it's me. Titine."

I let her in, watching the way her red curls bounced over her shoulders, but also noticing the way the spark had disappeared from her step.

"Titine, this is Antoine, Gisèle's brother."

She nodded at him, her expression grim. "I gathered as much from what happened downstairs." Then she switched her gaze over to me, the gray circles underneath her eyes even darker than they'd been this morning. "Ruby, I need to talk to you… in private."

I walked Antoine to the door, guided him into the hallway so we could be alone for just one more second.

"I'm sorry about what happened to your father, Ruby," he whispered. "Thank you for telling me."

I nodded, the lingering taste of his lips on mine still making my knees weak, taking my words away.

"And I will look into Thomas Riley, like I promised. In the meantime, stay safe. You have my number."

I leaned toward him, not able to stop myself from asking, "When will I see you?"

He brushed his soft lips against my cheek. I closed my eyes and inhaled his cool scent, never wanting him to walk away.

"Soon, Ruby. Soon."

<hr />

Titine paced back and forth in my small living room, kicking my high heels out of her way. She marched her feisty little frame up to me and shot a hand up to her hip.

"This isn't the time to get yourself wrapped up in another one of your dramatic love affairs, Ruby! For heaven's sake, you're being investigated for the murder of one of your friends, and now you're trotting around the city with her brother. What the hell are you thinking?"

She didn't give me a chance to answer because her little mouth kept on going as she resumed her pacing. "And now your picture is all over the papers with François Lefevre and you barge into the club and announce that he's dead! I mean, it's obvious that he would've killed himself, being the coward that he is. But you, Ruby. You were never a coward. And that's what you're going to become if you don't show up for the performance tonight."

She wiped her brow with the back of her arm, then puffed out a loud breath. "You've always known what you needed to do to make ends meet, to keep the show going. But ever since you fell yesterday, it's like you don't remember. You don't remember how important this was to you. To *both* of us. After all, you can't honestly think you're the only one who wants to perform for Robert Maxwell? Who wants a shot at something more than nightclubs and horny men? You may have lost your memory—and your personality, for that matter—but I know you're not stupid."

Titine plopped down onto the white couch, a sigh of exasperation escaping her lips.

"Titine, before I can agree to go onstage tonight, there's something I need to ask you. What was the *real* reason we left New York?"

Titine crossed her legs and gazed out the window, her tone impatient. "We left New York so we could come to Paris to dance at Jean-Pierre's club, like I told you yesterday morning after you woke up from your fall."

I needed to know more, though.

"Did it have to do with a man?"

"No, Ruby. We came here to perform. We were sick of the scene in New York. That's it."

"There's more, Titine. I know there is."

"You know, Ruby, in a way, this whole memory loss thing is a blessing. It gives you a chance to start fresh, to reinvent your life from here on out. So just go with it."

I stood up and walked into my bedroom, then returned with the torn photo. I handed it over to Titine. "I found this last night when I went through the apartment. He's here, Titine. He's in Paris, looking for me."

Titine glanced at the jagged photo pieces, her nostrils flaring, her breath quickening. "Get rid of that picture, Ruby. *Now.*"

"But I know he's here, Titine. I heard him last night on the bridge, and today, he was following me. I know it was him."

Titine closed her eyes for a second and sucked in a deep breath. "That's impossible," she finally said.

"How? I mean, maybe he followed us here. Is he—"

Titine shot up from the couch and pushed past me. "He's not here, Ruby. Now, throw the picture away and forget about him." She stormed toward the door, a little ball of red fury.

"His name is Thomas, isn't it?" I called after her. "Thomas Riley. And he gave me the scars I have on my back and stomach, didn't he?"

Titine stopped before she reached the door, and I noticed her hands trembling as she turned back around to face me.

"Yes, Ruby. Thomas gave you the scar on your back. And he's *not* in Paris. He won't find you here, I promise. You have to believe me."

"But I—"

"No buts. He's *not* here. Throw the picture away and promise me you'll stop thinking about him, and that you won't mention his name to a soul. It's in the past, and there's no need for you to remember how badly that man hurt you. Okay?"

I nodded, wondering why she wouldn't tell me more and why she was so sure he wouldn't find me in Paris. Because as I gazed back down at the eerie photo in my hands, I knew I hadn't been mistaken this morning. It had been *his* jet-black hair blowing in the wind, *his* unforgiving eyes staring me down, and *his* creepy, crooked smile shooting my way.

It was him. It was Thomas.

But when the skin underneath Titine's eyes turned gray again, weariness settling into the little lines on her forehead, I decided I'd better drop it for now.

She reached for the door, but gripped her stomach as she did so.

"Titine, are you okay?"

She closed her eyes and took another deep breath. "I'm fine. Just a little bug, like I told you." Dropping her hand from her stomach, she turned to me.

"The show starts at nine o'clock tonight, but we have to be downstairs for hair and makeup by eight. I know you're probably not going to show up, but I want you to remember, this isn't *only* about you. I need this job right now, more than you can possibly understand." She looked away, her jaw hardened, her eyes pained. "And if Robert is going to give Jean-Pierre money to keep this club going after everything that's happened, you need to do your part. All of the dancers here…whether they would say so or not, we're all counting on you, Ruby."

Titine stood in my doorway, so small and weak, the energy drained from her body.

And as I studied her face, her pale skin, the light freckles spotting her nose, I noticed for the first time how much she looked like my mom.

Suddenly Titine's words from earlier today raced through my mind.

You're not the only one with things going on, you know.

I need this job right now, more than you can possibly understand.

She slipped out the door, leaving me with a realization that was too enormous for me to even begin to wrap my head around.

Titine didn't have a bug.

She was pregnant. She was pregnant with my mother.

EIGHTEEN

I walked to the window, my mind a blurry, fuzzy haze that refused to believe the evidence staring me in the face. I closed my eyes and did the math again in my head.

If my mother had been born in August 1960, then Titine—my grandma Martine—would've gotten pregnant around November 1959. Which meant she was only four weeks pregnant at the most—but most definitely *pregnant*.

Down on the busy Parisian boulevard below my window, it was just another winter day in Paris, but so much had already happened today. Between the release of the incriminating photo in the papers, Thomas trailing me to François's apartment, finding François... *dead*, my own near brush with the murderer, Antoine fighting Jean-Pierre, the electric kiss I'd shared with Antoine...and now *this*, my mind was more jumbled and confused than ever.

I walked over to the desk, wracking my brain to find the true reason I'd been taken away from Édouard in the dance studio on the very day I'd found out I was having a baby girl, only to be dropped into a life where I was finding dead bodies left and right, and where my grandma was my best friend and was pregnant with my future mother.

Just thinking through all of that made me feel like a mental case.

Reaching for the desk drawer, I pulled out my thick scarlet journal and flipped right to the entry I was looking for. The words I'd written had faded even more since my first day here—making me fear that with each passing moment, I was losing my future as Claudia.

December 1, 1996

I spoke to my mom today, for the first time in six months. When I tried to tell her how beautiful it is out in California, and that I would love for her to come visit, she huffed into the phone and told me that if I expected her to come within a thousand-mile radius of Grandma Martine, I was nuts.

I know my mom sees my move out to San Diego to go to college near my grandmother as the ultimate betrayal. But besides the fact that Mom is prissy and uptight while Grandma Martine is kind, zany, and unpredictable, I've never fully understood why my mom refuses to even try to have a relationship with my grandmother. The two of them haven't spoken since before Dad died…and neither of them will ever open up as to why. They've never told me anything about my grandfather either. All I know about my mother's childhood is that she was raised in New York, and that she never got along with her mother.

And now, what little relationship I was able to hold onto with my mom after we lost Dad—amid the blame she dealt me for his death—has been obliterated by my choice to live near the one person in my family who makes me feel loved, and worthy of that love.

I wish things were different with my mom. I remember a time when she did love me, when she would pick me up in her arms and squeeze me so tight, I thought nothing bad could ever happen to me. But then something bad did happen. The worst thing of all.

I know my desire for my mom to forgive me, and for my mom and my grandma to be close, are just hopeless dreams. I can't change the past. So I need to stop trying.

I stared down at my own faded words, and as the last line disappeared before my eyes, I realized something. Claudia's *past* hadn't happened yet. Which meant I *could* change it.

Or I could damn well try.

I riffled through the mess on Ruby's desk, searching for a nice, clean piece of paper, something on which I could write a letter. But when I found a striking black-and-white postcard of the rooftops of Paris and La Tour Eiffel, just as I'd viewed it from Ruby's balcony, a rush of hope spread through me.

On the back of that vintage postcard, in Ruby's dainty handwriting, I composed the most important letter I would ever write.

A letter that, potentially, could change everything.

NINETEEN

A pair of round, perky breasts bounced frantically in my face as I opened the door that led backstage.

"Ruby! Where have you been? You were supposed to be down here half an hour ago! You still have to do makeup, and Jean-Pierre has been looking for you."

I barely heard the young dancer's shrieks or noticed how my brain had automatically translated her French into English. I couldn't take my eyes off her breasts and the skintight silver-and-black costume that revealed them.

On top of everything else that had happened today, would I be performing with my breasts hanging out? Why hadn't anyone told me about this?

Before I could get the question past my quivering lips, the dancer grabbed my arm and dragged me toward the dressing room. On the way there, my question was answered for me. There were breasts *everywhere*. Small ones, plump ones, lively ones, large but slightly saggy ones—you name it. They were all romping around, skittering through the backstage area in complete chaos.

With my eyes wide and my jaw permanently hinged open, I was led into the dressing room, where my gaze landed on a flashy, crimson-colored, sequined leotard—complete with a giant hole in the middle of both the back *and* the front—hanging next to a makeup station with *Ruby* written in red lipstick on the top of the mirror.

Dear God.

I shouldn't have been surprised that on a night as big as this, I would be performing in *that*. And really, after everything I'd been through today, baring my chest should've been the least of my worries.

Well, at least I'd be baring *Ruby's* chest.

As I took a seat at my mirror, swarms of tall, beautiful dancers flitted around the dressing room, applying another coat of deep-red lipstick and jet-black eyeliner, not seeming fazed in the slightest that their breasts were hanging out for the world to see *or* that one of their own had been murdered backstage just last weekend.

Ruby's own startling beauty reflected back at me in the mirror, and as I took her in once again, I knew in my gut that this would be her last performance. *My* last performance.

And even though I was doing this for Titine, deep down in this shared soul I now had with Ruby, I knew that I wanted to perform tonight. I remembered being here in this dressing room, breasts and makeup swirling around, French chatter and high-pitched, nervous laughter filling up the air. And I knew that when I'd been here before, I had loved this. Every last second of it.

As Ruby's hands, which were now my own, dug through the makeup case in front of me and applied a coat of light foundation to the pale skin under my eyes, I knew I could do this. I already *had* done this. And tonight would be no different...except for the fact that I was seeing everything with a new set of eyes—blue ones instead of green, to be exact.

While my hands went to work, I noticed that I didn't have to think about how to line my eyes without smudging or which colors to choose or how much or how little to put on. I just knew. And I *hadn't* known how to do this magnificent work of makeup artistry in my life as Claudia. I was lucky if I remembered to dab on a little lip gloss every morning.

After I finished brushing on the last coat of sparkly rose blush, I turned to face my costume...or, really, my lack of a costume. It was time for Ruby's perfect set of breasts to make their onstage debut. Well, I was sure this wasn't their *actual* onstage debut, but I could feel them quivering with nerves all the same.

Luckily, by the time I was slipping on the half leotard, the last dancer had cleared out of the dressing room and had closed the door behind her. I strapped on my sparkly red heels, attached a fan of black feathers to the curls I'd pinned atop my head, and spun around to take one last look in the mirror.

As I took all of Ruby in—her delicately arched dancer's feet, her bare, toned legs, her flat stomach and plump breasts—a nervous laugh escaped my lips. This was just insane. If I ever did get back to my life as Claudia and tried to tell someone about this—about me dancing around topless at a nightclub in Paris in this sex-bomb body—no one would ever believe me. Hell, I was *living* this, and even I was having a hard time believing it all.

The door swung open behind me and broke up my nervous giggling fit. I spun around to find a young dancer with large, brown doe eyes holding a full bouquet of dark-red roses.

"*Salut, Delphine,*" I said, her name instantly shooting from my lips.

She was the fourth dancer in the photo I'd found of Ruby, Gisèle, and Titine—the same one I remembered from my grandmother's photo album. And *she* was the dancer who'd originally discovered Gisèle's body.

"*Pour toi,*" she said, handing the roses over to me, an apprehensive look on her face.

"*Merci.*" I took the long-stemmed roses from her shaky hands.

She opened her mouth again as if she wanted to say something more, but quickly closed it.

"Is there something else?" I probed before she could race out the door.

She peered back over her shoulder at me, shaking her head profusely. "No, it is nothing," she said, her accent thick but endearing. "You are going to be *magnifique* tonight, Ruby, I know it."

As I watched her leave the dressing room, I felt as if I knew her from somewhere…but *not* from the memory I had of her finding Gisèle. It was something else, something eerily familiar, but I couldn't place it.

Amid the massive bunch of sweet-scented roses, I spotted a little white envelope tucked into the center of the bouquet. As I reached my hand in between the stems, a jagged thorn pricked my index finger. I yanked my hand back out, but a drop of my blood had already smeared the back of the envelope.

When I flipped the envelope over, I forgot about the prick in my finger or the blood that splattered in tiny droplets at my feet.

Because there, in bold red ink, was a name I did not expect to be written on that envelope.

Claudia.

—◆—

I dropped the blood-smeared envelope to the ground and stared at it. How? How could anyone here know that I'm Claudia? I thought back to the night I'd first woken up in this body. Had I said my name out loud to anyone besides Titine?

I breathed out a shaky sigh as I remembered that I *had*. I'd told Titine *and* Jean-Pierre that my name was Claudia, not Ruby. All of the other dancers had been standing around as well. So anyone could've done this.

This was obviously some sort of weird joke, and at least whoever had done it had paired the note with a stunning bouquet of roses.

But as I picked up the envelope and looked more closely at the edgy handwriting, I wasn't so sure this was a friendly prank. With trembling fingers, I slipped open the flap and pulled out the tiny white card.

Inside I found one lone sentence written in English in thick red print.

I know who you are.

I stared at the note, willing it to say something else—something that made sense, something that was kind and thoughtful. But no matter how many times I blinked and refocused my panicked pupils onto that scratchy, haunting red handwriting, the words wouldn't change.

Someone here knew *me*. Someone here knew *Claudia*.

Could it be Thomas? Or Véronique? Or was it possible that Delphine had something to do with this?

I smashed the roses and the note into the trash, not wanting my hands to be in contact with them for another second. I had to get out of here. I had to find Titine.

Flinging the door open, I scoured the backstage area for her red hair, her emerald eyes, and her dazzling smile. But all I found was a blur of bouncing breasts and silver and black sequins shimmering through clouds of cigarette smoke.

I pushed through the throngs of dancers until I reached a quiet hallway off to the side, but when I didn't find anyone back there, I turned around to head toward the wings. Just as I was almost around the corner though, a high-pitched voice crackled through the air. Whipping back around, I spotted a glimmer of light underneath a black door down the hallway. Inching closer, I sucked in a silent breath when I heard that same woman's voice on the other side—it was Titine.

But she wasn't alone. There was a man's voice too, and his was one I also recognized. When I closed my eyes and tried to place a face with his reassuring tone and his American accent, I couldn't.

"What are you talking about, Titine?" he asked.

"You know what I'm talking about. Don't play dumb with me," she said in her best tough-woman voice. But from knowing her so well, both in her young and old age, I could detect the real tone she was hiding underneath—my young grandmother was sad. She sounded broken.

"Gorgeous, I really have no idea. I've been away for the past four weeks on-site in Mexico. I just arrived in Paris this morning. How could I possibly know what it is you're upset about?"

"Don't call me gorgeous," she yelled, her voice strangling in her throat as a low sob escaped from her lips.

"Titine, baby. What is it? What's the matter?" the man asked, his voice softer now, endearing even.

After a long pause, she finally answered him. "I'm pregnant. And it's yours."

I swallowed hard as I realized what was going on. The man she was talking to was my grandfather.

"Get away from me!" Titine snapped. "Don't even try to touch me. I know what you're planning on doing tonight."

"My God, Titine. *What* are you talking about? What do you think I'm doing tonight?"

"You think I'm stupid? You sleep with me, tell me you're falling in love with me, get me pregnant, and then show up a month later and think you can just forget it all happened? If you're done with me and you're on to the next dancer, you might as well fess up and be a man about it."

"Fuck, Titine! What is going on? What do you mean, I'm on to the next dancer?"

"You're going to sleep with her tonight! She told me!"

"Who?"

I waited anxiously on the other side of the door, hoping, praying that the name she was about to say wasn't the one I thought it was going to be.

"Ruby. My *best friend*, Ruby."

The door handle jiggled, and I dashed behind a black curtain to my right to hide while Titine stormed away from the man who had gotten her pregnant, from the man who I was apparently supposed to sleep with later tonight, from the grandfather I'd never known in my life as Claudia.

As I peeked around the curtain and spotted the back of his head—his wavy blond hair and his medium, firm build—I knew it was him. Robert Maxwell.

"Titine, wait!" he called after her.

But it was too late. The haze of legs, sparkles, breasts, and smoke had already swallowed her up.

I sank to the ground and plunged my head into my hands in an attempt to stop the spinning, the confusion, and the nausea that was taking hold in my weak stomach.

No wonder I'd felt sick each time Jean-Pierre had mentioned Robert's name. He was my *grandfather*.

And now, Titine—the person I needed most in this life, and the only person I could talk to about the frightening note I'd just received and my fears that Thomas had resurfaced in Paris—thought I was going to sleep with the father of her unborn child later tonight.

As I squeezed myself into a tight ball, wishing I could hide out in this damp black corner forever, I peeked down at my naked chest pressing into the tops of my thighs and realized that after the latest turn of events, baring my breasts to a live audience suddenly didn't seem like such a big deal.

TWENTY

With ten minutes to showtime, I peeled myself off the floor, smoothed down my feathers, and headed toward the wings. I would follow through with this performance, breasts and all, but then things were going to change around here. Things *had* to change.

I obviously was not going to sleep with Robert. And although I knew that if I did not follow through with the *agreement*, Jean-Pierre would take away my apartment and my job, I didn't care. I was bound to lose them both soon anyway, simply because I wasn't willing to be Jean-Pierre's whore any longer.

Despite all of the other terrifying events that had taken place since I'd arrived in this life, I knew that right now, the most important thing I could do was to make things right with Titine. I had to let her know that no matter what kind of arrangement Robert had made with Jean-Pierre, I had no intention of following through.

With all of the threats coming my way, and less than four days left to accomplish whatever I'd been sent back to do, I couldn't leave Titine alone, thinking that I would actually sleep with the man she loved and had conceived a child with, just to snag a starring role in a film.

And if there had been any part of me in Ruby before I'd arrived here, I hoped she would never have committed such a hurtful act, especially not to her best friend.

Backstage, all of the scantily dressed dancers who'd been here just moments ago were now gone. They'd taken their places in the wings. Which meant I was late, and that Jean-Pierre was going to be furious.

But just as I picked up my pace, a deep whisper of a voice traveled past my ear.

I stopped and listened, hoping it had been my imagination.

"*Ruby.*"

My heart picked up its already staggering pace as I realized whose voice it was.

It was *his* voice. *His* whisper. The same one from the bridge.

Thomas.

My skin crawled with fear as my limbs froze in place, my heart thumping in my ears.

I closed my eyes and felt my feet go numb as he whispered my name again and again. Soft, but steady, he didn't stop, the rhythm of his voice lulling me into a trance.

Ruby, Ruby, Ruby.

I felt myself going deeper and deeper, my eyes unable to open, my feet plastered to the ground.

And there, in my darkness, I saw the long, nasty scar that wrapped around his hand, his fingers clutching the knife. The New York City skyline sparkled in the floor-to-ceiling window behind him, and when I lifted my eyes this time, I saw his face.

His angry black eyes glinted in the dim light of the apartment, flashing their control over me.

"Ruby," he whispered. "Don't run from me, Ruby. I'll find you. I'll always find you."

And he had. Thomas has found me.

As the sound of his voice laced through the air, I felt my entire body, my whole self—my dreams, my desires, all of me—succumbing to him. To the fear of what he would do to me if I resisted him.

But as my heart threatened to fold up into itself and never again resurface, it was then that I remembered.

I wasn't *only* Ruby anymore. I was Claudia now too. And between the two of us, we were strong enough to escape. Strong enough to fight back.

My eyelids shot open, but just as I took my first step toward the glaring red *Sortie* sign at the back of the building, a cool hand wrapped around my elbow. I ripped my arm away from the strong grasp and took off toward the door.

"Ruby! Where are you going? You're on in five minutes!"

My adrenaline-charged brain registered the voice that was yelling after me. It wasn't the same one I'd heard just moments before.

It was Jean-Pierre.

My lungs heaved for air as I took in the confusion on his face.

"Were you just whispering my name?" I called to him between gasps.

"*Quoi?* No, I was *yelling* your name, because *you're on in five minutes.* And in case you have forgotten, *Robert* is here."

"I don't think it's such a good idea for me to be here right now, Jean-Pierre."

He walked toward me, the coolness in his brown eyes not even remotely scary compared to the vision I'd just had of Thomas. "Thanks to you, my biggest investor in the club is dead. I do not care about what is going on in that messed up *tête* of yours. I promised Robert a night with the most beautiful girl in the club, and you will do it."

I broke Jean-Pierre's threatening gaze and cast my glance around the darkened backstage area, looking for a sign of the man I was sure I'd heard whispering my name just moments ago. But amid the shadows, I saw no one and heard nothing except the muffled sound of music playing in the front of the club and the dancers' feet clattering about in the wings.

Jean-Pierre grabbed my chin and whipped my face back toward his. "It's time, Ruby. Let's go."

+≕≔+

"*You give me fever,*" I purred into the microphone as my new, unabashed body strutted around the stage, my long legs straddling the red chair under the spotlight, my eyes flirting with every drooling man in the audience.

I let the muscle memory take over and guide me through this performance, knowing that of anything in this crazy life, the one thing I could trust was that Ruby's body was trained to captivate an audience like no other. And although my mind was running a mile a minute, and amid my flirtatious glances, I was actually scouring the shadowy faces in the audience for any sign of Thomas, I knew I could count on Ruby to be the dazzling, shining star she'd been before I'd arrived.

While I shimmied, kicked, straddled, and purred like the good little sex kitten the men expected me to be, I tried to keep the bile from rising in my throat each time I spied Robert in the front row, his California-blue eyes fixated on me throughout the entire performance. And I tried not to think about the whisper, or what had just happened to me backstage and why I'd gone into that strange trance at the frightening sound of Thomas's voice.

As I wrapped up the opening act of the show, my hips jutting out to the side, my long eyelashes batting at all the eager men in the crowd, I wondered where Thomas had been hiding, and most of all, why he hadn't taken me when he'd had the chance.

TWENTY-ONE

After the show, I spotted Titine backstage with a purple bag slung over her shoulder. Red circles dotted her cheeks. She took one look at me and made a mad dash for the exit.

"Titine!" I called as I ran to catch up, my legs sore and my voice scratchy from two hours of nonstop singing and dancing. "Please, Titine. I need to talk to you!"

But just as she flipped around to face me, a familiar hand took hold of my arm. It was Jean-Pierre smiling his greasy smile, Robert by his side.

"I'm sorry, I have to—" I began, but stopped when I saw the hurt look in Titine's eyes as she jetted through the door. *Damn.*

"Robert, this is the woman you've been waiting to meet," Jean-Pierre interrupted as he ushered us both toward the front of the club. "And Ruby, *this* is Robert Maxwell, the famous Hollywood film director who's come here to see *you.* Why don't you both enjoy a drink or two at the bar and get to know each other a little better?"

I opened my mouth, willing a spontaneous and brilliant excuse to come out, but when Jean-Pierre raised his stern eyebrows in my direction, I clamped my lips shut. Titine was long gone, so I had to focus on the task at hand. Getting a drink at the bar would give me a chance to find out if Robert was as dirty as Jean-Pierre or if he was actually a decent human being. Plus, being in a crowded area would hopefully keep me safe from Thomas *and* from whoever had sent that creepy note...unless, of course, they were one and the same.

The three of us emerged from backstage into a hazy cloud of smoke. Blinking my eyes, I fanned the gray swirls out of my face as we made our way through the front of the nightclub, which resembled a full-blown strip joint now that all of the topless dancers had come out to play. Two murders later and ties were still loosening, breasts were still bouncing, and massive doses of alcohol were being consumed, all in the name of what must've been considered *fun* in 1950s Paris.

This was *not* like any club I'd been to back home.

Jean-Pierre led us to the bustling bar in the corner, then slipped his hand around my waist and leaned into my ear, the strong stench of whiskey on his breath drowning out the staleness of his cigarettes. "*One night*, Ruby," he whispered. "One night to make your career and make us both rich. Don't blow it."

I feigned a giggle as I peeled Jean-Pierre's hand off of me and nodded for him to leave me alone with Robert. What I really wanted to do was kick Jean-Pierre in the groin, but I figured that wouldn't help my case at this point. Besides, Antoine had already taken care of Jean-Pierre earlier by giving him a nice, fat shiner over his left eye.

I needed to focus on finding out more about Robert and about his relationship with Titine. And more important, I had to figure out a way to ditch him. I knew I'd never get away from Robert with Jean-Pierre watching us like a hawk, though, so I linked my slender arm through Robert's muscular one and led him behind a thick cloud of smoke at the end of the bar.

He leaned close to me, the smell of his strong aftershave faintly familiar. "You were quite impressive up there tonight, Ruby. Even more so than the last time I saw you perform."

"Thank you," I said, combing my eyes over his tan skin and his white-blond hair, which was so out of place in France, let alone in this dungeon of a club.

"I spoke with Jean-Pierre about you earlier, and—"

"Let's order a drink, shall we?" I cut in, not wanting to solidify the evening plans, not wanting to hear those words out of his mouth.

He furrowed his blond eyebrows in confusion. "Sure, of course. You probably need to unwind a little before talking business."

Business? Was he referring to the business of sleeping with me or the business of casting me in one of his films? Or was it all one big package deal for him?

I leaned over the bar and ordered us both a vodka tonic, then downed the entire drink in one voracious gulp while trying to figure out a game plan.

"Wow, that was fast." His pearly-white teeth sparkled as he grinned, but I detected a hint of distress in his gaze. He'd just found out he was going to be a father, after all.

I motioned for the bartender to pass me another one, and when I glanced to the side, I noticed Robert's eyes bobbing toward my chest.

That was it. I couldn't pretend anymore. If this man was really my future grandfather, I had to be up-front with him. I was *not* going to sleep with him.

"Listen, Robert, I know what Jean-Pierre promised you, but it's not going to happen."

Robert blinked his big blue eyes as his face fell. "He told me you were extremely interested. Don't you want to know what the—"

"No, I'm not interested at all, you asshole. Titine is my best friend, and if you think—"

"Wait," he cut in, "I think you're misunderstanding me. I don't know what Jean-Pierre has been telling you and Titine, but I didn't fly all the way to France to sleep with you. Not that you're not every man's dream—you're a knockout—but no offense, you're not really my type."

"Oh…so you're really just here to talk to me about your film?"

He sighed as the tension in his face faded. "Yes. I think you'd be the perfect lead for my next film. It's about a dancer in a Paris nightclub, and who better to play that role than the rising star of one of the most popular clubs in Paris? But it's *Titine* I want to be with. I don't know what all this talk is about that I'm supposed to spend the night with you."

"You really want to be with Titine?"

"Yes, I haven't stopped thinking about her since I last saw her. And she told me something tonight…something important. I really want to be there for her. But I'm afraid she was given the same misinformation as you were, and now she's furious with me."

I smiled at him, feeling overjoyed that my grandfather was actually a decent man. That something in this life actually seemed to be going right for a change. "You need to go to Titine's apartment and make this right. Let her know that it was all a big misunderstanding that sleazy Jean-Pierre cooked up and that you didn't know anything about it. You didn't, did you?"

"Jean-Pierre said something about giving me a night with the most beautiful girl in the club. I'd just assumed that somehow he'd found out about Titine and me, and that that's what he'd meant. I had no idea he'd meant it was you. Again, no offense. You're stunning."

"None taken." I placed my hand on Robert's arm and leaned closer so the dancers behind him wouldn't hear. "Is there something for Jean-Pierre in all of this? Have you promised him anything?"

"Well, if I cast you as the lead in my film, it will provide amazing press for his club, you see. The star of Chez Gisèle landing the lead in a Hollywood film? It will make this place blow up. Crowds will flock to see you perform."

"Which will put more money in Jean-Pierre's pockets."

"Exactly," Robert said.

"But there was no other monetary agreement? Like you investing in the club?"

"No, nothing like that. I told Jean-Pierre I wanted to see you perform again and speak to you about my upcoming film. That's it."

"Well, just so you know, Jean-Pierre is expecting a bit more. In fact, he's just over there." I nodded to where Jean-Pierre sat at a table full of topless dancers, smoking a cigar and floating his eagle eyes toward us. "So, to keep him from acting like a maniac and thinking I've blown the deal, let's leave together, and then you can go to

Titine and explain everything to her. I know she'll understand, and she'll be happy to see that you're not with me."

Robert reached for my hand. "I like the way you think. Let's go."

I winked at Jean-Pierre from across the room as Robert led me out of the bouncing club, the music and smoke and breasts so overwhelming I couldn't wait to breathe in the crisp winter air.

But just as Robert was slipping his coat around my bare top, a pair of chilly hazel eyes appeared in the wings.

It was Véronique, watching us.

She narrowed her eyes to tiny slits, took a long puff of her cigarette, then her thin, wispy body disappeared into the crowd.

She must've been livid that Robert had asked to see me perform, that he was considering *me* for the lead role in his next film. I had enough problems to deal with right now, though. Jealousy was running low on the list.

I shook off the shiver that had run up my spine and followed Robert out of the club into the chilly Parisian night. On the corner of Boulevard Saint-Germain, I pointed Robert in the direction of Titine's apartment.

"Thank you, Ruby. I'll be in touch about the film. That is, if you're still interested."

I smiled. "As long as you don't mess things up with Titine, I'm interested."

He laughed. "You girls really do stick together, huh?"

"You have no idea." I noticed a dimple pressing into Robert's left cheek and remembered that my mom had one in the exact same spot. She had his eyes too, and his broad smile—that is, when she'd actually remembered to smile, which unfortunately, hadn't been too often.

I wondered why my mom had never met Robert. He seemed so intent on making things right with Titine. What could've gone wrong?

Robert kissed me on the cheek and squeezed my hand. "You're different from what I would've expected, Ruby. You're an incredible woman."

With his kind words, he took off down the dark Parisian boulevard, a harsh wind whipping at his silky blond hair, the scent of his aftershave like a salty ocean breeze lingering under my nose.

I leaned against the cool stones of the building and breathed in the cold air that was void of the suffocating cigarette smoke from the bar. I thought again about Robert's face, and how I had seen my mother in him. I tried to think back to a time when anyone in my family may have given me more information about my grandfather—something that I hadn't initially remembered. But all I could conjure up was the memory of my mom telling me at a young age that she'd never known her father, and that was that. I'd known not to question her or to bring it up ever again. And my grandma had never mentioned him to me either; I was sure of it. I didn't even remember seeing any photos of Robert in my grandma's old albums.

But as Robert disappeared around a corner, his heart and his feet carrying him to my young grandmother, I wondered if maybe what I had just done had changed the past.

The first time around, Ruby may not have overheard the argument between Titine and Robert, and she may have fully *intended* on sleeping with Robert. And that would've caused a permanent rift between Ruby and Titine, as well as made Titine decide never to speak with Robert again.

Which would explain why my mom had never known her father.

As I watched a graceful French woman stride down the dark Parisian sidewalk with her nose in the air and an eager man on her heels, I realized this was all just speculation. There was no way of knowing for sure what had really happened the first time around, and when I closed my eyes and tried to call up Ruby's memories of this night, of meeting Robert, of Titine's pregnancy, all that came to me was an uneasy feeling in the pit of my stomach.

I hoped the nausea wasn't a sign of things to come, but rather remnants of fear left over from all of the terrifying incidents that had taken place over the past two days. And above all, as I thought about my mom and about how she'd possessed neither the warmth that was my grandma's shining characteristic nor the charm or kindness I had seen tonight in Robert, I hoped I had stopped whatever had occurred the *first* time around that had taken my grandfather out of the picture.

TWENTY-TWO

A rush of violent wind snapped me from my thoughts and made me remember the whisper I'd heard before the show, the murderer on the loose, the disturbing note, and the bloodred roses.

Someone knew who I was.

I needed to get off of this shadowy Parisian boulevard and safely back into my locked apartment. *Now.*

I turned back toward the main entrance, but stopped when I spotted a tall man in a suit leaning against the club door, smoking a cigarette and eyeing me up. The streetlamp cast a dim glow on his slimy grin as he took a deliberate step in my direction.

His dusty-blond hair told me it wasn't Thomas, but by the determined look in his eye, it was clear that he wanted something from me. And I could take a pretty solid guess what that something might be.

Honestly, how many men had Ruby had in the wings before I arrived here?

I didn't have another second to curse Ruby's extracurricular activities, because the creepy man was advancing, and fast. I swiveled around on my heel and booked it toward the back entrance in the alley behind the club.

Footsteps pounded behind me. I pulled Robert's overcoat tighter around my shivering shoulders and took off in a run. But just as I rounded the corner, a brutal burst of wind plowed into me head-on, causing me to trip over my flimsy heels. My legs buckled, and I skidded to the ground, my knees and palms scraping against the dirty cobblestones, my forehead smacking up against the cold brick.

Scarlet-red drops splattered to the ground as I tried to scramble to my feet. Before I could make it up, a pair of shiny black shoes planted in front of my face and a sweaty palm wrapped around my wrist.

"Get off of me!" I screamed in French, pulling my wrist from his grasp and shooting to my feet. A primal grunt sounded from his throat as he shoved me back up against the wall, the force of his push knocking the wind out of me, bringing me back to my knees.

"Leave her alone." A firm male voice shot through the bitter night, its force drowning out the howling wind.

The knot in my chest immediately released.

It was a voice I knew. A voice I trusted.

Antoine.

Dressed in a long gray coat and a matching top hat, Antoine charged toward the coward hovering over me. The offending creep barely had time to whimper as Antoine grabbed him by the collar and slammed him up against the building.

"Ruby, is this him? Thomas Riley?" Antoine asked as the man struggled underneath his stronghold.

"No, it's not Thomas. I don't know this man," I said, forcing a breath into my heaving lungs.

Tense words flew between the two men, but the drumming inside my head drowned out the meaning. All I knew was that Antoine was here. He'd saved me once again.

After looking through the man's wallet for identification, Antoine issued one final warming then released him. The man hobbled down the alley, muttering French obscenities under his breath. I didn't even want to think about what he might've done to me if Antoine hadn't arrived.

A gust of wind stole the hat right off of Antoine's head as he bent down and scooped me off the ground. The fierce look in his stone-gray eyes told me he would've done anything to keep me safe that night...and that he hadn't been happy about letting that man walk away. But Antoine clearly knew how to choose his battles, and he knew that involving the police right now wouldn't help my case.

DANCING WITH PARIS

Resting my throbbing head on his shoulder, I wrapped my arms around his warm neck. "I can't go back to the club, Antoine. Please, don't take me back there."

"Come. I'll take you somewhere safe." Antoine carried me through the windy alley to a black taxi waiting at the corner then gingerly placed me in the backseat. After giving the driver directions in French, Antoine pulled a handkerchief from his breast pocket and dabbed at the cut on my head.

Choppy, shallow breaths struggled out of my lungs, my lips releasing little puffs of cold air with each attempt to exhale.

"It's okay, Ruby. You're safe now." Antoine's soothing voice was like a cup of chamomile tea to my rattled nerves. "You are absolutely sure you didn't know that man?" he asked once more, checking out my scraped palms.

"No—not that I can remember, anyway. He must've followed me outside the club, and he wanted...wanted—"

"Shhh, Ruby. I know. He will never bother you again, you can be sure of that. And you're here with me now." Antoine ran his hands up my arms and cupped my shoulders. It was only then that I realized my entire body was trembling.

The sincerity in his eyes poured into me, filling me up with a warmth that had been missing in my life—*Claudia's life*—for years...maybe even since my father's murder.

"I know you're scared, Ruby. But it's not too late for you."

One hot tear slid down my cheek. Antoine caught it before it slipped off my chin.

"I won't let anything happen to you. I promise." He leaned close, kissed me softly on the cheek, then pulled me tight while the night lights of Paris floated past our window.

We crossed over the Île de la Cité, catching once more that same view of Notre Dame I'd seen the night before from the bridge. But this time, from my vantage point inside the toasty car with Antoine's arms holding me close, the iconic Paris cathedral took on a warm yellow glow against the backdrop of the dark, indigo sky.

The city continued to light up as Antoine took me farther and farther away from that dark club, from its sleazy men, and from a life I had no desire to be living. The Palais du Louvre zoomed by to our right while the Seine flowed like a streaming sapphire ribbon to our left. Streetlamps lined the quai, their little round bubbles lighting up the night sky, coating the city in a magical haze, its charm unmatchable.

Antoine placed his thumb on my chin and swiveled my face to his. I breathed in his cool, masculine scent and remembered the way his lips had felt on mine. I wanted to feel them again, even though I knew, like he'd said, it would only complicate things.

Antoine's deep voice resonated through my pulsing body. "Your eyes are lighting up, Ruby…like it is the first time you've seen Paris at night."

"It *is* the first time I've seen Paris at night…*with you*," I replied softly. "It's more beautiful than anything I've ever seen."

Antoine ran his fingers down my neck then reached for my hand. He raised it to his lips and lifted his thick lashes, his smoky eyes full of desire, truth, and compassion. "*You*, Ruby, are more beautiful than anything I've ever seen."

Tingles rushed through my body as he kissed the back of my hand once, twice, and a third time. "Come, for one hour, let's forget everything that has happened. Let me show you my city." Antoine leaned forward, told the driver the new plan, then shot me a sexy wink.

A wave of intense heat spread up through my legs, fanned through my abdomen, and finally settled around my heart. The harsh freeze was gone, and my hands had finally stopped shaking.

Antoine held me tight in the backseat of the old 1950s taxicab as it chugged down the banks of the Seine, along the winding cobblestone streets, down the busy tree-lined boulevards, which were still bustling even after midnight. Crowded cafés boasted jovial crowds of Parisians steaming up the windows with their cigarette smoke, their laughter, and their late-night kisses. With Antoine by my side, the haunting, eerie city I'd become acquainted with these past two days took on an entirely new glow. The farther we drove from the shady, threatening world of the club, the more lively, thrilling, and sensual the city became.

After we rounded the tall, glowing Obelisk monument in the center of Place de la Concorde, we turned onto the famous, grand stretch of the Champs-Élysées. A gasp escaped my lips as I took in the endless rows of twinkling Christmas lights lining the boulevard, leading the path to the majestic Arc de Triomphe.

Antoine nudged my ear with his nose. "The Champs-Élysées is truly breathtaking this time of year, is it not?" His warm breath on my neck made it difficult for me to focus on his words. Instead I was craving his taste, his hands, and his lips. That familiar tingling sensation descended upon me once again, leaving me breathless in this magical moment in time…a moment that for once held no trace of the déjà-vu I'd been experiencing since I'd first arrived.

Which meant that even though I'd seen these glowing monuments, these charming streets, and these breathtaking city lights many times before as Ruby, I *hadn't* seen them through Claudia's crystal-blue eyes. I hadn't experienced Paris from the backseat of this old French car with Antoine's arms around me, his warm breath tickling my skin, his deep, knowing voice in my ear telling me the history of this beautiful city that he loved so much and knew like the back of his hand.

And while I didn't know what that meant for my time here as Ruby, or for my future as Claudia, all I *did* know was that I never wanted this thrilling moment to end.

⊢═‧═⊣

After the most stunning tour of the City of Lights, Antoine asked the driver to take us to his apartment at Place de l'Opéra. The regal Opéra Garnier towered over the square, its elegant archways, tall pillars, and golden statues giving off an air of royalty amid the nightlife that buzzed all around us.

JULIETTE SOBANET

Antoine held my hand as we squeezed into the miniature red elevator in his apartment building. Shivers combed through my body as his intense gaze locked onto mine.

"Are you still cold, Ruby? You're trembling again."

"Oh, I am?" A tingly flush spread up my neck, fanning onto my cheeks. "It's so windy out, you know." What I didn't tell Antoine was that Ruby and I must've had more in common than I'd originally thought.

I wasn't cold anymore. And I wasn't scared either.

I always shivered when I was falling for someone.

Inside Antoine's apartment, he turned on a dim lamp and immediately went to find a blanket. My sparkly heels clicked across the hardwood floors toward a set of French windows framing the sparsely decorated living room. A few random boxes lined the walls, and there were no pictures anywhere.

This apartment could definitely use a woman's touch.

I shook my head at my own preposterous thought. What was I thinking? What was I doing here? How would I ever explain who I really was? Not to mention the fact that I had a five-day limit to my time in Paris…and I was already two days in.

After my five days were up, would I ever see Antoine again?

I pressed my forehead and palms against the chilly glass to cool off the steamy cauldron of desire that bubbled and brewed inside of me. The blustering winds outside rattled the windows, but I was still searing with emotion. I had only felt this way with one other man in my life—a man who, strangely enough, loved Paris just as much as Antoine did.

Antoine wrapped a blanket around my shoulders then enveloped me in his strong arms as we gazed down at the beautiful view of the grand old opera house. And although I knew I should go, that I shouldn't complicate this already insane situation any further, my feet refused to budge, my back relaxing completely into Antoine's firm chest.

And for the first time since I'd arrived in Paris, I could breathe.

"I saved the best Paris moment for last," Antoine whispered.

"Oh?" I responded, not able to get another word past my lips. His deep voice in my ear, his breath on my neck, the strength of his embrace. It was almost too much to handle.

"Yes, the Opéra Garnier is my favorite place in Paris," Antoine said. "That is why I chose this apartment. The view of the opera house…it makes me feel hopeful. It makes me remember that there can be true beauty in this world, amid the chaos."

"It's gorgeous," I said, falling into a trance as our breathing filled the comfortable gaps of silence between us.

"Do you like the ballet?" he asked.

"I love the ballet. I haven't been since I was a little girl, though. My parents used to take me…before we lost my dad." I knew it was dangerous opening up to Antoine about my past as Claudia, but from the minute he had scooped me up off the cold sidewalk and saved me from that creep, I'd lost all of my defenses. And as long as his arms were around me, I wasn't sure I'd ever get them back.

"The ballet brings back memories of a happier time for me too." Antoine's voice was low and gravelly, his handsome gray eyes lost in a memory as he gazed down at the Palais Garnier. "My mother was a principal dancer in the Paris Opera Ballet. I grew up in this theater, watching her rehearse and perform. I was eight years old when my parents had Gisèle, and my mother had her in ballet slippers and tutus before she could walk.

"Gisèle loved performing almost even more than my mother did. The two of them would dance around the house for hours at night, laughing and twirling. My father and I always loved watching them dance, the joy on their faces…there's something about the sound of the dancers' feet on the stage, the music, the elegance of it all. It's such a contrast to my stressful world at the hospital, and it calms me. I need that calm in my life again. It's been missing for a long time."

I tipped my face back, catching a glimpse of the wistful look that passed through Antoine's eyes. I wondered what else had been going on in Antoine's life to take away his calm, his happiness.

"Did you ever learn how to dance?" I asked.

"Of course. It was a requirement in my house. Although I took after my father in my love for science, I couldn't grow up without learning a few dances. My favorite has always been the tango."

Chills slithered up my spine as I recalled my last night in San Diego…dancing the tango with Édouard in my grandmother's dance studio…it was the dance that had landed me *here*.

"Me too," I whispered. "It's always been my favorite. It was the first dance my grandmother taught me when I was a teenager."

Antoine placed his hands on my shoulders and turned me around until our noses almost touched.

"Before she died, my mother used to tell me that I would know when I'd found the right woman for me because our tango would be perfect."

The words slid from my lips before I could stop them. "And have you found her?"

Antoine searched my eyes, the truth in his gaze mixed with confusion, with longing, with desire.

Complicated or not, I wanted to forget about everything that had happened and feel his breath on my skin. His lips pressing against mine. His hands roaming my body.

"I was at the performance tonight, Ruby. I watched you dance."

I tried to lower my eyes, to avoid his intense gaze, but I couldn't. I couldn't turn away.

"I've seen you perform before. Many times. You were different up there tonight. Too different. You had an innocence, a lightness about your movements that you've never carried in the past. How can a person change so much in a matter of a day? Tell me the truth."

I opened my mouth to respond, but I didn't have an answer for him. I simply could not tell him about my time-traveling, past-life story. Forcing myself to turn away, I shifted out from under his warm touch and inquisitive gaze, wishing things were different. Wishing I weren't two different women hiding beneath this body of a dancer, of a prostitute, of a woman wanted for murder.

I could feel Antoine taking a step closer to me, the heat of his body making me surge with desire. With one finger on my chin, he swiveled my face back to his.

"I am a doctor, Ruby. I have built my career on medicine, on science, on logic, on *facts*." He brushed a strand of hair from my eyes and gazed into them so deeply, so intimately, I couldn't have escaped his hold on me if I'd tried. "But your eyes, Ruby, those eyes. Medicine does not give me an answer for why they are suddenly blue. Or for why you are suddenly the most beautiful woman I've ever seen. It's as if I didn't see you before. And even though I know I should not involve you in my complicated life right now, I cannot stop thinking about you. And I don't want to."

Antoine's eyes softened, his shield thrown to the wind. As his warm gaze washed down on me and his fingers traced the edge of my blushing face, down the curves of my neck, I remembered feeling this exact gush of warmth before. I remembered loving the way Antoine's chocolate-brown hair sat all wind-blown on his head, the way his cheeks and nose had turned pink from the cold, the way his touch had warmed me up and made me feel safe.

I remembered being with Antoine, except it wasn't here in this apartment. We were in Ruby's living room, gazing out at *her* gorgeous view of the lively streets of Paris. In the vivid memory that flashed through my mind, I knew that at that time, just as I felt in this moment, I didn't care where we were. I only cared that we were together.

I felt it then. I *knew*.

In this life before—as Ruby—I'd loved Antoine. I'd loved him more than anything in this entire world, and now, as we stood at the eye of this hurricane, surrounded by a whirlwind of mystery, emotions, and drama, I felt myself falling again. It made no sense, but somehow it made complete sense.

I was falling in love with Antoine.

As he wrapped his hands around my waist and pulled me to him, I forgot that I was in Ruby's body. Because by the way he looked at me, I knew that Antoine—and *only* Antoine—saw me for who I really was—a mixture of two totally different women who, in this moment, shared a soul.

I closed my eyes and let out a whimper as he pressed me up against the wall and kissed me on the lips, his hands finding their way underneath the large overcoat and roaming my waist, the bare skin on my back, and finally my breasts. Nothing had ever felt so good, so powerful, so fulfilling as having Antoine's hands on my body, his lips engulfing me with every kiss, his chest pressed firmly into mine, his body telling me he wanted every last part of me.

He slipped the coat off my shoulders, letting it drop to the ground, then took my face in his hands and pulled his lips from mine, our breath heavy and hot. He didn't say anything, but he didn't need to. The way he looked at me said it all. I knew he felt the same electricity I felt, and even though I'd only known him for two days, I felt as if it had been forever. And so I let him pick me up and carry me into his bedroom, where he laid me down on his smooth black sheets and slipped the sparkly red heels off my feet.

He ran his strong hands up my quivering legs as he climbed onto the bed, his body hovering over mine, our chests heaving for air. In that moment, I wanted nothing more than for him to devour me, kiss me, make love to me. I'd never wanted anyone or anything more in my life.

Antoine gazed down at me with a fierce hunger in his eyes as he rested his body on top of mine, his intense heat encapsulating me, making me feel a need I'd never felt before. He rolled to the side and removed what was left of my clothing in a few swift movements, then allowed me to rip off his pants and shirt, revealing a ripple of muscles down his shoulders, arms, and stomach. He rolled me over on top of him, his hot skin rubbing against mine, and slid his hand down in between my legs. My entire body throbbed and surged as he massaged me, making me moan and gasp for air.

"Take me," I breathed into his ear. "Take me."

Antoine rolled me back underneath his firm body as he brushed his soft lips over my neck, across the tops of my breasts, and down over my stomach. Each second that he wasn't inside of me made me pulse with anticipation. Finally he lifted himself back up, his eyes telling me he was ready to make love to me. And then I felt him thrust into me, the force, the weight, the depth making me cry out in pleasure. He continued to push deeper into my body, deeper into my soul, deeper into my memories as our bodies synced together in perfect unison, two becoming one, riding this intense connection, this inexplicable pull we had toward each other.

I relaxed completely into him, never wanting him to stop, never wanting to live another moment without his body wrapped around mine. Even the aggression of his kiss made sense to me. I felt that same violent urge as I dug my fingernails into his back and begged him not to stop.

Antoine breathed heavily into my neck as he pulled his weight off of me, flipped me over, then laid his glistening body on top of my back and slid into me. I grasped on to the satin sheets and let him take me. I let his scent, his masculine force engulf me as he pushed farther and farther into me, taking all of me and yet leaving me completely fulfilled in return.

Finally, as Antoine reached around and held my breasts in his trembling hands, our bodies enmeshed as two lost puzzle pieces that had finally found one another, I felt my insides rising, squirming, screaming, and I let out a cry as my entire body shook and exploded with heat. Antoine came with me, pushing deeper than he had before, his hands gripping me so hard it almost hurt. His heaving body collapsed on mine, the blood coursing through our veins, the only movement left in the steamy room as our bodies went limp on the silky black sheets.

TWENTY-THREE

"*Mon amour*, wake up. I want to show you something."

Antoine stood over the bed, his hand resting on my cheek, his gaze warm and soft as he peered down at me. I smiled up at him as he handed me a sparkly white sweater, a pair of sleek black pants, and a beautiful violet coat.

"What's this?" I asked.

"I went down to one of the shops near the Opéra to find you some warm clothes." He winked at me. "You're going to need them."

A man who makes passionate love to you all night then buys you beautiful clothes in the morning? I only wished I'd be able to tell my girlfriends back home about this one day.

"Thank you, Antoine. They're gorgeous."

He leaned down and kissed me softly on the lips. "Not as gorgeous as you, *ma belle*." His scruff brushed against my cheeks, the wintry scent on his clothes making me want to wrap myself up in him and never, ever let go.

"There's more." Antoine turned and grabbed a little black bag with a pink bow on the top. A clever grin peppered his rosy cheeks.

Inside the bag, I found a sexy white bra trimmed in pink lace, with a pair of dainty pink-and-white underwear to match.

I stood up and kissed Antoine once more. "You are unlike any man I've ever known. *Merci*, Antoine."

Antoine fitted the beautiful French bra perfectly onto my breasts, then turned me around and hooked it in the back. Gripping my waist, he ran his lips from the nape of my neck all the way down my spine to the sensitive curve of my lower back. I closed my eyes as he slipped the lacy panties onto me, running his hands over my hips, kissing my thighs, then spinning me back around and kissing my navel, then the tops of my breasts, and finally finding my lips once more.

Next, he slipped the soft white sweater over my head, and finally, with his hands running up my bare legs, his fingers sliding over the throbbing space in between, he slipped on my new pair of pants, zipped them up, and kissed me on the forehead.

Dear God. I didn't know it was possible to be this aroused while a man was putting your clothes *on.*

More than the intense sexual energy that danced so effortlessly between us, it was the deep emotional connection I felt with Antoine that made me light-headed…dizzy from love.

Even though I'd only known Antoine for the few days since I'd woken up as Ruby, I was certain that I'd known him before, that I'd *loved* him before, and that somehow those feelings, those memories, were still imprinted in Ruby's heart, and were now coming back to life…perhaps with a force even stronger and more powerful than the first time around.

I clasped Antoine's outstretched hand and immediately felt my body rush with the same tingling sensation I'd felt when he'd first touched me, kissed me, made love to me, and when he'd wrapped himself around me and fallen asleep. And as he led me out of the bedroom, I didn't bother to ask where he was taking me. I knew full well that I didn't care, that I would go anywhere with this man. Because despite the clear threats this life held for me, Antoine made me feel safe, like no one and nothing could harm me as long as my hand was intertwined in his.

The craziest part of all was that in my life as Claudia, I was nothing like this. I'd never been so love struck I would've blindly followed a man anywhere. I'd never fallen for someone in such a short period of time or felt such a deep connection with a man I barely knew.

Goose bumps prickled my skin when I remembered that I was wrong.

I *had* felt this way—*once.*

With Édouard.

But then, that had landed me here, hadn't it?

When Antoine opened the tall windows in his living room and led me out onto the black iron balcony, I forgot my train of thought and broke our comfortable silence with a gasp.

Big, fluffy snowflakes fell daintily from the sky, their crystal-white circles spinning so slowly toward the ground it looked as if thousands of dazzling white sparkles were suspended in midair in front of us, freezing this surreal moment in time.

I walked with Antoine to the center of the balcony and smiled as swirls of pink-and-purple light appeared off in the distance, the sun peeking through the cloudy morning sky, casting an orange glow over the snow-covered rooftops of Paris.

Antoine wrapped his arm around my shoulders and spun me in the other direction, where I spotted the tip of the Eiffel Tower off in the distance. Snowflakes floated around the tower as if they had no intention of ever landing on the ground but instead wanted to dangle from this beautiful Paris sky forever. I gazed back down to the Opéra Garnier, watched with Antoine as shimmering snowflakes coated its golden statues then fell to the skinny sidewalks below, where a group of young children were playing, balling up the snow and tossing it in the air, their laughter floating up to our perch on the balcony, warming my heart, calming my soul.

Antoine turned to me and wrapped his arms around my waist. "It is beautiful, is it not?"

I basked in the warmth of his smoky-gray eyes, knowing instantly that when I'd been Ruby before, these sweet moments with Antoine had been my happiest. I took a mental picture of the snow dusting the tips of his dark-brown hair, the shoulders of his coat, the top of his nose, and I smiled at him. "It's the most beautiful thing I've ever seen."

And as he leaned in and kissed me, his lips warm and moist against mine, I closed my eyes and kissed him back with a passion

I'd never known I was capable of. With our bodies and souls intertwined, it suddenly felt as if the balcony gave way under our feet, leaving us suspended in our own perfect little snow globe, the bubble of our love traveling through time, keeping us safe and warm.

But when our lips parted and I realized that my feet were still firmly planted on this earth, a gust of wind ripped past us, taking with it the perfect stillness of the snowy morning and instead leaving me with an icy chill down my spine. I shivered as Antoine wrapped his arms tighter around me and led me back into his apartment, the wind now whipping around us with a fury and slamming the window at our backs.

⊹≒≒⊹

After Antoine took me back to my apartment, I tried to control the thumping of my heart, the frenzied thoughts zipping through my head, and the butterflies doing laps around my stomach, but nothing worked.

So much had happened since I'd arrived in this life, I was having a hard time keeping it all straight. And with this most recent development...*falling in love with Antoine*...I could hardly keep myself from spinning around like a top on the living room floor.

Being Ruby was overwhelming, but after what I'd shared with Antoine, I wondered—if given the chance, would I still return to my life as Claudia?

Without thinking, I found myself running my hand over my flat stomach.

Tears rimmed my eyes, all of this emotion too much for me to bear.

I would go back. For my baby, I *had* to go back.

I'd given Antoine the torn photo of Thomas Riley, shown him the scars on my back and abdomen. I'd told him about Titine's reaction, her certainty that Thomas couldn't be here in Paris, her urgency that I tell no one about him. I believed Titine was just frightened, that she didn't want to face the possibility of such a dangerous man finding me again. And since she wouldn't tell me what exactly had gone on with Thomas, I'd had no choice but to take Antoine's offer for help.

Antoine had left to deliver the photo to his private investigator, and to stop by the hospital. He said he'd return in an hour, and that I should stay here with the doors locked until he came back.

But the urgent longing I felt in my heart for my unborn child suddenly boiled over inside of me, overpowering the strong love I already felt for Antoine. I couldn't sit here and wait for Thomas to find me, for another dead body to show up, for the police to knock on my door.

I thought back to my brief encounter with Madame Bouchard in the café, how she'd told me there wasn't a moment to waste, that I must fully engage in this life if I wanted any chance at saving my baby. I needed to find out more about past lives and reincarnation, find out what this all meant, if there was really any way to get back. But with no Internet, I would have to leave the apartment to complete my research. I would only leave for an hour.

I checked my purse to find that the gun was still firmly tucked inside. I rummaged through the desk to find my journal, my sonogram photo, and the copy of *People* magazine. If something were to happen to me, I wanted the remnants of my life as Claudia to be with me…just in case. And as I stuffed everything inside Ruby's small black purse, I spotted one more thing I couldn't forget.

The postcard.

✦

The blustering winds that had whipped through Paris the past two days had finally subsided, leaving tree branches and leaves scattered all over the snow-dusted sidewalks. After having mailed the postcard, and sending with it my hope for a happier future as Claudia,

I stood at the corner of rue de la Huchette and rue Saint-Jacques, the frosty waters of the Seine floating calmly before me as hordes of tourists, Parisians, and classic French cars combed the busy street. The trees that lined the river were bare save for a layer of sparkly white snow resting atop each scrawny branch. And even though the sun was making a brief appearance on this mild wintry morning, the entire city was bathed in an eerie gray light.

The scene that unfolded before me reminded me of the famous black-and-white photographs of Paris I'd seen in my life as Claudia. And as I stood alone on the corner as a real, live participant in this old snapshot of the past, with Notre Dame Cathedral looming across the river, art and souvenir vendors adorning the riverbanks, and snow crunching at my feet, I almost had to pinch myself. I still couldn't believe that I was here. *In Paris. In 1959.*

And that I'd just spent the most romantic night of my life with a man whose kisses were still making me weak in the knees, whose sweet words were swimming through my head, making me question my desire to find a way back to the future.

Who would ever believe me if I tried to tell them what had happened to me?

While I scanned the sidewalk to make sure there was no sign of a man with slick, black hair and haunting black eyes, a wild yet obvious thought occurred to me.

Were there others?

Could there be others walking these same streets, looking for the loophole in time and space that had landed them here, wondering what their purpose was, and how they could find their way back?

Madame Bouchard had said that these past-life revisits were rarely a walk in the park. Which meant there had to be others who'd been through the same thing.

The thought that I may not be the only person to have experienced something this crazy, something this impossible, made me all the more motivated to get to the bookstore and research this whole reincarnation business. Maybe I would find others. Maybe I would find someone who could help me figure out what in the hell was going on and how to make it back alive.

Adjusting the black hat that covered my curly blonde hair, the large black sunglasses shielding my blue eyes, and the small but heavy purse, which carried my loaded weapon, I headed east along the river. Right before I'd left my apartment, I'd had a vague memory of standing inside a charming little bookstore with a view of Notre Dame Cathedral just through the window. And now, as I walked with purpose, I hoped my memories would guide me back to that same place.

After passing by a few touristy cafés that looked familiar, I felt inclined to turn to the right. And there, set back from the crowded street, a green-and-yellow storefront caught my eye. The minute I spotted the sign above the door, which read *Shakespeare and Company*, I knew this was the place. I walked up the tree-lined path, and as I reached for the wooden door handle, I could already smell the pages of the old books.

Once inside, I peered back through the cramped rooms stacked with floor-to-ceiling books, and I had another strong flash of déjà-vu. I could see myself as Ruby standing in the back corner of the eclectic store, reading a book on the Paris Opera Ballet.

"Can I help you, miss?" the store clerk asked, snapping me from my memory.

"Do you have a section on past lives or reincarnation by any chance?"

"Straight back and to the right."

"*Merci.*"

In the back corner of the store, not far from where I remembered standing the last time I'd been here as Ruby, I thumbed through title after title on reincarnation and past lives, my hunger for information, for answers, insatiable. I wanted to know the real reason for my presence in this lifetime. How did I get here? Could I go back? Were there any documented cases of others just like me?

But all I found were different religions' takes on reincarnation, which all boiled down to one main idea—that after a person dies, his or her soul is reborn into a new form of life. There were stories of people *recalling* their past lives, but I couldn't find a single book on what *I* was experiencing. Apparently traveling back in time to reexperience a past life wasn't a common occurrence after all.

After frantically skimming every book I could find on the subject, then shoving them all back onto the shelf in frustration, I flopped my hands down at my sides, defeated. But just as I turned around to leave, my right foot bumped into something.

I peered down to find a tattered book that looked to be about a hundred years old, its worn purple cover void of words or pictures. As soon as my fingers touched the frayed spine, a jolt of electricity ran straight through me, jarring my insides and shoving me backward onto my butt. I sat there for a moment, stunned, wondering what in the hell had just happened when I realized my hands were still tingling. I remembered that familiar sensation. It was the same tingling I'd felt when I'd danced with Édouard. And it was the same feeling I'd experienced *every* time Antoine had touched me.

The book's energy, its pull, was so strong I couldn't resist. I grasped the book in my hands once more, the tingling and prickling intensifying. I didn't let go this time, though. I had to know what was inside.

Sneaking a quick peek around the shop to make sure no one was watching me, I leaned back against a bookshelf and opened the creaky cover.

On the first page I found what appeared to be a journal entry. I scanned the faded, unruly handwriting that scratched all over the page and felt my heartbeat quickening when I realized this was no ordinary diary.

April 4, 1945
   I don't know how I got here, but somehow I woke up in Rome yesterday morning. Not Dallas. Rome. And that ain't even the worst

of it. It's not 1988 anymore. It's 1945. At least that's what all these pussy willow Italian people keep telling me.

The craziest part of this whole messed-up mind trip is that I'm not me anymore. At least, I don't look like me. When I woke up, everyone was calling me Benito, and I told them they were all nuts. My name is Jackson, dammit. But when I looked in the mirror, damned if they weren't right. I have short black hair now, no more ponytail, I've lost about a hundred pounds, and I traded in my cowboy hat for a priest's getup. I told these people I ain't no priest, and that the closest I ever been to a Catholic church is to bury my great-aunt Jo, but they just think I'm losing my mind.

And I'm starting to think I am because everything and everyone I've met here so far is familiar. It's like having déjà-vu every single second of the day, but I have no idea what any of it means. And it's driving me insane. Oh yeah, and I speak Italian now. Kinda cool, but really fucking freaky at the same time.

I need to find a way back. I can't leave Tracy like this. Not with a little one at home and a second one on the way. I done found myself in some pickles before, but I'll be damned if I know my way out of this one.

Goose bumps prickled the skin on my arms as I flipped to the next page, thinking I would find another journal entry from Jackson, the cowboy who'd apparently lived through the same type of experience as me. But when my eyes combed over the frilly handwriting, I realized this entry wasn't Jackson's. It belonged to someone else.

July 14, 1789

Mother of God. What in the hell is going on? I must be going insane. Really, I must be clinically insane. I'm in Paris and it's 17 fucking 89. There are like people on horses trotting around outside, everyone's going crazy and revolting, and people are getting their heads chopped off by that guillotine thing I kinda sorta remember my French teacher spouting off about in French class one day.

But I don't live here. I live in L.A. in the year 2010! And my name is Reese! How many times do I have to tell these people I'm not Marie-Claire or whoever the fuck they think I am. The main problem, though, is that, somehow, I woke up in this chick's body wearing a corset and everything. And she's like really old. Like 35 or something. And she has kids! Those little brats think they're mine. I'm not your mom! I'm only 18!! And my name is Reese Carrington! WTF?!

I need to get home before one of these men galloping around on horses storms in here and takes me to the head-chopper thingy. This is freaking insane. I miss my mom. I miss L.A. I miss my life. How do I get home?

Sitting on the musty bookstore floor, I poured through the pages that followed, each one a journal entry of someone else who had jumped back in time to a past life, their confusion and desperation as strong as mine, their reasons for making the jump unknown.

The voracious hunger I had to learn everything I could about their experiences, and ultimately to find out what would happen to me, brought me all the way to the end of the journal, where, on the second to last page, I stopped.

There, in front of me, was my very own handwriting.

December 5, 1959

This morning I woke up in Paris in the body of a woman named Ruby Kerrigan. But my name isn't Ruby. My name is Claudia Marie Davis. I'm eighteen weeks pregnant with a little girl, and I have to find a way back to her…

It was the journal entry I'd written when I'd first arrived. When I was trying to figure out how in the hell I got here.

But how did *my* journal entry—the one I'd only written two nights ago—land in *this* book? And how were all of these other people's entries recorded in what I assumed was their own original handwriting?

And most important, why was any of this happening in the first place? Where was Madame Bouchard when I needed her?

Just as I was about to close the book and leave the store feeling more frustrated and crazy than when I had first come in, the handwriting on the very last page made me stop.

In bold red ink and slanted print that looked all too familiar, there was one final journal entry.

December 5, 1959

I made it back to Paris. And I won't be leaving until I've finished what I came here to do. That little bitch won't steal what's mine this time around, and she won't steal it from me in the future either.

I'll be sure of it.

My stomach turned sour when I realized that whoever had written this entry was here in Paris, right now.

And if my eyes weren't playing tricks on me, the slanted red handwriting on this page looked *exactly* like the handwriting from the note I'd found under my pillow on my first night here.

Whether it was Thomas who had written this or one of my other potential enemies, I was certain this note was for me.

I was *that little bitch.*

I had to get out of here.

I slammed the book shut, stood up, and charged toward the front of the store, knocking a crooked stack of books over on my way out.

"Excuse me, miss! You have to pay for that."

"Sorry, I…I'm in a hurry. I didn't mean to…here," I mumbled, handing the store clerk the ratty purple journal.

He turned the worn cover over in his hands, a puzzled expression washing over his face. Just as he was about to open the book, I lunged forward and grabbed hold of his arm to stop him.

"Is there a problem?" he asked, yanking his arm away.

"I…I'm sorry. Can I just pay for the book, please? I'm in a hurry."

Without responding, he opened the book before I could stop him. And inside, staring back at us, were completely *blank* pages. Each one was a shade whiter than the next—the handwriting, the notes, the stories I'd just read, all erased. I braced myself against the counter, suddenly feeling faint and sick to my stomach. Where had the words gone? How could they have been there one minute and gone the next?

Was I simply imagining this whole crazy escapade?

"Miss, this book isn't part of our inventory. I don't know how it got here, but there isn't anything printed inside. It's completely blank. See?" He flipped all the way through the book, again revealing the empty pages.

"You are welcome to take it with you at no charge, though, if you like. I don't see why you would want a book with no words, but…oh wait, here's something written on the inside back cover." He narrowed his eyes and lifted the book about an inch from his glasses.

"What is it?" I asked.

He shook his head before flipping the book toward me and revealing a tiny block of text printed on the bottom of the book flap.

Claudia,

When you find this, meet me at 46 rue de Passy in the 16th arrondissement. You are in grave danger. Come straightaway, as there is no time to waste.

Madame Bouchard

I snatched the book from the clerk's hands, ignored his startled expression, and fled from the bookstore.

As soon as I'd emerged onto the sidewalk, I opened the book back up.

And sure enough, every page was filled to the brim with the past-life stories I'd just devoured in the bookstore, the same ones that had somehow disappeared when the store clerk had looked inside.

Ignoring the little voice inside my head telling me I was officially losing it, I did a quick scan of my surroundings, then jogged up to the bustling Quai Saint-Michel to hail a cab.

TWENTY-FOUR

I bumped along in the back of the black Parisian taxi as the driver raced across the Pont Neuf, the oldest bridge in Paris, and the bridge where Antoine and I had been just one day earlier, right after I'd found François.

I didn't have time to process all of the déjà-vu flashes that popped into my brain as we sped over the tip of the Île de la Cité, then headed west up the right bank of the river, running through a red light and making three dangerous passes along the way. I searched around the stuffy cab for my seat belt, realizing that if Ruby's time was coming soon, I didn't want to die from something as stupid as not wearing a seat belt while this crazy taxi driver flew through Paris with me as his captive.

The Palais du Louvre flew by us as my heart rate sped up and my mind spun out of control. I gripped the purple book in my hands, my fingertips still tingling as they wrapped around the cover.

I was desperate to find out if the others had accomplished whatever monumental tasks they'd been sent back to their past lives to do, and I needed to know the *exact* reason I'd been brought back to my own dangerous, drama-filled past life. I was only hoping Madame Bouchard would have a more concrete answer for me this time. And preferably with instructions on how I could bring Antoine back with me.

After all, the clock was ticking.

Resting my throbbing temple against the cool window of the cab, I hugged my weapon-concealing purse tighter to my chest as we zoomed down the Seine, the Eiffel Tower shooting up toward the wispy gray clouds to my left. I felt a stab of guilt for having promised

Antoine I wouldn't run around the city alone, that I would be there waiting for him when he returned.

But if I really didn't have much time left in this life, I had no choice but to follow Madame Bouchard's instructions to meet her. I would demand that she tell me everything she knew, then I would head straight back to my apartment. I didn't want to miss Antoine when he came back for me. Just the thought of his deep-gray eyes, his strong hands on me, the way he'd made love to me, made me quiver in the backseat of the cab.

Before I had a chance to replay my entire night of passion over in my head again, the cab screeched to a stop in front of an ocean-blue door with the number forty-six overhead.

I thrust a wad of francs into the man's outstretched hand and climbed out of the old cab, its muffler huffing and puffing at me as I emerged onto the sidewalk and dodged three older women walking their miniature dogs through the posh neighborhood.

Scanning the list of tenants, I pushed the button next to the name *Bouchard*, the tips of my fingers still tingling and shaking.

But I didn't have time to be scared.

I had to find out what the heck I was doing here.

+≈≈+

The tall blue door buzzed and I hoisted it open. A damp, chilly hallway awaited me on the other side. Madame Bouchard's shadow beckoned at the end of the hallway, her tall, elegant frame filling up the doorway, a dim glow of light flickering behind her. As my feet glided forward, toward the knowledge I hoped she could provide me with, I realized that for the second time since I'd been in Ruby's body, I *wasn't* experiencing any trace of déjà-vu.

I *hadn't* been here before.

Silky shadows danced around the old woman's silhouette, pulling me to her, making me feel connected to her, entranced by her.

When we came face-to-face, the light was so dim that it allowed me to see only the silvery-gray hair that wrapped around her head and her deep-violet eyes that silently told me what I already knew.

I was in danger. And we didn't have a moment to waste.

"Claudia," she said, her voice deep and steady. "Follow me."

I didn't say a word as I trailed behind her, walking through a series of dark rooms and hallways, the only light coming from the flickering of candles that lined our path. Tall shadows flashed around us on the bare walls, their presence making me feel as if we were being watched.

The elegant Madame Bouchard led me into a scarcely decorated living room, the drapes drawn completely shut, blocking all light except for that of four lit candles, one in each corner of the room. She turned and placed her hand on my shoulder, then showed me to the couch and motioned for me to sit down. I breathed in deeply, taking in her rosy scent as she floated past and took a seat in the chair across from me.

Before I could begin pummeling her with questions, a lone object on the marble coffee table in front of me caught my eye.

The violet cover. The frayed spine.

The journal.

It was the same journal I'd been holding in my hands for the entire cab ride here. The one I'd stashed in my bag before I'd rung the doorbell.

I rummaged around in my purse, but the magic purple book was nowhere to be found.

"I see you've found the journal." She leaned back in her seat and focused her intense gaze on me.

I reached for the book on the coffee table, the one I was *certain* had just been in my purse, and jumped as that same shock of electricity coursed through me. But the shock neutralized and the tingling came to an abrupt halt as the woman leaned forward and placed her wrinkled hands on mine. She took the book from me and laid it gingerly back on the coffee table.

I gazed into her violet eyes, searching for answers, my mouth unable to form any words or spit out the thousands of questions I had swimming around in my head.

"I know you must be confused," she began as she crossed one long, thin leg over the other and placed a delicate hand on her knee. "But there is a reason for all of this. For every seemingly inexplicable thing you've experienced since you arrived here. There is a reason for *all* of it."

Suddenly, I found my voice again. "What *is* the reason, then? Why exactly am I here? What is this monumental task I'm supposed to accomplish in fewer than three days? Do you know why all of these other people have been sent back to their past lives? Did they make it back home? And do you know how in the hell this book even exists? And how it found me in the bookstore today? And how did it jump from my bag to the coffee table without me noticing? And how did you find me? Am I going crazy?"

"No, Claudia, you're not going crazy. I understand how you would feel like that, though. All of the others have felt the same. Like I told you in the café, these past-life revisits are never easy. Especially in your situation."

"Okay. We'll just pretend that's normal for a minute. And the journal?"

"The journal finds its way to those who've made the trip back so that you don't waste precious time wondering if you've gone mad. You haven't, and like you've read in these pages, there are others who've been in your shoes. But, like I've already warned you, you don't have much time, and if you read the last journal entry, I suspect you are aware that your position here in this life is not secure. I am meeting with you today to give you some information that may help you along this journey, but after that, the rest will be up to you."

"So why did I come back? What is the event I'm here to change, the one that will ultimately change the course of fate, as you said? And why did all the others travel back as well?"

"Traveling back in time to a past life is an extremely rare occurrence—so rare, in fact, that the only documentation of this ever happening is in the journal you found today, which I'm sure you noticed, only *you* can read. Most people wouldn't be able to understand this sort of occurrence, as it doesn't fit in with their two-dimensional view of the world, and that is why the journal is only visible to those who are experiencing this exact situation."

"But please just tell me *why*. Why am I here? I mean, so much has happened since I arrived, how do you expect me to figure this out on my own? Between the murder accusations, finding François Lefevre's dead body, a crazy ex-boyfriend stalker chasing me around the city, the threatening notes, Véronique's hatred for me, my sudden and overwhelming feelings for Antoine, and my young grandmother, who is my best friend and who is now pregnant with my mom…how in the hell do you expect me to decipher the *one* event I'm supposed to change? This is ludicrous!"

"As I explained to you in the café, the reason that you and the others you read about have been brought back is to *correct fate*."

I dug my nails into the smooth fabric on the sofa, gritting my teeth in frustration. "What do you even mean by that?"

"You see, sometimes a single event throws off the course of fate, and as a result, fate plays itself out in the wrong way for generations and generations thereafter. Usually, this inciting event is the result of great evil, and when it throws fate off its projected course for so many years, thereby negatively affecting so many lives, there are rare cases—such as yours—where the soul in question is given a second chance to go back and correct the mistake."

"So I'm one of the lucky ones who get to relive some awful event from the past. Fabulous."

"In the other cases you've seen in this journal, just like you, each person was brought back to their past life only a few days before the fate-changing event took place. And if you don't figure out a way to change that one event, it will happen again, and potentially have even greater repercussions than it did the first time around."

"Why do we only get a few days?"

"Because, while you and Ruby share a soul, as you've probably noticed, you are quite a different person than she. Faced with the same situations, you have already made drastically different decisions than she would have, and you have already begun to change things from the original way they happened. If you are given too many days here, with your free will, your knowledge, and your modern ideas acting out in Ruby's body, you may change things *too* much. Certain events are *supposed* to happen, no matter how negative they may seem to you, but there is *one* event that you are here to change. And *that* is your ultimate purpose for coming back."

"Does it have to do with my grandma? Or with Antoine? Or Ruby's death?"

"I do not know, my dear. Only you hold the answer to that question."

"So, all of these other people in the journal, were they able to figure it out in time and accomplish what they came here to do?"

"Not everyone, no."

"And what happens then?"

"Like I said before, the consequences of not correcting this error in fate can be catastrophic. Worse than the original time around."

"Suppose I am able to fix whatever went wrong last time, what happens to me then? Do I stay here or do I go back to my life as Claudia and pick up where things left off?"

"There is a portal by which you arrived here, and it is *only* through this exact portal that you will find your way back."

I rested my head in my hands, feeling so thoroughly confused that even the backs of my eyeballs were throbbing. "A portal? Like a hole in time and space or something like that?"

She smiled, but only for a second before she continued. "Yes, something like that. Don't worry about that right now, though. What you have to remember is that you are *here* now. You have to focus on the task at hand and not allow yourself to worry about the future. There is something you have been brought here to do, and if you follow your instincts, you will know the time and the place. You will know what actions to take. Don't let your intellect get in the way. Trust your gut, and you will succeed."

I noticed then that Madame Bouchard had been speaking English the entire time with no hint of a French accent. I wondered if that was even her real name. "Where are you from?" I asked her. "And how do you know so much about all of this?"

She leaned forward and picked up a small mug of steaming coffee, then tipped it past her thin lips and took a sip.

But there hadn't been anything except the purple journal on the coffee table when we'd first sat down. Had there?

I shook my head, the confusion setting in deeper as she curled her fingers around the mug, then lifted her eyes to mine once more, her penetrating gaze soaking right through me.

"Much of this experience will remain a mystery to you forever, Claudia. After all, the mere fact that you have traveled back in time to a past life is clearly not something that one can do in the physical, rational world we live in. Yet, here you are.

"My advice to you is to let the mysteries be mysteries. Trust that they have their place in this extraordinary experience, and focus on the events that you *can* control, which is the reason you've been brought here in the end. It is important to remember, though, that things may get worse before they get better. But even so, you mustn't give up. The fates of countless people will be changed for the better if you simply make one different choice this time around."

I circled my fingers over my throbbing temples, and while I was grateful for the clarification she was giving me, I needed to know more. "I think I understand. But I still have another question. You mentioned the last page of the journal earlier. Do you know who wrote that? Is there someone else after me, someone besides Thomas? Someone who has traveled to Paris, and possibly back in time, to find me?"

The old woman's expression became grave, the encouragement and motivation she'd been offering me just moments before disappearing.

"There is something else you must know about your particular situation," she said, her tone somber.

"What is it?"

"I don't normally visit with people a second time during their past-life journey. Usually the first visit coupled with the journal suffices in letting you know that this experience is real and that you have a job to do. But, your case is *different*...you see, something went wrong when you were sent back to this life. Something that, unfortunately, has never happened before."

Hairs prickled the back of my neck. How could this situation get any worse?

Madame Bouchard leaned forward in her chair, the seriousness in her gaze letting me know that all of the worries I'd had since I arrived here had been more than legitimate.

She continued, "Let me explain further. *Your* soul, Claudia, is *pure*. While in both of your lives you have made mistakes and you have, at times, acted in such a way that has been harmful to others, that is only human. At the core, you're a good soul with pure, honest intentions. Up until now, *only* pure souls have been given this chance to correct fate, to turn things around for the better. But when you were sent back, an impure soul, or an *evil* soul, was sucked into the time warp and sent along with you."

"So the last journal entry, it's from this person? This evil soul?"

She nodded. "Yes, and unfortunately, this makes your actions— and your purpose here—all the more urgent. All the more critical."

"Do you know who it is? Was it someone I knew in my life as Claudia? Someone who didn't like me for some reason and has come back here to harm me?"

"I do not know the identity of this person in your life as Claudia or in this life as Ruby. But what I can tell you that may be of use to you here is that when an impure soul is reincarnated, they do not change much. There is little to no growth; usually, there is negative growth. Their appearance may be similar, and they will repeat the same ill-motivated actions in each subsequent life, thereby interfering with and ruining the pure intentions and actions of a good soul, like you. Every soul has a purpose, an overall, grand purpose. Even impure souls have a purpose, wicked though it may be. And it appears that the soul who has been accidentally sent back to this life carries a grudge. And regrettably, you, my dear, are on the receiving end."

"So what am I supposed to do if you can't tell me who it is? I know that Ruby has a ton of enemies in this life, but as Claudia, I didn't really have enemies. I mean, not *real* enemies, anyway. God, this is insane. How am I supposed to figure this out? How am I supposed to stop this person?"

"I'm afraid I can't answer those questions for you. I am only here to make you aware of the fact that you are in grave danger, and that you will have to summon up the courage to take *whatever action necessary* to stop this evil from occurring again, from hindering your life purpose, before it's too late. And above all, you must act organically in each situation you encounter. Call up the strength you have stored from these two lifetimes, and know that when the time comes, you *will* make the right choice."

My hands shook in my lap, my voice a mere squeak as I asked her, "How do you know? How are you so certain I'll make the right choice?"

"The choice Ruby needed to make the first time around, she wasn't able to. She didn't have enough strength. But you, Claudia, you have different values, different strengths than Ruby, and you have been chosen to come back for a reason. You wouldn't have been sent back if you weren't strong enough. Trust in your strength. Trust in the inherent knowledge within. But take caution and know that you are up against a mighty force, for an evil soul who has come back to relive their past life possesses not one but *two* lives' worth of evil, of resentment, of vengeance. And it is up to you to stop it."

Just as she finished speaking, a clock began ticking on the wall behind me, each tick louder than the one before, making me wince at the noise.

Madame Bouchard's gaze landed just above my head before she folded her hands in her lap and nodded at me. "I'm afraid our time is up."

"But you *have* to know who wrote the last page of the journal. Was it Thomas? Was it Véronique? Was it François's wife? And how will I know what choice to make?" I fired my questions at her without taking a breath, not wanting to leave her presence until I had as much information as I could possibly squeeze out of her. But as I heard my own words echoing through the space between us, I realized I already knew her answer.

You'll just know.

She leaned forward once more, her hands resting on mine, and again I caught of whiff of her rose-scented perfume.

I closed my eyes and breathed it in, letting her scent soak into me, allowing it to penetrate my pores.

I recalled that first night in the dance studio, when she'd placed Grandma Martine's necklace on me.

The necklace.

Just as I was about to ask her what significance the necklace had in bringing me here, and if she knew if Ruby had actually been involved in Gisèle's murder, a brush of wind whipped past me, taking with it the strong scent of roses.

When my gaze searched the candlelit apartment, all I found were eerie shadows dancing around the walls.

Madame Bouchard had vanished, once again.

Before I could process what was happening, the wind whipped in circles around my head and the room began to spin. I closed my eyes once more, and there I saw the old woman's pretty face; her violet eyes transfusing confidence into my bones; her strong, weathered hands reaching out for me. But as I spun faster and faster, her comforting face disappeared, and in its place came bursts of intense light. And when the light became so bright I couldn't bear it, I finally stopped fighting and allowed its warmth to consume me.

And there, in my release, I found darkness.

TWENTY-FIVE

"Ruby? Are you okay?"

I rolled my head to the side, feeling a cool surface press against my burning cheek. Where was I?

"Ruby, what are you doing on the floor? Did you pass out again?"

I fluttered my eyes open until they focused on the face in front of me. Large brown doe eyes lined with long, curvy eyelashes batted at me. It was the young, beautiful Delphine, who'd handed me the flowers the night before at the show…who'd been the first to find Gisèle's murdered body.

"I…I'm not sure. Where are we?" I asked.

"You're in the dressing room. How long have you been in here? You missed morning rehearsal, and Jean-Pierre's been looking for you."

The burning lightbulbs shining above the mirrors blinded me. How did I get here?

Pushing myself up to a sitting position, I gazed into the young dancer's fearful eyes, memories of everything that had just happened flashing through my brain. The bookstore. The journal. The others. Madame Bouchard. Then the spinning.

I couldn't remember anything after that. But somehow, I'd woken up *here*.

Before I could overanalyze my latest voyage, the old woman's deep, soothing voice came soaring through my memory.

Let the mysteries be mysteries. Trust that they have their place in this extraordinary experience, and focus on the events that you can control, which is the reason you've been brought here in the end.

203

Peabody Public Library
Columbia City, IN

Whatever had happened in between me sitting on her couch and then landing back in the dressing room was definitely a mystery, but I needed to let it go. Plus, if everything she'd said was true, I didn't have much time, and I surely couldn't waste another second of it wallowing around in confusion.

Long green stems stuck out of the wastebasket at my feet, making me remember the bloodred roses and the haunting note that had accompanied them. Delphine crouched closer to me, her dainty hand resting lightly on my shoulder.

"The roses last night. Who were they from?" I asked her.

Her eyes darted toward the door. "I...I'm not sure, Ruby. I found them lying on the floor close to the dressing room. Are you okay? Should I call the doctor?"

I barely heard her questions. All I could think about was the envelope addressed to Claudia.

I searched Delphine's face for answers, for the truth. "How did you know those flowers were for me?"

"What do you mean, how did I know? Your name was on the card, of course."

"*My* name was on the card?"

"I think we should get you upstairs and call the doctor. I'll tell Jean-Pierre you're sick." Delphine's gaze darted around the room once more. There was something she wasn't telling me.

"I'm not sick," I snapped, shrugging her hand off of me then lunging toward the trash can. I peered down through the mass of long, prickly stems that stuck out of the bin, searching for the note. It had clearly read *Claudia* on the front, and I suspected the note had been written in the same slanted handwriting as that last journal entry I'd found.

When I didn't see the little white square, I ripped the roses out of the bin one by one and tossed them onto the floor, not caring that the thorns were pricking my fingers, not caring that drops of my own blood were spotting my clothes. I had to find it.

"Ruby, *mais qu'est-ce que tu fais?*" *What are you doing?*

Finally, at the bottom of the small trash bin, I found what I was looking for.

Before I looked at it myself, I thrust the envelope in the young girl's confused face. "Now tell me the truth. Tell me how you knew these flowers were for me. Who gave them to you?"

Delphine furrowed her eyebrows, causing little lines to stretch across her forehead. "What are you talking about, Ruby? It says your name right here on the envelope."

She flipped the envelope around, and there, plain as day, was the name *Ruby*.

But that couldn't be possible. I blinked my eyes to make sure I wasn't seeing things. No matter how many times I blinked, though, the name didn't change.

Ruby.

I turned back to the trash can to look for the note that had been meant for me—for Claudia.

But when I'd pulled out the square white piece of paper where just the night before I'd clearly read the words *I know who you are*, all I found this time were two completely blank sides. The writing was gone.

Just like when the bookstore clerk had looked through the journal and all of the entries were suddenly missing.

Apparently I could only *see* the writing when I was alone. Either that or I was heading deeper into the loony bin.

I gazed back up to Delphine, and the look in her flashing brown eyes made me remember the vision I'd had of the night we'd found Gisèle.

"What aren't you telling me, Delphine? Do you know who sent me these roses? Do you know who killed Gisèle?"

She shot up from the ground, suddenly not so concerned with my well-being. I scrambled to my feet and grabbed her skinny arm before she could flee the scene.

"I can see it in your eyes. You're afraid, and you know something. Tell me who is doing this, Delphine."

Tears grazed the tips of her long eyelashes as she bit her bottom lip. "I don't know what you're talking about, Ruby. I found Gisèle right before you did. I have no idea who killed her, and I don't know who gave you these roses." She yanked her arm from my grasp. "I'm sorry, but I have to go."

Something about her tone, her eyes, her full lips, made me remember her—but again, not from *this* life. She looked familiar, like someone I knew from my life as Claudia. But how was that possible?

"Ruby, why are you looking at me like that? *Qu'est-ce qu'il y a?*" *What's the matter?*

"Delphine, what's your last name?"

She started toward the door without giving me a response.

"Please, just tell me your last name," I called after her.

She stopped at the door, wiping a lone tear from her eye. "You *know* my last name, Ruby. It's Marceau."

I had to steady myself on the wall to keep from falling over, Édouard's words from my last night at the dance studio flashing through my confused head.

When I was growing up in Paris, it was my mother who taught me how to dance. You see, in the fifties, she was a dancer near the famous Latin Quarter of Paris.

Marceau. Édouard *Marceau*.

Her high cheekbones, her charming smile, her full lips.

Delphine was Édouard's mother.

⊹══·══⊹

Not sure what to do with this latest revelation, I let out a shaky breath, bent down, and picked up the envelope and the note.

And even though I'd been half expecting it, the hairs on my arms still stood on end when I found the name *Claudia* printed where just moments ago I'd seen *Ruby*. And on the square white piece of paper was the same red, slanted handwriting I'd clearly seen the night before, from someone telling me they knew who I was.

How? How was all of this happening? How could the words be there when I looked at the note, the envelope, the journal, but when someone else looked—Édouard's young mother, no less—they were gone? How in the hell was any of this happening?

Let the mysteries be mysteries.

Ignoring the fear that threatened to paralyze me, I located my purse lying just a few feet away, underneath a chair. After ransacking its contents, I found that the gun was still in its place, and more important, Madame Bouchard had let me keep the purple past-life journal.

Flipping to the very last page, I compared the threatening journal entry with the creepy roses note. The deep-red pen color was identical, and the writing was so thick the words seemed to elevate off the page. Besides the color and the thickness, the slants in the penmanship were *exactly* the same.

There was absolutely no doubt in my mind that whoever had sent me these roses had also written this journal entry. Which meant that someone had come to Paris specifically to hunt me down *and* that they knew my real identity. And while I feared it could be Thomas, I wondered how he would know that I'm Claudia, and how *his* journal entry would be in *this* book when the only stories found within the tattered journal were from people just like me—people who'd jumped back in time to a past life.

Did I know Thomas, or a version of him, in my future life?

And what did Delphine know about all of this? She'd clearly been hiding something.

Or could it be Véronique? Or François Lefevre's jealous wife?

I read over the journal entry once more, stopping on the part that frightened me the most.

That little bitch won't steal what's mine this time around, and she won't steal it from me in the future either.

I'll be sure of it.

Whoever had written this had carried a grievance for me in both of my lives, if that was even possible. But then again, what *was* possible or impossible at this point? I was reading a journal with words that disappeared when anyone else looked at them. I'd had three encounters with a mysterious old woman who knew about me and the journal, who drank coffee that had magically appeared, and who had somehow sent me to this dressing room where Édouard's young mother had found me. And I had no clue how I'd even arrived here.

So, really, who was I to decide what was possible or not?

The problem—among *many* others—was that I was now beyond confused trying to piece all of these clues together, trying to stay one step ahead of this person who had traveled here to find me. This person who, if I was reading their message correctly, wanted me *dead*.

And whether that person was Thomas or one of the other many suspects, none of it was adding up, and I wouldn't discover any new information sitting alone in this dressing room. Plus, Antoine would be coming back to my apartment soon, and I couldn't miss him. There was absolutely nothing in this life I was sure about—*except* my feelings for Antoine. Just thinking about him released a vat of butterflies in my stomach and made my cheeks and hands and toes tingle. I was madly in love. And while I couldn't tell him about all of this insane past-life business, I knew that seeing his face would give me hope.

I tucked the note and the envelope into the journal, noticing how my fingers still tingled just from touching the purple book. Then I squeezed the journal into my bag next to the gun and opened the dressing room door, hoping to slip through the backstage area unnoticed so I wouldn't have to deal with Jean-Pierre. I didn't have time for his games.

But as soon as I emerged, I noticed groups of long-legged dancers huddled around each other, hushed whispers passing back and forth between them. An ominous feeling rose up through my chest as I made my way around the girls and finally spotted Jean-Pierre at the other end of the room, shaking his head and mumbling something under his breath. I took a few steps to the left so I could see who he was speaking with, and there, facing Jean-Pierre, was Detective Duval.

Spinning around on my heel, I headed toward the staircase. I needed to get out of here as quickly as possible. Despite the dizziness that had just come over me, threatening to land me flat on my face, I gripped the banister and flew up the stairs to my apartment.

I had to hide the gun.

⊹⇒·⇐⊹

I barged into my apartment, but just as I was bolting the locks, I spotted a note that had been slipped underneath the door.

> *Ruby,*
> *I came back, but you weren't here. Please call me at the hospital when you get back. I want to make sure you are okay.*
> *Je ne cesse pas de penser à toi,*
> *Antoine*

"I can't stop thinking about you either," I whispered.

I ran to the phone, but as I picked it up, a harsh pounding on the door startled me, made me drop the receiver.

"Mademoiselle Kerrigan." It was Detective Duval's thick accent, his demanding voice reverberating through the door in between knocks. "*Ouvrez la porte.*"

With my heart beating so hard I could feel its rapid pulse in my temples, I opened the hall closet, threw my gun-concealing purse inside, then walked up to my front door where the banging persisted. But as I reached for the handle, I froze.

What if he was here to ask me more questions I couldn't answer about Gisèle's and François's murders? Or worse yet, what if he was here to arrest me for one—or *both*—of them?

I closed my eyes and swallowed hard. Whatever he was here for, I would just have to face it.

After I let the detective in, he strode past me, laid his black hat on the kitchen table, then took a seat. He nodded for me to join him as he reached for something in the breast pocket of his suit jacket.

At least he hadn't cuffed me yet. I would answer his questions as best I could, and hopefully I could ask him if he'd found anything out about Thomas Riley or François's wife.

But my thoughts roared to a halt when I caught a glimpse of the photo Detective Duval had slid across the table.

Crystal-blue eyes. Dashing blond hair. Glinting white teeth.

It was Robert Maxwell, my future grandfather.

"What happened after you left the club with Monsieur Maxwell last night?" the detective asked.

"Why? Did something happen to him? Is Robert okay?" I pressed my hands onto the table, my feet firmly into the ground, needing something to let me know that the world wasn't literally falling out from beneath me. The only reason he would be showing me a photo of Robert was if something bad had happened.

"Please answer the question, Mademoiselle."

"I walked Robert out of the club then he left."

"And where did he go?"

My heart thumped, my thoughts racing back to last night. I'd sent him to Titine's apartment, to make things right. Had something happened to him on his way there? Did he ever make it?

"*Mademoiselle, s'il vous plaît.*"

"I'm not sure where he was going. Back to his hotel, I presume."

Detective Duval lifted a brow, the lines around his eyes revealing the toll the last three days had taken on him. But I didn't care. I needed to know what was going on, and I wouldn't mention Titine's name until I knew it was safe to do so.

"Please, Detective. Tell me what is going on."

"Robert Maxwell's body was found on the quai of the Seine early this morning. Shot in the chest."

I tried to suck in a breath as I stared down at Robert's handsome smile…my mother's smile. But I couldn't. I couldn't breathe.

"Robert was…*murdered*?" I managed to spit out as I held my hands over my heart, the room spinning furiously around me.

"Yes, that is correct, Mademoiselle. I understand you had a performance *spéciale* for Monsieur Maxwell last night, no?"

I tore my eyes from the photo, barely hearing the words out of the detective's mouth. *This* was why my mother had never known her father. He'd been murdered. And I was here. I could've stopped it. I could've—

"Mademoiselle Kerrigan, please answer the question."

"I…I'm sorry. I just can't believe…"

"Mademoiselle Kerrigan, did you or did you not have a special performance for Monsieur Maxwell last night?"

"Yes," I sputtered. "Yes, that's correct."

"And, if I understand correctly, there was more to the *arrangement* than simply the performance. Is this true?"

"No, Detective. That part isn't true," I said, fighting the lump forming in my throat.

I glanced back down at the photo and saw traces of my mom in Robert's handsome face—her smile, her eyes, her dimple. This was so awful I couldn't begin to comprehend it. Why had I been brought back to this life to relive *this*? What was the point of being here if I couldn't stop this devastating event from occurring? This was why my grandmother had been a single mom. She'd never even been given the chance to make a life with the father of her child.

But then another horrific thought popped into my head as I remembered the words Madame Bouchard had spoken to me just this morning.

There is one event that you are here to change. And that is your ultimate purpose for coming back.

Was Robert's murder *the event* I'd been brought back to change? Was I supposed to have stopped it from occurring altogether? Had

I failed to change fate? Would the consequences now be even worse than the first time around?

"How did this happen?" I blurted. "Who would do this?"

"I am not free to discuss the details surrounding his death until I have questioned all the suspects." The corners of his mouth twitched, his expression relentless and hard. "Let us try this again. If you did not have another arrangement with Monsieur Maxwell, then why were you seen leaving the club with him last night? *Where* did you take him?"

If I explained to the detective that I'd sent Robert off to find Titine, the finger would be pointed straight at her. I couldn't do that to my young grandmother. She was already going to be devastated enough once she heard the news. The last thing she needed was to be accused of Robert's murder.

"Robert was considering casting me as the lead in his next film. Like I already told you, I walked outside with him so we could discuss the details a bit more, then he left. I'm assuming he was going back to his hotel. That was the last time I saw him."

He smirked as he snapped up the photo and tucked it back into his pocket. "Tell me, Mademoiselle, how is it that you are closely connected to *three* murders in one week, and you expect me to believe that you have nothing to do with any of them?"

Three murders. What a nightmare.

But I couldn't show my fear. It would only make me appear more suspicious.

"I'm innocent, Detective, and I'm afraid I won't be able to answer any more of your questions until I have my lawyer present."

A deep, sinister chuckle escaped from his lips. "Tell me, Mademoiselle, how exactly do you have the money to pay for a lawyer? I do not imagine you earn very much money dancing in this club. With Monsieur Lefevre *and* Monsieur Maxwell both dead, you must have other men willing to pay you for your services, no?"

Was he serious?

By the smug look on his face, I guessed that he was.

"I'm going to have to ask you to leave my apartment now, Detective. Like I already said, I'll be willing to speak with you once my lawyer is present." I was certain Ruby didn't *have* a lawyer, but I would figure all of that out later. I wasn't about to say anything more to this man that might incriminate me.

"Maybe that is the way things work over in your country, Mademoiselle Kerrigan, but that is not the way things work in France." Detective Duval stood from the table, his eyes combing my apartment and fixating on something across the room.

"Have you looked into that name I gave you yesterday? Thomas Riley? And have you located François Lefevre's wife?" I asked, but Detective Duval wasn't listening to me anymore.

I followed his gaze, but along the way, something shiny caught my eye. The closet door where I'd just stashed my purse was cracked open just a slit, and there, on the floor, peeking out of that tiny crack in the door, was the barrel of the gun, pointing straight at us.

Shit.

It must've slid out of my purse when I'd thrown it in the closet earlier. Why hadn't I been more careful?

The detective stood from the table and crossed the living room, his stride long and purposeful.

"Excuse me, what are you—" I began, but stopped when he snatched up a black overcoat from the couch.

The handsome jacket belonged to Robert. It was the one he'd lent me the night before when I'd walked him outside. I'd tossed it on the couch this morning without a second thought.

"What do you think you're doing?" I asked, charging toward him. "You can't just go through my things. Do you have a search warrant?"

"Monsieur Maxwell was found without a coat last night, which seemed odd considering the cold temperatures we have been experiencing in Paris recently, no?"

I grabbed at the jacket, but the detective was faster. Reaching into the breast pocket, he pulled out a little white card.

JULIETTE SOBANET

"Robert Maxwell. Film director. Hollywood, California," he read aloud, his strong accent removing the *H* from "Hollywood."

"Robert offered me his coat last night while we were talking outside," I said, feeling my cheeks flame up. I needed to get this guy out of here, *now*. "Like I told you before, I don't know anything about how Robert was killed. He was going to cast me as the lead in his upcoming film. Why on earth would I want to harm him?"

The detective gripped the coat and squared his face two inches from mine. "Do you have an alibi to cover what you were doing last night?"

A flash of Antoine's lips on mine, his body wrapped around me as we fell asleep in each other's arms, passed through my dazed head. He would vouch for me. I was sure of it.

"Yes, I was with Antoine Richard."

The detective raised an eyebrow. "Gisèle Richard's brother, the doctor?"

I nodded.

"*Intéressant.* And if I were to contact Monsieur Richard, you are certain he would tell the same story?"

"Yes, Detective. Right after Robert left, Antoine met me outside, and we went to his apartment."

"I see. Is he one of your *clients*?"

"No, it's not like that. We've just become close since Gisèle died. Because, like I told you, I was one of her best friends."

Detective Duval narrowed his eyes at me. "You are not to leave the City of Paris while these investigations are under way. You will be hearing from me shortly."

He held on to Robert's coat then glanced around my apartment once more. My heart pounded inside my ears, making me feel as if I might pass out.

Dear God. Please don't see the gun. Please.

But as he shook his head and walked toward the door, I let out my breath. I was in the clear. For now, anyway.

"Detective Duval. One more thing. Did you find anything on Thomas Riley? Or François's wife?"

"There are a hundred listings for Thomas Riley in New York City. And Madame Lefevre is grieving the loss of her husband. I do not have time for your distractions, Mademoiselle. Or for your lies."

After he'd gone, I bolted the door then stumbled backward into the armchair, my head a jumbled, confused mess. How could this have happened? Could Thomas have killed Robert? Could I have stopped this from happening? Had I already failed to accomplish what I was sent here to do? And why was this detective hell-bent on proving that I had something to do with all of these murders?

A stray tear rolled down my cheek as I thought about the fact that Titine had lost someone she loved, someone she'd created a child with, and that *this* was why my mom had never had a father.

But as I wiped my eyes dry, I knew I couldn't sit around and wonder about what could've been or if this was the event I was supposed to have changed.

Robert was gone. My grandfather had been killed. And if I didn't figure out what the hell was going on and who had done this, I was going to be next.

TWENTY-SIX

A cramp seized my side as I pounded on Titine's door. After the third knock, I rested my head against the wall and tried to catch my breath. I'd never run so fast in my life. I knew I needed to be with her right now. She may have already found out about what happened to Robert, and I had to make sure she was okay.

But she wasn't answering. Where could she be?

"Titine! Please open the door. It's me, Ruby."

Blocking out the loud voices that traveled down the miniscule stairway of her old Parisian apartment building, I pressed my ear up against Titine's door. But just as I was about to give up, the door-knob turned.

There, before me, stood my young grandmother, her eyes puffy and swollen, her cheeks stained with tears and mascara.

I reached for her, but she backed up and glared at me with an accusatory look in her eyes. She'd never looked at me that way before.

"Titine, I'm not sure what you know or don't know right now. But you have to believe me when I tell you that I didn't sleep with Robert last night. I know you loved him. I would never have done that to you."

"Then where was he all night?" she asked, her voice shrill. "Why didn't he come to see me?"

She didn't know yet.

"Titine, can I come in?" I asked softly as my stomach tightened at the thought of breaking this horrific news to her. I wanted to run the other way and pretend none of this had happened. I couldn't bear to watch her heart break right in front of me.

"No, you're not coming in here until you tell me where Robert was last night. He was with you. I know he was."

"He wasn't with me, Titine. He wanted to be with you. It was a big misunderstanding. Jean-Pierre told him that he could spend the night with the most beautiful girl in the club, and Robert thought that meant you. He'd never planned on spending the night with me. He only wanted to speak with me about the film."

A glimmer of hope returned to Titine's swollen eyes. "Really?"

I nodded. "Can I just come in, Titine? I need to talk to you."

She relaxed her stance at the door and let me pass by. Immediately, as I entered Titine's apartment and smelled her lavender-scented perfume, a flood of memories surged into my brain. I remembered being here with Titine and Gisèle, drinking wine after our shows, giggling as we talked about how much we couldn't stand Véronique and how handsome the men in the audience had been.

But when Titine's voice came soft and shaky from behind me, I remembered something else. I remembered standing here, giving her this exact same news once before. And I remembered feeling like nothing had ever hurt me more than telling her that Robert was gone.

"Ruby, what is it? What's the matter?"

As I stood before her, trying to call up the strength I'd had in my life as Claudia when I'd counseled patients through grief, loss, and devastation, I couldn't. As Claudia, I'd been strong for my clients, for people I didn't know all that well, but after my father died, I'd learned to keep a safe distance from friends and family. And especially from men. I'd never wanted to love anyone again so much that I would break when they broke...or when they were gone.

But as I stood before Titine, I remembered that I wasn't *only* Claudia anymore. I was Ruby too.

I took Titine by the hand and led her over to the couch, knowing in my heart that Ruby had the strength to handle this. Ruby could break this news and not crumble.

"Titine, last night, after the show, I talked with Robert and we figured out the misunderstanding. He let me know that you'd told him something important last night, and that he wanted to be there for you. So, I pointed him in the direction of your apartment, and he left to come talk to you."

Confusion passed through Titine's piercing green eyes. "But then why didn't he ever come?"

I took Titine's other hand in mine and looked her in the eye. "I'm sorry, Titine, but I just found out this morning that something happened to Robert last night."

The perplexed look in Titine's eyes deepened as her tiny hands squeezed me so tightly I thought I would break. But I didn't. I wouldn't. I had to be strong for her. I had to tell her the truth.

"Robert's been murdered, Titine. I'm so sorry."

I scooped her frail, shaking body into my arms before she could protest, and I held her as sobs raked her chest, ravaging what was left of the flicker of hope she'd had just moments ago.

I didn't let go until she pushed back and looked me in the eye.

"How? How did it happen? Who would want to hurt Robert?"

"The detective told me—"

"The detective? You talked to the police about this?" Her tearstained eyes darted frantically back and forth over my face.

"Yes, Detective Duval came to talk to me this morning. I was the last one seen with Robert, so they had to question me."

Titine grasped my arm. "Oh, God. Someone killed him, and you…you probably thought it was Thomas. You probably told the police that it was him. Didn't you?"

"Titine, I know you told me earlier that Thomas couldn't be here, but I really believe that he is. I think he may have had something to do with Robert's murder, and possibly with François's and Gisèle's as well."

Titine's face turned so red it was almost purple before she stood up and knocked a stack of papers off her coffee table. "No!" she screamed, her voice rising with hysteria. "Thomas isn't *here*, Ruby. I told you, he's not here! Don't ever mention his name again. Do you hear me, Ruby? Never!" She stormed through her apartment, seized a picture of us off the windowsill, then smashed it to smithereens at her feet.

"Titine!" I rushed over to her, but she flung me off and continued on her rampage.

"This is all your fault, Ruby. If you wouldn't have sent Robert to me, nothing would've happened to him. You should've just spent the night with him. You should've just fucked him like you fuck everyone else! And now I have his baby. I have his *baby*, Ruby. What am I going to do? What am I supposed to do without him?"

Titine crashed into my arms, a heap of despair in the aftermath of loss. I stroked her head as I brought her down to the floor with me. "Shhh. I'm not going to let anything happen to you. You're going to get through this."

But just as the words came out of my mouth, Titine's head slumped farther into my chest, her arms going limp at her sides.

"Titine? Titine, wake up. Wake up!"

But her body stayed as limp as a rag doll.

I hoisted her up and onto the couch, and when I pulled my hand out from under her legs, I noticed a dot of red, silky liquid gleaming on my finger. I peered back over to where Titine had just been lying, and there, on the ground, was a small red puddle.

I quickly rolled Titine onto her side and gasped as my worst fears were confirmed.

It was blood. It was Titine's blood.

And if I didn't act fast, she was going to lose her baby.

TWENTY-SEVEN

After what felt like hours, the strange, piercing sound of French sirens blasted underneath Titine's apartment window. Knowing the paramedics were here didn't calm the panic surging through me, though. I wouldn't feel calm again until I knew for certain that my young grandmother was going to be okay, and that the baby inside of her—my mother—would survive this ordeal.

Because if there was no more Titine and no more baby, that meant I would lose my mother, my grandmother, and ultimately, my entire future as Claudia.

And I refused to let that happen.

I swung the door open before the paramedics had a chance to knock then led them over to Titine, who was lying on the couch, drifting in and out of consciousness. The emergency workers carefully lifted her onto a stretcher, the bloodstained towel I'd placed beneath her spilling to the floor—a reminder of what could be lost if they didn't get her to the hospital fast enough.

I rode beside Titine in the ambulance, squeezing her limp hand in my shaky palm as the paramedics worked swiftly around me, taking her vital signs, hooking her up to an IV, doing their best to stop the bleeding. They fired questions at me about what had happened, and while I barely heard myself or noticed I was speaking French, I still managed to tell them about Titine's pregnancy. The murder. Titine's hysteria. And finally, her blood on the floor.

Once they'd heard the whole story, they continued to work on stabilizing her. I remained quiet as I focused on Titine's pale skin, which had turned a sickening shade of gray, the freckles that dotted her nose, and the long locks of red hair that sprawled out from underneath her head and cascaded along the edge of the stretcher.

I pressed her hand to my forehead, willing her to hang on. Willing her to keep this baby, and to stay strong.

And in that moment, with my young grandmother's clammy palm pressed to my head, I felt her pulse speed up and beat in time with mine. I didn't notice the ambulance racing down the bumpy Parisian boulevards any longer, nor did I hear the siren wailing just overhead.

Instead, I heard my grandmother saying Ruby's name back at the dance studio the night I'd passed out in Édouard's arms. Somehow, she'd known that I'd been Ruby in my past life. That we'd been best friends.

And here, in the ambulance, as her heart continued to beat with mine, I felt as if our souls were merging, as if there was suddenly no separation between our two beings, between time and space and past lives and future lives.

In this silence, I knew I could speak to her. I could communicate with her. And although there was no rational explanation, I knew she would hear me.

I lowered Titine's hand to my chest and placed it over my heart. With my eyes closed, I told her that she needed to stay strong. I told her that she needed to keep this baby because someday, she would have a granddaughter named Claudia, and that we would be the best of friends. I told her that our bond would withstand the test of time, and that if she could just hang on a little bit longer, everything would be okay.

It had to be.

The ambulance came to an abrupt stop, and while the fast-working paramedics wheeled Titine away from me, I hoped that my presence here hadn't somehow messed with fate or changed the way things were originally meant to happen. What if my actions here had actually led to this moment? What if they had led me to losing my grandmother, my mother, and my future all in one blow?

The old woman had told me that I'd already begun to change things from the way they'd originally played out. What if *this* was my fault?

I shook my head and snapped myself back to reality. There wasn't any time for speculation. Titine and her baby would be okay. They had to be.

Not wanting Titine to be alone, I plowed through the double doors, hoping to follow along wherever they were taking her, but a woman clad in a crisp white polyester dress and a pointy nurse's hat stopped me.

"You cannot go in with them, Mademoiselle. You will have to stay here in the waiting room until they stabilize your friend."

Her French words whistled through my head, automatically translating into English, but only some of them stuck as I glanced around the pale-blue walls of the waiting room, the smell of stale hospital air, medications, and plastic pitchers of water so familiar to me I could hardly keep my balance.

I'd been here before.

If this had happened to Titine the first time around in this life, then of course I'd been here before.

But as I turned back to the nurse, I knew I'd been here for another purpose.

Antoine.

I needed to know which hospital this was. "*Excusez-moi, dans quel hôpital sommes-nous?*"

"*L'hôpital* Hôtel-Dieu," she answered, completely unaware of what those words meant to me.

"*Merci,*" I called over my shoulder before slamming through the doors marked *For Patients and Staff Only*. No visitors allowed.

"*Mademoiselle!*" she shrieked after me. But I was already down the hallway, winding through the hospital from muscle memory, heading to the one man who I knew could save Titine and her baby.

"Ruby, what are you doing here? Are you okay?" Antoine stared at me with wide eyes as he rustled some papers around on his desk then shoved them into the top drawer.

"It's Titine. She's here—and her baby. You have to help, Antoine." I knew I wasn't making any sense, but after sprinting across the entire hospital and up three flights of stairs, my lungs starving for anything resembling fresh air, I didn't care. I needed Antoine to come with me.

Antoine met me on the other side of his desk and placed his warm hands on my trembling shoulders. "Ruby, what is going on? What happened to Titine?"

"I don't have time to explain, but something horrible has happened, and you are the only one who can save Titine and her baby. I need you to come with me now."

Antoine grabbed my hand and led me out of his office.

As we raced to the emergency room, I gave him as much information as I could about Titine's pregnancy, the murder, and the bleeding that had started after she'd found out about Robert's death. Antoine didn't miss a beat. He located Titine's room in the ER, then turned and kissed me on the forehead.

"I will take care of Titine for you. You don't need to worry." He squeezed my hands then pushed through the double doors, leaving me alone in the hallway, with nothing but spots of memories flashing through my dazed mind and a cold draft on my palms where his hands had been.

As I steadied myself against the wall, I remembered standing outside this room once before, feeling just as terrified and alone as I had back then. I tried to picture the outcome—Antoine walking out of the hospital room telling me that Titine and the baby were both healthy, that everything was going to be fine. But I couldn't see the future. Whether bad or good, I couldn't see it. I could only grasp those vivid moments of déjà-vu as they passed through me like a hot summer rain pouring down so hard I couldn't ignore them, then coming to an abrupt halt before I could see what would happen next.

I slid down to the cold tiles of the hospital floor, a wintry draft whipping through the hallway, leaving a chill on the back of my neck where I'd been sweating. I thought back over everything that had happened since I'd arrived in this life a couple of days ago, and Madame Bouchard's mention of fate popped into my rattled mind.

I'd never believed in fate before. In my practical existence as a therapist, I'd counseled people on rational ways to improve their relationships, their careers, and their lives. I hadn't saved any room for fate or what it might hold for us. I'd believed that if you made good, solid decisions and nurtured your relationships with clear communication, compassion, and hard work, you would see positive results. Things like trusting in fate and following your gut instincts were *not* things to pay attention to, let alone to live by.

But ever since I'd been zapped back to the past, all I'd had to go on were my instincts and the overwhelming gut reactions I couldn't have ignored if I'd tried. There was no reason to the madness of this situation, no practicality. Nothing here made sense.

Yet when I thought of the bond I had with my grandmother in my life as Claudia and the close friendship I shared with her here as Ruby, somehow it did make sense. And when I thought of how amazing I felt with Antoine—as if I'd known him forever, as if our souls were meant to be together—I realized that I did believe in fate.

I didn't understand it. I couldn't explain it. I just suddenly believed.

And if fate was guiding *this* course, I could only hope that it would be kind enough to replay itself one more time and save my grandmother's life.

TWENTY-EIGHT

An hour later, Antoine emerged from the double doors of the emergency room and spotted me curled in a ball on the scuffed tile floor.

I stood and grabbed on to his arm as the blood drained from my head. I refused to give in to the urge to throw up, to pass out, or to collapse into a heap on the ground. Titine was going to be okay. She had to be.

"How is she?" I asked. "And the baby?"

"We've stabilized Titine for the moment, we managed to stop the bleeding, and the baby still has a steady heartbeat. We will have to run several more tests and monitor both Titine and the baby over the next few days to rule out any serious conditions, but it looks as if her body went into shock after hearing the news. A reaction this strong can put severe stress on the baby and can cause major complications. We will do everything we can to make sure they are okay, but unfortunately, I cannot give you any guarantees at this point."

"You mean there's a chance she might not make it? And the baby too?" I asked as tears rimmed my eyelids.

Antoine blinked a few times, but his gaze never faltered. "I will do everything I can to make sure that both of them get through this, Ruby. I know it will be difficult for you, but please try not to worry. They are in good hands."

I felt myself collapsing into Antoine's arms, his strong embrace more comforting than I ever could've asked for.

"Thank you so much, Antoine. Thank you."

He lifted my chin and wiped the lone tear that had streaked down my cheek. "It was smart of you to come to me. The doctor on staff in the ER doesn't have as much experience in this domain as I do. How did you know where to find me?"

"Oh…I asked one of the nurses and followed my instincts the rest of the way."

Antoine arched an eyebrow, his smoldering gray eyes piercing through me just as they had the night before. He ran a finger down my cheekbone then tucked a fallen strand of hair behind my ear. "I've never met anyone like you before, Ruby. And I know I never will again."

Despite the grim circumstances for me being here, I still felt my lips relax and even smile as Antoine leaned in and kissed me on the forehead.

"Can I see her?" I asked as he kissed me once more on the cheek and then at the corner of my mouth.

"Yes. She is still very tired, but I'm sure she would like your company."

"Thank you again, Antoine. You saved her. Thank you so much."

He squeezed my arm and ushered me into the pale-white room, where my young grandmother lay in a metal hospital bed, tubes poking out of her arms, a steady *beep*ing noise emanating from a rickety machine next to the bed.

"I'll be right out here whenever you're finished, okay?" Antoine squeezed my hand one last time and left me alone with Titine.

I walked up to her bedside, placed my purse on the ground, and took a seat next to her. The sight of her sunken eyes and her pale skin frightened me, making me fear the worst.

But she was alive. She was still here, breathing, and her baby had a heartbeat. My mom had a heartbeat.

I clasped Titine's hand and watched as her tiny chest rose and fell, her breath blowing lightly out of her mouth, her eyelids fluttering open and closed.

Amid the distinct sense that I'd been here before, that I'd held Titine's hand just like this in these exact circumstances, Madame Bouchard's voice came flooding back to me.

Certain events are supposed to happen, no matter how negative they may seem to you, but there is one event that you are here to change. And that is your ultimate purpose for coming back.

If you follow your instincts, you will know the time and the place. You will know what actions to take. Don't let your intellect get in the way. Trust your gut, and you will succeed.

Once again, I felt Titine's pulse beating in time with mine, our hearts, our bodies, our souls completely in sync with one another.

And it was then that I knew with absolute certainty, this *wasn't* the event I was here to correct. And Robert's death, no matter how untimely, no matter how horrible, no matter what it meant for my grandmother's, my mother's, and my own future, was *not* the event.

Because as I ran through the decisions I'd made the night before, I was certain that at the time, I had done the right thing. I'd straightened out the misunderstanding that Jean-Pierre had created, and I'd sent Robert off to explain things to Titine. To the woman he loved.

I'd followed my gut instincts. And at the time, there'd been no way to know what was going to happen to Robert. As much as I didn't want to accept his death, and as easy as it could've been to blame it on myself and think that I'd already failed to accomplish what I'd been sent here to do, I knew that it wasn't my fault. That wasn't my event.

Madame Bouchard's words continued to resound in my consciousness, their meaning finally taking hold. For the first time since I'd woken up as Ruby, I felt certain that my presence here in this life was vital. And while I hadn't a clue what awaited me, I knew I hadn't yet accomplished what I'd been sent back to do.

"Ruby." Titine's scratchy whisper cut through my thoughts as she gave my hand a light squeeze.

"Titine, you're awake." I smiled down at her, feeling immensely grateful that she was here. She was going to be okay. I knew she would be okay.

"The baby?" she asked, the fear in her eyes palpable.

"The baby is okay, Titine. And you're going to be okay too. They just have to run some tests to make sure that there's nothing more serious going on, but Antoine thinks it was just your body going into shock."

The pained expression from earlier returned to her face with a vengeance. She must've momentarily forgotten what had happened—that Robert was gone.

I leaned forward and hugged her before she had a chance to say anything. "I'm sorry, Titine. I'm so sorry."

She rested her head on my shoulder and gripped my arms with her shaky, frail fingers. "What am I going to do?" she whispered. "I can't raise this baby by myself, Ruby. I can't."

I pulled away from her and rested my hands on her shoulders. "You *can*, Titine. You're going to be an amazing mother."

"No, Ruby. You're wrong. I'll make a horrible mother. I've never even wanted children. I'm a dancer. I like to drink and stay out late. I want to stay in Paris and live in my studio apartment and not have to worry about taking care of someone else all by myself…" She paused, her green eyes void of their characteristic sparkle, her flame momentarily doused. "I'll have the baby, and I'll give it to my parents to raise back in the States. God knows they were never proud of anything *I've* done, so maybe this will give them someone else to be proud of for once."

I stared at Titine, speechless, my words caught in my throat. So *this* is what had happened. Titine had given the baby to her parents. My mother had been raised by *them* in the United States, not by my grandma Martine. No wonder my mother and my grandma had never had a good relationship. And no wonder my mom had always lacked the warmth of other mothers, and had so easily abandoned me after my father was killed.

Her own mother had abandoned her.

And I couldn't let it happen again.

"Titine, you have to listen to me. You *have* to keep the baby and raise her yourself. I know under these circumstances that that seems unfathomable. It seems like your entire world is crumbling. But I'm here for you, and I'll help you. You can't give her away, Titine. You have to promise me you won't give her away."

Titine's green eyes flickered just the tiniest bit. "Ruby?"

"Yes?"

"How do you know it's a girl?"

I smiled at her, feeling a warm tear bubble up under my eyelid. "I just know. You can trust me on this one. And she'll need her mom. You will be the most important person in her life. You can't abandon her."

"But how will I afford a baby? I barely make enough money at the club to get by on my own, let alone support a child. Plus, we work nights. Who will watch the baby while we're at the club?"

"I don't know how it will all work out, Titine, but you have to trust that it will. The alternative is that you give your child to your parents, they raise her, and someday, when you *are* ready to have kids, you'll have this child out there who doesn't know you, who thinks you don't love her. I know you, Titine. And I know you will regret it."

A tear streamed down her cheek as she squeezed my hand. "Thank you, Ruby. Thank you for being there for me. I'm so sorry about what I said to you earlier. What happened to Robert is not your fault. And I had no right to say those things to you. You're my best friend. You're my family. I wouldn't be who I am without you."

I took Titine's other hand in mine, feeling our pulses beating in tune yet again, and I smiled at her. "You're my best friend too, Titine. And you *always* will be. You'll get through all of this. I promise you, you'll be okay."

Titine's eyelids began to droop, and I noticed the fatigue, the weariness settling into the tiny lines around her eyes.

"You should get some rest," I said, wiping one last tear from her cheek.

But before her eyelids closed, she turned to me, her voice barely a whisper. "If the police come to talk to you again, remember, *don't* mention Thomas Riley's name."

She drifted off to sleep, leaving me to wonder what exactly I didn't know about Thomas yet, and *why* I shouldn't have mentioned his name to the police.

I needed to talk all of this through with Antoine. Of anyone in this life, I knew that he would help me.

As I stood to leave, I noticed my red journal protruding out of the top of my purse. I remembered the way the pages had been fading right in front of my eyes. After the conversation I'd just had with Titine, I needed to see if my future life was still disappearing.

I sat back down and opened the worn, old book.

Goose bumps prickled my arms as I found that every single entry had faded away to almost nothing. I flipped to the page I'd read only a day earlier—the entry about my mother and my grandmother—but when I reached the spot in the journal where I was certain it had been, I only found a blank page. My words had vanished completely.

I clutched the scarlet binding, hoping against all hope that the disappearance of my words on the page meant that I was changing the future—for the better. But when I flipped another page, my hope vanished.

Because there, staring back at me, was my faded sonogram photo, the black-and-white specs almost completely gone, the date at the bottom erased.

Fighting back the tears that threatened to spill down my cheeks, I emerged from Titine's hospital room and spotted Antoine waiting for me in his long white coat, just as he'd said he would be.

He paid no attention to the nurses swirling around us in the hallway and instead wrapped his arms around me and pulled me close. I buried my face in his chest, willing myself to pull it together, to keep the truth inside, even though I so desperately wanted to tell Antoine everything. Tell him who I really was. That in my other life I was pregnant.

And that I had to find a way back or I would lose my baby. I was losing her already.

"Come, Ruby. I'll take you back to my office." Antoine took my hand in his, our fingers intertwined in a perfect fit as I followed him through the hospital back to the labor and delivery wing.

Inside Antoine's dark, cozy office, he leaned against the desk and pulled me close, tucking a wavy strand of blonde hair behind my ear.

"Where were you today, Ruby? I came back to your apartment, I searched the club, but no one knew where you had gone."

I blinked, trying to avoid Antoine's gaze, but I couldn't. He was so honest, so caring, and I hated lying to him. But what was I supposed to tell him?

"I'm sorry I wasn't there. I...I had a few things I needed to take care of, and I thought I would be back in time, but it took longer than I expected."

Antoine brushed his fingers up and down my arms, his touch sending tingles throughout my entire body. "It is not safe for you to be out alone, especially after what just happened to Robert Maxwell." Antoine cupped my face in his hands, then leaned down and kissed me tenderly on the lips. "I can't let anything happen to you. I won't."

I let my body relax into the safety of his kiss, my tense muscles softening at his touch.

And as he pressed his lips a little harder into mine, his hands roaming down to the curves of my waist, I felt the fear, the exhaustion, and the confusion that had been consuming me these past few days melt away. And in their place came an intense desire, an overwhelming urge to be with Antoine again, to feel his body against mine. Because in his arms, I felt safe. In his arms, I could forget about my worries for the future.

I pulled my lips from his and whispered in his ear, "Make love to me."

Antoine raised an eyebrow, and normally I would've raised an eyebrow at me too. In my life as Claudia, I would've never dreamed of making love to someone inside an office with people milling around just outside the door, especially when smack in the middle of figuring out some insane past-life murder crisis.

But I felt different now. I wasn't *only* Claudia anymore. I was bolder, more daring, more confident—more like *Ruby*.

"Right now," I breathed into his ear before brushing my lips across his flushed cheek and squeezing his shoulders in my palms.

I didn't have to ask twice.

Antoine pulled me closer to him as he ran his lips down my neck and sent his hands roaming up under my shirt. Then he sat me down on the desk in front of him, and while I slipped off his white coat and unbuttoned his red collared shirt, I wrapped my legs around his body and felt his firm groin press into me. He slipped my sweater over my head then cupped my breasts in his strong hands before unhooking my bra and pushing his heaving body against my bare chest.

I reached down and unhooked his belt, wanting him, needing him inside of me. His pants fell to his ankles, followed by his underwear, as I admired his lean, firm body, the cuts of muscle in his stomach and arms so defined, so unbearably sexy I could hardly stand it.

As a low moan escaped from his lips, he pulled my pants and lacy pink-and-white panties off in one quick swoop, squared his face in front of mine, and with eyes full of lust, need, and love, he wrapped his arms around my bare waist, then thrust deep inside of me. I gripped the side of the desk as Antoine pushed deeper and deeper into me, both his body and his passion so strong, I could hardly take in another breath.

He ran his tongue down my neck and over the tops of my breasts before gently grazing my nipples, his hands making their way to my inner thighs, and finally massaging me while he continued to thrust farther inside. My entire body pulsated with pleasure as I grabbed on to his shoulders and tipped my head back, letting him take me, letting this new love that somehow felt timeless and more pure than anything I'd ever felt before engulf me and erase all of my doubts or worries about what might happen when this perfect moment was over.

Because in that moment, the future didn't exist. There was only me and Antoine, and all I needed in this world, in this life, was his love.

He laid me down on the desk, his lean body fitting perfectly on top of mine, and sent neat stacks of papers and yellow file folders flying to the ground. I let out a moan of pure ecstasy as I wrapped my legs around Antoine's back and felt him press into me once more. He went so deep this time, I could barely see straight. Then, as his hips rocked with mine, our bodies shaking the desk, making it pound into the floor, he sped up and I felt him growing harder and firmer inside of me.

His hand cupped my breast, his fingers running back and forth over my sensitive nipple as his other hand pushed down in between my thighs and caressed that even more sensitive area. He continued to press into me in firm, even strokes that became harder and faster while his lips roamed over my neck, breasts, and shoulders until finally I couldn't take it anymore. I felt the desire rising in my chest and shooting down in between my thighs before I let out a muffled cry, an explosion setting off inside of me.

Antoine wasn't far behind. He lifted his face to mine and kissed me on the lips as his body tensed up, then released while he throbbed and pulsated inside of me, his ultimate pleasure, his climax reached.

He collapsed on top of me, his breath rough and heavy in my ear, our naked bodies still connected in the most perfect way. And in that moment, as I listened to Antoine's heart beating, his chest pulsing into mine, I knew without a doubt that I loved this man. Nothing about these last few days had made as much sense as me being here with Antoine.

He propped himself up on his elbows and gazed down at me with a sweet, inquisitive look in his eyes. "Do you believe in fate, Ruby?"

Fate. There was that infamous word again. "I…I'm not sure. I'm beginning to think I do. What about you?"

"I never believed in fate before. I did not believe in much of anything after I lost my parents. But now, even though I have lost Gisèle, I am realizing that this strange course of events has led me to you. And, Ruby, I do not know what has gotten into me, but I feel as if I've known you forever. I feel like I was meant to be with you, to spend my life with you. I've never felt this way before. Not even close. And if it is fate that has brought me to you, then yes, I believe in it."

Antoine's words momentarily erased all of the angst I'd been carrying around since I'd arrived in this life, and especially since this morning's grueling string of events. I stared deep into his smoky-gray eyes, never wanting to leave his side, never wanting to have another moment without his face in front of mine, his warm hands on my skin.

"I've never felt this way either, Antoine. And I can't explain it, but I know it's right. In fact, it's the only thing in this life that feels right to me."

Antoine leaned down, kissing me softly on the lips. "I'm falling in love with you, Ruby. I'm falling head over heels in love with you."

I smiled, feeling as though nothing in the world could be more perfect, more fulfilling than this feeling. "I love you too, Antoine."

He brushed a strand of hair off my cheek and smiled. "Fate brought us together. And I won't let anything take you from me. I promise."

As I melted into the sincerity of his words, I refused to acknowledge the voice in the back of my head reminding me that my time here was limited. And I rejected the doubt that had lodged itself in my chest like an ax in a tree trunk.

The love I felt for Antoine was an entity all unto its own—something I'd never known I was capable of feeling. So even with the fear that at any moment I could be ripped away from him and sent back to my future life, I had to trust that a love this strong could survive anything.

Because no matter what awaited me, I knew I wasn't willing to lose Antoine.

But then, I wasn't willing to lose my baby either.

If only I could have them both.

TWENTY-NINE

Once we'd dressed and caught our breath, we sat together at the desk, trying to piece together the confusing events of the past few days.

"Let's start with the most recent incident. How did you find out about Robert Maxwell's murder?" Antoine asked.

"Detective Duval came to my apartment to question me. I was the last one seen with Robert last night outside the club, so now I'm a suspect. But they found Robert's body on the quai of the Seine early this morning, with a bullet wound to his chest."

"Which means someone killed him late last night, while you were with me," Antoine said.

"Yes, and I'm afraid that whoever did it also may have had something to do with François's murder...and possibly with Gisèle's. And they're trying to frame me for all three."

Suddenly I remembered the note I'd received when I'd first arrived here. The one telling me not to talk to *A*. "There's something else I forgot to show you." I riffled through my purse to find the square piece of paper I'd stuffed inside earlier.

"Ruby, did you tell the detective that you were with me last night? That you have an alibi?"

I stopped my search for a moment to face Antoine. "Yes, I did. I'm sure they'll want to question you about it later today. But they'll probably be suspicious of anything you say too—" I stopped talking because the color had drained from Antoine's face.

"Antoine, what is it?"

He shook his head, forced himself to take in a breath. "It's...it's nothing, Ruby. What were you going to show me?"

I found the small, creepy note inside my purse and handed it to Antoine. "After I fell the other morning, I came back up to my apartment to lie down. This was underneath my pillow. I'm not sure what it means or who it's from, but I'm assuming whoever it was didn't want me talking to you."

I wished I could tell Antoine that the handwriting on this note matched the handwriting from the scary past-life journal entry I'd found earlier today, but this would have to do for now.

"I was thinking maybe you could pass this along to the private investigator you're working—" I started, but Antoine's startled expression stopped me cold.

"You said this was underneath your pillow? Are you certain?" Antoine said, his intense gaze not leaving the loopy handwriting on the page.

"Yes, I'm certain. Do you know who wrote it? Based on everything that's happened so far, and by the initials on the note, I think it could be from Thomas, but it's hard to make them out."

Antoine rubbed his forehead, muttering something incomprehensible under his breath.

"What is it, Antoine? What's going on?"

He stood from the desk, tucking the note into his pocket. Then he leaned down and grabbed my shoulders, his expression deadpanning into mine. "Lock the door behind me, and promise me you will not leave this room, Ruby. You are not safe anywhere else."

"Of course, but where are you going? Tell me what's going on."

Antoine kissed me on the forehead then headed toward the door. "I'll explain everything soon. But there isn't time right now. You must promise me you won't leave, Ruby. Promise me."

"I promise," I said breathlessly.

And with a whip of the door, he was gone, leaving me alone in his office wondering what he'd seen in that note that had spooked him so badly.

The clock ticking above Antoine's desk told me he'd only been gone for five minutes, but it felt like an eternity. What was going on? What wasn't he telling me?

With shaky legs, I stood from my seat at the desk and began cleaning up all of the papers we'd knocked to the floor just moments earlier. I couldn't just sit here and wait patiently. Not with the way he'd run out of here like a bat out of hell after he'd seen that note. And why had he acted strangely about me telling the police he'd been with me the night before?

Bending down to gather the last stack of files from the floor, I was just about to stand up when something caught my eye. Half of a black-and-white photograph stuck out of Antoine's top drawer, its corner bent and smashed into the desk. I stole a quick glance at the door, but with no sign of Antoine, curiosity overpowered my nerves.

After retrieving the old picture from the drawer, I tilted it toward the lamp to get a better look.

But the scene staring back at me made my stomach curl.

Antoine stood at the altar of a church, wearing a spiffy tux and a gleam in his eye. His arm was wrapped tightly around a petite woman whose long black hair cascaded in waves down the back of her sparkling white gown.

A bride. A wedding.

Oh, God.

Antoine is married.

I blinked away the tears that sprang to my eyes without warning, but gasped when I noticed something else in the photograph. Something that made this inconceivable situation even worse than it already was.

Amid the woman's Medusa-like black locks, strings of diamonds dangled from her ears.

I closed my eyes and felt myself immediately being transported back to the night I'd found Gisèle.

I could see her now. The silhouette of the woman outside the club. That long, dangling diamond that sparkled underneath the dim light of the streetlamp.

Except she wasn't a silhouette any longer.

It was her. The same woman in the photo.

Antoine's wife.

In a frantic haze, I riffled through the rest of Antoine's desk drawer, telling myself that this couldn't be true. Antoine couldn't really be married. He'd taken me to his apartment, and there'd been no sign of another woman, no sign of a *wife*. Surely he would have an explanation for the photograph. But what could possibly explain this woman's presence at the club the night of Gisèle's death? And her earring at the scene of François's murder?

When my search yielded a silver wedding band hiding in the back of the drawer, I pounded my fists on the desk in frustration.

How could he have done this to me? Were the two of them in on this together? Framing me for all of these murders? What in the hell was going on? How could I have been so stupid to fall for him?

Gathering every ounce of courage I had left in me, I placed the ring on the desk where Antoine would see it when he returned, tucked the sickening photograph of him and his wife into my purse, and ran out of his office.

I didn't care that I'd promised him I wouldn't leave.

After all, *his* promises clearly hadn't meant a thing.

+≈•≈+

Rain poured from the sky in sheets as I exited the hospital, my entire world turned upside down once again. The fat raindrops running down my face were the only tears I could cry at the moment.

Antoine, the only person who'd made me feel safe in this god-forsaken life, had betrayed me. My baby was disappearing by the minute. I was wanted for three murders. And Titine was passed out in a hospital bed.

My numb legs carried me down the sidewalk, toward the wet, busy Parisian street. Where would I go? Who could help me now?

JULIETTE SOBANET

When the rain had sufficiently soaked through my clothes and I began to shiver so hard I could barely feel my hands, I spotted a black taxicab coming to a stop just ahead. Running to catch up with it, I yanked open the door and slid into the backseat, my wet clothes squeaking against the cool leather.

"To the police station, please," I called to the driver as I rested my throbbing head against the window. I had no other choice but to bring the wedding photograph to Detective Duval. Show him the earrings in the picture and tell him about the note and how Antoine had bolted from his office the minute he'd seen it.

Besides, the police station was the *only* place I would be safe at this point.

A grunt sounded from the taxi driver as he sped through a stop sign and left the hospital in a rainy haze behind us. He weaved in and out of traffic, a wild runaway train with no brakes. Why was he going so fast?

My stomach lurched from the rapid stops and starts, the erratic turns and jerks we made through the narrow city streets.

I reached forward and wrapped my hands around the front seat so I could lean closer to the driver and ask him to slow down, but I stopped when a solid mass brushed against my fingertips.

It felt like clothing, and when I reached my hands around just a little bit farther, tilting my head to the side to see what exactly my hands were touching, I had to stifle my scream.

A thin woman sat slumped over in the passenger seat, her head and neck completely curled down over her chest, her body still warm but motionless.

It was when I noticed her icy profile and her high cheekbones that the whimper escaped my lips.

It was Véronique.

I yanked my trembling hands back as the car made a sharp turn into a tiny alley. The driver slammed on the brakes and flipped his face around to give me a full view.

240

When his wicked black gaze met mine, the full-blown panic set in and the air refused to move in and out of my constricted lungs.

Underneath the black top hat he was wearing, the man's slick black hair protruded down toward his black shirt collar, and his jet-black eyes, void of kindness or humanity, bored into me. Then his top lip, adorned with a jagged scar, curled up into a snarl.

The man driving the car looked like the man who'd followed me to François's apartment.

It was Thomas. Thomas Riley was driving this car.

And he'd already killed Véronique.

As this realization set in, my entire body began to shake from the inside out. But when I tried to move, to scream, to reach for the car handle, my body wouldn't budge, my voice wouldn't come out. It was exactly like the nightmares I'd had as a little girl, after I'd witnessed my father's murder, when the man in the black mask had been chasing me, and every time I screamed, no sound would come out. Here, in the car, I was just like that little girl—glued to the seat and paralyzed with pure terror.

Thomas didn't move or speak either as he fixed his gaze on me, his jaw locked, his silence more powerful than any words he could possibly say.

If I made one move to get out of this car, he would stop me.

He would kill me.

But as I thought of my future baby, I knew I couldn't let that happen. I had to get out of here. I had to at least try.

Just as I reached for the handle, the car door flew open from the outside. I squinted as a blast of freezing rain blew into my eyes, but when I blinked them open to see who had opened the door, a cool, hard object smacked me upside the head. I winced as my body was shoved farther into the car, and then another blow came hard and fast, this time to the other side of my face.

I vaguely heard the slamming of a car door and felt us moving again as I fluttered my eyes open and closed, willing myself to stay conscious, to fight back.

"Thomas," I managed to whisper. "Please, no. No, Thomas, no."

But the pounding in my skull kept my eyes closed, and my body remained limp on the seat.

And just before I passed out completely, a woman's voice laced through the air and into my consciousness.

Her tone was sinister, evil, making my blood curl.

"You stupid bitch," she growled. "You're even dumber than I thought."

And with that, she dealt me one final blow to the head, and I was out cold.

THIRTY

The woman's threatening voice woke me from my sleep, her broken words weaving in and out of my consciousness.

Antoine. The police. Dump her body.

What was going on?

My arms were twisted behind my back, my wrists bound together, my eyes plastered shut. A warm drop of liquid oozed down the side of my face and over a patch of raw skin. I was too dazed to let out a reaction to the burning I felt as the wound absorbed the wetness.

She kept talking. Barking orders.

How did I know that voice—that soulless, lifeless voice?

"Park behind the building and don't leave until you see that we've gotten in without any problems."

I struggled to drag my eyes open but a fierce pain shot through my jaw, making me wince. I tried to suck in a breath, but the throbbing intensified, ruthless and unrelenting, preventing all air from moving in or out, stopping my eyes from opening to see what in the hell was going on.

"Perfect timing," the woman whispered in my ear as she slipped something onto the bridge of my nose and over my ears. Then I felt a cold, firm object press into the side of my stomach as the car jerked to the side.

"Claudia," she sang into my ear. "Oh, Claudia. It's time to wake up."

I forced my eyelids open as her menacing tone rang in my ears, the pain in my head so strong I felt like I might throw up.

How did she know my name? How did she know I was Claudia?

When my eyes finally batted open, the scene before me was a blurry, dark haze.

Wondering why it seemed as if a black screen had been pulled over my eyes, I felt the rigid object push farther into my side.

"When the car stops, you're going to come with me. And you won't say a word to anyone. If you do, you're dead. Understand?"

"Who...who are you?" I sputtered as my vision settled and I made out the figure of a woman through the dark shades.

She let out a deep, sinister laugh. "We'll have *plenty* of time to get to know each other, but for now, you'll keep your mouth shut and come with me." She dug her fingernails into my arm and continued to press the cool, cylinder-shaped object into my side, and despite the dizziness, the nausea, and the throbbing, my understanding of what was going on finally began to kick in.

It was a gun.

This woman, whose voice I recognized but couldn't quite place, was holding a gun to my side.

And it was then that I remembered what had happened before I'd passed out.

Thomas.

Thomas had been driving the car. He'd killed Véronique, and then he'd taken me. And just as I had tried to escape, this woman had jumped into the car and bludgeoned me over the head.

God only knew how much time had passed since I'd been out or where they were taking me.

Was Thomas still in the car? And *who* was this woman?

I lifted my chin off my chest and tried to look toward the front seat to see Thomas, but all I could make out were dim, shifting shadows. The rain still poured down outside, puddles spraying the side of the car.

"Alexandre, you're clear on the plan?" she barked to the front.

Alexandre?

A grunt traveled back from the front seat. Then a voice. "You're on your own after this. Don't forget to clean up your mess, and don't come crying to me when you get caught." As his bitter tone traveled through my ears, chills of terror weaved down my spine.

That *wasn't* the same voice I'd heard on the bridge or backstage before the show.

She let out a low, grumbling laugh. "I thought you knew me better than that, Alexandre. As long as *you* don't fuck up, I won't get caught. Pick up the pace, will you? We don't have much time before Antoine will come looking for his latest slut."

She spat the word *slut* into my face, her saliva landing right inside the slice on my cheek.

She knew Antoine.

Was she...could she be the woman from the photograph? Antoine's bride? The one with a crazy look in her eye and a pair of dangly diamond earrings?

And I'd been sure the man driving the car was Thomas. But his voice was different. And she'd clearly called him Alexandre.

Since I couldn't see the driver's face anymore, the front seat a blurry dark shadow blocking his true identity and mocking me in the process, I closed my eyes and called to memory the face that had glared at me earlier in the car, before Megabitch had taken over.

I easily recalled his coal-black eyes, his slick black hair underneath the black top hat, and his fixed, defined jawline. They were the exact same features of the man who'd followed me to François's apartment only yesterday, the man who, *at the time*, I'd been sure was Thomas.

But when I remembered the way the driver had snarled at me in the car earlier, like a dog that would bite my head off if I so much as made a sound, something struck me. He had a scar—a crooked, long scar that jutted out above his lip.

And in the photo I'd found of me and Thomas—the photo I'd stared at for close to an hour before bed that night, memorizing every line, every crevice of his face—I *hadn't* seen a scar. Despite the way his possessive gaze had chilled me to the bone, I remembered thinking that Thomas's face was flawless, even strangely handsome in its iciness. But in that photo, Thomas definitely did not have a scar.

Which meant that while the man sitting in front of me held a striking resemblance to Thomas, he wasn't Thomas after all. He was someone called Alexandre, and just like me, I sensed that he was at the mercy of this merciless woman.

My eyes shot open once more as the car came to an abrupt halt and the woman tightened her death grip on my arm. I tensed my muscles, refusing to move.

But with my head pounding so hard it was making me dizzy, my injured jaw screaming in pain, and my blurry vision threatening to suck me into a black tunnel, my body finally gave in to her violent pulls and tugs.

"Get out of the car," she growled, "and come with me."

Jabbing the gun into my ribs, she wrapped her other arm around my waist and hoisted me up and out of the car. I blinked my eyes as the rain showered down on us, making it even harder for me to see through what I now realized were a large pair of sunglasses.

"Where are you taking me?" I cried out in panic. "Are you…are you Antoine's wife?"

I wriggled my hands behind my back, the rope that bound them together digging into the skin on my bony wrists.

"Don't say another fucking word," she hissed over the sound of the pouring rain as she yanked me forward.

I walked with her, my heels sliding on the wet sidewalk, my heart now pounding louder than the pain throbbing through my face and head.

This was out of control. Where was she taking me? Someone had to help me. Someone would see us. Someone would see her shoving a gun into my side, my hands tied behind my back. But as the wind whipped around us, blowing sheets of rain into the wounds on my face and completely obstructing my vision, I felt my long peacoat draped around me, which meant that even if anyone saw us through this wicked storm, they wouldn't see my hands tied behind my back, nor the gun at my side.

I couldn't count on anyone else to help me. I had to get out of this on my own. I had to escape.

But suddenly the rain stopped pelting me and what little light there'd been disappeared.

"I...I can't see," I started, but before I could finish my sentence, her arm tightened around my waist and she shoved the gun deeper into my side.

"That's the point, you stupid bitch. Shut up and keep walking."

I put one foot in front of the other, trying to keep up with her rapid pace as I tried to figure out why her threatening voice sounded so familiar. But after walking down some sort of long hallway, I stepped onto something soft and cushy and the scent of fresh flowers drifted past my nose, causing my thoughts to halt. Light returned to my vision, and as I peeked upward, I could see the outline of a chandelier. I blinked my eyes as it shimmered above me, and as my heels dug into the soft carpet, I felt that unmistakable jolt of déjà-vu.

The flowery scent, the chandeliers, the soft carpet, her hand digging into my waist.

I'd smelled, seen, felt all of this before.

Her hand left my waist while the gun remained firmly pointed into my side, and as I heard a key turning in a lock, another flash of déjà-vu rattled me.

"Move," the woman barked in my ear as she shoved the sunglasses back up my face and pushed me forward into the apartment, snapping me from the memory dying to break through.

She slammed me against the wall and held me there as she let out a disturbing cackle and bolted the door behind her.

Her gun traced my body and finally landed on my temple.

The dizziness I'd felt from the blows she'd dealt me earlier vanished. The haze lifted. Blood coursed through my veins at warp speed as my senses jolted into overdrive.

Madame Bouchard had said I would know when the moment had arrived...the moment where I would have the opportunity to change my entire ill-fated life course.

It was here. My moment.

But as the woman who held a gun to my head ripped the sunglasses from my face and finally graced me with the chance to gaze into her silvery-black eyes, I realized that the one thing I did *not* know was how I would stop *Antoine's wife* from killing me.

THIRTY-ONE

"Claudia," she sang in a low, eerie tone as her cool breath grazed over my face, leaving goose bumps in its wake. "You're much more appealing to the eye as Ruby. It's a shame you won't get to enjoy this body much longer...or *any* body, for that matter." She laughed again, her throaty, deranged cackle making the knot in my stomach spread upward and lodge firmly in my chest.

That wild, unhinged look in her eyes made me remember her, but it wasn't just from the wedding photograph. It was from my life as Claudia. But just as I felt the memory flittering through my brain, she flipped me around, pushed me into the living room, and shoved me onto the floor, where my head banged up against the wall.

Pain seared through my face, my wrists, my arms, and my head. A pair of black leather boots paced back and forth in front of me, their thin heels piercing the hardwood floor with each purposeful step, the sound like a hammer to my already throbbing temples.

The evil woman's tangled, jet-black hair shot all the way down her back while heavy raindrops rolled off the uneven ends, dripping down her slick, black trench coat. Adorning her pale, bony neck was a bloodred scarf that had been matched to perfection with the color of her lipstick, and that contrasted with her snow-white complexion. As she flashed her silvery-black eyes at me once more, she looked like a vampire, hungry and ready to strike.

"Tell me your name." My weak, hoarse voice struggled its way out, and I immediately wished I'd sounded stronger, more daring and more confident.

She ignored my question and continued pacing, her steps becoming heavier, angrier as she carelessly waved the gun around like a child would a sparkler on the Fourth of July.

But as I took in that head of Medusa hair, those compassionless eyes, those crimson lips, and those long, stringy legs, the memory I had of her came soaring into my brain.

Those features belonged to someone I'd *definitely* seen before in my life as Claudia.

It was uncanny. They looked almost identical.

And as I blinked my eyes to make sure I wasn't imagining the similarities, Madame Bouchard's words rushed back to me.

When an impure soul is reincarnated, they do not change much. There is little to no growth; usually, there is negative growth. Their appearance may be similar, and they will repeat the same ill-motivated actions in each subsequent life, thereby interfering with and ruining the pure intentions and actions of a good soul, like you.

I combed my eyes up and down her body once more, noticing her wispy, thin figure and her ice-cold features—the same chilly features she'd flaunted on the cover of *People* magazine, with her fiancé, *Édouard*.

It was Solange. Solange Raspail.

She paced before me in an even more hauntingly beautiful body than the one she would inhabit in the future, but her demeanor was colder now, more threatening.

Every time I'd looked at the cover of the *People* magazine that had traveled back in time with me, I'd known in my gut that something was off about that woman. And now, as I looked her dead in the eye, I knew I'd been right all along. I should've listened to my instincts. It was just that at the time, I'd had no idea how accurate they could be.

"Solange," I called out, my voice steady and firm, holding no trace of the fear and weakness I'd demonstrated earlier.

A disturbing grin spread across her thin, red lips as she stopped pacing and turned to face me. She positioned one manicured hand on her hip, the other still waving the gun around like a toy.

"*Now* we're getting somewhere," she said, a hint of hysteria peeking out behind her cool façade.

She raised one perfectly arched eyebrow as she bore down on me with her menacing glare. "*You*," she spat. "I knew you were in love with him the minute I saw you gazing up at him with those big, pathetic puppy-dog eyes at the dance studio." She took a step closer to me, pointing the barrel of the gun right at my face, her eyes suddenly wide and frantic.

"But who are you? You're *nobody*. I told myself I was crazy to think Édouard would have eyes for you. To think that my attractive, accomplished fiancé would ever find someone as *pathetic* as you beautiful. You were just his dance partner, Claudia, and you'll never be anything more."

I suppressed the panic that coursed through my body, forced myself to forget about the pain surging through my head, and looked her straight in the eye. "Solange, there was never anything going on between me and Édouard. You're his fiancée. *You* are the one he loves." But as the words exited my mouth, I thought of the way Édouard had looked at me in the dance studio, just a few nights ago. I remembered the way his hand had rested on my waist, so comfortable, like it belonged there. And every time we'd danced together, something magical happened. And Édouard had felt it too, I was sure of it.

"*I know* I'm the one he loves, you stupid bitch. You think I don't know that? He just needed a little reminder, that's all. Which is why I told the press we were engaged. I knew it would make him come back to me, make him remember how perfect we were together."

Suddenly I remembered how angry Édouard had become when he'd seen the *People* magazine in the dance studio that night. And

I could still see him frantically trying to tell me something as I'd slipped away.

He was trying to tell me that it wasn't true. He wasn't engaged to Solange. He never had been.

Solange resumed her pacing. "I followed him to the studio that night; he was being so stubborn. I just needed to make him understand that I was the one for him. That *I* was the one he was meant to spend his life with." Her eyes darted throughout the apartment, the sound of her heels beating against the hardwood floors making me jump with each step. "But then he told me to leave before he rushed into that dance studio, and when I followed him in, I saw you, Claudia. I saw you dancing with him. And the way he touched you…the way he was looking at you…" She turned to me once more, aiming the gun straight at my head. "I won't let you take him from me. I won't."

"Solange, wait, please. I'm not taking Édouard from you. You don't have to do this. He wouldn't want you to do this."

She narrowed her eyes at me and tightened her grip on the gun.

"You still don't get it do you? Oh, poor Claudia. You've been so confused since you arrived here. You don't think I'd come all this way and kill you just because of the way you looked at Édouard, do you? I mean, surely I'm not that desperate."

Before I could tell her that I'd already figured out who she was in *this* life too—*Antoine's wife*—a startling ring pierced through the air.

She flipped around and glared down the hallway. It was a telephone.

"Fucking Antoine," she murmured under her breath as she tore through the living room and headed down the hallway.

Had Antoine really been working with this evil woman the whole time to frame me for all of these murders?

But what about his beloved sister, Gisèle? Surely he couldn't have had anything to do with her death.

What in the hell was going on?

I knew there was something I was missing—something *huge*—but I didn't have time to figure it out because I only had a few seconds before she would fly back into this room and point that gun at my head again. I struggled to my feet and scoured the room for something sharp that I could use to cut the rope off my wrists. Spotting a glass coffee table, I ran over, crouched down and rubbed the rope against the corner as rapidly as I could manage.

The shrill ringing continued while Solange's boots thumped down the hallway on a tile floor, and she hurled incoherent words through the air. I pulled my wrists as hard as I could to loosen the rope while I continued scraping it along the sharp edge of the coffee table, hoping, praying, I could free my hands and get the hell out of this apartment before this woman did what she'd come back to this lifetime to do.

The phone stopped ringing, and with it, my heart ceased its beating as I waited for the sound of Solange's boots to come roaring back down the hall. But as the rope loosened just the slightest bit, my wrists screaming in pain to be released, the phone rang again, and this time brought with it the sound of cupboards slamming then glass breaking.

"This is *my* fucking house," she screamed from down the hall-way, more dishes and more glass clattering to the floor.

I rubbed the rope at an inhuman speed, pulling and pushing as hard as I could to get out of my binding. I had to get out of here. This woman was beyond insane. Madame Bouchard had been right—Solange was an evil soul, and I had to escape. I couldn't let her take me down again.

The rope loosened another millimeter or two, but then the shattering came to a halt. My heart slammed into my chest, sweat dripping down my neck as Solange's boots pounded back down the hall.

"Did you hear me, you dumb slut? This is *my fucking house. Mine!*" She charged into the room, her wet hair plastered around her face while fiery red blotches splashed onto her cheeks and her eyes raged with a fury I hadn't yet seen.

I slumped to the ground next to the coffee table, still pulling at my wrists, determined to free my hands, determined to stop this crazy woman from hurting me.

She didn't seem to notice my new location or my struggle to break the rope as she marched in circles around the living room, knocking over vases, pulling framed pictures off the walls and throwing them to the ground. "This is my house!" she screamed again. "And *you*, you little dancing slut, you think you're going to get to live here."

Solange ripped a framed photograph off the coffee table and marched it over to me. It was a photograph of Antoine and Gisèle. His smile was so bright and happy, his eyes shining and carefree as he hugged her close.

Antoine would never have hurt his sister. And he wouldn't have harmed me either, not in a million years.

But this woman—the woman he'd married—*she* would've. I only wished he'd told me about his raging bitch of a wife before I'd found myself tied up at her mercy.

"You look so confused, Ruby," she spat. "So lost. Like you have no idea that you're sleeping with Antoine—my *husband*. Like you have no idea that you stormed back to this life, seduced him just like you did the first time around, and made him think he's in love with you. Well, he's not! He's mine. This house is mine. Antoine is mine. And his money is mine. You're stealing him away from me just like you're going to try to steal Édouard in the future. And I won't let it happen!" She hurled the framed photo across the room, where it smacked against the wall, its glass shattering all over the sparkly wood floors.

As my brain continued to piece together this deranged woman's story, my gaze traveled from the broken frame and stopped on another object carelessly strewn on the apartment floor.

It was the magical purple journal, resting next to my purse, which was crumpled on the ground only about five feet away from me. Solange must've carried my purse in with her when she'd forced me into the apartment.

Eyeing the journal, I remembered the last entry and the chilling words that I hadn't truly understood until this moment.

> *That little bitch won't steal what's mine this time around, and she won't steal it from me in the future either.*
> *I'll be sure of it.*

It seemed impossible, but as I watched the woman who was raging around the house before me, I knew that in this insane past-life experience, the impossible wasn't only possible, it was *real*.

I had to repeat it over and over in my head though before I truly believed it.

Solange Raspail, Édouard's fiancée from the year 2012, was *Antoine's wife* in her past life.

Unbelievable.

When I'd passed out in Édouard's arms and had traveled back in time to my past life as Ruby, Solange's evil soul had been sucked back in time to *her* past life as well.

But as Madame Bouchard had said, this wasn't supposed to have happened. *Solange* was not supposed to have been sent back. And as this vengeful, maniac wife of the man I was in love with destroyed what I now realized was Antoine's apartment while she waved her gun through the air, I understood why.

"Do you get it now? Are the pieces coming together in that dim-witted dancer brain of yours?" she spat.

"You don't even love Antoine," I said, ignoring my more rational side, which was telling me to keep my mouth shut and not provoke her any further.

Solange's hands trembled as she lifted the gun once more and walked slowly and deliberately in my direction. "Of course I love him. Why else do you think I'd be protecting him from you?"

"If you really loved him, then why did you kill his only sister?" I was assuming this insane woman had been the culprit behind *all* of the murders that had gone down in the past week, but I wanted to be sure.

"You want to know why I killed Gisèle, that dirty whore of a sister?" She let out a loud, dramatic sigh as she advanced toward me, knelt down, and pushed the cool barrel of the gun straight into my cheek. "Ruby, Ruby, Ruby. Claudia, Claudia, Claudia." The edgy, hysterical sound of her voice was like nails down a chalkboard. I pulled at my wrists, but the rope was still too tight. I couldn't free them.

She leaned into my face, her breath chilly despite the heat that emanated from her body. "Don't you remember how this all played out the first time around? It was perfect. Oh so perfect. And now, I have the *pleasure* of making it all happen again."

This was it. This crazy murderer was going to shoot me right here and now, and with my hands bound together and my body weakened from the struggle, there was nothing I could do. If I bit her, if I kicked, if I screamed, she would shoot me.

There was no way I could stop this horrific event from taking place again.

I'd been sent back to stop this event, to stop my own murder, and because I'd stepped into that damn car without being absolutely sure that the man in the driver's seat was a real taxi driver, I was about to fail.

And failing in this instance meant my own death.

Just as a tear escaped out of the corner of my eye, I jumped at the sound of footsteps in the hallway.

Solange wasn't startled, though. She smiled that sickening, evil smile before lifting the gun to my temple and standing up in front of me. "Right. On. Time."

I whipped my head up and felt relief flood course through my veins as Antoine took a step toward us, his smoky-gray eyes not wavering for a second as he reached his hand out to Solange.

Thank God this woman had been dumb enough to take me to what was obviously their *former* apartment.

I'd never been so happy to see anyone in my entire life…or *lives*.

"Solange," he said without even a hint of panic in his tone. "Give me the gun."

I wondered how Antoine knew her name would be Solange in the future, but then I remembered what Madame Bouchard had said about evil souls not changing much when they're reincarnated. Solange must've stayed so similar—so *corrupt*—that she'd even kept the *same name* from one life to the next.

Solange tilted her head back and laughed so hard that tears sprang from her eyes. "Let me guess. You want to make amends now. Now that I have a gun to Ruby's head, you want to make it all better. Just to save the girl who's fucking you senseless and making you think you love her. Well, it won't work, Antoine. It didn't work the first time around, and it won't work this time either."

Antoine didn't do as great a job hiding the confusion that passed through his eyes as he looked from Solange to me and back to Solange. "What do you mean, *the first time around*?"

Solange peeked down at me and winked. "He doesn't know about our little secret, Claudia. I don't think I should keep this juicy story to myself, though. It's just too good not to share." Keeping the gun at my temple, she turned back to Antoine.

"You see, the *first time* we were married, I was sick of you hanging around that sleazy club and watching out for your trashy little sister. I mean, you're a renowned surgeon, for God's sake! Spending your nights in that dungeon of a club. And you *know* the kind of family I come from, and there you are, supporting that slutty sister of yours and making my family name look bad. Making *me* look bad. Plus, I knew it was only a matter of time before one of those hookers got their paws on you and made you cheat on me.

"So, after you made the biggest mistake of your life and tried to divorce me, I used little miss Véronique to help me rid the earth of your low-class sister. But just as I was about to leave her bleeding body behind, I heard your precious Ruby here fucking that sleaze-bag politician François Lefevre in the office next door. And when she walked him out of the club, her necklace fell to the floor." Solange peered down at me and snickered. "Things must've been getting a little rough in there, hmm?"

She leveled her gaze back at Antoine and continued on her diatribe. "It couldn't have been a more perfect setup if I'd planned it myself. I snatched up the necklace and planted it underneath Gisèle's body. The police would find the necklace, trace it back to Ruby, throw her in prison for the rest of her life, and you, *Antoine*, you would come crawling right back to me.

"But then those fucking imbecile police thought the necklace belonged to Gisèle and gave it to you, leading you to Miss Star of the Show here. Then, Véronique, God rest her soul, was kind enough to inform me that Ruby, the new, undeserving star, was making a move on *my* husband."

"You killed Véronique too?" Antoine said, taking a step toward Solange.

She lowered her eyes to me once more, expelling daggers with her gaze. "Véronique was an efficient partner in crime, but she knew entirely too much, didn't she, Claudia? After I arrived here from the future and got my bearings on what the hell was going on, Véronique came to me and told me that the star of the show had fallen, that she had suddenly lost her memory, and that she was claiming to be someone named Claudia. That's when it all clicked for me. That's when I knew what I was sent back here to do. I tried to be nice to you, Claudia, by warning you with those gorgeous roses and those sweet notes, but you poor, lost girl. You didn't get it. You clearly didn't adjust to this whole past-life adventure as well as I did."

"*You* were responsible for Gisèle's death," Antoine cut her off as a new rage fired up in his eyes. "You killed my sister, and Véronique too. And now you're talking about arriving from the future and past lives?" He stopped speaking, his grave expression making it clear that he had *much* more to say to her, but as his eyes darted back and forth from her wild face to the gun in her hands, he demanded in a calm, cool tone, "*Hand me the gun.*"

She laughed again, the sound so sickening and evil I felt my body shaking as the vibrations ravaged me.

"I didn't have my way with *only* your perfect little Gisèle, Antoine. Or with Véronique, my informant. My brother, Alexandre, and I also had a little fun with that low-life politician François, *and* that sexy film director, Robert. I framed Ruby for both of their murders, of course, but when those idiot police failed to arrest her, I remembered the beautiful way things had happened last time and realized I wouldn't need to rely on Ruby getting locked up for life. I wanted to take care of her myself. And so here we are."

So it hadn't been Thomas all along like I'd thought. That explained the first creepy note I'd received under my pillow, with the clear warning not to speak with *A.*, or Antoine, and the ambiguous signature. I'd thought it had been signed "*T. R.*" for Thomas Riley, but I'd been wrong. It had been "*S. R.*" for Solange Richard *and* Solange Raspail.

The red roses and the note addressed to Claudia also made sense now—in the most deranged way. Solange—and *only* Solange—understood who I really was because she'd made the same past-life trip as me.

And now I understood why the memory of that dangly diamond earring had stood out to me from the night of Gisèle's murder, and why I'd found the same earring at the scene of François's murder. *She'd* been responsible for all of it. Even my own grandfather's death. And it just so happened that her brother, Alexandre, held a striking resemblance to Thomas, which reminded me that we *still* didn't know if he too was hunting me down in Paris.

The determination in Solange's eyes made me forget all about Thomas. Nothing would stop this woman. We had to get that gun out of her hands before she killed us both.

"Solange, did you ever think about the fact that maybe what happened last time didn't work out so well for you in the end?" I asked, stalling for time. "And that maybe you've been given a second chance so that you can change things...for the *better*?" As Solange tapped her boot on the ground and mulled this over for a second, I flicked my gaze over to Antoine and noticed the confusion in his eyes. Seeing as how he had absolutely no clue what I was talking about with second chances, and the *last* time this had all happened, I would have been confused too. I didn't care, though. I just hoped he would go along with whatever I was saying because we had to do *something* to stop her from pulling that trigger.

"Nice try, Miss Psychologist. You can't use your dumb therapy tricks to talk me out of this, you little smart-ass. I'm going to do exactly what I did last time, but this time it will be even better. This time, the effects will last forever. You see, last time we all did this little dance I killed you and framed Antoine for your murder. Then when you were reborn as Claudia, like the dumb girl you are, you repeated the *same damn mistakes.* You'd think you'd have learned from the first time around and *not* tried to steal my man from me again. But you did. So the beauty of tonight is that *this* time, when I kill you, your soul won't ever be reborn. You, *Claudia Davis*, will never exist. This way, Édouard will be mine, and the world will be rid of you forever."

As she cocked the trigger, my entire body tensed up in anticipation of the blow. But the ear-piercing sound I was expecting never came, and instead the gun suddenly went flying from Solange's hands. She lunged for it, but Antoine was quicker as he tackled her to the floor.

She flailed and screamed beneath him as he struggled to pin her arms above her head and keep her wiry, frantic legs down at the same time.

I rose to my feet and tugged so hard that one of my wrists finally slipped out of the binding. And just as Antoine turned toward me, I spotted something shiny in Solange's hand.

It was a jagged piece of glass from the picture frame she'd thrown across the room.

Flashes of déjà-vu paralyzed me as Ruby's memories came into full view. I remembered exactly what had happened the first time around.

Solange had lied earlier. She hadn't killed me and then framed Antoine for my murder.

She'd sliced Antoine's neck with the glass, killing him, and then she'd shot me in the head.

And she would do it again if I didn't stop her.

My muscle memory jumped into action, all of the strength and force I'd built up from these two lifetimes kicking in and telling me *exactly* what I needed to do.

I lunged for my purse, dug inside, and withdrew the loaded gun I'd been carrying around all day.

I'd had a feeling I would need it.

And just as I turned around and pointed the gun toward Solange, who was still flailing and struggling beneath Antoine's strong hold, a startling realization washed over me. Staring down the barrel of the gun, I had a vivid memory of myself as Ruby pointing this exact gun at someone else before.

The struggle between and Antoine and Solange went black, and replacing them, a man now stood before me. The memory was so clear, so real, it took my breath away.

Thomas Riley stood in front of me. Thomas with his slick black hair, his wild black eyes, and his perfect, clear skin that didn't carry so much as a freckle, let alone a scar.

Something shiny was in his hand too. It was a knife, and he was pointing it straight at my chest.

"Put the gun down, Ruby." There it was. That same controlling whisper. The same one I'd heard on the bridge and in the dressing room. "Put it down or you know I'll make that scar on your back a lot deeper than it already is."

I could still feel the blood that had drained down my back and poured down my bare legs. He'd sliced me with that knife. And as I stared at his cowardly face down the barrel of this cold black pistol, I'd known that if I didn't want to die, there was no other way.

And in a split-second decision, I pulled the trigger.

The realization of what I'd done—what *Ruby* had done—came like a literal shot to the head—just not my own. It was a shot to Thomas's head, and *I'd* been the shooter.

Which meant that Thomas was *dead*.

All along, when I'd thought he'd been following me, that he'd sent me those flowers, that he was after me, he was actually dead. He hadn't followed me to François's apartment—it was Alexandre, Solange's brother—the man who bore an uncanny resemblance to Thomas.

What about the whispers, though? They'd sounded so real. Had it been Ruby's subconscious haunting me? Or could it have been Thomas as a ghost?

As my memory served up the image of Thomas lying on the floor, his black eyes staring blankly up at the ceiling while blood ran down his forehead and covered the wood floor around him, I knew it didn't matter if the voice had really been him or not. What mattered was that he was gone.

And Titine knew. She knew I'd killed Thomas.

That's why we'd fled New York and come to Paris. And that's why she hadn't wanted me to mention his name to the police. Because I was the one responsible for his murder. And since she thought I had amnesia, she must've reasoned it would be better for me not to know what I'd done, so that I could never admit to it if questioned.

A loud shout brought me back to the present. It was Antoine.

"Ruby, put the gun down and call the police!" he shouted over his shoulder.

But just as he was turning his head back around toward Solange, she wrapped one leg around his back and kicked him right in the spine with her pointy heel, causing him to lose his tight hold on her. She capitalized on his brief moment of weakness by wriggling her arm free of his grasp. And in that clenched fist of hers, she still held the shiny piece of glass—the piece of glass she would kill him with if I didn't get to her first.

As I ran toward them, pointing the gun right at her head, I knew that the first time around, I'd hesitated for a second too long, the memories of my fight with Thomas revisiting me, making me terrified to take another person's life, even if it *was* in self-defense.

Solange's arm swung toward Antoine's face. As if in slow motion, my hands moved into place, my fingers tightening around the trigger, Madame Bouchard's warning ringing loudly in my ears, as if she was right there in the room with me.

You will have to summon up the courage to take whatever action necessary *to stop this evil from occurring again.*

And this time, the courage I needed to rewrite history was there. I didn't hesitate. I didn't even blink.

Instead, I pulled the trigger.

THIRTY-TWO

Antoine held me in his arms in the cold, dreary police station, the reality of what had just happened settling in my bones.

I'd killed someone. I, Claudia Davis, had actually *killed* someone.

I'd pulled the trigger and shot Solange, then I'd watched as the blood had pooled out from the back of her head while her silvery-black eyes stared straight at me, void of life but still as haunting and deadly as when she'd had breath in her lungs.

Each time I closed my eyes, I could see her lying there in that ever-growing puddle of her own silky red blood. I could see the shard of glass that had tumbled from her hand as soon as I'd shot her. The glass she would've used to kill Antoine if I hadn't pulled the trigger.

Antoine placed his hands on my shoulders and squared his gaze on me, his expression one of true regret. "I am sorry I didn't tell you about my marriage, Ruby. It was wrong of me to keep it from you."

"Were you married a long time?" I asked.

"Only about a year and a half. Unfortunately, after only a few months, it was clear that she hadn't married me out of love."

"Why did she marry you then?"

"For Solange, it was a marriage built on money. On status. I'd always made it clear to her that I became a surgeon to help people, to save lives. I didn't do it for the money or the social status it provided. But unfortunately, a few months into the marriage, it became obvious that she'd only married me to appease her wealthy family. She didn't love me. She never had. And she was insanely jealous of my close relationship with Gisèle..." Antoine paused, his gaze traveling out the window, where the strong rain continued to drown out the sound of the howling wind. "I filed for divorce almost a year ago. But she refused to sign the papers. The past year has been a nightmare. She wasn't the woman I thought I'd married. But I never imagined she was capable of...of murder."

Antoine cleared his throat, taking my hands in his. "I avoided seeing other women this year because I wanted to wait until the divorce was final. But this past week with you, Ruby, I...I couldn't stop myself. It was a force so strong that I couldn't have stopped it if I tried. And when you showed me that note today, I immediately recognized her handwriting, her signature. I knew it was Solange. I left you in the office to alert the hospital security, and to call the police. I didn't want to alarm you without having the chance to explain first. But when I returned, you were gone, and you'd found the ring and the photo."

"If you were finished with your marriage, why did you keep your wedding ring and that photo in your desk?"

Antoine shook his head. "I didn't. I'd left the ring with Solange when we separated, and I hadn't seen that photograph since I left her. She must've been following you, Ruby. This whole time. She followed you to the hospital and planted the picture and the ring... and she had her brother wait for you outside. She knew you would run away as soon as you realized I was married."

I let out a shaky breath. That woman was out of control. And as difficult as it had been to take her life, I couldn't say I was sorry that she was gone.

"I didn't tell you about my marriage at first because I did not want to bring you into this mess, Ruby. I knew that if Solange found out about us, she would make it even more difficult for me to divorce her. But I never imagined she would take it this far."

I squeezed Antoine's hands. "It's okay, Antoine. I understand now. You couldn't have possibly known what would happen."

Antoine lifted his hand to my face, cupping my cheek in his palm. "Ruby, you are my angel. You saved me today. You saved us both."

I leaned into his strong, safe embrace as a stray tear slid down my cheek. "But what if it isn't enough? What if the police don't believe us?"

"It's all going to be okay, Ruby. Once the police check out our story, they'll let us go. It was self-defense. You don't need to be scared."

I tried to open my mouth to tell him thank you, to tell him I trusted him and that I knew this would all work out, but I could hardly breathe. I could hardly see straight. So instead of talking, I rested my head on his shoulder and closed my eyes. Then I replayed our conversations with the police over and over in my head until I felt like I would explode.

After we'd called the police, they'd taken us to the station and questioned us for hours on everything that had happened. We told them everything Solange had admitted to, including her involvement in Gisèle's, François's, and Robert's murders; her brother, Alexandre, taking Véronique's body somewhere outside the city; and I gave them the wedding photo of Antoine and Solange, explaining the diamond earring connection. I told them to cross-check this with the earring found at the scene of François's murder, as well as with the earring pictured on the female silhouette in the photograph of me and François taken the night Gisèle was murdered.

And although my face was beat to hell and the bloody rings around my wrists surely proved that I'd been tied up against my will, Detective Duval was still skeptical. After all, he'd just been after me earlier today, thinking *I* was the main suspect in Robert's murder, and when he'd arrived at the scene of the crime tonight, he found a doctor and his lover alive, the soon-to-be ex-wife shot in the head.

I'd be suspicious too, if I were him.

Antoine placed a finger on my chin and tipped my face up to meet his. "No matter what happens, I will make sure you're okay,

Ruby. You have to trust me. I won't stop until the police believe our story. I'll do whatever it takes."

I still couldn't speak. All of the energy, the fight, had been drained out of me. And all I could do now was hope that I'd made the right choice. I'd trusted my gut and I'd taken the life of an evil woman, and in doing so had stopped both my own murder *and* Antoine's.

I'd done what fate had sent me back here to do, and now I just had to hope that fate would have my back—*our* backs.

Just then, the office door was flung open. It was Detective Duval.

He sat down across the desk from us and raised an eyebrow in my direction. "You have had quite the day, Mademoiselle Kerrigan, have you not?"

I had no room left for his dry humor or his rough accent, so I just stared back at him, hoping and praying he wasn't going to arrest us.

"I am afraid that we are going to have to retain each of you tonight for further questioning," Detective Duval stated flatly. "We have not yet located Mademoiselle Véronique or Solange's brother, Alex—"

A harsh rapping on the office door interrupted Detective Duval. With a perturbed look on his face, he stood to open the door, but whoever was on the other side wasn't waiting.

"Detective," a young officer called as he barged in. "Delphine Marceau is here, the woman who found Gisèle—"

"Yes, I know who Mademoiselle Marceau is," Detective Duval snapped in French.

"She said she has information pertaining to the murders this week. She needs to speak with you right away."

Detective Duval leveled his glare at us. "Stay here."

⊹═⋅═⊹

An hour of nail biting and praying later, the detective reappeared, and trailing behind him was a terrified Delphine Marceau.

She nodded at me as she shuffled into the cramped space then hovered by the door until Detective Duval motioned for her to take a seat.

"Mademoiselle Marceau, would you like to tell Ruby and Antoine what you've just told me?" The detective leaned back in his seat, tapping a pen against the hard wooden desk, the sound like a nail drilling into my skull.

What was Delphine here to do? Point the finger at me?

Delphine's long lashes batted over her big brown doe eyes before she spoke. "I know who murdered Gisèle. I know it wasn't you, Ruby. I've known all along. And I'm so sorry I didn't say anything, but she's been threatening me to keep quiet. She told me she would kill me and my family if I went to the police. I saw her that night in the wings. I saw her running from Gisèle's dressing room right after I heard the shot." Delphine turned her gaze to Antoine. "It was Solange, your ex-wife. I'm only sorry that I didn't have the courage to say something sooner. I could've saved all of these people from getting killed." She looked over to me, the guilt in her eyes almost unbearable. "I'm sorry, Ruby, I'm so, so sorry." Then she buried her sweet, innocent face in her hands and cried.

I reached over and took her hand in mine. "Thank you for coming forward, Delphine. For telling the truth." The realization that Delphine was Édouard's mother hit me over the head once more, the *full* truth of this situation too much for me to grasp at the moment.

Detective Duval cleared his throat. "In addition to this latest confession, it seems there is more news to support your defense, Mademoiselle Kerrigan. My partner has located Alexandre's car. And just as you said, Véronique's body is inside."

"Was Alexandre in the car?" Antoine asked.

The detective shook his head. "No, but we have dispatched a team to locate him."

Relief surged through my body, all of the tension, the fear, the anticipation that had built up in my chest finally releasing. "So, does this mean…?"

Detective Duval nodded at me, the tiniest hint of kindness in his voice. "Mademoiselle Kerrigan, I apologize for making the assumptions I'd made earlier today regarding your involvement in the death of Robert Maxwell. It is clear now that you and Docteur Richard were the victims of a woman who would stop at nothing to get her revenge. Go home and get some rest. We'll notify you as soon as we have found Alexandre. In the meantime, though, you may want to see a doctor. Those bruises on your face are quite severe."

"Thank you, Detective," Antoine said for me as I sat in my chair, unable to speak or move, the relief so great it had paralyzed me. "I'll see to it that Ruby is taken care of."

Delphine blinked over at me one last time on her way out of the office. "I wanted to tell you, Ruby, you were stunning up there last night. You've never danced so well. It was almost as if…"

"What is it, Delphine?" I asked, knowing by the look in her eyes that she was onto me. She knew I wasn't the same Ruby she'd known before.

She bit her bottom lip, a tiny grin popping onto her face, instantly making me remember Édouard's handsome, charming smile. "You've changed, Ruby," she said. "And I like the new you."

Delphine left the musty police station, taking with her the dark cloud that had hovered so closely these past few days.

Antoine and I stood to leave, but the detective held his hand up to stop us.

"There is just one last thing before you go." Detective Duval cast a curious glance in my direction. "This ex-boyfriend of yours, Thomas Riley?"

I swallowed hard, wishing I had listened to Titine and kept my mouth shut about Thomas.

"We looked into it, and it appears there was a Monsieur Riley who matches the profile of the man you described. He was shot and killed in his Brooklyn apartment last year. They never found the murderer."

His words lingered in the air around us while I forced myself to keep a neutral expression.

"It also appears that this man was notorious for beating up the women he dated. With no leads on the case, the New York police have closed the investigation. Which means you have nothing to worry about, Mademoiselle Kerrigan, and you can go home."

I released the breath I'd been holding, thankful that I'd made it out of this insane nightmare alive, and with Antoine by my side. "Thank you, Detective. Thank you so much."

Antoine held me tight, kissing me on the forehead. "It's over now. Let's go home."

As Antoine took my hand and led me out of the police station, I noticed that day had turned into night and the rain had finally stopped. We passed by a smoky club in the Latin Quarter and slowed our walk as a sultry jazz tune filled the night air. And as the piano notes calmed my frayed nerves, I suddenly realized that nothing about this moment felt familiar to me.

The déjà-vu was gone.

I'd stopped my own murder from taking place, which meant that each new moment was fresh and had never been lived before.

I squeezed Antoine's hand and rested my head on his shoulder as we strolled down the narrow cobblestone sidewalk together and let out a collective sigh.

I knew then, deep down, that everything would be okay. I'd made the right decision. I'd accomplished what I'd been sent back to do and had corrected the gross error in fate that Solange's evil heart had caused.

But as we walked down a road we'd never traveled before, with only the glow of a dim Paris streetlamp to light our way, I thought of my baby, the little girl that awaited me in my life as Claudia, and one blaring question remained.

What would happen next?

THIRTY-THREE

Four months later

With the sun shining high in the sky and gorgeous, fluffy white clouds floating calmly overhead, I strolled down the bustling Boulevard Saint-Michel and hummed a tune to myself as the scent of tulips, buttery croissants, and steaming coffee danced around me. I stopped walking for a moment and smiled as I took it all in, this place I now called home.

Springtime in Paris in the fifties was absolutely magical. And what was even more delightful was that I was experiencing it all for the *very first time*. Gone were the jarring flashes of déjà-vu, the ominous memories and premonitions that had plagued me when I'd first arrived. Instead I felt more vibrant, more alive, and more at home here each day than I ever thought possible.

Those first few days in Paris felt light-years away as I stopped at a charming flower shop on the corner and bought a bouquet of pink roses, then took off down the street and found myself walking right by the tree-lined boulevard that led to Jean-Pierre's nightclub without giving it so much as a passing glance. The club had since been shut down after one too many dancers had accused Jean-Pierre of sexual harassment and had quit the show, leaving him with a mountain of debt and an even bigger pile of enemies.

Breathing in the scent of the roses, I continued my leisurely stroll and shook off my memories of Jean-Pierre, eternally grateful that both Titine and I had had the courage to quit dancing for him and to tell that sleazy *drageur*, as they say in French, to take his nasty advances and shove them up his you-know-what.

As I crossed through Place Saint-Michel and reached the Seine River, its waters glistening in the sunlight, the trees that lined the riverbanks swaying softly in the breeze, I thought about how drastically the world around me had shifted since that night just four months ago—the night I'd taken Solange's life in order to save both Antoine's and my own.

It was as if, ever since that night, the universe had gone into a permanent state of joyous celebration. Wrongs were righted, and my life—*Ruby's* life—as well as the lives of everyone around me, began to work themselves out.

I'd succeeded in stopping Solange's evil soul from derailing fate, and in doing so, an outpouring of love, joy, and hope had resulted.

And each day that I was here, that joy, that hope, swelled in my heart. I felt it each time Antoine gazed into my eyes and told me he loved me, each time I visited Titine and saw the healing that was replacing her despair over losing Robert.

But even with all of the positive changes this new life had brought for me, I still couldn't help but wonder if in stopping my own murder, I had completely erased my future as Claudia. The journal that had traveled back in time with me was now completely empty, every last line erased, except for the one entry I'd written with Ruby's hand when I first arrived. And the cover of the *People* magazine had changed too. Solange's face had faded to the point where she was completely unrecognizable...of course *that* was okay with me.

The one thing that wasn't okay with me, though, was the fact that my ultrasound photo had *also* continued fading. It was now just a washed-out blur of black and white. The outline of my baby girl, the date of the sonogram, even my name...it was all gone.

The magical Madame Bouchard hadn't made any more appearances either, so while I desperately wanted answers about the future, especially about my baby, it didn't seem they were coming anytime soon.

On the one hand, I couldn't imagine leaving the beautiful life I'd built here with Antoine; but on the other, I still couldn't shake the idea that the portal Madame Bouchard had spoken about was somewhere out there, just waiting for me to find it. Waiting to suck me back in and take me away from this man I'd fallen head over heels in love with, from a life I'd grown to adore, and transport me back to my future life, my future baby—the baby I felt certain I was destined to have. I wondered constantly if the next day, the next hour, the next moment would be my last here in this life.

And if given the chance, which life would I choose?

A siren blared down the street, snapping me from my thoughts, my worries, from these frantic emotions that raced through my head without pause. And just like I had each day for the past four months, I bottled them up and told myself that my life here was amazing, that I should be thankful, and that when the time was right, I could have a baby *here*, with Antoine.

But as I repeated those positive thoughts in my head to drown out the worries, one more nagging concern crept up.

What if I had a baby here with Antoine and then somehow stumbled across the portal and was sent back to my life as Claudia? What would happen to my child here? To Antoine? Would I lose yet another possibility of a real family?

I shook my head and gazed up at the fancy apartment building in front of me, then told myself to stop worrying and just live my life in the here and now.

After all, if this past-life experience had taught me anything, it was that all I had was the current moment. And after everything I'd been through, everything I'd done to right the wrongs of the past, I had to trust that fate was on my side now.

I rang the buzzer, glancing up toward the sky as I waited, wondering if fate was some entity that I could talk to, or if Madame Bouchard was listening.

You'll take care of me, won't you? I asked the clouds, hoping they'd deliver the message.

But instead of some powerful voice traveling down from the heavens, it was Titine's.

"Come on in!" she cooed through the speaker in the new sing-songy tone she'd recently adopted.

I laughed up at the sky, the sound of her voice reminding me that life here *was* good, then let myself in and took the elevator up to the top floor. Just two months ago, Titine had moved into a gorgeous penthouse apartment, and with its perfect view of the Seine River, it was a far cry from the tiny studio she used to call home.

Such a high standard of living never would've been possible for Titine before, but when Robert's parents got wind that Titine was pregnant with their only grandchild—by way of me and Antoine—they'd bought it for her free and clear, and had sent with it a hefty portion of the money Robert had left for them in his will. The apartment and the money hadn't erased the pain of losing the father of her child and the man she loved, but it had certainly given Titine hope that she could raise this child on her own and that life could, and *would*, get better. And after what Titine had been through—after what we'd *all* been through—we couldn't place a price tag on hope.

"Hey, sweetie, thanks for coming," she said, opening the door and pecking me on the cheeks. "The paint in the nursery is finally dry, so we can start hanging things on the walls now. And whenever that handsome fiancé of yours is available, I'm ready for him to come over and put the crib together."

"Got it, chief," I said, smiling at her growing belly. Titine was five months along now, and she was glowing from head to toe. I handed her the bouquet of pink roses as we walked into her apartment together.

"Thanks, love. How sweet! I'll put them in the nursery. They'll be baby Adeline's first flowers."

I stopped when I heard the name Adeline roll off her tongue. It was the first time she'd mentioned it.

And *Adeline*, as I knew from my life as Claudia, had been my mother's birth name. Although later in her life, after my mom had officially cut off all contact with my grandma, she'd legally changed her name to the very simple *Jane*.

I reminded myself though that things were different this time around, and hopefully my mother would never feel the need to change her name just to spite my grandmother.

Titine stopped and placed a hand on my arm. "There you go again with that far-off look in your eyes. You do like the name Adeline, don't you? I came across it in that baby-name book you gave me last week, and I just fell in love with it. You don't think it sounds too much like my name, right? I mean, I could always go back to Martine, but that just feels so old, and I'm so used to people calling me Titine, you know? Okay, I'm babbling."

I laughed as we walked down the shiny hardwood floors toward the nursery. "I love the name Adeline," I told her. "It's beautiful."

"Oh good." She rubbed her belly and smiled at me. "I had a feeling you would like it. I'm still going on your *insistence* that it's a girl, you know. I mean, we don't know for sure."

"Trust me, Titine," I said with a smile, "it's a girl."

"All right, all right. You better be right, because I don't know what I would do with a boy. I mean, with a girl, I can teach her to dance, speak French, we can play dolls together, have tea parties. It's going to be so much fun."

I stepped into the newly painted nursery, the walls now a light shade of pink, and couldn't help but think of how my mother—when *I'd* known her, at least—had loathed the color pink. She hadn't been girly at all. She'd never been fun or adventurous in the way that Titine would surely be. She'd never played games with me or encouraged me to be creative. I knew she would come out differently this time around, though, and I was certain that there was no way this new beginning to her life *couldn't* change everything.

"What do you think of the paint? It's not *too* pink, is it?"

"It's perfect," I said, feeling a strange tug at my stomach, a twinge of a feeling I wasn't yet ready to admit I was having.

"I'm going to go put these gorgeous roses in a vase. I'll be right back." Titine bounced into the hallway, leaving me alone in the empty nursery—the nursery that in another four months would hold a beautiful baby girl who had no idea that things had happened *so* differently the first time around. She wouldn't have the faintest clue that in the first version of her life, she hadn't even been given the chance to get to know her shining, young dancer of a mother, but instead had been shipped off to the States and raised by her strict, older grandparents, and consequently had lived her life with a steel wall surrounding her, the pain of having been abandoned by her mother making her afraid to let anyone in.

My mother's future was more promising now, and of all of the wonderful changes that had occurred since the night I'd changed fate, I knew that *this* change, this renewed outlook for my mom, was one of the best.

Still, though, as I traced my hand along the smooth walls and breathed in the scent of the new paint, there was that feeling again.

The *what if.*

What if I had lost my only chance at having a baby when I left my life as Claudia? What if that was my one opportunity to correct all the wrongs my own mother had done, and to create my own little family, as imperfect as it might have been without a father in the picture. What would happen now? Where would that baby go? That baby who was destined to be born to Claudia?

I shook my head and fought off the thoughts of need, of want, of jealousy over Titine's excitement for the baby who would be sleeping in a crib in this very room in just a few short months. I was happy for her, thrilled that after that horrific day at the hospital, both she and the baby had recovered. Even though she'd lost Robert, she'd stayed strong and had decided to keep the baby and to raise her herself.

But in my heart, there was that pang, that longing for my own child. And I knew that no matter how wonderful my new life as Ruby was turning out, no matter how in love I was with Antoine, no matter how fun it was going to be getting to know my young grandmother as a new mom, I couldn't shake that intense longing.

But since I wasn't sure if I would ever return to my life as Claudia, since I didn't know if the portal Madame Bouchard had spoken about was just around the corner, or if it had disappeared forever, I knew my only choice was to take action here and now, in this life. In my fresh, unwritten existence as Ruby.

Perhaps that baby *was* still out there, just waiting to be mine.

Titine floated back in the room, interrupting me from my thoughts, and as I turned to face her, my heart swelled. I had to tell her.

"I want to have a baby," I announced, beaming from ear to ear. "I know we haven't set a date for the wedding yet, but I want to have a baby with Antoine."

But in Titine's eyes, instead of the excitement and maybe even the hint of surprise I was expecting, I saw a trace of something else—of *pity*.

She walked over to me and placed her hand on my shoulder, the sad look in her green eyes intensifying.

"What is it, Titine? Why are you looking at me like that?"

"You don't remember, do you, Ruby?"

"Remember what?"

She took in a deep breath and didn't let go of her grip on my shoulder. "When we were living in New York, and you were with Thomas..." She stopped, her voice suspended in midair and her gaze traveling to the floor, to the window—anywhere but to me.

"What, Titine? What happened with Thomas that I don't already know?" I felt the panic rising, the hysteria that I hadn't experienced since my first few chaotic days as Ruby boiling to the surface once again.

She cleared her throat, and as she finally lifted her eyes to meet mine, I recognized in them the same determination I'd felt when I'd had to tell her about Robert's murder. And before she even spoke, my insides crumbled.

"Ruby, you *were* pregnant once. With Thomas's baby. That's why, even though he was so awful to you, you wouldn't leave him. And one night, when you were about six months along, the two of you had a really bad fight. Well, you were always having bad fights, but this one was the worst. Thomas hit you really hard, Ruby... in the stomach. You passed out, started bleeding, and like the sick bastard he was, he just left you there...to die.

"I tried calling you late that night, and when you didn't answer, I just had this gut feeling that something bad had happened with Thomas, so I rushed over, and you...you were...oh, God, Ruby. It was a nightmare. They had to perform emergency surgery to stop the bleeding. You lost the baby that night...and the damage was so severe that you had to have a complete hysterectomy."

My hand shot to my lower abdomen. "The scar on my stomach...it wasn't from Thomas. It was from the surgery."

Titine nodded, the sorrow in her eyes unbearable. "When we first arrived in Paris, you made me promise never to bring it up again. It was all too painful. And then after you had that fall during rehearsal and you kept asking if you'd lost your baby, I didn't have the heart to tell you *again* that you had. I thought by now that surely you would've remembered on your own. I'm so sorry, Ruby."

"So I'll never be able to have my own children. *That's* why I hated him so much. That's why I..."

Titine nodded. I didn't need to say it. I hadn't *only* killed Thomas out of self-defense. I'd also killed him because he'd taken my baby away from me.

I stared back at my sweet, young grandmother, the closest friend I'd ever had in my life, and as she tried to comfort me, telling me that I would be like a second mom to her child, that Antoine and I could adopt, that it would all be okay, I stopped listening, my heart closing up inside my chest, my hope, my soul deflated. And as she wrapped her tiny arms around me, her full, round belly pressing against my stomach, all I could think was *why*.

After everything I'd done to change fate, after I'd called up the strength to literally kill an evil soul and in doing so had erased all of the wrong that soul would bring if left to her own devices, after I'd rebuilt not only Ruby's mess of a life, but the shattered lives of Titine and Antoine, *why* would I be denied the chance to have my own children? Why would I be brought back here, with no obvious prospect of getting through the portal, and still not be able to have the one thing I felt so sure that I was destined to do?

I lifted my face from Titine's shoulder and glared at the happy white clouds floating along outside the window, as if nothing could faze them. As if nothing monumental had just occurred. I wanted to scream at them to pass along another message for me, to tell fate or Madame Bouchard or whoever the hell was listening that this wasn't fair, this wasn't how it was supposed to be. I'd done what they wanted! And where were they now, when I needed them the most? Who was calling the shots here? Where was the silver-haired woman who'd brought me back here in the first place? Where was the big man in the sky, patting me on the back, telling me I'd done a good job, that I'd accomplished what I'd been sent back to do and now I could finally have my dream of a real family?

As it turned out, fate didn't have my back after all. Fate didn't care about all the good that I'd done.

I didn't scream at the clouds, though. I didn't have the fight left in me.

Instead, for the first time since Solange had held the gun to my head that terrifying night four months ago, since that hopeless moment where she'd made me feel as if my presence here was all for nothing, I cried.

+≡──≡+

I didn't end up helping Titine decorate the nursery that afternoon. Instead, I left her there with piles of girly paintings, fluffy baby bunnies and teddy bears, boxes of pink and white furniture yet to be assembled, and her dwindled excitement. I promised her that I would come back to help tomorrow, but told her that today, I needed to get some air, clear my head, and spend some time alone.

She reluctantly let me go, that look of pity never leaving her eyes. And I couldn't take it; I couldn't bear the way she looked at me. I had to get out of there. I had to break out of those four pink walls that would soon house a baby.

And most important, I had to figure out what was next, since it was becoming clear that I would never have my own.

Winding endlessly through the streets of Paris, I didn't pay attention to where I was going or where I would end up. The only marker of how far I'd gone was the tip of the Eiffel Tower, which appeared through the trees or in between buildings every so often.

How would I continue on in this life when, on the inside, I was still holding onto the remnants of my hopes and dreams from my life as Claudia? When I couldn't answer the questions Antoine had been asking about why my eyes were a different color now, why I talked differently and acted differently from the old Ruby? About why the story I'd told him about my father's murder didn't match up with stories Titine had mentioned to him about my family.

I wanted so badly to tell him that even though I was Ruby—and I *did* feel at home here, in this life and in her body—I still wasn't *only* her. I was someone else too. I was a woman who'd grown up feeling unloved by my own mother. A woman who'd been independent ever since that fateful day when I'd lost my father and realized my mother would never forgive me for his death. I was a woman who'd studied psychology in college and had become a therapist so that I could help others avoid the problems I'd dealt with in my own family. I'd counseled couples on how to get along, how to raise their children, how to overcome setbacks when I, myself, had never been able to see a relationship through to marriage.

I was a woman who'd been pregnant once, and who desperately wanted to find my baby.

Those qualities, those experiences, those hardships were just as much me as the boldness I now felt living in Ruby's body, the fluent French that flowed from my tongue, the unabashed confidence I demonstrated each time I danced or sang a song with my new, beautiful voice.

I was both Ruby and Claudia, and I wondered how that could really work long-term. I wondered if I could exist like this, knowing that there was this whole other part of me, thirty-five years of a different life I had lived, about which I could never tell a soul.

And with the recent news Titine had delivered, I now walked through the darkening streets of Paris with a weight on my shoulders and a heaviness in my heart that I wasn't sure how long I could carry on my own.

When a cold wind blew past me and a drop of rain landed on the tip of my nose, I realized I had roamed all the way over to the sixteenth arrondissement, to the rue de Passy. As I gazed down the street, past all of the fancy shops that adorned this ritzy neighborhood, I remembered that the apartment where I'd met with Madame Bouchard was only a few blocks away.

The drops fell harder and faster, running down my face and leaving a chill in my bones. As the rain wilted my hair and soaked through my clothes, I thought about ringing the buzzer to see if the mysterious old woman was there so I could demand answers, ask her what I should do. But before I even took a step in the direction of the apartment, I realized she wouldn't be there. She had never lived there to begin with. And I didn't need to go through the trouble of asking the current tenant if an older, elegant woman named Madame Bouchard had recently moved out. They would look at me like I was crazy and tell me they'd lived there for the past twenty years.

I was living a new life now. I was in unchartered territory. *This* course of fate had yet to be written, and there was no one to guide me down this path, no magical journal or wise old woman to hand me the answers.

So, under the spring shower that poured over Paris, I shook away all of my worries and fears and let the rain wash them straight down the gutter at my feet. Then I turned away from Madame Bouchard's mystical apartment, and with a determined step, I set off to find the man I loved.

It was time to tell Antoine the truth about who I really was.

THIRTY-FOUR

"Where have you been?" Antoine asked as I let myself into the elegant apartment we now shared overlooking the grand Opéra Garnier.

When I didn't respond, he ran his hands over my wet hair, then held on to my shoulders and pulled me in tight. "Are you okay? I was starting to get worried. We had dinner plans, remember?"

As I breathed in the scent of his clean clothes and nestled my face in his shirt collar, I willed the courage I'd felt on the cab ride home to return. Because to say everything I was planning on telling him, I was going to need it.

"I'm fine, Antoine. I'm so sorry to have kept you waiting. There's something I need to talk to you about, though. Do you mind if we sit down?"

A curious look passed through his smoky-gray eyes as he ran his strong hands down my arms and took my hands in his. He led me into our cozy living room, then slipped my wet jacket off my shoulders and wrapped a warm blanket around me as I sat down next to him.

The comforting scent of spring rain floated into our apartment from the open window opposite us, and as I breathed it in, I knew it was time.

But just as I opened my mouth, Antoine spoke.

"I've been waiting for you to tell me what's really been going on, Ruby. I know you haven't lost your memory. Your blue eyes, the way you talk, like you're not from here, like you know so much more than you're telling me. I know there's more to it than amnesia. But whatever it is, I can handle it."

His tone was reassuring, but the look in his eyes told me that he was scared.

And if the truth be told, I wasn't all too hyped at the idea of telling him about revisiting past lives, finding magical journals, and correcting errors in fate. Could our love really survive such an outlandish story?

But as Antoine kept his sweet gaze on me and squeezed my hands, I knew that he deserved the truth. We were engaged to be married, and I couldn't walk down the aisle without being completely honest about who I was, where I'd come from, and what I wanted in life. It wasn't fair to him, and it wasn't fair to me.

And so, on that rainy Paris night, I looked deep into my love's eyes and started from the beginning.

The color had drained from Antoine's face, and he stared at me in silence after I'd told him the entire story. The story of two lives woven into one—a story about love, revenge, and the ties that carry people from one life into the next, and then back again.

I reached my hand out to touch him, willing him to say something, anything. Hoping he didn't think I was a verifiable nutcase and ship me off to a mental institution to live out the rest of my life in a padded cell.

"Antoine," I said, resting a hand on his knee. "I know. I know this is the craziest story you've ever heard, and it defies all logic. It defies everything we know about how the world works, but I'm telling you the truth. And if we're going to be married…if you still *want* to marry me, that is, you need to know who I really am."

He cleared his throat and blinked his eyes at me as if he was trying to decipher if I was even real, or if the woman sitting in front of him spouting off all of this nonsense had just been a figment of his imagination.

Finally, he spoke. "That night with Solange…she called you Claudia. She said something about you being a psychologist. She mentioned a man named Édouard. And she kept referring to the way things had happened the *first time* around. You're saying that what she was saying was valid? That she wasn't as insane as we thought?"

"Well, she was clearly insane, but insane with revenge. And she'd carried that revenge back from her future life, as Solange Raspail, the actress."

"And your eyes. Your beautiful blue eyes. You're saying they're Claudia's?"

I nodded.

"And the story you told me about your father being murdered… that never happened to Ruby? It happened to you, as Claudia, in the future? That's why you were always so guarded any time Titine would talk about your family in front of me?"

"Yes. I knew it was a risk telling you the truth about my father, and I knew it wouldn't match up with Ruby's past, but when I saw you hurting so badly after losing Gisèle, I couldn't hold it in. I couldn't let you think you were alone." I squeezed Antoine's hand, hoping, praying that he believed me.

He stayed silent for a few moments, and I could almost see the smoke rising from his brain as it worked overtime to process all of the unbelievable information I'd just crammed in there.

"There's one more thing I can show you that might help," I said, remembering the three items that had made the voyage with me. And although they were faded, there was one point of proof that would show Antoine that this outrageous story was real.

That, or it would make him run for the hills.

After digging to the bottom of my lingerie drawer, I found what I was looking for.

I emerged from our bedroom with the faded *People* magazine, the blurry ultrasound photo, and my now-empty journal.

"These three items traveled back in time with me." I handed Antoine the magazine first. "The picture on the cover started fading as soon as I arrived here, and ever since Solange died, her face has completely faded. But you can still make out the names, as well as part of Édouard's face."

Antoine held the magazine and narrowed his eyes before reading aloud, "Édouard Marceau and Solange Raspail. *Engaged*."

I pointed to the top of the page. "And the date. You can still see it."

"*December 5, 2012*," Antoine whispered. He dropped the magazine onto the coffee table and turned to me at a complete loss for words.

I handed him my thick scarlet-red journal. "This used to be full of entries from my life as Claudia, but as soon as I arrived here, the entries started fading, and now they're completely gone. The only one left is the one I wrote when I first arrived in Paris."

After Antoine read over the entry, he spoke softly. "So, this Édouard Marceau…do you miss him? Do you want to go back to him?"

I shook my head. "I did love him, *before* I met you. And it's hard to explain, but the minute I met you in the wings that day, I…I knew I was falling for you. I knew I had to be with you. And I'm not normally like this, running from one man to the next. But I've totally and completely fallen in love with you, Antoine. You make me feel safe, alive, and happier than I've ever been, and I never want to leave you."

The worry didn't leave his eyes, though. "What about your baby? If you could go back to her, would you?"

I swallowed, knowing deep down that the answer to that question wasn't one I could admit to Antoine. Not yet, anyway. Instead, I handed him the final piece of proof: my sonogram photo.

"This is an ultrasound photograph of the baby. It's just a blur now, but if you could've seen it before, it was really amazing."

"This is incredible. We are only just beginning to develop this technology." Antoine shook his head in disbelief as he stared at the hazy photograph. "The date, it says December 18, 2012. The same month as the magazine. And the same date as your birthday, Ruby."

"December 18? That can't be right. Besides, the last time I looked at the picture, the date had already faded. I got my ultrasound on December 5. I'll never forget because that was the day I found out I was having a baby girl."

Antoine held the photograph up for me to see.

He was right.

A *new* date had appeared.

December 18, 2012.

Chills traveled up my spine as I blinked over and over, certain my eyes were playing tricks on me.

But they weren't.

What did this new date mean for me? For Antoine? For Claudia and my baby?

Antoine took the photo and laid it on the coffee table with the rest of the evidence. He didn't speak for a few minutes. He just sat there, staring, mulling over the most improbable story of all time.

Finally his big, smoky eyes lifted to mine. "Do you still want to have children someday? With me?"

A knife twisted into my heart, hot tears threatening to spill over.

"Ruby, what is it?"

Clutching the edge of the couch, I forced myself to get it together. "I *do* want a baby with you, Antoine. More than anything. But today, Titine told me that I can't…I'm not able to have children."

A silence as thick as an early morning fog settled between us, the shock of my latest confession rattling us both to the core.

Antoine finally spoke, his voice raspy, shaken, and confused. "Why, Ruby? What happened?"

"I *was* pregnant once, when I was with Thomas. But during one of our many horrible fights, he hit me, and I…I lost the baby. Titine said the damage was so severe that I had to have a hysterectomy."

Antoine bit his lower lip as he gazed out at the drizzling rain pattering on the windowsill, his silence saying more than words ever could.

He wanted children too. He'd never asked for this.

"I'm so sorry, Antoine. I didn't know. I didn't remember." Warm, relentless tears broke free, streaming down my face.

And just when I thought he was going to stand up and tell me to leave, that he'd had it with my talk of portals in time and space, past lives and future lives, abusive boyfriends, changing ultrasound dates, lost children, and infertility, he turned to me and pulled me close.

"It's okay, Ruby. I'm here, and I'm not going anywhere." Antoine ran his soothing hands over my back until I calmed down. He tucked a strand of hair behind my ear, then rested his forehead against mine. "I'm so sorry that that happened to you, *mon amour*. That he took so much away from you."

"From *us*," I whispered, swallowing a hiccup.

Antoine took my chin in his hand and ran his thumb over my cheek, wiping away the last of the tears. "I know better than anyone that there are no guarantees in this crazy life. All we can hope for is that we find someone to love who will love us in return. And I have found that in you, *ma chère* Ruby. *You* are the one I love. The one I will always love, no matter what comes our way. If we want to have children one day, we can adopt. Or we can travel the world together. Now that we have found each other, the possibilities are endless."

Unable and unwilling to control the swell of emotion, of pure, sweet love I felt for Antoine, I showered his cheeks, forehead, and lips with kisses.

He laughed as he pulled me in for one more spine-tingling, warm embrace.

"So what happens next?" Antoine said with that sweet twinkle of curiosity in his eyes that I'd so grown to love.

"I don't have a clue. None of this has happened before. We didn't survive the first time around, yet here we are."

He leaned forward, his lips hovering so close to mine that I forgot about the new date on the ultrasound photo and about how badly I wanted my baby. At least I had Antoine now. I had found the love of a lifetime.

"You do realize, if you told this story to anyone else, they'd think you've completely lost your mind," he whispered, nuzzling his cheek against mine.

I couldn't help but laugh as he took my chin in his hand then traced the outline of my face with his finger.

"When I came to you in the wings that day, the day you'd fallen, I still remember the way you looked at me—like you'd never seen me before. And later that night in the café, when I noticed that your eyes had changed color, I knew, Ruby. I just knew you weren't the same person. That something had happened to you. But I have spent my life researching science, studying and believing in tangible, real facts. I never could've imagined..." He trailed off, his gaze softening into mine, his warm hand still caressing my face. "I believe you, Ruby. Every insane, unbelievable word of your story. I believe it all."

I smiled as he lowered his handsome face to mine and his full, soft lips brushed over my eyelids, then the tip of my nose, and finally my mouth. He kissed me with such passion that I plummeted even further into the depths of my love for this man, for the man I'd traveled back in time to meet, the man who was, undoubtedly, my soul mate.

And when our lips parted and he gazed at me again, the confusion he'd held in his eyes just an hour ago had been replaced by complete love and understanding.

"I think I might have something that will cheer you up," Antoine announced.

"You do?" *What on earth could he have up his sleeve?*

A sly grin slid over his lips, making his already handsome face all the more irresistible. "Come with me. It's a surprise."

On our way out of the apartment, a strange feeling flooded my gut.

"Antoine, just give me a second. I forgot something."

I ran back into our beautiful Parisian living room, and taking one last glance around the apartment, I scooped up the magazine, my red journal, and my sonogram photo. And before I met Antoine outside, I swapped my tall black boots for a pair of sparkly red dancing heels.

I had a strange feeling I might need them.

+≈≈+

"Ready?" Antoine stood behind me, his hands covering my eyes.

"Ready," I answered, the excitement and anticipation building up inside of me, ready to explode. Where had he taken me? What could this possibly be?

Antoine slid his hands down to my shoulders, and as I blinked, taking in my surroundings, warm tears filled up my eyelids.

It was a dance studio—a huge, gorgeous new dance studio. Shiny hardwood floors glistened underneath our feet, and tall, sparkling mirrors studded the four walls that surrounded us.

"It's yours," he said. "I bought it for you and Titine, so the two of you can finally open up your own studio and teach dance lessons, just like you've been talking about."

I turned to him, feeling more gratitude, more love than I knew how to express in that moment. So instead, I said a simple, heartfelt *"Merci."*

Antoine grinned from ear to ear and gestured around the beautiful studio. "What do you think? Is it as nice as your grandma's studio in the future?"

I couldn't help but laugh. How could he still be here after everything I'd told him?

"It's better," I said.

His eyes lit up as he shot me an ornery grin. "I have another surprise for you. Wait here."

He turned on his heel, his dark-chocolate hair bouncing as he ran over to a record player in the corner. I watched the way the muscles in his back pushed through his white collared shirt as he reached up to the windowsill for a record he'd obviously left there for just this occasion.

How? How had *I* ended up with the sweetest, sexiest, most loving and considerate man on this entire planet?

I shook my head and grinned, not believing that after this insane journey, here I was, about to dance in my very own dance studio with the man I loved and adored more than anything or anyone in this world.

Suddenly, a spicy tango tune traveled through the beautiful space as Antoine strutted back over to me.

That song.

Where did I know it from?

Before I could place it, Antoine reached into his pocket then stretched his hand out to me.

And there, dangling from his fingers was the heart-shaped ruby pendant.

Goose bumps prickled the back of my neck as I stared down at the deep-red stone, sparkling underneath the soft lighting in the dance studio.

I realized instantly that in my rush to tell Antoine the story of me traveling back in time to my past life, I'd forgotten to mention *the necklace.* I'd forgotten to tell him how *that* necklace, the one floating so elegantly from his hands, had much more of a story to it than the one he knew from this life.

"I bought you a new silver chain and had it polished up a bit. It's beautiful, is it not?" Antoine said, smiling his handsome, charming smile.

I nodded, unable to speak, to move, to think as Antoine slipped his hands underneath my hair and fastened the necklace.

He slid the ruby heart pendant around the chain and placed it ever so gently on my chest.

Breathless, I reached up to touch it.

Sparks sizzled underneath my fingertips…just like the first time.

"Do you like it?" Antoine asked, an expectant look passing through his eyes.

I smiled back up at him, forcing the tears that wanted to spill onto my cheeks back in their place. "I love it, Antoine. It's gorgeous."

The tango beat picked up and swirled around us, electricity lacing through the air.

Antoine gazed down at me, the gleam in his eyes suddenly making me remember this feeling. This moment.

"Dance with me, Ruby," he said, stretching out his hand.

I knew then. I knew where I was.

The shiny dance studio. These beautiful mirrored walls. My sparkly red heels. The tango tune moving through the speakers. The ruby-red necklace.

Antoine with his smoky gaze, hand outstretched, waiting for me to take it. Waiting for me to dance with him. *My soul mate.*

I'd found the portal.

Antoine had created it for me without even knowing it.

I ran my hand over my flat stomach, thinking of my baby girl.

But how could I leave Antoine? And how could I leave Titine while she was pregnant?

Traveling back in time to live out these past four months with Antoine was my destiny, I knew that now.

But deep in my soul, I also knew that being Claudia was just as much my destiny as being Ruby. And even more so, being a mother to my baby girl…*that* was my destiny.

As I ran my fingers once again over the ruby pendant that rested over my heart, I could almost hear her whispering to me, *Take his hand. I'll be waiting for you on the other side.*

Tears of anticipation, sadness, and joy glazed over my eyes as I smiled up at Antoine. The love of my life. The man I would never forget.

It only took a puff of air, a tiny swell of energy for me to say the word that lingered so heavily at the tip of my tongue.

"Yes."

I placed my shaky palm in Antoine's and let him sweep me up in his arms and twirl me around the dance floor. As we swayed in time to the sexy music, our bodies, our souls connecting, I leaned closer to him and whispered in his ear, "I love you, Antoine. No matter what happens, know that I will love you forever. *You* are the reason I came back."

Antoine smiled warmly as he pressed his chest so close to mine, it felt as if our hearts were now beating as one. "I love you too, Ruby. You are the most incredible woman I've ever met, and I've waited my whole life for you. I'll never let you go, ever."

Just as I felt my heart overflowing with love, my body buzzing with desire, and my brain telling me that maybe this *wasn't* the portal after all, a harsh wind whipped through the dance studio, the windows and doors banging open and closed. Antoine pulled me in tighter, then leaned down and kissed me.

A jarring pain ripped through my chest, just underneath the ruby-red pendant. But I didn't break our kiss. I didn't let go.

The pain spread from my chest, up to my head and down to my toes. Sparks crackled beneath my fingertips as I held on to Antoine.

"I love you, Ruby. I'll always love you," he whispered in my ear.

As the wind picked up, whirling around us with a fury, I whispered back, "Come with me, Antoine. Please come with me."

Every ounce of power within me strained to hold on.

I will not lose him. I traveled so far to find him. I can't lose him now.

The room spun around us, flashes of red, silver, and black swirling past our heads, until finally the blackness swallowed up every last color. Every last sound.

But one spark remained.

One little piece of light led the way.

The gleam in Antoine's smoky-gray eyes.

THIRTY-FIVE

Beep…beep…beep.

At first it was a distant, faraway sound, a faint, steady beeping that was almost comforting. But then, as the sound moved closer to me, growing in intensity but never losing its firm pace, I realized it was right next to my head.

Where was I? And what was that noise?

I blinked a few times, but everything blurred together, one big swirl of silver and red. My mouth was so dry I could hardly swallow, and it felt as if someone had beaten the insides of my head with a hammer. I wished that beeping sound would stop. Where was it coming from?

I blinked again, this time forcing my eyelids open.

"Claudia? Claudia, sweetie, you're awake."

A petite woman with short blonde hair sat next to me. It was my mom, Jane. She squeezed my hand in hers as she blinked a stream of tears from her eyes.

There was something different about her…something new about the way she looked at me. Before I could figure it out, she leaned forward, laying her tiny little frame over me, letting her warm tears splash onto my cheeks. "Oh, sweetie, I'm so glad you're okay. You gave us such a scare. I love you so much."

My mom never said *I love you*. And she didn't hug me.

And she *never* cried.

What was going on?

"Mom," I croaked, my voice all hoarse and scratchy. "What's going on? Where am I?"

A worried look passed through my mother's eyes—another expression I don't ever remember seeing in her normally icy features. "The doctor said you may not remember everything right away. You hit your head pretty hard when you fell. Maybe I should call the nurse."

But I grabbed onto my mom's hand, not wanting this moment to end. Not wanting her to leave my side. She was finally here. The mother I'd always wanted. The caring, loving, motherly woman who had been hiding underneath that cool façade for all those years—she was here. And I didn't want to lose another second with her.

"Wait, Mom. Don't leave, okay? Stay with me."

She sat back down and tucked a strand of hair behind my ear. "Don't worry, sweetie. I'm not going anywhere. Let's just take it slow, okay?"

I nodded and coughed as I tried to swallow. "Could I get some water?"

"Of course, dear." She grabbed a pink plastic pitcher from the tray next to the bed and poured me a glass.

After gulping down the entire cup, I cast a confused glance around me. Bland white curtains enclosed the small room, and a metal railing lined the uncomfortable bed I was lying in. Wires and tape covered my hands, while an IV dripped steadily by my side. "What happened, Mom? Why am I in the emergency ro—?" But I stopped as I noticed the gorgeous, sparkling silver dress I was wearing.

And even more surprising than the designer gown spread over my figure was the firm bump that protruded up from the dress, in the exact spot where my stomach should've been.

I ran my hands over the bump, realizing that the small basketball beneath the dress *was* my stomach. And as my hands rested on the top, I felt a small kick.

The fog that had surrounded me lifted, the grogginess gone.

I'm pregnant.

And that annoying beeping sound next to my bed was suddenly the most glorious sound I'd ever heard. It was my baby's heartbeat.

My baby.

I was going to be a mom.

I looked over to my own mother, who was now blinking back the tears even more fiercely, though not allowing the relieved smile to leave her dainty little face. "The baby is going to be fine, Claudia. The paramedics who brought you in said her vitals look good. They just want to get you in a hospital gown so they can do a quick ultrasound to be sure everything is okay."

"It's a girl?" I asked as another tiny kick protruded from my growing tummy.

She nodded as she laid her hand over mine.

"Yes, sweetie," she said. "You're having a baby girl. Isn't it just wonderful? You only found out last week. I don't think I've ever seen you more excited, although now the trick will be choosing a name. There are so many good girl names. But at least the two of you have another few months to decide."

What did she mean, *the two of you*?

Before I had a chance to ask who she was referring to or why I was wearing a sparkly silver gown, the white curtain swished open and a gorgeous older woman entered the room. She had strawberry-red hair pulled back into a bun, crystal-green eyes, and an elegant violet scarf adorning her neck.

It was Grandma Martine.

Her emerald eyes danced the minute she realized that I was awake, and in that moment, I remembered.

I remembered everything.

I remembered my young grandma, *Titine*. Her baby, *my mom*. The pink nursery. Robert and his untimely death.

And then I remembered Ruby. I remembered living in her body, and falling in love…with Antoine.

My mind raced to decipher if the vivid memories swimming around in my head were real or imaginary, but before I could figure it all out, my mom stood and rushed over to my grandmother, where the two of them embraced and whispered to each other, then walked back over to me, motherly smiles masking their concern but not their relief.

I'd never seen them hug, *ever*.

They took post on either side of my hospital bed, and as they held my hands in their own, I felt all of our pulses beating in time with my baby's heartbeat, a symbol of the life force that held all four of us together. And I knew in that moment that this powerful bond, this strong love, would never again be broken.

I looked from my beautiful grandmother over to my warm, caring mother, and it was then that a *new* rush of memories flooded my brain.

Closing my eyes, I saw myself as a little girl dressed in a frilly pink dress, my mom swinging me around and laughing as she pulled me in close for a hug and told me how much she loved me. I remembered family gatherings with my mom and grandma laughing side by side, their smiles almost identical, their eyes full of love and gratitude for each other. I saw myself dancing from a young age, taking lessons in the evenings with my grandma Martine.

"How are you feeling, Miss Claudia?" my beautiful grandmother said, squeezing my hand.

Just hearing her voice brought tears to my eyes. It was Titine, my best friend. And she was as beautiful and sweet as I remembered from my days with her in Paris.

My mom mouthed something over to my grandma, but her voice was so low I couldn't make out what she'd said. Then she turned to me and smiled. "I'll be right back, sweetie. I'm just going to go find the nurse to let her know you've woken up. And hopefully once the doctor clears you and the baby, we can get you out of this emergency room."

My mom left the two of us alone, and again as I gazed up at my grandma, I recalled the details of the life I'd just lived in Paris with her, and with Antoine. The life that felt as if it was only yesterday, but at the same time felt light-years away.

And as I remembered that very last night, the night Antoine had given me that shiny new dance studio, along with the ruby-red necklace, I recalled the choice I'd made to take his hand. To come back to my baby. But I'd held on to him. I'd tried to take him with me.

In a panic, my eyes scanned the room. Was he here? Had he made it?

"What is it, dear? What are you looking for?" Grandma Martine asked.

"Grandma, where's Antoine? Is he here?"

Confusion swept over her face as she blinked and focused in on me, as if she hadn't heard me correctly. "Now, what made you think of Antoine? I don't think I've talked to you about him since you were a little girl."

"I just need to know, Grandma. Please. What happened to him? And to Ruby?" I said, not able to hide the desperation I felt to find the love of my life. To feel his touch again. To find out where he'd gone after the wind had swept through the dance studio on that mysterious night in Paris, so long ago.

"Just calm down, dear," she soothed before beginning the story. "As you may remember, Ruby was my very best friend. She and Antoine helped me raise your mother after your grandfather passed away. They were the most amazing friends I could've ever asked for—an absolute godsend. Antoine bought me and Ruby our very own dance studio in Paris after we'd quit dancing at the nightclub. The two of us taught dance lessons together for several years after."

My grandma's words caused a new rush of memories to fill my brain. I remembered teaching lessons in the studio that Antoine had given us. I remembered walking down the cobblestone streets of Paris with Titine pushing my little mom in a stroller. I remembered it all. It had happened. Life hadn't stopped for us when I'd taken Antoine's hand and danced with him.

But then how was I here now?

"What happened then, Grandma? Where are Ruby and Antoine now?"

She patted my hand, a faraway look entering her eyes. "Well, when your mother was about ten years old, I decided to move to California so I could raise her here, near her father's family. I loved Paris, but I knew it was time for me to come back. And as for Ruby and Antoine, they couldn't have their own children, so they decided to take off for a few years and travel the world. I received postcards from them from every corner of the earth, places you couldn't imagine. Tropical islands in the Pacific, South America, Australia, New Zealand…"

As she listed the places we'd gone, I remembered each and every one. I remembered lying on sun-kissed beaches, Antoine's gorgeous body by my side, his handsome grin shining down on me as I wrote yet another postcard to Titine, telling her what a wonderful time we were having, but how much we missed her and baby Adeline.

It occurred to me then, that in my new batch of memories, both from my life as Ruby and Claudia, my mother was always called Adeline. She *hadn't* changed her name over to Jane. Clearly, *this* time around, she'd had no reason to.

My grandma stopped speaking for a moment, and as the corners of her mouth turned down just the slightest bit, I realized that after all the travel, something must've happened to Ruby. Otherwise how could I have been reborn as Claudia?

"Then what, Grandma?"

"Well, dear, after spending a few years traveling the entire world together, I received word that they had finally decided to return to Paris. By that time, Antoine had gotten his pilot's license, so he chartered a small plane just for the two of them. But something happened…my dear Ruby and her love, Antoine, they never did make it back to Paris."

"You mean the plane crashed?"

My grandma shook her head. "No, dear. There was never any record of a plane crash. It just…it disappeared."

"Disappeared? But how is that possible?"

"I've never understood it myself. After their disappearance, I was absolutely devastated. Your mom was only seventeen then, and she really carried me through that period. It was one of the worst times in my life. I couldn't stop worrying about where they'd gone, what had happened to them. But then, about two months later, your mom came home one day and told me she was pregnant. It was quite a shocker, seeing as how she was just a teenager, but the wonderful part was that she was pregnant with *you*, Claudia."

My grandma smiled down at me, the years of life experience evident in the tiny lines around her green eyes. "And nine months later, you came along, my little angel, and you took all of my pain away. It was as if, the minute you arrived here on this earth, I felt like I had found my best friend again. But when you fell earlier today, I…I couldn't imagine anything ever happening to you. You are the light of my life, Claudia. And I'm so happy you're going to be okay."

I managed a smile as my grandmother's sweet words attempted to comfort me, but all I could think about was that plane ride as my eyes grew drowsy and I drifted off to sleep.

⊹═══⊹

Dressed in his spiffy new pilot outfit, Antoine shoots me a disarming grin.

"Where to next, *ma chérie*?" he shouts over the roaring engine of the tiny plane we chartered from Tahiti, the last stop on our long list of exotic places to visit.

I giggle as my gaze fixes on the orange-and-pink swirls floating over the vast Pacific Ocean, the brilliant hues creating the most magical sunset I've ever seen.

"Surprise me," I say to him with a wink.

Antoine's knowing smile melts me to the core as we fly off into the fiery orange sunset together.

+=·=+

Lying in the hospital bed, I blinked my eyes open, trying to remember where Antoine had taken me. Where we'd landed next. But all I could see was a deep-orange sunset just beyond Antoine's handsome smile.

It was my last memory of him.

Hot tears rushed down my cheeks as my grandmother's voice reminded me where I was.

I was Claudia now. Lying in a hospital bed in a beautiful silver dress, pregnant with a baby girl. I had a wonderful, supportive family to see me through this. But something was missing. It was more than Antoine being gone. There was a big, gaping hole in this new picture of my life, and when I couldn't figure it out, I began to cry even harder.

"Oh, dear, I didn't mean to make you cry. I shouldn't have told you that sad story when you're lying here pregnant in a hospital bed. I'm so sorry, Claudia." She wiped the tears from my eyes and kissed me on the forehead. "You don't need to worry about any of that. You and your dear little girl are going to be just fine. And that big, burly dad of yours should be here any minute now to cheer you up. He'll be so happy to see you awake. He's been worried sick."

My dad?

As soon as I thought his name, that filmstrip of memories resumed playing through my head, and a new one popped to the forefront of my mind.

It was a memory of me on my first day of college in San Diego, moving into my dorm room. The room was exactly as I remembered it that day, empty except for a few suitcases that I'd begun to unpack. Suddenly, there was a knock at the door. I glanced up, and there, in the doorway, was my tall, handsome, jovial father. He smiled at me as he barged into the room carrying a tall stack of boxes. "Here you go, sweetie. I think this is everything!"

JULIETTE SOBANET

Back in the hospital bed, with the beeping ever steady in my ear, I shook my head. That couldn't be right. My dad hadn't been alive when I moved into college…but when I tried to recall the memory that was buried somewhere deep in my subconscious, the one where he'd died, the one where I'd failed to save him, I couldn't.

It was gone.

And when I opened my eyes, there, standing at the foot of my hospital bed, was my father.

"*Dad*," I called out to him, barely believing the words coming out of my own mouth.

"Claudia," he said, rounding the bed and taking my hand in his. "You are the only woman I know who can still look beautiful lying in a hospital bed." Then he winked over at my grandma. "No offense, Martine."

She giggled softly as she left us alone in the hospital room.

"Dad, I can't believe it's you," I said as more warm tears spilled down my cheeks. I didn't want to cry again, but I couldn't possibly hold them back. "You're really here, Dad. You're really here."

He chuckled as he wiped the tears from my eyes. "Don't cry, honey. Of course I'm here. Where else do you think I'd be?" He leaned down and held me tightly in his warm embrace. I breathed in the scent of his cologne, felt the strength of his arms around me. How many days had I longed to see him again, to hug him, to hear his deep, happy voice.

My dad was really alive. But how? How had things happened so differently this time?

Once I caught my breath, my dad pulled up a chair and held my hand.

"Honey, why are you looking at me like that?" he asked.

"Dad, are you…are you a politician?"

A hearty laugh erupted from his lips. "You really did bop your head pretty hard, didn't you, honey?"

"So you're not a politician?"

My dad shook his head, a flare of curiosity passing through his ocean-blue gaze.

"What is it, Dad?"

"It's just funny that you would ask that, sweetie. You know, I don't think I've ever told you this, but when I was really young, that's all I dreamed about. With my dad and my grandfather being in politics their whole lives, I wanted to follow in their footsteps, but I was determined to go higher. I even had dreams of becoming the president one day. Then when I was really little, maybe about ten or eleven years old, something changed my mind."

My heart sped up. "What was it?"

My dad hesitated, searching my eyes, before finally reaching into his pocket and pulling out his wallet. But before he unfolded the brown leather, he glanced back up at me. "I've never shown this to your mother…she gets spooked about this kind of stuff. So let's just keep this between us, okay?" He winked as he dug to the back of his wallet and removed a worn, faded postcard, folded into four squares. He unfolded it before handing it over to me.

A stunning black-and-white photograph of the Eiffel Tower stared back at me. My hands shook as I remembered this postcard. I remembered holding it in Ruby's beautiful hands.

I turned it over and gasped as her handwriting—*my handwriting*—filled up the postcard.

December 6, 1959

Bonjour from Paris, Anthony! My name is Ruby Kerrigan, and I'm an old family friend. I wanted to tell you that I've heard what a smart young man you are becoming. I've heard that you're thinking of following in your dad's footsteps and becoming a politician one day. That's a big dream, Anthony, and your father knows that if anyone can make it happen, you can.

Peabody Public Library
Columbia City, IN

But that's the thing about dreams, sometimes all it takes is knowing that your family believes in you to make you realize that the dream you once had as a little boy may not be your destiny.

Remember this always:

Your destiny is yours to create.

Know that your parents will love you and support you no matter what path you choose.

And one day, when you're older, I'll make the trip from Paris to meet this boy I've been hearing so much about. You can count on it.

From Paris with love,

Ruby

My dad wiped another tear from my cheek. "The funny thing was, Claudia, the day that postcard arrived in the mail, my parents said they didn't know anyone named Ruby. And they didn't know anyone living in Paris. But after my parents read the words this mystery woman had written to me, they sat me down and told me that what Ruby had said was true. That my destiny was mine to create. That I didn't need to follow in my father's footsteps for them to be proud of me. They said they loved me just the way I was, and that they knew I would accomplish amazing things when I grew up. So over the next several years, I asked my dad tons of questions about his career. And by the time I was heading off to college, I knew that the life of a politician wasn't for me."

"So what did you decide to do?"

Concern swept over his face. "Claudia, honey, you really don't remember what I do?"

I rubbed my head and closed my eyes, willing the rest of my memories to come into focus. The slideshow that had begun earlier picked up again, and as it sped along, it replaced the void where the old memories had been and took with it the longing I'd felt my whole life for a real family who loved and cared for each other, for a mother who loved me unconditionally, and a father who hadn't been taken from us unfairly.

My second chance at Ruby's life had given me a second chance as Claudia—a chance at a happy, functional family. *I'd* done this. I'd changed my destiny, and that of my entire family, and fate had rewarded me by bringing me here to this moment. To this incredible reunion with my dad.

Opening my eyes, I smiled warmly over at my father. "You're a professor. A political science professor here in San Diego."

He laughed. "There's my girl. I told your mother a little bump on the head was no match for my Claudia. Except there is one thing you don't seem to remember."

"What is it, Dad?"

"We're not in San Diego right now, dear. We're up in LA for the weekend."

"What are we doing here?"

My dad glanced over his shoulder and stood up as a knowing grin spread over his handsome face. "Why don't I let your husband refresh your memory?"

"My *husband*?" I said, barely believing my ears. I glanced down at my left hand, and there on my ring finger was a gorgeous diamond shimmering in the dim hospital light. When I closed my eyes, I could picture a man placing that ring on my finger, but before I could make out his face in my memory, a voice called my name.

I flicked my gaze just past my father, and there, to my astonishment, stood a handsome vision of a man in a tux.

Except this *wasn't* a vision.

With his jet-black, wavy hair and rugged five o'clock shadow, he was as real as the baby kicking away in my belly.

It was *Édouard*.

He rushed toward me, the relief in his charcoal-gray eyes palpable. Reaching for my hands, he leaned over and showered my forehead and my cheeks with warm, sweet kisses.

And as he sat down at my bedside and smiled at me, that same disarming smile I remembered from our night at the dance studio, that last, missing puzzle piece finally came into view.

"This is our baby?" I asked him.

His hearty, warm laugh filled up the room. "Yes, Claudia. She's ours. And you're awake. God, I'm so happy you're awake. And I just spoke with the doctors. They said the baby is doing fine." As he squeezed my hands in his, I noticed my dad quietly slipping out of the room, leaving us alone.

"How are you feeling?" he asked.

"I was a little confused when I first woke up…" I trailed off as I gazed into Édouard's eyes, feeling a sudden bliss wash over me while the last flood of new memories set in.

I remembered Édouard standing underneath a white archway in a loose, white collared shirt, his dark hair blowing in the breeze, the fiery orange sun setting over the ocean behind him. I held on to my father's arm and walked down the sandy aisle past familiar, smiling faces as my flowing white gown gathered at my bare feet. As I reached Édouard and took his outstretched hand, I gazed into his handsome gray eyes and felt an overwhelming sense of love, of compassion, of protection emanating from them. It was a feeling I'd felt before. As Ruby.

I blinked away the happy memory and focused in on those same eyes that held my gaze back in the hospital room, and I realized I knew *those* eyes. Those loving, warm gray eyes.

They belonged to Antoine.

Was it possible? When Antoine and Ruby had set off into the sunset, had Antoine traveled to this life as Édouard? Just so we could be together again?

"Are you still feeling confused, love?" Édouard asked, his deep, strong voice pulling me from my new memories, my old ones, and the biggest question of all.

I searched his eyes for the answer, and as their warmth penetrated my heart, my soul, my experience between these two lives, just as Madame Bouchard had told me I would, I simply *knew*.

I knew the answer.

"It's you," I said, breathless and relieved, the smile on my face growing as I realized that my soul mate had traveled with me, that we'd found each other in this life, that we'd never again be apart.

"Were you expecting someone else?" he asked, a playful twinkle in his eye.

"*You* are the one I was waiting for, Édouard. You are the one I was hoping would be here."

He leaned forward and brushed his hand along the edge of my face, sending those familiar tingles skittering and dancing through my body. The same tingles that *only* Édouard and Antoine could give me. My soul mate from two lives, wrapped into this one body, this one love who now sat by my side.

Édouard was my husband. This baby was ours. Everything had changed. And when I'd gone back to relive that patch of my life as Ruby, I'd changed it all.

But when a flash of wavy black hair and silvery-black eyes entered my mind, my tingles turned to chills.

"Claudia, what's the matter? You're looking a little pale all of a sudden. Are you feeling okay?"

"What happened to Solange?" I asked him.

Édouard stifled a laugh. "The cat is *fine*, Claudia. We fed her before making the trip up to LA this morning. And the neighbors are watching her while we're away."

"The *cat*?"

"Yes, Claudia. Our cat, Solange. I thought it was strange to give a cat that name, but you insisted."

"So you were never engaged before me? To a woman named Solange?"

"Are you sure you're okay, Claudia?"

"Just answer me, Édouard."

"No, love. I was never engaged before you. I don't know any-one named Solange—anyone apart from that annoying black cat of ours, who you love to death."

I let out the breath I'd been holding, relief flooding through me. With that bullet, I'd ended Solange. I'd ended her evil soul, and now, she was only...*a cat.*

But, just in case..."Édouard?"

"Yes, Claudia?"

"I don't know how safe it is to have a cat around a newborn. Maybe we should consider asking my parents to take her for a little while...the cat, that is."

Édouard laughed. "Whatever you want, love. Solange *has* been a little hostile lately."

"And by the way, what are we all doing in Los Angeles? And why am I in this dress? And you in a tux?"

"It's for the film premiere, don't you remember? When you were getting ready earlier in the hotel room, you tripped on those red sparkly heels you always insist on wearing, and you hit your head as you fell. You passed out and gave us all a bad scare, so that's why we're here."

"My red sparkly heels, are they here?"

He chuckled. "You're not going to give up on those, no matter how pregnant you get, are you?" He leaned below the bed and emerged holding the sparkling, strappy red heels. The shoes I'd danced so many dances in.

As I turned the beautiful heels over in my hands, admiring their grace, their pizzazz, and their beauty, I knew there was one more event these shoes needed to attend.

"What time is the film premiere?" I asked Édouard.

"Claudia, you can't possibly be feeling—"

In one swift movement, I swung my legs over the side of the bed and planted my lips on Édouard's. If I'd doubted it at all before, his passionate, sweet kiss was the final proof.

Édouard was my love, my Antoine, my soul mate.

As our lips parted, Édouard traced the outline of my face with his finger. "Wow. Maybe you should bump your head and pass out more often."

I nudged him. "Help me put these heels back on and take me to the red carpet."

+======+

An hour later, Édouard and I were cozied up in the back of a crowded limo, our families dressed to the nines, clinking their bubbly glasses of champagne and prepping to make their very first appearance on the red carpet.

Apparently this wasn't the first time I'd accompanied Édouard to one of these glitzy events, but it was the first time *I* was a guest of honor.

Because this time around, in my new, corrected course of fate, I wasn't a therapist anymore. I was a dance teacher, and most recently, I'd become the screenwriter for Édouard's film directing debut.

"How ever did you think of the idea for this movie, Claudia?" It was Delphine Marceau, Édouard's elegant mother, who I remembered so very well from my life as Ruby. After all, if it weren't for her confession, I may still be locked up in a French prison for the murder of a certain black-haired Medusa woman. "Soul mates traveling back in time to be with each other in a past life, how very romantic," she continued. "And set in Paris, it couldn't be more perfect. Please, tell me. How do you come up with a story this beautiful, this original?"

I smiled over at my chic French mother-in-law. "It came to me in a dream one night, and I knew I just had to tell their story."

Édouard kissed me on the cheek. "My talented, beautiful wife. How did I ever get so lucky?"

I cuddled a little closer to my husband. "I'm asking myself the same question."

As excited chatter filled up the limo, a peculiar gleam shone in Édouard's dark-gray eyes.

"What is it?" I asked, suddenly feeling as light as a feather, as if the burden of carrying these two lives had finally lifted. I could just be *me* now. *Claudia*. It was a relief larger than I could express.

"I thought of a name for the baby," Édouard said. "Would you like to hear it?"

I nodded, thinking about how fun this was going to be: picking out baby names, decorating the nursery, preparing the world for a sweet, loving baby girl who would be mine, who would be *ours*.

"I don't know if you'll like it, but it came to me earlier in the hospital while we were waiting for you to wake up. I haven't been able to stop thinking about it."

"What is it?"

"What do you think of the name *Ruby*?"

I smiled, feeling a tear bubble over my eyelid and run down my cheek. "Baby Ruby. It's perfect."

He had no idea how perfect it really was.

Just then, the limo pulled to a stop. Excited fans crowded the sidewalks to either side of the red carpet. Photographers stood poised on the sidelines, ready to shoot.

My stomach tightened with nerves at the sight of all these people. Were they really here for us?

Édouard squeezed my hand. "Are you sure you're ready for this, *chérie*?"

Before I answered him, I remembered my days as Ruby, strutting my stuff onstage, not a nervous bone in my body. I'd adored the crowds, craved the attention.

Smiling over at Édouard, I realized I wasn't *only* Claudia. Ruby still lived inside of me. She always would.

And Ruby would've *loved* the red carpet.

"I was born ready," I said to my husband, shooting him a sexy wink.

But just as I was about to follow Édouard's lead, the strong scent of roses drifted past me.

Flicking my gaze toward the front of the limo, I noticed the driver opening the partition. A weathered hand stretched through the open space, and dangling from her fingers was none other than a ruby-red pendant in the shape of a heart.

"Mademoiselle Claudia, I think you may have dropped this."

With her striking violet eyes and silvery hair, there was no mistaking the elegant, ever-mysterious Madame Bouchard.

When we met eyes, she cast a knowing glance toward my belly. "You see, *this* is how it was all supposed to turn out."

"Thank you. Thank you so much," I said to her, not sure how else to demonstrate the immense gratitude I felt at having my dad and my baby back. And above all, my soul mate, Édouard.

That familiar, mischievous glimmer appeared in her eyes as she leaned forward and lowered her voice to barely a whisper. "Don't thank me, Claudia. *You* did this. All of it." She dangled the necklace closer to me and raised a silvery brow. "Would you like to wear this tonight? It would look stunning with your dress."

Running my hands over my growing belly, I shook my head and grinned at the beautiful old woman. "No, thanks. I have everything I need right here."

A soft chuckle escaped her lips, the lines around her eyes crinkling. "Very well. But you must know that this necklace has a way of finding its owner, no matter what the circumstances."

"I'm not *traveling* again, if that's what you're implying," I said firmly.

Madame Bouchard's kind regard hardened just the slightest bit before she spoke. "No, my dear. *Your* travels are complete. But there is something you must know before your daughter arrives."

A knot formed in my throat as I stared back at her, wondering what more there could possibly be. Shielding my belly from her penetrating gaze, I forced the words out. "What is it?"

"These past-life revisits…they run in your family, Claudia."

"*Chérie*, are you coming?" Édouard's adorable grin appeared just outside the limo, inviting me to follow him, but Madame Bouchard's words kept me planted in my seat.

"One second," I told him, casting another glance toward the front of the limo.

But just as I feared she would be, the mysterious old woman was already gone, leaving only a whiff of her rose-scented perfume and the hefty weight of her words for me to ponder.

With one sparkly high heel on the red carpet, I took Édouard's outstretched hand, pushed Madame Bouchard's haunting last statement from my mind, and made a silent promise to my baby that I would never let anyone take her away from me.

And so, with my dashing husband by my side and my baby girl kicking up a storm inside my belly, this happy little family who'd traveled so far to be together worked the red carpet like no other. And when the camera flashes died down, we settled in to watch a bold, heartwarming tale set in the heart of 1950s Paris, about two soul mates who would stop at nothing to be together, and the unbreakable ties that carried them from one life into the next, and back again.

As the opening credits rolled over a breathtaking nighttime view of Paris and Peggy Lee's "Fever" filled up the darkened theater, I thought of Ruby and how she would've adored the title... *There's No Place Like Paris.*

+⟞⟝+

Applause thundered through the theater as the film, which was dearer to my heart than anyone could've possibly understood, came to a close.

Édouard turned to me and wiped a tear from my cheek, his smoky-gray eyes dancing over my face. "It was *magnifique*, was it not?"

I nodded, unable to get a single word past my lips, the emotions from seeing my past-life experience on screen almost too much to bear...and if I was being honest with myself, Madame Bouchard's words were still swimming through my head, threatening to swallow me whole. Had other women in my family traveled back in time to their own past lives? Would my daughter one day be expected to do the same?

"I have a present for you." Édouard interrupted my frantic thoughts as he pulled a red velvet box from inside his coat pocket.

"You didn't have to—" I started, but the minute he placed the box in my hands, a familiar tingling sensation sparked underneath my skin. I opened the lid and gasped when my eyes met the ruby-red heart pendant that had just been dangling from Madame Bouchard's fingers in the limo, only a few hours ago.

"It's a ruby," Édouard said, pulling the necklace from the box and clasping it around my neck. "And maybe one day when she's old enough, you can pass it along to *our* little Ruby."

Running my tingling fingers over the beautiful stone, I smiled back at the man who I adored more than life itself, the man who I had loved longer than he would ever comprehend. And instead of telling him that our daughter would never wear this necklace, I sent a silent message to Madame Bouchard, letting her know that no matter what tricks she had up her sleeve, *our little Ruby* would *never* be taking a voyage like the one we'd just watched on screen…not if I had anything to say about it.

Once I'd passed along my silent warning, I turned to my sweet, handsome husband and pushed all worries out of my mind. "It's stunning, Édouard. Thank you so much."

Édouard leaned in, sliding an arm around my waist. "It *is* gorgeous, but nothing could ever outshine you, *mon amour*."

Then, in the middle of the crowded, buzzing theater, my man, the love of my life, gave me the kiss to end all kisses—a toe-curling, butterfly-inducing, electrifying, heart-swelling kiss.

When our lips finally parted, a sultry grin spread over his sexy face before he winked at me. "Don't worry, *ma belle*, there is plenty more where that came from."

I wrapped my hands around his neck, running my fingers through his thick, wavy head of hair. And before I kissed him one more time, I whispered in his ear, "There better be."

Peabody Public Library
Columbia City, IN

ACKNOWLEDGMENTS

I am forever grateful to the amazing team of people who helped me bring this story to life. To my agent, Kevan Lyon, and my editors, Kelli Martin and Andrea Hurst. Each of you has inspired me to write better, dig deeper, and make this story more unique and exciting than I ever could've hoped it would be. Thank you a million times over for your passion and enthusiasm for this novel. And to the team at Montlake Romance, I am so thankful for everything you've done to bring *Dancing with Paris* to my readers.

To my talented critique partners, Karen, Sharon, Mary, Alison, Tracy, and Marion. Your help with this novel was invaluable, and your support through this wild writing journey keeps me smiling. Special thanks to Alison for flying to France with me at a moment's notice and for our fabulous brainstorming sessions over croissants.

I would like to thank my husband for listening to me talk about my characters as if they are actually real people, and for loving me anyway. To my mom, thank you for always encouraging me to dream. Those dreams have become my stories. And to my Grandma Martha, thank you for inspiring me to write the character of Titine. I think the two of you would've been great friends.

Finally, my stories wouldn't have a home if not for my loyal readers. I write these books for you, and I am immensely grateful for your support and for your belief in my work. Paris is an endless source of inspiration, so there will be many more novels to come!

ABOUT THE AUTHOR

Juliette Sobanet earned a BA from Georgetown University and an MA from New York University in France, living and studying in both Lyon and Paris. She worked as a French professor before turning a new page in her career, penning romantic women's fiction with a French twist. Today she lives with her husband and two cats in San Diego, where she devotes her time to writing and dreaming about her next trip to France.

20487134R00189

Peabody Public Library
Columbia City, IN

Made in the USA
Charleston, SC
12 July 2013